# THE
# DAWN
# *of a* DREAM

## Books by Ann Shorey

### AT HOME IN BELDON GROVE

*The Edge of Light*
*The Promise of Morning*
*The Dawn of a Dream*

AT HOME IN *Beldon Grove*
BOOK 3

# THE
# DAWN
# *of a* DREAM

## ANN
## SHOREY

Revell
a division of Baker Publishing Group
Grand Rapids, Michigan

© 2011 by Ann Shorey

Published by Revell
a division of Baker Publishing Group
P.O. Box 6287, Grand Rapids, MI 49516-6287
www.revellbooks.com

Printed in the United States of America

Library of Congress Cataloging-in-Publication Data
Shorey, Ann Kirk, 1941–
    The dawn of a dream / Ann Shorey.
        p.   cm. — (At home in Beldon Grove ; bk. 3)
    ISBN 978-0-8007-3334-6 (pbk.)
    I. Title.
PS3619.H666D39 2011
813'.6—dc22                                                    2010050632

Scripture used in this book, whether quoted or paraphrased by the characters, is taken from the King James Version of the Bible.

11   12   13   14   15   16   17        7   6   5   4   3   2   1

This book is dedicated with love to my brother,

Joe Matot.

You're the best!

# 1

*Beldon Grove, Illinois*
*August 14, 1857*

Luellen O'Connell aligned the edge of a flower-bordered table-cloth and stepped back to admire her handiwork. She wondered if Brendan would remember what day it was.

Whether her husband remembered or not, she still had tasks to complete before he came home. She hurried into their bedroom and gathered an accumulation of papers from the top of a bookshelf. For a moment, her eyes rested on an envelope from Allenwood Normal School. Luellen shook her head. Life was full of choices. She'd made hers. She dropped the papers behind a row of books.

A breeze lifted the curtains. Luellen removed her glasses and wiped perspiration that collected across the bridge of her nose. The past week had been unbearably hot. She hoped the evening would bring a cooling thundershower. Brendan returned home after each day's work out of sorts and silent. She could hardly blame him—hauling freight in the blazing sun day after day would tire anybody.

After sweeping dust out the front door, she returned to the bedroom and opened her bridal chest. Her white dimity petticoat, trimmed with blue tatting, lay folded inside. Luellen smiled and slipped the garment on under her skirt. It was too hot to wear petticoats, but the memory of Brendan removing it on their wedding night sent an anticipatory tingle through her.

One more thing to do. In the kitchen she tested a cooling loaf cake with her fingertip, checking whether it was ready for frosting. The fragrance of cinnamon filled her senses while she beat sugar into egg whites. Humming, she spread the sweetened mixture over the cake and placed the decorated treat in the center of the table.

At the sound of jingling harnesses, she dashed to the door in time to see Brendan drive his freight wagon toward the barn. Luellen slipped her glasses into her apron pocket. She wanted to look especially pretty for him this evening.

Brendan shoved the last bite of cake into his mouth. From the time he stomped through the door, red-faced and sweating, he'd said less than two words. Now he pushed his chair away from the table and slapped the armrests. Thick cinnamon-colored hair matting his forearms made him look bearlike.

Tears swam in Luellen's eyes. She couldn't read his expression, but the tension of an unspoken message simmered between them. "What is it?" She fought to keep her voice from trembling.

"Got something to tell you." He leaned back and folded his arms.

Luellen took a breath and held it for a moment. "It must be terrible. Did you lose your job?"

"Still got the job." He took a swallow of tea. "I'm going to

Chicago. Tomorrow. Boss says he can use me there. More freight coming in on the railroads. More business."

Luellen's jaw dropped. "Is that what's bothering you? I'm sure Papa will help me pack our household so I can join you." She moved behind him and slid her arms around his neck, kissing the top of his head.

Brendan reached up and disengaged her hold. "Your father won't be helping you go no place. I already got a wife waiting there."

The room turned gray, then red. Luellen pivoted to face him. "You can't be serious. You married me! A month ago today, in case you've forgotten." She yanked her glasses from her pocket and put them on with shaking hands.

He stood, smirking. "'Twas no other way to get you into my bed, lass. You and those glasses—you should be happy you had this much time with a man." He reached behind her head and jerked the silk net from her hair, spilling the long dark waves over her shoulders. "This hair is the only thing I'll miss. 'Tis truly lovely."

She slapped the net from his hands. Grabbing the rest of the cake, she dumped it over his head. "Get out! Now!"

Brendan wiped frosting out of his beard and glared at her. "I'll get my things." He turned toward the bedroom.

"You have two minutes. I want you out of this house, out of Beldon Grove." Her voice shook with anger. "You're a filthy, lying—" She sputtered to a stop, unable to think of a vile enough insult.

He banged into the bedroom, snatched his valise from under the bed, and stuffed in handfuls of clothing. On his way out the door, he picked up his razor and strop from the washstand and dropped them into the open bag.

"Time's up. Go on with you." Luellen's hands clenched into fists.

He sent her his easy grin. "With your hair blowing wild like that and the roses in your cheeks, you're a fetching sight. Maybe the day will come you can find some other man." Brendan turned on his heel and strode toward the stable.

She grabbed his shaving mug and threw it after him. It shattered on the ground. For the first time, she was glad their cottage sat far from the center of town. No one would notice when he drove away.

Thunder cracked. Wind flapped the bedroom curtains and the scent of rain filled the air. Luellen had no idea how much time had passed since Brendan left. She'd been too busy removing all traces of his presence from the cottage. Bedding lay in a heap on the floor, waiting for the wash kettle to heat. The kitchen felt stifling, but the bolted door represented safety. Nothing could hurt her as long as she stayed inside.

Jaw clenched, she opened the firebox on the stove, lifted her skirt, and jerked off the dimity petticoat, shoving the garment into the fire. Flames caught the lace tatting, then burst through the white skirt. Luellen stalked to the bedroom and snatched her ruffled nightdress from its peg on the wall. It followed the petticoat into the stove.

Her eyes landed on the Rose of Sharon quilt she and her mother had stitched for her bridal chest. What a great joke. No husband, but she still had the quilt. She gathered the red and green flowered coverlet into her arms, trying to roll it small enough to fit through the firebox door. The flames had subsided, smothered by the weight of her voluminous nightgown. By poking and shoving, she forced one end of the quilt over the gown. As she did, her eyes rested on the embroidered message her mother had stitched onto one corner. "*Jeremiah 29:11 For I know the thoughts that I think toward you, saith the* LORD, *thoughts of peace, and not of evil . . .*"

"Oh, Mama." Luellen pulled the quilt free of the firebox and slumped to the floor. A brown singe had eaten its way onto one of the roses, but the rest of the design was unharmed. "How can this be thoughts of peace and not evil?" Shattered, she buried her face in the soft folds and screamed her pain into the deserted room.

❧

"Luellen?" Her younger sister Lily's voice sounded outside. "Are you ill? Why is the door bolted?"

Luellen glanced around the cottage. Broken dishes swept up, bed remade with clean linens, stovetop shining with fresh polish. Everything looked normal . . . except no Brendan. She'd wondered how long it would take for her family to check on her. Usually she visited their house every day, especially with Lily's wedding so near.

Feeling a hundred years old, she slid back the bolt and opened the door. Lily burst inside and hugged her.

"Thank the Lord. When you and Brendan didn't come to church yesterday, Papa wanted to come see you, but Mama said you were probably enjoying each other's company." Lily blushed. "In another week, Edmund and I will be together too. I can't wait."

Luellen said nothing. Her sister's happiness seemed to mock her own feelings of desolation and betrayal.

Lily stepped back. "You look terrible. What's happened?" She glanced around the cottage, pausing at the open bedroom door-way. "Where's your Rose of Sharon quilt?" Her gaze landed on the table standing against the kitchen wall. "And the embroidered tablecloth I made for you? Your new dishes—what did you do with them?" She placed a hand to her throat. "Something's dreadfully wrong." She took Luellen's hand and drew her to one of the chairs next to the table. "Tell me."

It seemed odd to her that Lily should be offering comfort. Luellen had always been the one to give advice and guidance. She clasped her hands in her lap and stared into Lily's brown eyes. "Brendan is gone." As she said the words, cold, hard shame stiffened her body. She'd given herself to a man who already had a wife. She was no longer pure. When word got out, she'd be humiliated in the eyes of the town.

*Marry in haste, repent at leisure.* Wasn't that what Mama said when she and Brendan told her they'd eloped? Repent at leisure was one thing. Being ridiculed was quite another.

Lily's voice drew her out of her thoughts. "What do you mean, gone? He hauls freight for the railroad every week. He's always gone."

"Gone for good. Back to Chicago." Luellen's voice cracked. "Lily, he already has a wife." She covered her face with her hands. "He just married me to have a woman to bed while he jobbed in our county."

"No. It can't be true."

"I wish it weren't." Tears slid down her cheeks. "How will I ever face Mama and Papa?" Her voice turned mocking. "I thought my job serving meals at the hotel made me a good judge of people. After all, we fed dozens of men a week. I could tell which ones were up to no good—or so I believed."

Lily knelt in front of her. "They'll understand. He fooled them too, with that handsome face and his charming ways. He fooled all of us."

Love for her sister filled her heart. Lily's wedding was days away. Luellen couldn't let her troubles spoil the event. She drew Lily to her feet. "Let's go home. I'm sure Mama has things for me to do." She squared her shoulders. "I need to tell them sooner or later. Might as well be now."

# 2

Arm in arm, Luellen and Lily covered the distance to their parents' home, their footsteps loud on the boardwalk along Adams Street. A buggy rolled past and turned left at the corner of Monroe.

"Wonder who that was," Lily said. "Ever since the railroad came through, we get more strangers all the time." She clapped a hand over her mouth. "Oh, I'm sorry. I didn't mean Brendan."

"I know you didn't. But it's true. His was a new face—someone different than the boys I grew up with. I was so sure—" Her voice caught.

Lily squeezed Luellen's arm. "We're almost home. Take a deep breath. We've got to act calm. Mama's going to be beside herself when she hears."

Luellen slowed her steps when they passed the cabin where she'd lived most of her growing-up years. Now clapboarded and painted white, it held her father's medical office and infirmary. It still felt like home in spite of the sign facing the street that read KARL SPENGLER, PHYSICIAN.

"Maybe we could tell Papa, and let him talk to Mama."

"It would be best coming from you. She'd just want you to repeat everything, anyway."

Luellen sighed. "You're right."

They mounted the steps of the veranda and entered the front door of the spacious two-story house their parents built after Lily finished her schooling. The high-ceilinged entry felt cool after being out in the midday sun. Luellen removed her bonnet and fanned herself, gathering courage.

Their mother, Molly Spengler, stepped out of the kitchen, wiping her hands on her apron. "There you are. We missed you yesterday." The corner of her mouth twitched in a smile. "I expect you and Brendan decided to keep the weekend to yourselves."

Luellen released a slow breath. "Is Papa home?"

Mama stepped closer, frowning. "You don't look well. Your eyes are all red. Do you need Papa to give you a tonic?"

Her careful composure fled. "I . . . I need to talk to both of you." She felt herself tremble.

Mama rested a hand on her forehead.

"I'm not sick. Please. Get Papa."

Mama turned to Lily. "He's in the kitchen. Ask him to come in here."

When her parents were seated, Luellen bowed her head and pressed her hands together. "Brendan's gone . . . back to his wife in Chicago." She stuttered out the words. Tears threatened to spill when she saw the shock on their faces.

"No. It can't be." Mama jumped to her feet and circled Luellen with her arms. "My poor baby girl." She patted her on the back as though she were soothing a skinned knee.

Papa's face flamed with anger. "When?"

"Friday."

"Why didn't you tell us right away? I could've chased him down, brought him back."

She met his eyes. "To do what? He's married to someone else."

Her face burned. "How could I have been so easily deceived? Why on earth didn't I wait until we knew more about him?"

"He was awfully charming," Lily said in a small voice. "We all thought so."

"Charming. Yes, that he was. Charmed me right into bed with him."

"Luellen!" Mama said. "That's no way for a lady to speak."

"Am I still a lady? I'm ruined. How can I face people?"

"People. Oh my word. The wedding Saturday." Mama rubbed her forehead. "We just won't say anything. Who's to know?" She paced the length of the room and turned. "That's it. By the time folks realize he's gone for good, we'll have an explanation."

Papa rose and took Luellen's hands. "You'll always be a lady. It's what's in your heart that makes you who you are. We'll get through this—all of us together."

Grateful, she leaned into the comfort of his arms.

"But first we have to think of Lily's wedding." Mama continued to pace. "We have guests coming. Edmund's family will be here. We can't have scandal ruining everything."

"You sound like Ellie's aunt Ruby, God rest her soul," Papa said, referring to his sister-in-law's aunt. "We won't say anything for now, but we can't present a lie to the community forever." He squeezed Luellen's shoulder. "Come stay with us. Everyone will think you're here to be of more help."

Dizzy, she sagged into a chair. After Saturday, then what?

Early Saturday morning, Luellen stepped into the decorated parlor to add fresh bouquets of daisies and maidenhair ferns to the mantel. Her uncle Matthew, pastor of Beldon Grove's leading church, would stand before the screened fireplace to perform the wedding ceremony.

Glad for a few minutes of quiet before the guests arrived, she stepped back and surveyed the chairs to be certain they'd provided enough seating. She counted as she mentally ran through the expected attendees—Uncle Matthew's wife, Ellie, with their two youngest children, Sarah and Robert. Lily's fiancé's parents would be there, of course, as would Ellie's uncle Arthur, friends of the family from the community, and several of Lily's former schoolmates.

Luellen blinked back tears. Her sister's wedding would be beautiful—nothing like her own marriage ceremony before a judge in the county courthouse. Brendan had assured her it wouldn't matter. Now she knew why. She'd traded years of work toward a higher education for the persuasive promises of a man she hardly knew.

She wiped her eyes. "How could I have done such a thing?"

"Done what?" Papa walked up behind her and rested his hands on her shoulders.

She turned and met his gaze. "Made such a terrible mistake."

"Would it be easier for you to rest in your room during the ceremony? Having our guests question you about your missing husband is bound to be a trial."

"Thank you, but no. I want to be here for Lily."

He settled in one of the chairs. "It's too bad James will miss it, and Franklin, too, looks like."

"I knew James wouldn't be able to travel all the way from Philadelphia, but I'd hoped to see Franklin. It's been months." Luellen sat beside him and smoothed her rose-colored taffeta skirt. Sitting with Papa in the quiet room calmed her spirit. She knew these were likely to be the last peaceful moments they'd have today.

"Franklin must be off scouting. He didn't reply to your mama's letter, and she sent it in plenty of time." Sadness touched his eyes.

"You miss the boys, don't you?"

Papa nodded. "And after the wedding Lily will be living in Springfield. Thankfully, we'll have you at home with us."

His words rang an alarm bell in her head. Would that be her future? To be the unmarried daughter spending her life at home with her parents?

Luellen paused inside the kitchen to gather courage before taking her seat in the parlor. She needed to hurry. Lily and Edmund would make their entrance at any moment.

A strong arm seized her around the middle. A hand covered her mouth. As she struggled to free herself, a masculine voice spoke in her ear. "Shh. Don't say anything and I'll let go."

She nodded, and the hand withdrew. Her captor stepped in front of her, grinning.

"Franklin!"

"Quiet. I want to surprise everyone."

Luellen grabbed her brother in a hug. "It's wonderful to see you. Mama and Papa will be thrilled." She stepped back, studying him, noting his tanned face and his dark hair worn at collar length. He wore wedding attire—gray trousers and a frock coat over his white shirt, but his feet were shod in moccasins.

"No wonder you crept up on me." She pointed. "Shouldn't you be wearing boots?"

"Don't have to shine moccasins." Franklin winked at her, then beckoned toward the open back door. "Come in, Ward."

A man in dark blue Army dress stepped into the room. Shorter than Franklin by about four inches, and stocky where Franklin was lithe, he whipped off his black felt hat and bowed in her direction.

"This is Lieutenant Ward Calder, a friend of mine from Jefferson

17

Barracks. He's likable in spite of the fact he's an officer." Franklin shot a teasing glance in the lieutenant's direction. "Ward, this is my sister, Luellen O'Connell."

Lieutenant Calder bowed again. "A pleasure, ma'am."

Franklin rubbed his hands together. "Now that we've dispensed with the formalities, let's join the wedding party. If I figured right, isn't it almost time for Uncle Matthew to tie the knot on our little sister and her intended?"

Luellen nodded, amused. Franklin's cheerful outlook never failed to lift her spirits.

As they started toward the parlor, he whispered, "Is your husband already seated? I want to meet the man who changed your mind about marriage." He glanced at Lieutenant Calder. "My sister always swore she didn't want to marry, but O'Connell won her over."

Her momentary lightheartedness evaporated. "He couldn't be here today." She hurried forward and opened the door, standing aside so her parents could see Franklin.

The wedding breakfast covered the dining room table. Fresh peaches swam in a bowl of cream. On a round platter, sliced chicken surrounded fried sweet potatoes, and muffins were stacked in a pyramid on a footed glass plate. A sideboard under the window held the wedding cake. Luellen stood near the kitchen and helped with serving, hoping hunger would keep their guests from pressing her with questions about Brendan.

She couldn't help but contrast today's elegant meal with the contents of the dinner pail she and Brendan had shared on their way back to Beldon Grove to tell her parents of their marriage.

Cold ham sandwiches could have been a special memory between the two of them—if there were still two of them.

She gave herself a mental shake and forced a smile at Lily and Edmund, who stood near the sideboard, waiting for the cake to be served. "I imagine you're eager to start on your journey," she said as she inserted a knife into the fruit-laden pastry.

Lily blushed. "Yes. The train north will be here around two. We're planning to stop in New Roanoke for the first night."

Edmund looked down at his bride. "Long train trips are fatiguing. For Lily's sake, we'll make the journey in short segments."

Once the cake had been shared among the guests, Lily hurried upstairs to change into her traveling costume.

Luellen joined her in the bedroom. "It was a perfect wedding." She lifted her sister's green and blue checked shawl from the bed. "Too bad Maria and Graciana had to miss it. You three have always been as close as sisters."

"Those two." Lily's smile carried the fondness she felt for her cousins. "Marrying brothers, living next door to each other in Quincy, expecting their babies the same month. I wonder if their children will grow up as close as we were."

"I don't see how they can help it." Luellen settled the shawl over Lily's shoulders, arranging the fringe so it fell smoothly over her hoop-skirted, oyster-gray dress.

Lily turned and clasped Luellen's hands. "Thank you for all you've done to make my wedding special. I know how hard it's been for you to keep smiling." She kissed her cheek. "God has something better planned for your life than Brendan."

Luellen stopped, hand on the knob of the kitchen door. Voices from inside carried through the polished walnut panel.

"Did you see how she's dressed? No hoops—just those heavy petticoats."

"And those eyeglasses. She looks like she's forty years old. No wonder her husband left."

Luellen self-consciously tucked her glasses in her pocket. Her face burned. If Lily's friends knew, the news had to be all over town. No wonder few of the guests had mentioned Brendan.

She pushed the door open and strode into the room. Two young women stood at the counter, washing dishes from the wedding breakfast. They sprang apart, their hoopskirts swaying.

"Luellen! We thought you were . . ." Abigail's fair skin flushed scarlet.

"Mama's resting. I told her I'd give you girls a hand." Luellen gave them her sweetest smile. "Why don't you join the others? My brother's around someplace with that friend he brought with him. I'm sure they'd enjoy some fashionable company."

"How kind of you. We'd love to visit with Franklin, wouldn't we? He's been away for ever so long." Abigail preceded her companion through the doorway, tipping her hoops sideways to negotiate the narrow opening.

The other girl swept by with embarrassed words of thanks. They hurried through the dining room, past the table covered with the family's best linen, and into the parlor where the last guests lingered.

Once they were out of sight, Luellen rested against the edge of the counter and leaned forward, eyes closed. At one time, she'd wanted more from life than a husband. Why did she ever let Brendan change her mind? She knew why. Loneliness. The flattery of

20

his Irish charm worked its way into her heart and she'd dropped her guard.

She pushed up the lace-trimmed undersleeves of her dress and settled a stack of sticky plates into the basin. Cloudy water covered her hands. She couldn't see her task any more clearly than she could see her future.

# 3

When the last plate was washed and replaced on the shelf, Luellen slipped out the back door and headed toward Papa's office. He wouldn't be there, but neither would anyone else. She wanted time alone.

Franklin rounded the corner of the house and planted himself in front of her. "Did you loose those simpering girls on me?"

Luellen managed a smile. "Better you than me. I'm tired of being gossiped about behind my back."

"Don't let them bother you. Not one of them has half your brains."

"Brains weren't enough—" She cleared her throat. As far as she knew, her parents had kept the news about Brendan from him. But who knew if he'd heard the gossip?

She changed subjects. "It's just not fair. You're twenty-five, and no one talks about you." Luellen mimicked a high-pitched voice. "He's not married. Why do you suppose that is?"

Franklin swept his fingers through his straight hair, pushing it behind his ears. "Who'd marry a person who spends his time scouting for the Army? I'd make a terrible husband." He turned toward Lieutenant Calder, who stood a few feet away listening to the exchange. "Ask Ward here. Am I husband material?"

Lieutenant Calder shook his head. "Don't expect me to answer that. Mrs. O'Connell, what would you call husband material?"

"I don't think about it. I'm through looking for a husband." She hoped her words were ambiguous enough not to be an outright lie.

"That puts you in the minority, it would seem." His words carried a touch of sarcasm.

Franklin glanced between them. "My sister has always had her own way of looking at the world." He took Luellen's elbow. "Were you going for a walk when we interrupted you?"

"No. I wanted to be alone in Papa's office." She disengaged her arm and turned toward the clapboarded cabin. "I need some time to think."

"We'll leave you to it." He strode toward his friend. "I want to show Ward around town. Tell Mother not to wait supper. We'll get something at the hotel."

The mingled aromas of camphor and various tinctures greeted her when she opened the office door and slipped inside. In an adjoining room, Papa had established a small three-bed infirmary. Shadows cast by the silver maple behind the building created fluid images of dark and light on the floor beneath the window.

She walked past the unoccupied beds and settled in a chair. Memories surrounded her. Here she'd grown up, studied her lessons, and dreamed of a life beyond Beldon Grove. Now those dreams seemed to rise and mock her.

She started at the sound of the door opening and closing. Franklin hesitated at the entrance to the infirmary, then moved toward her.

Luellen glanced behind him, expecting to see Lieutenant Calder.

"I sent him on ahead. The hotel's not that hard to find." Franklin grinned and sat on the edge of a bed facing her.

"I told you I wanted to be alone."

He leaned forward, forearms resting on his thighs, hands clasped between his knees. "That girl—Abigail—told me about your husband leaving." Anger darkened his expression. "I asked her if she had proof, and she said she heard the story through some of the railroad workers staying at the hotel. From there . . . well, you know how folks love to talk."

Luellen cringed. "It's worse than I feared. I'd hoped they were just guessing. Did she enjoy telling everyone at the wedding?"

"I put a flea in her ear—told her if she said another word to anyone, I had a story or two of my own to tell." He chuckled. "Not that I have anything, but she doesn't know that." Franklin's eyes searched hers, depth meeting depth. "I teased you when we were growing up, but I've always been proud of you and your goals. Don't give up now, Lulie."

Sighing, she rested her head against the back of her chair and stared at the ceiling. "I'm still so shocked I hardly know which way to turn. Today Papa said something about me being the only one left at home. He sounded so sad." She studied her brother's face, hoping he could understand her dilemma. "You know I wanted to be a teacher. I've worked at the hotel for the past four years saving money to attend normal school. Even if they'd admit me now, as a married woman, how can I disappoint Papa?"

A moment of quiet rested between them. Franklin stood, his expression unreadable. "I'm your friend, as well as your brother, but the decision is yours."

Luellen walked toward the cottage she and Brendan had shared. She knew Mama and Papa wanted her to move back into their home, but she saw that as the first step in a commitment to a life of spinsterhood. Monday she'd call on the hotel's proprietor and ask to be rehired. If she could resume cooking in the hotel kitchen, and if the rent on the cottage could be reduced, she'd remain where she was. Beyond that, she had no plan.

When she opened the door, her skin prickled. The room felt different. Her eyes darted to the corners. No one there. Turning, she entered the bedroom and stopped short. The low shelf under the window was missing. Her books and papers lay strewn over the floor. The wool blanket that covered the bed had been taken. *Brendan.*

Luellen dashed into the kitchen and unlatched the cupboard. The brown crockery she'd borrowed from her mother was shoved to one side. The dishes Brendan bought were gone. Frantic, she ran back into the bedroom and flung open the trunk where she'd stored her Rose of Sharon quilt. The vines and flowers stitched along the border greeted her eyes. She collapsed on the floor, weak with relief. From what she could see, Brendan had returned and taken everything he'd contributed to their brief life together, but he'd left her possessions undisturbed.

Where was he? Didn't he go to Chicago?

"Miz O'Connell?"

She jumped at the sound of a man's voice. Their landlord stood in the open doorway, an apologetic expression on his face.

"Mr. Pitt. You startled me." Luellen stood, trying to smooth her rumpled skirt. "I was just . . ." She waved her hand vaguely in the direction of the scattered books.

"I'm sorry to scare you. I came by to see when it is you're leaving."

"Leaving?"

"Yup. Your husband stopped in yesterday and told me you folks was moving out. I refunded him the rest of the rent." He looked at the disarray surrounding her. "'Course I'll expect you to leave it good as you found it, or I'll have to charge you some."

She threw her shoulders back. "It'll be perfectly clean before I go tomorrow."

"Figured it would." He lingered against the door frame. "You're headed for Chicago, he said? That'll be hard on your mama."

"Mr. O'Connell will be in Chicago." Luellen bit her lip, deciding he needed no further explanation.

When she didn't elaborate, Mr. Pitt raised his eyebrows in a question. "And you?"

The sadness she'd seen in Papa's eyes haunted her. "I haven't decided."

Once the landlord departed, Luellen removed her best dress and all but one petticoat, and slipped into a simple cotton gown and apron. With Brendan's possessions gone, little needed to be done to tidy the cottage. She surveyed the kitchen–sitting area. The cookware borrowed from her mother could be returned tomorrow. Her meager furnishings—table, two chairs, and a bedstead—likewise belonged to her parents and would be replaced in their home. Would she, too, return to her parents' care?

Kneeling in the bedroom, she gathered her scattered books. *Shakespeare's Collected Works*, Cooper's *The Deerslayer*, and her well-worn copy of Longfellow's *Ballads and Other Poems* were packed in a trunk, along with history and geography texts. After the last book was stored, she felt under the bed to be sure none had been kicked out of reach.

Her fingers grasped a thick envelope. Resting on her heels, Luellen reread the first page. *Miss Luellen McGarvie is accepted for admission to Allenwood Normal School, Allenwood, Illinois.*

*Fall term to begin September 14, 1857.* The next two sheets outlined courses she would need, described the residence hall, and listed names of families in Allenwood who were willing to board students.

⌒

The next morning, Luellen sat at the table sipping a mug of tea and nibbling a muffin left from yesterday's wedding breakfast. Her trunks were packed and ready to be taken to her parents' house, along with their furnishings. She'd take the key back to Mr. Pitt at his blacksmith shop that afternoon.

The door latch lifted. She dropped the muffin and braced herself, fearing Brendan had returned yet again. Instead, Franklin stepped into the room, followed by Lieutenant Calder.

"Mother sent us to escort you to church," Franklin said.

"I wasn't planning to go this morning. I don't feel like being a cynosure."

Franklin blinked. "What's that?"

"Something that strongly attracts attention," Lieutenant Calder answered for her.

Pleased to hear from someone who shared her love of language, Luellen flashed him a smile. "Thank you. Someone has to help Franklin learn words of more than one syllable."

Franklin picked up a muffin. "I was just waiting to see if Ward knew what it meant."

Luellen chuckled, then quieted. "I'd rather stay here."

"Don't worry. We'll be there with you, won't we?" Franklin turned to Lieutenant Calder, who nodded.

"But I've packed my Sunday dress."

"What you're wearing looks fine." Franklin popped the muffin into his mouth and moved toward the door.

"I know it's not my affair, Mrs. O'Connell, but my experience has been that the sooner one faces down opposition, the sooner it passes." Lieutenant Calder bowed in her direction and held out his arm, crooked at the elbow. "Allow me."

"All right."

Sighing, she stood and laid her hand on his arm. Franklin stepped to her other side. Once outdoors, he helped her into his rented buggy.

Dogwood trees provided scattered shade along the route to Uncle Matthew's church. Lieutenant Calder removed his black felt hat and wiped his forehead. "Where I come from out east, we don't have this unending humidity."

"And where is that?" Luellen asked, more out of politeness than any real interest.

"Northern Pennsylvania. Athens."

"You're a long way from home."

Franklin laughed. "The Army is Ward's home. He lives and breathes drills and excursions."

When the whitewashed siding of the church came into view, Franklin slowed the horse to a walk. "I noticed you're packed to leave," he said to Luellen. "You've made your decision?"

She shook her head. "I can't stop thinking about Papa's face when he said I was the only one left. I'm packed because I promised the landlord I'd be out today." She preferred not to discuss family matters in front of a stranger, but it seemed Lieutenant Calder would be at Franklin's side for the remainder of his visit. She bit her lip before continuing. "Brendan told Mr. Pitt we were leaving. He pocketed the rent refund and, I hope, left for Chicago."

Lieutenant Calder stirred next to her. "If you'll excuse my saying so, you're a brave woman. In your circumstances most females of my acquaintance would take to their beds with the vapors."

"Not my sister," Franklin said, guiding the horse to a hitching rail. "I told you she has her own way of looking at the world."

The two men flanked Luellen as they walked into the nearly full church. A few heads turned. One woman covered her mouth with her hand and spoke into another's ear.

"Hold your chin up and look everyone in the eye," Lieutenant Calder whispered.

They found vacant seats next to her parents as the congregation rose to sing the opening hymn. When the words of "Just As I Am" flowed over her, some of the defilement she felt from Brendan's betrayal washed away. She was who she was, and she couldn't help what people thought of her. She would make her decisions and accept the consequences.

Uncle Matthew stepped to the pulpit. Amused, Luellen noticed that his graying hair had been slicked flat, but wiry strands had sprung loose along the sides of his head. She couldn't remember ever seeing him with his hair under control. The effect made his words seem fervent, even when he uttered the most commonplace statements.

Following prayer, he opened his Bible. "Our scripture for today is found in Jeremiah, chapter 29." While he read the text, Luellen visualized the words stitched on the back of her Rose of Sharon quilt. "... *thoughts of peace, and not of evil.*" Would her decision bring peace—or more evil?

Late Sunday afternoon, Luellen and her parents accompanied Franklin and Lieutenant Calder to the railroad depot where they'd board the train for the first leg of their journey to St. Louis. The sun's red-gold light reflected against the windows of the passenger carriage as they approached, which added to the fearsome

dragonlike effect of smoke and sparks billowing from the locomotive's stack.

Luellen clung to Franklin's arm. "I'll miss you more than ever."

"Wish we could stay longer, but Ward had to talk hard to get
this much furlough. I'll haunt the post waiting for your letters."
He bent close to her ear. "Still undecided?"

She nodded, turning to say good-bye to Lieutenant Calder,
who stood with her parents.

"I'm grateful for your hospitality," he said, shaking Papa's hand.
"It's a treat for me to spend time with a family." He removed his
hat and ran his fingers through his russet-brown hair. "My mother
and father have been gone for some years."

Mama's face showed sympathy. "You have no brothers or sisters?"

"No, ma'am."

"Well, you're welcome in our home anytime."

He dipped his head, acknowledging her words. "Thank you."

"Bo-oard!" the conductor called from the steps of the carriage.
Steam from the locomotive poured over the platform.

Franklin and Lieutenant Calder climbed aboard and after a
moment leaned out one of the open windows, waving good-bye.

Luellen and her parents waved back, watching until the train
resembled a centipede in the distance. "That poor boy," Mama
said. "No family."

Papa slipped his arm around her shoulders. "It's unfortunate,
but he's not a boy. He's thirty, according to Franklin."

"Nevertheless, I meant it when I said he was welcome in our
home. Everyone needs to belong somewhere."

He gave her a one-armed hug, then turned to Luellen. "I have
something serious to discuss with you when we get home."

# 4

Luellen took her father's arm when they left the train platform. "What do you want to talk to me about?"

"I'd rather wait until we get home."

Did he know of her letter from Allenwood Normal School? She didn't recall mentioning it.

Was he sick? Her stomach clenched at the idea. He looked tired and drawn, but she attributed that to the fatigue of wedding preparations. Papa had been her rock since she was four, when he married Mama. He couldn't be sick. She shoved the thought away.

More than likely, he assumed that by bringing her possessions back home she meant to stay. She swallowed hard. Why did they need to have this discussion today?

They entered the front door and turned into the sitting area. Mama and Papa took seats side by side on the divan. He removed his cravat and unfastened the top button of his high-necked shirt, resting his feet on a cushioned stool.

Mama lifted a fan from a side table and waved it in front of her perspiring face. "I'm glad to be out of that sun. Today's the hottest it's been all week."

Papa pointed to an armchair near the hearth. "Sit down and rest, Lulie. You worked for days on your sister's wedding. It's been hard on you, I know. You're tired—we're all tired."

Luellen sank into the chair. Bending over, she worked the buttons on her boots open and slid them off, wiggling her toes against the polished oak floor. "We're home now. What did you want to discuss?" Her nerves trilled while she waited his answer.

"I spoke to Elihu Stebbins about your situation after church this morning."

"The lawyer? Why?"

He took Mama's hand. Clearly, she already knew what he planned to say. Her eyes glittered with tears.

"You have to undo your marriage," he said. "File for divorce."

Stunned, Luellen stared at him. "Divorce? But I'm not really married. Brendan already had a wife."

Mama rose and crossed the room, laying a hand on Luellen's shoulder. "Your marriage in front of the judge was legal according to Illinois law." She brushed stray curls off Luellen's cheek. "To be able to remarry you need to dissolve the bonds once and for all."

"Remarry? Nothing could be farther from my mind."

"Maybe not now . . ."

Luellen sought Papa's face. "Can't we just let things go on this way? He won't dare—" Then she thought of him coming back to get his possessions while she was away from the cottage. No telling what Brendan would dare. She slumped against the back of the chair. "This is a nightmare. Even if I leave Beldon Grove, I'll be branded as a divorced woman wherever I go." Luellen covered her face with her hands, feeling tears against her fingers.

"People forget, quicker than you think." Papa's deep voice rumbled comfort.

Mama kissed the top of her head. "Hold your chin up and look them in the eye."

Luellen sniffled, remembering. Lieutenant Calder had said the same thing when they entered the church that morning.

Smoke and cinders billowed through the open windows of the passenger carriage. Ward Calder shifted on the iron-bordered wooden seat. "Why can't they build these cars for comfort?"

Franklin chuckled. "Beats riding a horse for days out in the sun. We should be back at the barracks by tomorrow morning, if nothing happens to the train along the way." He picked a cinder from the leg of his trousers and dropped it out the window. "A weekend furlough wouldn't have been enough to get us to Beldon Grove without this smoking beast."

Ward nodded. "I like your family. Thanks for asking me."

"Sorry you had to walk into my sister's domestic troubles." He shook his head. "I couldn't believe it when Mother wrote she'd run off and got married. Luellen of all people."

"Everybody needs someone to love." Ward clenched his jaw. Why'd he say that? He sounded like a woman.

Franklin gave him a surprised look. "Thought you loved the Army."

"I was referring to your sister. Women have those instincts." Discomfited, he stood, wishing he'd never opened his mouth. He brought his bag down from the overhead rack and rummaged through it until he found his canteen. At that moment, a water boy walked through the car carrying a bucket with a dipper hooked to the side. Franklin motioned him over.

"You thirsty?" he asked Ward.

He held up his canteen. "Brought my own."

After taking a long drink, Franklin gave the boy a coin and resumed his seat. To Ward's dismay, he jumped back into their previous conversation.

"I could never understand how a man could spend his life in

the Army, being ordered around every day." He leaned back and locked his fingers behind his head, stretching his long legs in the aisle. "The commander at Jefferson Barracks pays me to scout the trail to Santa Fe, but he doesn't own me. Merchants in St. Louis want to get their goods to New Mexico Territory. If something happens, they blame the Army, not me."

Ward studied his friend. What a difference between Franklin's beliefs and his own. If he'd grown up with a family like Franklin's, maybe he'd feel the same way. But he didn't. He turned and stared out at the prairie sliding past the window like a bronze river. "I like the assurance the Army offers," he said, half to himself. "The rules and order. The predictability. When things go well, it's like the poet said, 'God's in his heaven, all's right with the world.'"

Franklin snorted. "You get all that from some fat captain hollering at you when you're five minutes late? If you really want to see God in his heaven, come with me the next time I go out on the trail. The sky pulses with stars. I think of them as sparks burned through a canvas, letting heaven's light pour down."

Ward felt exposed to be talking so freely about feelings. He looked out the window again, noticing purple dusk shading the scenery. "Let's get some sleep. The commander may not own *you*, but I have to be ready to go first thing tomorrow." He rolled his coat into a pillow and tried to get comfortable on the wooden bench.

In Alton, Ward and Franklin hurried from the depot to the ferry landing. Once across the Mississippi, they retrieved their mounts from a livery stable and rode toward Jefferson Barracks.

As the men approached the post, Ward saw new recruits on the parade ground going through drills. Morning sun illuminated limestone buildings arranged in a semicircle on a bluff overlooking the river.

Franklin looked at him. "How late are you?"

"Maybe an hour."

"Will it do any good to tell the captain we missed the ferry and had to wait?"

"What do you think?"

Franklin reined in his horse. "Wish I could help." He raised an eyebrow. "Good luck." He rode toward the enlisted men's quarters, his home when he wasn't on the trail.

Ward took a deep breath, girding himself for the encounter with the post commander. Captain Block's temper was one of the predictable features of Army life that he could do without.

After stabling his horse, he entered the headquarters building. A musty, mildewed smell wrinkled his nose. The older buildings on the post were poorly built, with damp masonry floors and roofs that leaked. He was tempted to leave the front door ajar to gain air circulation, but the captain had forbidden the action. Jefferson Barracks was headquarters for the Department of the West, and as such needed to display formality.

In line with formal requirements, Ward straightened his coat and shined the toe of each boot on the back of his trouser legs. Shoulders squared, he strode down a hall and entered Captain Block's domain.

His superior officer raised his head when Ward entered. Gray hair parted on one side framed his craggy face. The buttons on his single-breasted coat shone in the lance of sunlight penetrating the room.

Captain Block stood, leaning forward. "Lieutenant Calder. How good of you to drop by." His voice sounded gentle.

Ward braced himself.

"Do you think you're living on some soft Southern plantation?"

the captain roared. "You were to report in hours ago. Are you, or are you not, planning on a career as an Army engineer?"

"I am, sir."

"Does the Corps allow its men to live by their own rules?"

"No, sir."

"Then what are you playing at, Lieutenant?"

"Nothing, sir. It was an unavoidable circumstance."

Captain Block drew a deep breath and blew it out with an exasperated snort. "Circumstances, by their very nature, are unavoidable. Don't engineers know that?"

"Yes, sir, they do."

The captain resumed his seat, leaning one elbow on the arm of his chair. "So, have you completed mapping your last survey?" His voice took on normal tones.

From experience, Ward knew the storm had passed. He fought an impulse to whip out his handkerchief and mop his sweating forehead. "Yes, sir."

Pretending to search his desktop, Captain Block said, "I don't see it."

"The maps are in my quarters, sir. I'll have them here in ten minutes."

"I'll be waiting."

Ward strode across the grounds toward the officers' quarters. He banged in the front door and took the stairs two at a time. Once in his room, he threw off his hat and coat and dropped them on the bed. The portfolio that held his maps lay on the desk. He grabbed it, unfastening the loop holding the flap closed. A stack of maps slid onto the desktop. He glanced at the top page, then took a second look. Where was the overview? The sheet that held the name and location of the area surveyed, along with the outside boundaries, was missing.

He fanned the right-hand corners, thinking he'd accidentally shoved the first page behind the other sheets. Nothing out of order. He scrubbed his fingers through his hair. He knew he'd completed the task—he remembered initialing each page as he placed his work in the portfolio.

"Looking for something?" Lieutenant Mark Campion leaned against the doorframe, his round face mocking.

Ward surveyed Lieutenant Campion through narrowed eyes. They'd both graduated from the Academy in the same class, Ward near the top, Campion next to the bottom. They hadn't been friends during their years of study, and proximity at the Army post hadn't brought them any closer. "The first page of my survey seems to have disappeared. Know anything about it?"

"I might." He slid his hand into his pants pocket and pulled the lining out. "Empty. I could use a little help until we get paid."

Ward shook his head. "Sorry."

"You can afford it. Everyone knows your old man left you a pile of money."

"Is that what everyone knows? Well, now they'll know I don't respond to extortion." He grasped the edge of the door and pushed it in Campion's face.

"You'll be sorry, Calder."

"I doubt it." The latch clicked and he heard Campion stalk away.

At Captain Block's request, he'd spent hours combining the results of several separate surveys to produce the front matter. Gritting his teeth, he tucked the portfolio under his arm and headed for the captain's office. Ward could only guess at how he'd react to the news that the survey was another day or two away from completion.

# 5

On Monday, Luellen walked the five blocks to Bryant House. Early morning air carried the fragrance of wood smoke from neighbors' cookstoves. As she passed the town square, she heard blue jays squabbling over breakfast among the branches of elm trees.

Luellen loved walking early in the morning. In her imagination, she pretended she was alone on the prairie, back in the days when there were no houses. A locomotive approaching the station jolted her back to present-day Beldon Grove and the reason she was hurrying toward the hotel.

How would Mr. Bryant react when she asked to be rehired? More than that, how would she handle the regular customers' reactions when they saw her there?

She cut around behind the building and entered through the kitchen door. A woman she didn't know stood in front of the range, cracking eggs into a skillet. For a moment, Luellen pictured herself standing there, and Brendan sitting at the worktable chatting with her while she cooked.

He'd stopped into the kitchen shortly after he arrived in Beldon Grove to tell her he'd enjoyed her lovely supper. Blue eyes twinkling, he offered to be her official food taster. As days went by, she heard his woebegone tale of loneliness for his family back in Ireland. She couldn't resist offering words of comfort—he was so grateful—and soon found herself spending all her free time with him. She blinked, and the vision disappeared.

The woman at the range dropped the last eggshell into a pail. "Morning. You looking for work?"

"I'm Luellen Mc—O'Connell. I used to be the cook here."

"Martha Dolan. Mr. Bryant hired me last month. You must be the gal who up and got married." She wiped her hands on her apron and pointed at the coffee boiler. "Help yourself. Reckon you know where everything is." Martha picked up a spatula. "I've got to tend to these eggs."

Martha looked to be around thirty or so, broad-shouldered, wearing a harassed expression. Luellen filled a mug and sat at one of the chairs around the long worktable. "Where's your helper? When I worked here Mr. Bryant had a girl come in mornings to get breakfast out quickly for the workers."

"Haven't seen her for a week. Heard he's looking for someone else." Martha used the back of her arm to brush trailing brown hair from her forehead. Her freckled cheeks were red from the range's heat. Using both hands, she lifted the skillet by its long handle and expertly slid a dozen eggs onto a waiting platter. A nearby bowl of biscuits sent a tantalizing fragrance through the room.

"How'd you like to carry these eggs into the dining room? I'll be right behind you with the biscuits." She clanged the empty skillet onto the stovetop. "I need this job, but if you want to take over helping, we'll talk to Mr. Bryant when the rush is over."

Luellen grasped the crockery platter with both hands and pushed through the door that led to the dining room. Several men dressed in work clothes looked up eagerly when she appeared.

"'Bout time," one of them grumbled.

Martha slapped the pan of biscuits on the long table. "Takes

39

longer to cook this than it does for you to eat it." She jammed her hands on her hips and surveyed the complainer. "But you'd best keep a civil tongue in your head. I can't work faster, but I sure can move slower." With a grin, she returned to the kitchen.

Luellen turned to follow her when one of the men put out a hand and grabbed her wrist. "Say, aren't you the gal that Brendan O'Connell married? Heard he went back to Chicago." He looked her up and down. "How come you're still here?"

She jerked her hand away, her mind searching for a response.

Another customer poked the man on the shoulder. "Tell you later." He arched an eyebrow at Luellen. "You looking for someone to take O'Connell's place?"

Luellen stared at him until he lowered his eyes. Now all of the men were watching her, silent, waiting. "In case any of you have the same question, the answer is no. Not now, not ever." She took a deep breath and cocked her head toward the kitchen. "Anyone want more coffee?"

Mr. Bryant came in while Martha and Luellen were washing breakfast dishes. "One of the boarders told me you was here," he said to Luellen. "I heard about O'Connell—your uncle Arthur stopped by yesterday."

Uncle Arthur's habits were as predictable as the sunrise. Sunday dinner at the hotel, Monday at her parents' home, Tuesday at Uncle Matthew's, and so on through his list of friends and family. In a way she was relieved not to have to make an announcement to Mr. Bryant. He'd voiced his disapproval of Brendan almost as soon as the two of them met. A warning she shouldn't have ignored.

Martha set a cup of coffee and two buttered biscuits in front of him. He nodded his thanks and continued talking to Luellen. "So you're back. Martha here's doing fine—we don't need two cooks. Are you willing to serve meals and do washing up?"

Luellen thought about facing the railroad workers every day. As cook, she'd had limited contact with the men. If she were to hire on as kitchen maid, she'd have to cope with customers like this morning's questioner at each meal. The letter from Allenwood Normal School flashed into her mind. If not now, when?

"Cat got your tongue?" Mr. Bryant took a bite of biscuit.

Luellen perched on the edge of a chair facing him. "I'll work for two weeks, if that's suitable. Then I'm leaving Beldon Grove."

As Luellen walked home late that afternoon, gusty wind blew grit from the road onto her perspiring face. Several buggies rolled by on the stage road and she heard a locomotive clang its way into the station. Excitement rose in her throat. Before long, she'd be going somewhere too.

Her steps slowed. First, she needed to tell Mama and Papa about Allenwood. *Lord, please help them understand.*

Her parents smiled at her from their seats on the veranda when she came up the front steps. "Looks like Jack Bryant gave you your job back," Papa said.

"Not quite." She sat in a rocking chair facing them. "He has a new cook. I'm hired as kitchen maid for the next two weeks."

"What happens then?"

She leaned forward. "I'm leaving for Allenwood. Upstairs, I have a letter from the Normal School. In June, I was accepted into their teaching program, but by then I'd met Brendan. I thought I had to choose." She made a harsh sound in her throat. "He chose for me."

Papa's face sagged. Luellen noticed how gray had overtaken the blond in his thinning hair. Pouches of fatigue rested under his eyes.

She surveyed her mother. Silver wings fanned through her

41

gleaming black hair. Her once-trim figure had turned matronly. How long had it been since she really looked at them?

"Your impulsiveness is going to be the ruin of you." Mama shook her head. "First you run off and get married. Now you want to travel almost two hundred miles north and have a career." She twisted a lace-trimmed handkerchief between her fingers. "Once James graduates, I doubt he'll come back. Franklin's in Missouri. Now Lily's gone. Please, let some time pass before you decide."

"I want to be a teacher. I've told you that before and you didn't take me seriously."

"That's the trouble," Papa said. "You've talked about going away to school for years, but you're still here. We stopped paying attention."

Excuses trembled behind Luellen's lips. She'd needed to save money. She had to find a school that accepted women. She had to stay and help them with the move into the new house. Swallowing, she stared at her hands. In truth, she hadn't left because of her fear of the unknown. It was easier to remain at home and talk about leaving than it was to pack her bags and set off.

Something clicked into place today at Bryant House. If she remained in Beldon Grove, she'd be gossiped about by everyone in town. At the hotel it would be no time at all before every man who came through thought she was an easy target.

She met Papa's eyes. "I don't blame you for not paying attention. As time went by, I stopped listening to myself. But now I have a second chance and I'm going to take it."

For a moment, no one said anything. The mantel clock inside chimed a quarter past six. When Mama looked up, tears glistened in her eyes. "If you leave, all my children will be gone."

"James said he'd be back when he finished medical school."

Papa folded his arms over his chest. "Maybe. His letters sound like he's pretty well settled there in Philadelphia."

"Lily and Edmund will visit."

"It's not the same thing." Mama wiped her eyes with her handkerchief. "Edmund's business is in Springfield."

Luellen longed to capitulate, to promise to stay, anything to wipe the sorrow from her parents' faces. But she couldn't. Postponing her decision had brought her to this point—now she had to act.

Papa used the arm of his chair to boost himself to his feet. "No school would waste a teaching certificate on a married woman." He cleared his throat. "I'll take you to Elihu Stebbins's office tomorrow whenever you're able to leave the hotel. He can draw up a divorce petition for us."

Hands on the clock in the hotel kitchen pointed at thirty minutes past ten when Papa appeared at the door. As soon as Luellen saw him, she hung her apron on a peg and waved at Martha. "I'll be back before noon."

Martha looked up from rolling a pie crust. "Good luck to you. Tell me what it's like, in case I take a notion." She grinned.

Luellen smiled back, appreciating the other woman's attempt to make light of a serious matter. "I'll write everything down." Her smile faded. She checked to be sure her gored brown skirt wasn't stained from breakfast and joined Papa at the door.

They crossed the road and walked three blocks up Jefferson Street to the Bryant County Bank, where Elihu Stebbins occupied an office at the east end of the modest brick building. Luellen followed Papa inside, her heart thudding in her chest. A lamp burning on a desk tried valiantly to push gloom out of the dark recesses of the rectangular space. Mr. Stebbins rose and extended his hand. His thin hair had been raked in neat furrows across his pink scalp. "Dr. Spengler. I appreciate you coming to me with this delicate matter." His voice was as papery as the books that lined the walls.

He nodded at Luellen. "Mrs. O'Connell. Your father has told me of your unfortunate . . . experience. I will do all I can to bring this matter to a speedy conclusion." He gestured toward two straight-backed chairs on her side of the desk. "Please sit."

Luellen chose the seat nearest the lamp and waited. Mr. Stebbins drew an open volume toward himself and ran his finger down the page. Without looking up, he said, "I understand this is a case of bigamy. The defendant's name is Brendan O'Connell, is that correct?"

"Yes." Luellen felt naked before the blunt legal terms. The excitement of meeting and marrying Brendan had become something shameful. It took strength of will to continue to hold her head erect and listen to the lawyer as though she were unaffected by his words. Papa reached over and grasped her hand.

Mr. Stebbins dipped a pen in an inkpot and held it poised over a sheet of paper. "Where is Mr. O'Connell now?"

"Chicago, I believe."

"Do you have an address?"

She almost laughed. Why would she have his address? "No."

"You understand that once the bill of divorce is filed, a subpoena will be issued in chancery ordering Brendan O'Connell to appear in court to answer the charge of bigamy." He laid the pen down. "Your father tells me Mr. O'Connell works for a freighting company?"

"Yes."

"We'll make inquiries to find him."

A flush traveled up her body. "You mean he has to come back here? I have to see him?"

Papa squeezed her hand as Mr. Stebbins answered. "He is required to appear if he contests the charge." His voice softened. "In my experience, if the defendant is clearly in the wrong, he most often will ignore the summons. Please don't distress yourself."

"What happens next?"

He leaned back in his chair. "If he doesn't appear, the charges will be taken as confessed. The Circuit Court will hear the case and grant your petition. There should be time within this term of court to complete the matter. You will be free of the man."

His words hung in the musty air. She'd be freed from Brendan, but she'd carry the stigma of divorce forever.

The lawyer continued. "I'll prepare the papers for your signature. They will be ready by tomorrow afternoon."

"Thank you." Luellen stood, trembling. She needed to get outside before she collapsed.

Papa rose and slid his arm around her waist. "We'll be here around three o'clock."

Once on the board sidewalk, Luellen leaned against him and took in gulps of air.

"Relax," Papa said. "If you faint out here on the street, you'll really give folks gossip fodder." He chuckled.

"I've caused you so much trouble and embarrassment. Can you ever forgive me?"

He turned her toward him and took both of her hands. "There's nothing to forgive. We've all done things we wish we could undo, but life doesn't work that way. Someday we'll see how this has brought good to all of us."

Luellen doubted it, but she kissed his cheek and walked in the direction of Bryant House while Papa crossed Jefferson Street and headed back to his office. As she passed the town square, her pace slowed. They couldn't have spent more than thirty minutes with Mr. Stebbins. If she hurried, she could take one more step toward Allenwood before returning to work.

She turned east and strode toward Clark Street.

# 6

On her way home after work, Luellen wondered what her mother's reaction would be to the morning's events. Now she needed to tell both of them about the mission she'd completed before returning to the hotel. Conscious of the turmoil she'd brought to her parents' lives, she wavered. Perhaps the visit to the lawyer was enough for one day. Ahead, fading sunset painted their house with a golden brush, touching Mama and Papa as they rested in their after-supper chairs on the veranda.

The papers in Luellen's reticule whispered their promise of a new life. Her stomach fluttered with a mixture of anticipation and fear.

She climbed the steps, meeting Mama's welcoming smile with one of her own, and settled into a chair facing them.

"You're late this evening," Papa said.

"I stayed longer to make up for being away this morning."

"You weren't gone that long. It's past seven thirty now—much more than an extra hour."

Luellen removed pasteboard squares from her reticule. "I went to the train depot before returning to the hotel. These are my tickets to Allenwood."

He scanned them and whistled. "Pretty steep price."

Luellen nodded. The flutter in her stomach was back. "I didn't expect the fare to cost so much. I won't be able to come home very often." She darted a glance at her mother, expecting to see tears.

Instead, Mama asked, "When are you leaving?" in a matter-of-fact voice.

"September 7. It's a Monday."

"So your mind is made up."

"Absolutely." Luellen wished she felt as certain on the inside as she sounded on the outside. She took her mother's hand. "I'm sorry, Mama. If I don't do this now, I'm afraid I never will."

"Don't be sorry. I've thought about your plans all day. I understand your determination."

"You do?"

Mama leaned forward. "I remember how I felt when I wanted to leave your uncle Matthew's house and find my own cabin. You were too young to understand then, but my brother opposed my leaving. Even after Uncle Arthur found me that little place north of town, Matt kept after me to come back and live with them. Worrying about Franklin, trying to take care of you children, and fighting my brother all at the same time was one of the hardest things I ever had to do."

"But she did it," Papa said. "I'd never seen anyone like her. She won my heart without even trying."

Mama flashed him a smile and turned back to Luellen. "After I recalled all that, I realized I was doing the same thing to you by wanting you to stay here with us." She shook her head. "It was wrong then, and it would be wrong now. Go to Allenwood. You have my blessing."

Luellen exhaled and leaned back in her chair. Of all the reactions Mama might have chosen, this was one she hadn't anticipated. Love for her mother brought sudden tears to her eyes. "I

48

remember that cabin. We weren't there long. After that we lived in Mr. Pitt's house. I guess I never thought about how you felt—you were just Mama, busy all the time."

"I'm still Mama." She grinned. "We have less than two weeks to get your things together before you leave." Standing, she looked at Papa. "Did Mr. Stebbins say how long they'd wait to hear back from Brendan?"

He shook his head. "We'll find out tomorrow."

Brendan. His unseen presence threatened to unravel her plans. Papa was right—the Normal School wouldn't waste a teaching certificate on a married woman.

Smoke from the locomotive rose in the distance. The tracks next to the platform hummed with the vibration of the approaching train. Luellen looked down to be sure her trunk waited at her side.

Papa laughed. "It hasn't moved since you checked last time."

After years of dreaming, the moment had arrived. Nervous perspiration moistened her palms. What if she couldn't find a place to live? She'd finished her formal schooling four years ago—could she study at Normal School level? She sucked in a deep breath and held it until her lungs ached. Most frightening of all, what if Brendan responded to her suit and delayed the decree? Representing herself as Luellen McGarvie before her divorce was granted could get her dismissed from school. Her heart pounded at the thought.

The locomotive roared into the station, bell clanging, steam pouring from beneath the engine. The cars clashed together as the train stopped. A worker hopped down from the baggage car and approached them. "This your trunk, miss?"

Luellen nodded.

He hefted it onto his shoulder and dropped it in the car, then walked to the next passengers to collect their luggage.

Luellen kissed her parents. Good-byes had already been said, over and over. There was nothing left to do but board the train. Chin uplifted, she entered the passenger carriage. She didn't look back.

Weary, dusty, and stiff-limbed, Luellen stepped onto the train platform in Allenwood. Setting sun threw orange light over the bustling depot. While she waited for her trunk, Luellen studied her surroundings. Three omnibuses waited for passengers. Looking beyond them into town, she saw a large shopping district bounded by wooden sidewalks and the gabled roofs of homes spread as far as she could see.

A freight wagon rumbled past. In spite of herself, Luellen turned, following the driver with her eyes. An older man in a slouch hat. Not Brendan.

"Miss?"

She jumped when one of the omnibus drivers spoke. "Do you require transportation?"

"Yes."

"Where are you going?"

"Allenwood Normal School." She studied the crumpled paper in her hand. "But now I need to find Mrs. Hawks's boardinghouse."

The driver touched the brim of his cap. "Miz Hawks's place is on College Avenue—not far from the school. It's on my route." He pointed at the first of the three omnibuses. "Please seat yourself."

"Thank you. My trunk is over there. Could you fetch it for me?"

"Be happy to. As soon as I have a few more passengers, we'll be on our way."

She settled in one of the empty seats below the driver's bench. Another woman sat alone at the back, and an older man who reminded her of Uncle Arthur sat near the middle. She heard a thud overhead and assumed the driver had dropped her trunk next to the other baggage stowed between iron rails on the roof. Luellen stared straight ahead, trying to look like she rode public transportation every day. The men and women who passed by on the street paid no attention to the buses or the departing train. In Beldon Grove, this much activity would have drawn a crowd.

She'd had a skimpy meal earlier at a relay station, and now her stomach grumbled with hunger. Maybe there'd be a late supper available at the boardinghouse.

After a half dozen more people boarded the bus, the driver took his seat outside and shook the reins over the horses' backs. They rumbled through the center of town, passing more shops than Luellen had ever seen in one place before. One side of the street was lined with a dry goods store, a butcher shop, a boot maker, and a bookstore. The other side boasted a hotel, a jeweler, a barber, a dressmaker, and a milliner. The bus stopped in front of the hotel and most of the passengers disembarked. Once the driver carried their luggage inside, he climbed back onto his seat and drove past more businesses into a residential area.

"This here's College Avenue," he called down. "The Normal School is at the corner of College and Chestnut—about a half mile on." He slowed the wagon and stopped in front of a modest frame house. "Miz Hawks's place." The omnibus jounced as he climbed off his perch outside and opened the rear door. "This is your stop, miss," he said to the woman sitting in the back.

Glad for a companion, Luellen turned and smiled at her. "Did you just arrive in Allenwood too?"

"Yes." Her fair skin looked flushed. When she stood, her dress snagged on the arm of the seat. Luellen heard cloth tear as she jerked it free. "Drat these hoops anyway!" The woman stomped down the steps and stood tapping her foot while the driver climbed back up to retrieve the baggage.

Luellen descended and stood beside her. "I hope your dress isn't too badly torn."

"No. I can mend it." She turned round blue eyes on Luellen. "My mama insisted I dress properly for the trip." She glanced at Luellen's skirt and put her fingers to her lips. "Oh! I'm sorry! I don't mean to imply you're not—"

"Don't apologize. I despise hoops and won't wear them. My mama gave up a long time ago."

The other woman, who looked to be not more than sixteen, extended a lace-gloved hand. "I'm Liberty Belle Brownlee. Isn't that the most dreadful name? Please call me Belle."

"I'm happy to make your acquaintance, Belle. I'm Luellen . . . McGarvie."

Luellen heard a tap on her door the next morning and opened it to see Belle standing in the hallway. She slipped into the room and brushed her hand across the skirt of her green calico print dress. "Look, no hoops. You won't write my mama and tell her, will you?"

"I'll keep your secret." Luellen smiled and turned back to the mirror to slip a silk net over the coil of braids at the back of her head. "After breakfast, would you like to accompany me to the Normal School? I need to make residence arrangements as soon as possible. At two dollars a night here, I'll run through my savings in no time."

"The very thing I planned to do myself." Belle faced Luellen, excitement sparkling in her eyes. "I'm so pleased we met. I want to be a teacher in the worst way, but must confess to being frightened at leaving home."

Looking at her, Luellen felt older than her years. "You're fortunate to obtain your schooling while you're still so young."

"Twenty-one's not young. Most girls my age are married."

At Luellen's surprised expression, she continued, "It's this round face of mine. People treat me like a child. I worry that I won't be able to enforce discipline when we do our practice teaching—that's a big part of the training here."

Luellen's stomach tightened. "Right now, I'm worried about all of it. The course listing mentions zoology and botany—they weren't taught in my school."

Belle tilted her head. "Do you understand algebra?"

"A little."

"We'll help each other. If we register together, perhaps they'll allow us to share a room." The brown curls at the back of her neck bounced as she opened the door and preceded Luellen down the stairs to breakfast.

The campus of Allenwood Normal School spread over a broad grassy area. Graveled pathways formed a T in front of a four-story red brick building that dominated the landscape. Maple trees grew at regularly spaced intervals across the lawn, their leaves showing the first tints of autumn. At one end of the path stood a broad two-story building. The school chapel, a square edifice with a cross atop the bell tower, faced Chestnut Street.

The words "Allenwood Hall" were carved into the stone frieze above the double front doors of the administration building. A bronze plaque set into the brick entry read *The highest object of education must be that of living a life in accordance with God's will.*

"The drawings in the brochure didn't do justice to the size of this place," Luellen said, awed.

"The state capitol at home in Springfield isn't this tall, but it's much grander. I've visited there with my papa more than once."

Surprised, Luellen glanced at her new friend. Perhaps they had less in common than she first believed.

After the two women entered Allenwood Hall, they followed an arrow pointing toward the registrar's office. Their footsteps echoed along the passageway.

"It's quiet here. I wonder if we're the first students to arrive," Belle said.

"Maybe. We're a week early. I wanted plenty of time to get settled." Luellen clutched her acceptance letter, hoping her moist palms wouldn't smear the ink.

A young man looked up from a desk covered with papers. "New students, or returning?"

"New." A wave of joy swept over Luellen. She was really here, registering for school. "Here's my acceptance." She thrust the wrinkled envelope at him.

"Here's mine," Belle said. "I'm new too."

"The registrar will see you one at a time." He smoothed his sparse moustache and lifted Luellen's letter. "You may go first. Take this with you. Dr. Alexander's office is directly to your left."

The registrar rose when she entered. His height and his wiry hair reminded her of Uncle Matthew. "Welcome. You're the first student to register for this term, Miss—" He took the envelope, removed the contents, and scanned the first page. "Miss McGarvie."

She dropped her gaze, feeling a flush rise in her cheeks at his use of her maiden name. Two more weeks to wait. If Brendan failed to appear, which Mr. Stebbins believed to be likely, the circuit court would grant her petition.

The registrar's voice cut through her thoughts. "Please sit."

Luellen glanced around. The chairs were piled with books. She hesitated, then lifted a stack onto the floor and settled in a chair facing his desk.

"You've had a secondary education in Bryant County, I see."

"Yes." She locked her fingers together to keep her hands from trembling.

"It's our policy to test all students who come to us from the rural areas. I trust you're prepared to take a placement examination this morning?"

Luellen tried to hide her dismay. Nothing in the acceptance letter had mentioned a qualifying test. The trembling in her hands spread through her body. "Yes, sir. I'm prepared."

"Excellent." Dr. Alexander stood and walked to the door. "Down the hall to your right, you will see a room marked 'Testing—Do Not Disturb.' Just go on in. Mrs. Hale is waiting—she will be the proctor. Once your examination is reviewed, if your scores are acceptable, we'll complete the registration process." His stern face cracked into a smile. "Don't look so frightened. Most applicants do very well."

As she walked through the anteroom, she met Belle's questioning gaze. "I have to take a placement test."

Belle gasped. "Oh my word. Do you suppose he'll make me take one too?"

"Depends on where you went to school," the young man at the desk answered. "Small towns, yes. Cities, no."

Luellen tried to focus on the test packet, but her eyes kept drooping shut. She wanted nothing more than to lay her head on the table and sleep. An hour to go. She unbuttoned the first two buttons on her bodice and fanned herself. If it weren't so hot in the room, she knew she'd be better able to concentrate. Mrs. Hale had a book open on her desk, but more than once Luellen caught her nodding off.

The clock ticked toward noon. Luellen turned the next page in the booklet. No. Not zoology. She flipped to the next section. Botany. Swallowing hard, she turned the page again. Literature. She could answer those questions. Relieved, she wrote until the bell in the church steeple tolled twelve.

Mrs. Hale stood. "Time. Be back here at two. We'll have the results for you."

# 7

Luellen stumbled out of Allenwood Hall without waiting to find Belle. She knew the blank sections in her test would send her back to Beldon Grove on the next train. But now all she could think of was sleep. She'd never been so tired.

An omnibus and several carriages passed by on College Avenue as she hurried toward Mrs. Hawks's house. Once there, she climbed the stairs to her room and opened her trunk. Her Rose of Sharon quilt lay atop books and clothing. She hugged it to her and stretched out on the bed.

Tears trickled from the corners of her eyes. All her plans, her dreams, seemed to lie beyond her reach. Why hadn't she asked about requirements? She'd assumed an acceptance letter was a guarantee. Luellen rolled on her side, heedless of the wrinkles she was causing in her skirt. She pulled the quilt next to her face and felt the scratchy edge where the fire had singed Mama's embroidery. How appropriate. Singed was just how she felt.

A fly crawling over her cheek awakened her. She brushed at it, but the annoying insect flew in a circle and landed on her face again. How long had she slept? Luellen sat up, dizzy, and settled her glasses back on her nose. Her quilt had fallen to the floor, adding to the clutter in the room. She studied her surroundings for a moment. Enough self-pity. She didn't get this far by giving up and she wouldn't quit now.

Opening her reticule, she checked to be sure the bank draft she'd brought to pay for the first term was safely inside. After tucking it under her handkerchief, Luellen smoothed her skirt, folded the quilt across the end of the bed, and straightened her scattered belongings. She tied her bonnet under her chin and closed the door behind her.

Halfway along College Avenue, she heard the bell toll two o'clock. Picking up her pace, she hurried the last blocks to the school. The corridor in Allenwood Hall felt blessedly cool after the heat outside. She strode toward Dr. Alexander's office.

The young man at the front desk looked up. "Miss McGarvie. You're expected. Go on back."

She lifted her head, remembering with a smile Franklin's friend, Lieutenant Calder. *Hold your chin up and look everyone in the eye*, he'd said. Somewhere in his life he must've had reason to put his own advice into practice, or he wouldn't know it worked.

Dr. Alexander stood until she'd seated herself, then lifted her test papers from a stack on his desk. His eyes met hers. "I'm sure you must realize your answers in many places were insufficient. In addition to practice teaching in our Model School, our students are expected to reach high standards academically. You cannot teach what you do not know. Allenwood is not organized to compensate for the failures of secondary schools."

His words stung. Luellen had been at the top of her class every year. She'd read all the books her school offered, and purchased as many others as she could afford. She rose, resting her fingertips on the edge of his desk.

"May I propose a bargain? Admit me for this term and allow me to study the areas I don't yet know. I'm certain Allenwood's library can provide the materials. Then let me take the test again. If my answers are still inadequate, I'll leave. If I succeed, enroll me in the following term without reservations."

Dr. Alexander studied her, a smile twitching at the corner of his mouth. "Fair enough. I must say, with that attitude you're several steps ahead as far as classroom control is concerned."

He gestured toward the chair. "Please sit. I need to enter your name in the registry." An oversized ledger lay open beside his right hand. "You're aware of our fees?"

"The acceptance letter spelled them out quite clearly. Ten dollars for the term, and thirty-five for room and board on campus—is that correct?" She placed her hand over her reticule.

"Yes. You will lodge in the Ladies Hall. You may have noticed the building to the left when you entered."

She nodded.

"Matron Bledsoe will assign your room." He held out his hand. "On receipt of satisfactory fees, you may have your possessions delivered there at any time."

Luellen passed the draft across his desk.

He hesitated.

"Isn't that the correct amount?"

"It is, but since last month's bank panic in New York, local bankers have put severe restrictions on even routine transactions. I'm reluctant to accept a draft. Would you be able to pay in specie? Gold or silver coin?"

A headache squeezed her temples. Where would she get forty-five dollars in coin? Were her savings in Bryant County Bank at risk? "I could go to the railroad depot and telegraph my father." Her voice wobbled. "Even if he's able to help, it will take time."

Dr. Alexander cupped his hand over his mouth and studied her. A compassionate expression crossed his face. Again, he reminded her of Uncle Matthew. "Let me see what our bursar advises." He made a notation in the ledger. "Meantime, feel free to occupy a room in the Ladies Hall. Classes will start next Monday. My assistant has the schedule."

She stood and extended her hand. "Thank you, Dr. Alexander. For everything." Luellen left the office, her head spinning. She'd been allowed to register, but for how long? Could a bank failure in New York affect her savings in Illinois?

Belle called a greeting from the parlor when Luellen entered the rooming house. "Come sit with me." She waved her hand at a pitcher and two glasses on a serving table between upholstered chairs. "Mrs. Hawks has treated us to lemonade."

"That sounds delightful." Luellen struggled to act nonchalant. No doubt Belle hadn't had the same experience she did at school that day. Guilt at passing herself off as Miss McGarvie, worries about additional studies on top of regular classes, and now financial concerns left her feeling drained. She leaned back and closed her eyes.

"Are you unwell?"

"Just tired. Too much in one day."

Belle eyed her with sympathy. "I was sorry you had to take that test. You must have passed—you're registered, aren't you?"

"Just barely. Dr. Alexander is going to permit me to study independently and test again at the end of the term."

"Extra studies? In what?"

"Botany and zoology, chiefly." She removed her bonnet and smoothed her hair. "I need to locate the necessary textbooks in the school library." Fatigue settled in her bones. She couldn't have studied a nursery rhyme and made sense of it.

"I went to the Ladies Hall while you were occupied." Belle handed Luellen a glass of lemonade. "Mrs. Bledsoe, the matron, said we couldn't share a room, but she did assign us adjoining quarters. I've already made arrangements for a delivery man to take our things to the campus."

"Oh, thank you! I'm grateful for your help. I'm feeling quite overwhelmed." She sipped the tart beverage while calculating the amount of cash left in her reticule. "What will he charge?"

"I don't know." Belle waved a hand. "Not much, I shouldn't think. My father told me not to worry about expenses. He's a banker, so he knows all about money."

The following Monday, Luellen woke early and dressed by lamplight. Breakfast in the ladies' dining room would be served at seven. At eight the bell would toll for her first class as an Allenwood student.

Her eyes ached from studying late into the night. A zoology textbook lay open on the table under the window, and two more books were stacked on the rug next to the single bed. She fluffed her pillow, tucking it with her nightgown under the Rose of Sharon quilt. Her few garments hung inside a pine wardrobe next to a two-drawer chest that held her underthings. After living in her parents' home in Beldon Grove, she felt confined in a space smaller than the bedroom she'd shared with Lily.

Luellen looked out at the approaching dawn, remembering how the prairie turned golden at daylight. Here all she saw were brick and stone buildings. She sighed. In due time, she'd take her certificate and return to the prairie to teach. Farmers' children deserved more than the rod and rote memorization.

She blew out the lamp and stepped into the hallway, stopping at the next room. "Belle. Are you awake?"

The door opened. "I've been up for an hour. I heard you moving around in there." Belle rubbed her hands together. "Let's have breakfast and go to our lecture class early."

"I'm glad geography is the first session," Luellen said as they descended the stairs. "I've always done well with maps."

"I don't know south from west." Belle giggled, dimples accenting her cheeks. "The good thing about maps is that little arrow at the top pointing north. Keeps me straight."

After the meal, Luellen and Belle, along with other women boarders, headed across the campus toward the ladies' entrance to the lecture hall. Male students joined them on the pathway, but according to the rules, no conversation between the sexes was allowed. Upon reaching the building, the men entered by a separate door.

Inside, tables were arranged in two columns with an aisle in the middle. Clerestory windows let in morning light and lamps were lit along the walls. The men sat on the right side of the hall. Luellen and Belle found seats among the other female students on the left.

Promptly at eight the instructor entered, stepped to the podium, and class began. After aiming at this goal for four years, Luellen wanted to pinch herself to be sure she wasn't dreaming. She couldn't stop the smile that crossed her face when she opened the textbook to the first page.

The week slipped by in a blur of studies. When Luellen hadn't heard from the registrar about her financial status by Friday, she went to Allenwood Hall after her last class of the day.

"May I see Dr. Alexander, please?" she asked the young man in the anteroom.

"I remember you. You're Miss McGarvie."

"That's right." The lie pricked her conscience. God willing, in one more week it would be the truth. She took a closer look at him—sandy hair, pale gray eyes, wispy moustache, maybe mid-twenties. "You must see dozens of students a day. I'm surprised you recalled my name."

He stood and bowed in her direction, scattering papers on the floor as he did so. "You're a striking woman, if you'll pardon my boldness. I hoped I'd see you again." A blush covered his pale cheeks.

She swallowed. His comments boosted her spirits, laid low after Brendan's devastating departure. But unlike some of the girls on campus, she hadn't come to Allenwood to find a husband. If she had, there'd be no shortage of men to choose from. Allenwood's population appeared to be several men to every woman.

Realizing he was waiting for a response, she said, "Well, here I am. Now, is Dr. Alexander available?"

He cleared his throat. "Sorry. Forgive my impudence." He bent and gathered up the dropped papers, clutching them in his right hand. "I'll go—"

"Who's out there, Mr. Price?" Dr. Alexander stepped out of his office. "Miss McGarvie. I was planning to send for you. Come in, please."

She followed him, sensing Mr. Price's gaze tracking her down the hallway. Dr. Alexander drew a chair out for her and took his place at his desk. A stack of paper rested on the open pages of a ledger. "I've heard from the bursar."

Tension prickled over Luellen. She tightened her grip on the arms of the chair. "Yes?"

"Have you contacted your father yet?"

"No." She looked down at her hands. "I hoped I wouldn't have to."

"I suggest you do. The bursar was able to negotiate your draft, but further financial problems have come to light."

She sucked in a breath.

"Not with you personally. With the country in general. The reports from New York are not good." His voice softened and took on a fatherly tone. "If you have funds in a bank in your hometown, it would be a good idea to convert them to gold as quickly as possible."

"I appreciate your candid advice. I'll telegraph my father soon."

He glanced at a case clock standing between bookcases. "The telegraph office closes at five. It's three now. You'd best take care of this matter today."

She stood to leave, her mind racing. The fare and gratuity for the omnibus ride to the railroad depot would be an expense, as would the telegram. She hadn't planned on all of the secondary costs of life in Allenwood, and certainly hadn't planned on having her savings disappear. There had to be a way to stay in school beyond this term.

The train platform was deserted. Carriages and riders on horseback filled the street behind the depot. A water wagon had evidently passed by earlier, since the traffic raised no dust. Cool wind blew around the corner of the building, ruffling Luellen's skirts. She hurried toward the telegraph operator's office, praying she wasn't too late.

The operator, a red-faced man, stopped scribbling and glanced up at her. "It's going on five. Hope what you've got won't take long."

"I need to send a telegram to Dr. Karl Spengler in Beldon Grove, in Bryant County." She handed him the message she'd composed during the omnibus ride. "I've never sent anything by telegraph before."

He scanned the words she'd written, then pushed a blank lined page and a pencil across the counter. "Print what you want to say on this form, and I'll send it for you." He tapped the paper she'd handed him. "We charge by the word. It will cost a pretty penny if you don't shorten this. You're not writing a book, you know."

Luellen rubbed her fingers across her lips, wondering if rudeness came with the man's job. She picked up the pencil and printed her name and address on the top line, Papa's information on the next, then wrote, "Please go to bank and change my savings to gold. Will write a letter explaining everything. Love, Luellen."

The red-faced man heaved himself to his feet and read what she'd written, shaking his head. He plucked the pencil from her hand, turned the paper around, and struck through half of her words. He replaced every period by drawing a line through the punctuation mark and writing "stop" in its place. The corrected message read, "Go to bank stop change savings to gold stop letter follows stop Luellen."

"Can't put in them marks," he said. "Gotta use a word." He placed the page next to the telegraph key. "That'll be sixty cents."

She gasped. "I had no idea." Fumbling in her reticule, she handed him the coins.

He grunted, dropped the money in a cash box, and took his seat, fingers clicking the telegraph key. Luellen watched, fascinated at the rhythmic ticks sending her words hundreds of miles away. After several moments, he looked up. "No need to wait here. If there's a reply, I have a messenger boy who delivers." He pointed at the top of the form. "You're at the Normal School?"

"Yes."

"He'll find you."

The omnibus ride back seemed much slower than it had on the day she'd arrived in Allenwood. Luellen dozed in her seat.

She'd lost two hours of study time, and once she returned to campus, the first thing she'd need to do was write a long letter home explaining the reason behind her terse telegram. If only she weren't so tired.

By the time the driver stopped at the corner of College and Chestnut, Luellen was the only passenger left on the bus.

He held out a hand to help her down. "Looks like you're late for supper. Ain't nobody around."

"Couldn't be helped." She handed him the fare.

"Maybe they saved you a bite."

"Maybe." She plodded toward the Ladies Hall, intending to go straight to her room and write a letter to Papa while she could still stay awake.

Belle stopped her at the door. "Where were you? Matron Bledsoe was concerned."

"I've been to the depot. I had to send a telegram home."

Belle's eyebrows shot up. "You went to the depot without a chaperone?"

Luellen put her hands on her hips. "I came from Beldon Grove without one. I certainly don't need protection between here and the depot. I'm used to being on my own."

"Well, you can expect a visit from Matron Bledsoe anyway. You know how she is." Belle took Luellen's arm. "Supper was perfectly revolting—codfish balls—but I sneaked out some bread and butter for you." She held up a napkin-wrapped bundle. "Come up to my room and we'll have a picnic. I visited Mrs. Hawks this afternoon and she sent us a jar of peach preserves."

Luellen's mouth watered. "All right, but just for a few minutes. I must write a letter to my father. I want to post it first thing tomorrow."

"Speaking of mail, there was a letter for you on the table

downstairs." Belle reached in her pocket and handed an envelope to Luellen.

"It's from my brother Franklin." The evening brightened. She
slid her thumb under the flap. "I can't wait to read about his lat-
est adventures."

# 8

Ward Calder lay in his bedroll, savoring the stars strewn across the deep black sky. The heavens shimmered with light. No wonder Franklin believed the thousands of tiny specks were glimpses of glory. They'd traveled three days northwest of Independence, and each night had been more radiant than the last.

Across the campfire, Franklin stirred and said something.

Ward peered through the darkness. "What did you say?"

Franklin sat up, wrapped in a blanket. "I said, we'd better get moving. We're pushing daylight." He slipped on his buckskins and moccasins. "I'll stir the coals and put coffee on."

Ward wrapped his bedroll and tied it with a leather strap. Early on this survey expedition, the two men had established a routine. Ward packed their simple camp while Franklin cooked breakfast. Now Ward gathered bedrolls under one arm and loaded them on the back of a mule tethered a short distance away.

He shivered in the crisp morning air. The sun touched the eastern horizon, but did little to warm the morning. A coyote yipped in the distance. The aroma of boiling coffee drew him to the campfire, tin cup in hand. "Got our gear stowed. We can be on the trail soon as we eat."

"Where to today, Lieutenant?"

"Funny." Ward cuffed Franklin on the shoulder. "You're supposed to be guiding me. Captain Block would never have given permission if he'd known what a lark this was."

"Well, I didn't tell him. He asked if I'd guide you on a survey since I've been through this country before." Franklin grinned. "I acted like we'd face Indian peril daily once we got off the steamer at Independence. You saw the Indians at Shawnee Mission—no peril there."

"Yeah. Sad."

"It is." Franklin pushed a skillet into the coals. "When I was a boy, they still had their own hunting lands. Now they're pushed out all along the trail. Railroads are going to finish the job."

Ward looked over the landscape. He'd never experienced such freedom. He could imagine himself and Franklin as the only people on the prairie. He kicked at a clod of dirt. "I know."

His survey equipment waited in one of the panniers on the mule's back. Railroad speculators wanted a line between Independence and St. Joseph. Once he took his report back to Jefferson Barracks, he'd be one of the people responsible for destroying the peace that surrounded them. He hunkered down across the fire from Franklin. "Until I saw this country for myself, it was easy to map out roads and railways. Now I'd rather be posted somewhere out west, watching the sun go down."

"You'll never get a promotion if you say that back at the barracks."

Ward tossed the remains of his coffee on a clump of switchgrass. "Right now rank doesn't seem important."

Franklin scraped bacon onto two plates. They stood, backs to the fire, contemplating the vastness around them while they ate.

Ward placed a ranging rod at a destination point in the survey, then walked back to where he'd left the Gunter's chain.

Franklin rose to his feet. "Ready?"

"Yes." While he worked, Ward thought about locomotives shattering the quiet. The finches and sparrows feeding on seed heads around them would be driven away, as would cottontail rabbits and prairie dogs. He recorded measurements in his notebook and moved rods without enthusiasm.

What would happen if he turned in a negative report? If he claimed the terrain was unsuitable for development, perhaps the idea of a rail line would be abandoned. His conscience clamored that the idea was dishonest. Could he propose an alternate route? One farther east, through established settlements? He considered the plan. The Army expected him to follow orders, not be an independent thinker. He knew what would happen to his career if he were found out. On the other hand, he knew what would happen here if he endorsed the speculator's plans.

"Almost finished," he called to Franklin. "We should be at Fort Leavenworth tomorrow. Then it's back downriver." Ward lifted one end of the chain and folded it while walking toward Franklin, who mirrored his actions.

As they rode away, Ward leaned forward in the saddle and pointed east. A dark mass covered the prairie near the horizon. "Was there a fire? See how black the grass is."

"All that mapping has weakened your eyes. Those are buffalo." Franklin's horse snorted and sidestepped when he halted the animal to study the herd. "Hundreds."

Ward slowed as the herd came closer. Fascinated, he watched the dark mass separate into a wall of shaggy beasts. Huge and broad-shouldered, the animals rumbled in his direction, flattening grass and raising clouds of dust.

One more reason to keep railroads off the prairie.

Luellen entered the foyer of the Ladies Hall and checked the mail rack suspended next to the entry bench. *A letter from Papa!* She tucked her parcel and the letter under one arm and hurried up the stairs to her room, shoving her key in the lock.

"Miss McGarvie." Matron Bledsoe puffed up to the landing. A dumpling of a woman, her round cheeks were pink from exertion. "A word with you, please."

Shoulders slumped, Luellen turned the key and opened the door. She yearned to rip open Papa's letter and read the news from home. Dealing with Mrs. Bledsoe's fluttery reprimands was the last thing she welcomed, now or at any time. "Come in. I just arrived from town, so I'm afraid my room may be a bit cluttered."

"That is exactly what I wish to speak to you about."

"My cluttered room?"

Mrs. Bledsoe splayed her fingers across her chest and sucked in gasps of air. "No. Your unchaperoned trips to town." She dropped into a chair.

Luellen placed her paper-wrapped parcel and Papa's letter on the table. She remained standing. "I needed to visit the bookstore. They had a zoology text that Allenwood's library lacked." She hung her bonnet and shawl on a peg. "Why would I need a chaperone to visit a bookstore?"

"My dear, anything could happen to you." Her several chins wobbled. "In the absence of your parents, I am responsible for you girls. We can't allow questionable activities. I've spoken to

71

you in the past regarding your behavior. Any more infractions and I'm afraid I'll have no choice but to speak to Dr. Alexander."

Luellen pinned her with a look. "I'm an independent woman, Matron Bledsoe. I earned a living before coming here, and needed no one's help to pay my way. By my standards, that sets me beyond the seventeen- and eighteen-year-olds who arrive straight from the bosom of their families. If I ever give you cause for suspicion, you'll have every right to report me. But in the meantime, please allow me the same freedom you enjoy."

"Well!" The matron plucked a handkerchief from her sleeve and dabbed at her eyes. "I'm only looking out for your reputation, and this is the thanks I get." She sniffled.

*Lord have mercy!* Luellen softened her tone. "I apologize. My words were too sharp. I've had a trying day, but I shouldn't take my frustrations out on you." She slid open the top drawer of the chest and removed a bag of peppermints Belle had shared with her. "Would you care for a sweet?"

"Why, thank you, dear. I would." Mrs. Bledsoe tucked a mint into her cheek and palmed two more, which she dropped into the pocket of her flowered calico skirt. She stood and patted Luellen's arm. "I enjoyed our little talk. Feel free to come to me anytime."

Luellen closed the door behind her and leaned against the solid wood. Five weeks under Mrs. Bledsoe's watchful eye already felt like months. Somehow when she'd dreamed of an education, she hadn't taken the Mrs. Bledsoes of the world into account.

"Luellen?" Belle's voice carried through the door. "Are you receiving guests?"

Chuckling, Luellen stepped aside. "Why yes, do come in." She hugged Belle when she entered the room.

Belle walked to the table and took a peppermint. "Matron

waddled past me down the stairs just now. What did she want this time?"

"I went to town without a chaperone again." Luellen lifted the parcel from the table and removed the string and paper, revealing an olive-colored volume. "*Elements of Zoology*. Once I master this I'll be ready to be tested again."

"You're pushing yourself too much." Belle's forehead wrinkled with concern. "You don't look well—you have dark smudges around your eyes."

Luellen rubbed her temples. "I admit I'm always tired, but I don't know what else to do. The term ends in late November, and you know the bargain I struck with Dr. Alexander."

"I don't think he expected you to memorize the entire discipline." Belle held out her hand. "The Literary Society is meeting tonight. We're discussing *Uncle Tom's Cabin*. It's bound to be a stimulating evening."

"I wish I could spare the time. It's a fascinating book. I'd love to hear what others think of the issues Mrs. Stowe raises." She shook her head. "But I really must study. If I can finish early enough, maybe I'll get a full night's sleep for a change."

"Well, at least come to supper with me. Who knows? Perhaps they'll serve something edible."

As soon as she returned from supper, Luellen removed her tight brown skirt and changed into her nightgown and wrapper. As bland as the food tasted, she still felt herself gaining weight. At home, meals didn't rely on bread and gravy at the expense of vegetables and meat. Her mouth watered when she remembered Mama's savory stews, filled with venison and carrots. And her apple dumplings . . . Next month couldn't come soon enough.

Luellen picked up Papa's letter and stretched out on her quilt to read it.

*September 30, 1857*

She'd sent the telegram on the eighteenth of September. Now they were partway through October. Why did he take so long to write?

> *I've delayed responding to your telegraph so I could*
> *include all the news. What I have to tell you is both*
> *good and bad. I know you're anxious for the good*
> *news first, so here it is—the Circuit Court granted*
> *your divorce from Brendan yesterday. He did not*
> *appear. Thankfully, you are now free to be Luellen*
> *McGarvie again.*

Luellen dropped the letter to her lap and closed her eyes. Tears slipped from under her lashes. Beneath her humiliation and anger ran a stream of sorrow. She'd given herself to Brendan believing he loved her as much as she loved him. Love dies, but it won't be buried. A corner of her heart still treasured the joy she'd felt during their brief courtship and even briefer marriage.

She let out her breath in a long sigh, blotted her tears, and continued reading.

> *My other news is not so uplifting. Bryant County*
> *Bank allowed me fifty cents on the dollar in gold*
> *for our savings. It's a good thing you telegraphed*
> *when you did. They've promised to make good the*
> *rest of it as soon as current economic conditions*
> *improve. I had no choice but to accept the offer—I*
> *couldn't risk leaving the funds there in case of bank*
> *failures like the ones during Jackson's presidency.*

Half her savings, gone in an instant. Luellen's mind raced. How could she earn enough to make up for her losses and finish her schooling? She stood and paced the room, considering her options. There must be jobs available at the school, or even in town. During vacations she could tutor children in Beldon Grove as well as work at the hotel.

Stopping at the window, she surveyed the campus. Most of the women she roomed with were walking along the gravel path toward the lecture hall for the literary meeting. With the exception of Belle, she hardly knew any of them. She'd hoped to forge friendships once this term ended, but if she had to work after classes . . .

Luellen shuffled through the papers on her desk, looking for the school calendar. First, she'd calculate the amount of money left to her, then decide how much she'd need to earn for the next three terms. She ran her finger along the calendar spaces, counting weeks. Suddenly she stopped, perspiration prickling her body. How long had it been since she'd had her monthly flow? She sank into the chair and rested her head in her hands. It was before Brendan left. Luellen feared she might faint. *I'm going to have his child.*

# 9

After a sleepless night, Luellen rose at dawn and selected the work dress she'd often worn at the hotel. Round-necked and high-waisted, it would be more comfortable than the brown skirt and tucked bodice she'd been wearing.

Luellen lifted her nightgown, studying her body for signs of pregnancy. Her abdomen looked slightly rounded, her breasts were fuller, but all in all she didn't see much change. If she could conceal her condition, she'd be able to complete the school year.

*Lord, why? You know how much I want to teach.*

The breakfast bell tolled across the campus. Luellen jerked the laces of her corset together, dropped a chemise over her head, and buttoned the soft yellow calico dress. Dipping a comb into the water pitcher, she swirled her hair up at the back of her head, pinning the curls in place.

She grabbed her books and opened the door just as Belle stepped into the hall from the next room. "We're both late," she said. "If we hurry we'll have time to eat."

Sounds of chatter and clinking cutlery greeted them as they dashed down the stairs. Once in the dining hall they collected their plates from the cook's assistant, who dropped viscous white globs onto slices of bread. "Ham gravy this morning, girls," she said. "Enjoy your breakfast."

Choosing a table near the door, Luellen and Belle joined three women who were finishing their meal. The one in the center, a serious-looking person with hair pinned tightly to the back of her head, smiled at them. "You'd better eat quickly. The bell for class will chime in a few minutes."

Belle scrutinized her plate. "Quickly is the only way to eat the food here. If you stopped to think about it, you'd die of starvation."

Chuckling, the three girls stood and headed for the door.

Luellen raked her fork through the gravy, her stomach protesting at the sight. "It's been a day or two since ham was anywhere near this stuff. Looks like flour paste to me."

"Probably tastes like it too."

"Well, we better eat it. Dinner is a long ways off." Luellen lifted a bowl from the center of the table. "I'm going to put applesauce on mine. Might make it taste better."

Belle scooped a spoonful of butter onto her plate. "I'll try this." She cut a corner from the bread. Around a mouthful she said, "Are you ready for the constitutional history examination this morning?"

Luellen choked on a bite. "I forgot all about it!" Her mind jumped to the instructor's lectures. Maybe she could dredge enough from her memory to pass the test.

"I thought you stayed in last night to study. How could you forget the examination?"

"I must've been distracted." Luellen kept her eyes on her plate.

Fighting drowsiness, Luellen entered the Ladies Hall after her last class. Her corset pinched her waist. As soon as she reached her room, she'd be able to loosen the strings and breathe.

"Miss McGarvie." Matron Bledsoe appeared at the doorway of the parlor. "You have a visitor."

"Who is it?"

"Mr. Price, from the registrar's office."

Luellen swallowed. Had she broken one too many rules? She tried to read Mrs. Bledsoe's features to see whether she'd made good her promise to report her to Dr. Alexander. The matron's face was expressionless.

She led the way into the parlor, Luellen following. As soon as they appeared, Mr. Price jumped to his feet, knocking a stack of books off the table in the process. "So sorry." He bent and scooped the books from the floor.

"Please, do sit down," Mrs. Bledsoe said. "You young people have your conversation. Pay no attention to me." She settled her bulk into an overstuffed chair and picked up a piece of needlepoint.

Luellen glanced between the matron and Mr. Price and chose a chair across from him. "How is it you are able to call on me? Isn't it against school policy for male and female students to spend time together outside of class?"

Mr. Price opened his mouth to reply, but before he could say anything, Mrs. Bledsoe cleared her throat. "Absolutely. However, Mr. Price isn't a student here. He's an employee of Allenwood, and as such has permission to come to the Ladies Hall as long as it's on school business." She pointed her needle at him. "He assured me this is a school matter."

The young man's face flushed. "Dr. Alexander sent me to escort you to his office. That is, if this is a convenient time for you, Miss McGarvie." He ran a finger under the high collar of his shirt.

Luellen's heart pounded. What did the registrar want? Was she to be expelled? Besides the unchaperoned trips to town, she'd obeyed every rule. Or had she? Was there some infraction she'd committed unknowingly? Her hands dropped to her abdomen. It wasn't possible for Dr. Alexander to know her secret. No one knew.

"Miss McGarvie?" Mr. Price looked at her. "Would another time be better?"

"No. This is fine. Please give me a moment to put my papers away. I'll join you directly."

Mr. Price walked close at Luellen's side as they paced along the corridor toward the registrar's office. Overhead, footsteps sounded from the men's housing on the upper floor. He pointed at the ceiling. "All those students sound like a herd of cattle. Makes it hard to get my work done." The aroma of peppermint filled the air as he spoke.

She glanced at him. He wore his self-importance like an ill-fitting coat. Luellen wondered how long he'd been in his position as assistant to the registrar.

Dr. Alexander stood when she entered his office. "I appreciate your coming, Miss McGarvie. A matter has come up that I wish to discuss with you."

"Yes?" Her pulse drummed in her throat.

He lifted a paper from his desk. "This is last Saturday's *Harper's Weekly*. Were you aware that banking has been suspended in New York and parts of New England?"

"No." She felt the blood drain from her face.

"Please sit down." His eyes widened in alarm. "Are you feeling faint? Would you like a glass of water?"

Without waiting for her answer, he stepped to the door and called into the anteroom. "Mr. Price. Please bring a pitcher of water and two glasses."

Luellen heard a scrambling sound. Footsteps retreated down

the hall. Dr. Alexander turned and studied her face. "I apologize for being so abrupt with such shocking news. When I read the article, my first thought was of your situation. Forgive the personal question, but were you able to contact your father regarding your funds?"

She took a deep breath and held it for a moment. "I heard from him yesterday. He's been able to secure part of my savings, as well as a portion of his own."

Mr. Price barged into the room with the requested water. He nodded at Luellen and placed a tray on a table next to the wall. After glancing at the registrar, he poured a glassful, the lip of the pitcher clinking against the rim, and handed it to Luellen.

"Thank you." She sipped it, realizing her mouth had gone dry.

"My pleasure."

Dr. Alexander cleared his throat. "That will be all for now, Price."

Once the clerk left, Dr. Alexander leaned against his desk, arms folded across his chest. "Of course, we don't know yet whether this incident will affect banks in Illinois. One hopes it will not. Nevertheless, I was concerned about you when the *Weekly* arrived."

"You're extremely kind to take this much interest in my welfare. Forgive my asking, but are you this attentive to the finances of all your students?"

He stuck his thumbs in the pockets of his waistcoat. "Each student is different, Miss McGarvie. You're excellent teacher material—it's in the interest of Allenwood's reputation to assist you in every way I can."

"I'm very appreciative." Her heart warmed at his praise. For the moment she pushed the worry about her pregnancy to the back of her mind. She'd think about it later.

"I have a daughter around your age." His mouth tightened. "She showed the same potential you do, but unfortunately she chose an early marriage and now has two children. She's been a severe disappointment to me."

Luellen cringed inside. She knew what a blow her marriage to Brendan must have been to her parents. Somehow she would get through the program at Allenwood without disappointing them or Dr. Alexander.

He walked back around his desk. "The first session of our Model School begins on Monday. Based on your exemplary work thus far, I'm recommending you for practice teaching right away, rather than waiting for the next term."

She swallowed hard at the thought of additional work added to what she was already doing. "I'll try to live up to your faith in me."

He raised an eyebrow. "How are you progressing with your botany studies? I understand you've completed the primary zoology text."

"I have. I'm working on botany drawings each evening after my regular classwork."

"Excellent. I'm sure you'll sail through the examination next month."

Luellen wished she were as convinced.

When she emerged from Dr. Alexander's office, Mr. Price jumped to his feet. "I'll be happy to escort you across the campus."

"Thank you, but that won't be—"

"You're needed here, Mr. Price," the registrar's voice thundered. "Please tend to those reports."

He flushed bright red and fell back in his chair. "Some other time," he said, keeping his head down.

Luellen almost felt sorry for him, but at the same time she couldn't understand his interest. There were plenty of other girls on campus for him to pursue. As for her, she couldn't be more ineligible than she was now.

○

On Monday morning, icy rain pecked at the window while Luellen dressed. She laced her corset loosely, wishing she had more than one high-waisted gown in her wardrobe. She tried on the brown gored skirt, but it was uncomfortably tight. If she had time this evening, she'd let out the seams. A shawl would cover the alterations. In the meantime, she'd wear the yellow dress again.

Her nerves fluttered as she swept her hair up and covered it with her green silk net. Was she ready to face a roomful of youngsters? What if she couldn't hold their attention?

Belle rapped on her door, using their special signal of three taps followed by two quick ones. "Are you ready?" she asked when she stepped into the room.

"Much as I'll ever be." Luellen gathered the primer and first reader that the classroom instructor had given her for review. "I remember the teacher I had when I was six. He was so harsh to us little ones. My prayer is that I can guide these children without crushing their spirits."

Belle pretended to applaud. "That sounds like a commencement speech."

"That'll be next year." Luellen chuckled. "I know I sound high blown, but truly that's been my motive all along."

"I know. I feel the same way. My younger brother was so taxed by one of his teachers that he just quit learning. He's eighteen now, and can hardly read or write, much to my parents' dismay."

"I've seen that too. Especially with lively young boys. How

anyone can whip a small child . . ." Luellen shook her head. "Anyway, I hope to change that—in my classroom at least."

After breakfast they left together, wrapped in cloaks against the blowing rain. When they reached the gravel walkway, Luellen turned east toward the Model School, situated across from the chapel on Chestnut Street.

Belle waved as she walked to the Lecture Hall. "Best of luck. I know you'll be successful."

Fourteen curious faces turned in Luellen's direction when she entered the schoolroom. Pausing to hang her cloak on a peg, she was engulfed by the aroma of damp wool and oiled floors. Between the windows on one side, a stove glowed with heat.

A stocky woman turned from the blackboard where she'd written practice words for the day's lesson. "Children, this is Miss McGarvie. She will be your teacher this morning." She left the board and held out her hand. "I'm Mrs. Guthrie. I graduated from Allenwood's program two years ago."

Luellen clasped Mrs. Guthrie's hand. The teacher's glasses, perched at the end of a round nose, magnified her pale blue eyes.

"I'm happy to meet you," Luellen said. "Please tell me what you'd like me to cover today."

The children whispered and fidgeted in their seats while Mrs. Guthrie showed her the place in the first reader that she'd been using when she wrote on the blackboard. The whispering grew louder. Smiling, Mrs. Guthrie bent her head near Luellen's ear. "They're all yours. I will be in the back of the room, but only as an observer." She whisked away.

Luellen stepped to the front of the room, her nerves jumping. Folding her arms across her middle, she arranged her face in a pleasant expression and waited, her eyes moving around the room. Each desk held two children, and had been arranged so the smallest ones sat in front. Gradually the whispers stopped.

"I see you have new words this morning," she said. "Can anyone read these for me?" She fought to keep her voice from shaking.

Hands waved in the air.

A round-cheeked boy bounced in his seat. He looked as though he'd burst if he didn't get to recite what was written on the blackboard.

Luellen pointed at him. "What is your name?"

"Joshua."

"All right, Joshua. Please read the first two words."

He stood. Luellen noticed he seemed small for a six- or seven-year-old. His dark hair had obviously been cut by using a bowl for shape, and his shirt was patched. "Good. Rolled. Every." Joshua sat down, looking pleased with himself.

She shot a glance at the back of the room. How would Mrs. Guthrie handle this? Taking a deep breath, she forged ahead. "Very good. But that was three words, wasn't it?"

"Joshua always does that, Teacher," a blonde girl said. "He thinks he's so smart."

"Do not."

Luellen cocked her head, folded her arms again, and waited. The children glanced at one another, then focused their attention on her.

"There will be enough time for each of you to read to me today. But you must wait until I call on you." She turned to the blonde girl. "What is your name?"

"Cassie."

"Would you read me the next two words, please, Cassie?"

"Af-ter. Be-gan." She smoothed the skirt of her long-sleeved brown dress.

"Thank you." Luellen called on children until all the words on the board had been pronounced, then sat behind the teacher's desk and lifted the reader. "Open your books to the pancake story, please."

The rustle of pages filled the room as books were opened, one to a desk. Heads bent together over the readers.

"Who'd like to read first?"

Joshua's hand sprang into the air.

Luellen smiled at him. "Let's give someone else a chance." Her eyes found one of the girls toward the back. Curly hair fought with the braids she wore—the curls winning. She reminded Luellen of herself as a child. "What is your name, dear?"

"Elizabeth Goins. Can I read?"

"*May* I read. Yes, please do."

Elizabeth bent over the book, her finger following the text. "A big fat cook made a big fat pan . . . cake. Near the cook were seven hun . . . hun . . ."

"Hungry!" Joshua shouted.

Luellen held up her index finger. "Manners, Joshua. It's Elizabeth's turn. Please apologize."

Joshua blushed and lowered his head. "Sorry."

Elizabeth resumed the story. When she finished the page, her seatmate had a turn. Once the children had read to the end of the tale, it was time for sums, geography, and finally, dinner. The room filled with the sound of pails being opened and food being unwrapped.

Luellen's stomach growled. She'd been too nervous to eat much breakfast, and now she felt ready to collapse. The noon bell rang from the chapel tower. If she hurried, she could arrive in the dining hall in time for the meal. But first, she needed to hear the teacher's assessment of her performance. Her hands shook as she waited.

"You were wonderful," Mrs. Guthrie said in a voice meant for Luellen's ears alone. "The children responded to you very well. I'm going to enjoy working with you this term." She patted Luellen's shoulder. "Now, I imagine you're ready for some food. Go on with you. I'll see you tomorrow."

Luellen blew out a breath. "Thank you. I'll be here."

When she stepped outside, the wind caught at her hood and blew it off her head. Rain splattered her face. She pulled the hood up, holding it with one hand while she darted across the street and into the Ladies Hall.

She inhaled. Pea soup. She hoped they had cornbread with it. Luellen shook the rain from her cloak and hung it near the door. If she hurried, she could have dinner and still arrive at the afternoon elocution class on time.

As she walked toward the dining room, part of her mind remained on the children in the Model School. Joshua was such a darling boy, so precocious. And Elizabeth—she'd love to take her under her wing and help her become an avid reader. For the first time, the child she carried in her womb became real to her. Would it be a boy or a girl? What would he or she look like?

When she passed the parlor, Mrs. Bledsoe intercepted her.

"You have a visitor, Miss McGarvie. Your cousin, from Chicago."

# 10

Luellen reached out and steadied herself against the wall. She had no cousin in Chicago. Her visitor could only be one person. Heart pounding, she followed the matron into the parlor and found herself face-to-face with Brendan O'Connell.

He stepped forward and took her hand. "Darlin' Luellen. It's been a long time."

She stared at him, speechless.

"You're surprised. I should've written first, but I hardly had time, what with one thing and another." His grip on her hand tightened.

Mrs. Bledsoe bustled over, obviously taken in by his handsome face and broad-shouldered build. "Do sit down, Mr. O'Connell. How kind of you to pay a visit to your cousin." A puzzled expression crossed her face. "With that Irish accent, how is it you and Miss McGarvie are cousins?"

"By marriage, ma'am."

Luellen found her voice. "Actually, a former marriage, Mrs. Bledsoe. Technically, we are no longer related." She jerked her hand free.

The matron stared from one to the other. "This is all too confusing for me." She turned to Brendan and pointed at a chair next to the fire. "Won't you have a seat? I'm sure you and Miss McGarvie have much to talk about."

"Indeed we do, but I'd rather escort my cousin on a walk around the grounds." He gripped Luellen's elbow. "Wouldn't you like to show me your school?"

"But it's raining," Mrs. Bledsoe said. "Surely you'd be more comfortable in here."

"Ah, we Irish are used to rain. Reminds us of home." He propelled Luellen toward the door. "Let's get our wraps and step out into the lovely afternoon."

Once in the entryway, he released her arm and dropped an oilcloth poncho over his head. Fuming, she threw her cloak over her shoulders and stalked to the door.

"Allow me." Brendan held the door open for her. Turning toward Mrs. Bledsoe, he said, "I'll have her back shortly. Thank you for being so gracious."

"Well . . . I'm not sure . . . this is irregular . . ." The matron wrung her hands.

Brendan sent her a wink. "I won't tell anyone if you don't." He closed the door in her flushed face.

Luellen strode ahead of him along the gravel path toward Allenwood Hall's covered front steps. Brendan grabbed her arm. "Slow down."

She shook him loose. "I'm not going to get soaked. You can tell me what you're doing here as soon as we get out of the rain." She covered the remaining distance at a trot and turned to face him when she reached the top of the stairs. "Talk. How did you find me?"

"'Twasn't that hard. You mooned over that Allenwood letter every time you thought I wasn't looking. So I had to read it, didn't I? And here you are, sure."

"What do you want?"

He stood close enough for her to see drops of moisture beading on his chestnut curls. "You caused me a great deal of grief, sending that sheriff after me with a subpoena." His blue eyes shot fury. "I had to talk fast to keep my father-in-law from booting me out of the house."

"*I* caused *you* trouble? What do you think you've done to me?" She started to throw the fact of her pregnancy in his face, but stopped short. No. He'd have no part of this baby.

Brendan stepped closer, pinning Luellen against the wall by resting one hand on the bricks behind her. His breath smelled of ale. "Looks like I did you a favor. Now you can do one for me."

"Why would I—"

"Just stay away from me and my life. No subpoenas, no lawyers. I'm done with you, Luellen."

She pushed him away. "You should've read that subpoena instead of trying to lie your way out of it. You wasted a trip. We're divorced. I never want to see you again."

"Miss McGarvie?" Mr. Price stood next to the open door, staring between her and Brendan.

She clapped a hand over her lips. How much had he heard?

"Are you all right?" He moved to her side. "Is this gentleman bothering you?"

Brendan faced him. "I was just leaving, laddie." The corner of his mouth twisted in a sneer. "*Miss* McGarvie and me are done with our conversation."

Luellen watched him stride away, her heart pounding in her throat. Thank goodness he lived in Chicago. They'd never cross paths again.

Mr. Price lifted an umbrella from a wooden stand near the door and fumbled it open. "I was just going to deliver a message to the Lecture Hall. May I escort you to your next class?"

She bit the inside of her lip. "Yes, please. I would appreciate an escort."

❧

November arrived, and with it the looming date for examinations. With a zoology textbook open, Luellen sorted a list of animals into their proper classifications. Horses, snakes, frogs, falcons—each had to be placed under their correct heading. If the test were timed, she'd need her placement to be automatic. She rested her head on one hand and turned to another list. Her eyes hurt, and so did her back.

*Tap, tap, tap. Tap tap.* Belle pushed the door open. "Brought you some shortbread. My mother sent a box of treats." Her face lacked its usual bright smile.

Luellen leaned back in her chair. "You're heaven sent. I've been looking for an excuse to stop studying."

"No better reason than enjoying some of my mother's baking. I hope someday to be half the cook she is."

"Our mothers spend more time cooking than we do." Luellen took a shortbread square and bit into it. Buttery softness spread over her tongue. "Delicious." She pushed the tin toward Belle. "Join me."

Belle heaved a deep sigh. "Not right now." She flopped on Luellen's bed. "Mother sent a letter with the sweets. Things are not going well for my father's bank. They'll be traveling to New York at the end of the month to meet with investors."

"The end of the month? But that's when winter vacation begins." Luellen stood, careful to keep her shawl draped over her midsection. "You won't be at home by yourself, will you?"

"I won't be home at all—at least not until they return. My father has made arrangements for me to stay here until mid-December."

Her eyes shone with unshed tears. "I'm trying to be brave, but . . . oh, Luellen, I'm so disappointed! I know we don't have to be back until February, but I'll miss nearly a month at home." She put her hands over her face and sobbed. "Can you imagine what it'll be like? Just me and Mrs. Bledsoe?"

Luellen sat next to Belle and hugged her. She'd never seen her sunny friend so upset. "I don't blame you for crying. The thought of spending a month in Mrs. Bledsoe's company would send me into hysterics."

Belle sniffled. "Maybe I could ask my father to allow me to stay at Mrs. Hawks's boardinghouse. She's a dear soul."

"Let me pray about this. Maybe there's something we can do." An idea glimmered at the back of Luellen's mind. She handed Belle a clean handkerchief.

"I'm open to suggestions." She glanced at the textbook and papers on the table. "You go on with your studies. I'll see you in the morning."

Instead of returning to her zoology lists after her friend left, Luellen closed the book and stared out at the black night. Her thoughtful face reflected back at her in the glass. She took a blank sheet of paper and scribbled a hasty note to her parents. If it went into the post tomorrow, perhaps they'd receive it before winter vacation.

Luellen rolled her shoulders to loosen tight muscles. Mrs. Hale, the proctor, looked up from her desk at the front of the examination room. "Are you finished, Miss McGarvie?"

"No. Just taking a breath. How much more time do I have?"

Mrs. Hale checked a pocket watch lying open on the desktop. "Half an hour."

Closing her eyes, Luellen tried to picture the structure of a flower from the botany textbook. Which was the stigma, and which was the anther? After two hours of answering questions and illustrating her responses, her mind felt drained of knowledge. She turned the page. Almost finished. She dipped her pen and filled in the last answers, closing the examination booklet just as the supper bell rang.

"Time." Mrs. Hale collected the booklet. "If you wish, you may stop by Dr. Alexander's office in the morning for the results. I'm sure you'd like to know how you fared before leaving for winter vacation."

"Thank you, Mrs. Hale. I appreciate it." Luellen knew the woman's offer meant she'd be spending her evening grading the answers. She rubbed the bridge of her nose. "It's kind of you to do this for me."

"Dr. Alexander specifically requested that I give him the results as soon as possible." Her eyes appraised Luellen. "He's taken quite an interest in you, it seems."

Luellen couldn't stop the guilty flush that rose to her cheeks. What would he think if he knew she was a divorced woman, and pregnant to boot? He mustn't find out.

She hurried from the room and dashed through a light rainfall that misted the campus. Belle greeted her when she entered the Ladies Hall. "Well? How was the examination?"

"I had answers to the questions. Tomorrow I'll learn whether they were the right ones." Luellen shook raindrops from her cloak and hung it on a peg. "What are we being served tonight?"

Belle sniffed the air. "Something disgusting involving cabbage, I'd say." She linked her arm through Luellen's. "Let's go get it over with."

The following morning Luellen dressed carefully. Her blue shawl with the long fringe contrasted well with her yellow calico dress. By cinching her corset as tight as possible, her rounded abdomen wasn't apparent. Mentally, she apologized to her baby for squeezing him or her. As soon as she got home, she'd sew another dress or two designed to conceal her figure. Could she make the new clothes without telling her mother why she needed them?

After dropping her cloak over her shoulders, she left the room. She'd worry about her mother later—now examination results were paramount in her thoughts.

Last night's rain and subsequent freeze had left the gravel walk icy. As Luellen picked her way toward Allenwood Hall, she observed the deserted campus. Most of the students had left for vacation as soon as their last classes ended. She wondered whether Mr. Price would be on duty.

When she entered the anteroom outside Dr. Alexander's office, Mr. Price's desk was cleaned off. Apparently he too was at home with family. Too bad. His flattering attention would have boosted her flagging confidence. What if she'd failed the examination? She shook her head to rid herself of the thought, knocking on the registrar's door with a shaky hand.

"Come in." Dr. Alexander's face broke into a smile when he saw Luellen. "I have good news for you, Miss McGarvie." He held up the booklet. "You breezed through these questions with scarcely an incorrect answer. I commend your diligence." He leaned back in his chair, fingers laced over his midsection. "Rarely have we had a student with such promise. You may register for the next term with no reservations whatsoever."

"Thank you. That's welcome news."

Relief flooded through her—one hurdle crossed. But two higher ones waited. By February, how much would her pregnancy show? And would she be able to earn enough over the break to return at all?

# 11

Luellen rubbed condensation off the window and peered out as the train rolled in to the Beldon Grove depot. "There they are," she said to Belle. She pointed across the platform at two figures sheltering under the building's overhang. Papa had his arm around her mother's shoulders.

She jumped to her feet. "I didn't realize how much I missed them until now."

A shadow crossed Belle's face. "I miss my parents too. I so appreciate your invitation to spend the month with you."

"It's selfish on my part. I'll be lonesome when you go back to Springfield."

Mama enfolded her in a hug when she stepped onto the platform. "It's wonderful to have you home. I've been lonely with all my children gone." She turned to Belle. "This must be Liberty Belle Brownlee."

"Just 'Belle,' please." She took Mama's outstretched hand. "I'm grateful for your hospitality. My parents send their thanks, as well."

A cutting wind tore along the tracks. Papa greeted both girls and directed the baggage handler toward their buggy. The women followed him, cloaks pulled tight against the late November weather.

Luellen felt a tingle of apprehension as the buggy rolled down

Adams Street toward her family's home. How long would she be able to keep her secret? Might it be better to tell Mama and Papa and be done with deception? Belle's presence allowed her conscience the excuse she needed to conceal her pregnancy. Her condition was a family matter, not one for outsiders.

Papa stopped at the hitching post in front of the picket fence. The climbing roses that covered the fence during the summer had faded to orange seed pods. Between their house and Papa's office the silver maple stood bare before the weather, its leaves scattered by prairie winds. To everything there is a season, Luellen thought. The coming years were her season for school, and nothing would stop her.

She noticed light spilling from the sitting room windows. Her parents would never go off and leave a lamp burning. "Is someone here?"

The door swung open, and Aunt Ellie ran onto the veranda. "Welcome home!"

Uncle Matthew stepped around her and strode toward the buggy. He held out his arms to Luellen. "Come here and give your old uncle a hug." Wind ruffled his hair and beard.

"What a wonderful surprise." She embraced him, turning when Belle descended. "This is my dear friend, Belle Brownlee. Belle, my uncle, Matthew Craig."

"Miss Brownlee. Luellen mentions you in all of her letters."

"I'm surprised she has time to write letters at all. She's a dreadful bookworm."

Luellen made a face at Belle. "It was worth it, wasn't it? I'm on equal footing with you for next term."

"Come in," Aunt Ellie called. "You'll all catch your death standing out there in the cold."

Luellen hurried up the steps. Bending slightly, she kissed her aunt on the cheek. After introducing Belle, she looked over Aunt Ellie's shoulder into the entry hall. "Where are Sarah and Robert?"

"In the kitchen, I expect. Your mama made a pan of her wonderful shortbread. They're probably sneaking bites."

Mama entered the house, Uncle Matthew's arm around her shoulders. "My husband is putting up the team. He'll be here in a moment," she told Belle.

The commotion stirred up by her arrival warmed Luellen. How dear everyone was. She looked around at her home—fire burning in the sitting room grate, long dining table lined with chairs—and heaved a sigh of contentment. The faint aroma of caraway drifted from the kitchen. She took Belle's hand. "Let's go sample the shortbread before my cousins eat it all."

Later, as the family sat around the table after supper, Luellen listened to Aunt Ellie go on about her grandchildren, Maria's and Graciana's babies. "Quincy's so far away. I've only seen them once," she said. "But they are the prettiest girls you ever saw." She looked at Uncle Matthew. "Next to ours, of course."

He kissed his fingertips and rested them against her cheek. "With such a lovely grandmother, how could they miss?"

"Grandchildren and children at the same time. God has surely blessed us." Aunt Ellie sent a soft smile toward ten-year-old Sarah and her younger brother, Robert. They both looked bored at the grown-up conversation swirling around the table.

Mama sighed. "Lily's our only hope right now, and so far, no news."

Luellen looked at her hands. She'd never considered the possibility that her mother might long for a grandchild. When she glanced up, she caught Papa studying her.

Toward the end of Belle's visit, Luellen sat at the table after breakfast, paging through her mother's copies of *Godey's Lady's Book*. Her gaze stopped on a picture of a traveling sacque worn over a wide skirt. With the jacket, the silhouette was one of a continuous bell shape from shoulders to hem.

Her mother walked past and paused to look over her shoulder. "There will be time to sew a winter outfit while you're home. Fitted bodices are the fashion right now." She chuckled and patted her rounded figure. "I can't wear them, but you girls can—isn't that right, Belle?"

Belle lifted her head from another issue of the magazine. "Indeed we can, Mrs. Spengler. There's a gown here that's caught my eye." She slid the book across the table, pointing at an illustration of a narrow-waisted dress with a wide skirt and ruffled bodice and undersleeves.

Luellen raised an eyebrow. "You'd need to wear hoops."

"You're right." She turned the page.

Mama slipped into a chair next to Luellen. "Let's decide on a style you like. After Christmas, you'll be home for another month and a half. Plenty of time to sew a dress or two."

Luellen's wardrobe needed refreshing, but not for the reasons Mama assumed. The yellow calico she wore with a shawl or covered by an apron was the only comfortable dress she had left. She'd need another outfit and a change before she returned to Allenwood. The difficulty lay in choosing styles that would conceal her figure without announcing her condition.

She removed her glasses and polished the lenses with a corner of her skirt. "I do need something warmer for winter."

"Wonderful. Mr. Wolcott recently enlarged his store and made space just for cloth and notions." Mama glanced at Belle. "We can all visit the mercantile together."

"Excellent idea. I'll buy a Christmas gift for my family while I'm there."

"We'll go this afternoon."

The back door banged shut. Papa appeared in the kitchen doorway. "Lulie, would you be able to spare me some time? I'd like your help in my office."

What could be so important that Papa needed her right now? Why not ask Mama?

She looked at Belle. "Would you excuse me for a bit?" Her voice held an apology.

"Of course." Belle stood, turning to Mama. "I noticed you have a copy of Sir Walter Scott's *The Betrothed* on the shelf in the sitting room. May I borrow it to read?"

Mama's face flushed.

Papa grinned. "That's one of her special favorites. I'm sure she'd be happy to share it with you."

"Karl, stop it." Her eyes twinkled. "You're such a tease."

Luellen remembered the day she and her brother James had brought the book home to their mother, a gift from Mr. Pitt. She wondered if that might have been the day Papa decided to step up his courtship a notch. In any case, she'd always been thankful that it was he, and not Jared Pitt, who'd won her mother's heart.

Papa cleared his throat, bringing her back to the present. She jumped to her feet, careful to keep her shawl crossed in front of her. "What do you want help with?"

He rested a hand on her shoulder, guiding her from the room. "Just a few things. We shouldn't be long."

Once inside his office, Papa slid a chair away from the wall and held it for her. Then he seated himself on the edge of the examination table. In the wintery light coming through the window, he appeared old and tired.

She looked around the room, but couldn't see any undone tasks. As always, the odor of medicines tickled her nostrils. Maybe he wanted her to wash out the bottles he used when he filled his bag to make house calls. She opened her mouth to ask again what he needed, when he straightened his shoulders and rested his hands on his knees.

"Do you have something to tell me, Luellen?"

A wave of heat washed over her. She should have known she couldn't hide her condition from him. She looked down, rubbing at a spot on her apron. In a tiny voice, she asked, "How did you know?"

He slid off the table and tucked his thumb under her chin. His eyes met hers. "Your face is fuller and so is your body, in spite of the way you keep yourself wrapped in that shawl." Papa drew her to his chest and stroked her hair. "How long did you think you could keep it from us?"

Luellen gasped. "Does Mama know?" Her words were muffled against his shirt.

"I'm sure she suspects."

"Would you please tell her for me? I've caused so much distress already—I can't bear to upset her further."

He stepped back and leaned against the examination table. "My dear girl, this isn't something that's going to be over tomorrow. She'll be on your side. Remember, Lily was born after your father died. If anyone can understand, it'll be your mother."

His compassionate tone tore at her heart. She covered her face and sobbed. "I made such an awful mistake. I'm so sorry. You and Mama don't deserve to suffer for my troubles."

"Hush now." He kissed the top of her head and offered her a handkerchief. "A new baby in the family isn't a tragedy. I'll be right here to look after you until your child is born."

"I'm not staying home." Luellen wiped tears from her cheeks. "School's too important to me to—"

Papa held up a hand, palm out. "He or she will arrive sometime in May, perhaps before the term ends. You can't tax yourself during those last months. You've been part of a doctor's family for too many years not to know the risks you'd be taking."

"Please, Papa." She seized his hands. "I'm afraid if I leave now I'll never go back."

"Even if you complete this term, there's still one more year. I assume you'll stay home until your child is older, then finish."

"No. The Model School instructor is a widow with a young child. If she earned a teaching certificate under those circumstances, so can I."

A muscle twitched in Papa's cheek. Shoving his hands in his pockets, he paced the length of the room, turning to face her. "Why don't you wait on that decision until May? Perhaps you'll feel differently after the baby's born."

If Papa were focused on next year . . . "So you won't object if I return in February?"

"I didn't say that. I worry about—" He paled and drew several deep breaths.

"Papa?"

He shook his head. "It's nothing." He sucked in another breath and released it in a heavy sigh. "You've already overcome a great deal to reach your goal. I won't stand in your way now. But keep in mind you're gambling with a human life."

Preoccupied, Luellen walked along Monroe Street toward Wolcott's Mercantile with her mother and Belle. She hadn't considered her ambition as gambling with her baby's life. The baby *was* more

100

important. But school was important too. Why couldn't she have both?

She hunched her shoulders against a gust of wind, drawing her cloak close to her throat. Belle squeezed her arm. "You're awfully quiet this afternoon. Is something troubling you?"

Mama turned to face them, apparently listening for Luellen's response.

"Not at all," she lied. "I'm just wondering what colors I should choose for my new dresses."

Belle inclined her head, studying Luellen's face. "Let's look for a deep green or gold to highlight your brown eyes."

Once inside the mercantile, Mama led the way to the dry goods section. The odor of fresh paint mingled with the smell of fabric dyes and stiffeners. After a pleasant half hour contemplating all possible combinations, Luellen chose a golden brown wool challis for a dress and matching sacque, and a green worsted for her second dress.

Ben Wolcott joined them, carrying a pair of shears. "Miss Luellen. A pleasure to see you again. I trust all the books I sold you have been a help in Allenwood?"

"Indeed they have." Luellen surveyed their family's longtime friend. Though he was well over sixty, Mr. Wolcott moved with the bounce of a man twenty years younger. What was left of his hair was plastered to his scalp with sweet-smelling oil.

He brandished the scissors. "And now you've come for some cloth?"

She laid her hand on one of the two bolts of woolen material resting on the cutting table. "I need ten yards of the green." She consulted her notes. "And fourteen yards of the challis."

He cut and folded the fabric and carried it to the front counter. Mama and Belle followed him, adding their purchases to the stack. Luellen watched his efficient movements, happy memories of childhood visits to the mercantile filling her mind. The store had stood on the same spot ever since she could remember. More businesses had come to town, but Wolcott's Mercantile was the only place Mama would trade.

He snapped off the end of a string binding their packages. "The boy will deliver this later this afternoon."

Mama smiled at him. "Thank you, Ben."

When they left the store, they decided to take advantage of the rare December sunshine. They strolled along the board sidewalk, passing the post office, a grocer, a millinery, and a drugstore. When they reached Hancock Street, Luellen noticed a Closed sign in the window of the Bryant County Bank.

Her throat constricted. "Mama?" She pointed at the darkened building. "When did that happen?"

"Just before you came home. There wasn't time to write you. Hasn't Papa talked to you about your finances?"

"No." Her thoughts spun. "Why didn't you tell me before I bought all that fabric? I could've gotten by with one dress."

Mama skewered her with a glance. "No you couldn't. Not—" She looked at Belle and cleared her throat. "Not with winter coming on."

Luellen swallowed, grateful her mother had said nothing further.

# 12

Once the three women returned home, Mama turned to Luellen. "Do you want to put your feet up for a bit?"

So this is how it would be. Oversolicitation. "No, Mama. I'm not tired. I've been thinking about how good your ginger cake would taste." She looked at Belle. "We need cooking practice, don't we? Let's make a cake."

"Sounds delicious."

Mama patted Luellen's shoulder. "You hardly need practice after cooking at the hotel for so long. But ginger cake does sound good, and there's time to get it in the oven before supper. You know where I keep my recipe book?"

"Of course."

"Then I'm going upstairs and lie down for a while."

Luellen gazed at her mother, surprised. It wasn't like her to rest during the day.

By late afternoon, Luellen and Belle were in the kitchen measuring ginger and cinnamon into the molasses-laced cake batter. Luellen handed a bowl of beaten egg whites to Belle. "Would you please fold these in while I butter the pan?"

Belle dipped a finger into the batter and smacked her lips. "I could eat this plain. No need to bake it—let's just pour it into bowls."

Luellen giggled. "I don't think that's what Mama had in mind."

The spoon clicked against the side of the bowl while Belle blended the batter through the fluffy egg whites. "Would your mother mind if I copied this recipe and took it home with me?"

"Not at all. She'd be pleased." Luellen turned at the sound of a knock on the back door. "That must be our parcels from the mercantile." A stab of guilt returned at the thought of the money she'd just spent. One thing about cut fabric—it couldn't be replaced on the bolt. She sighed and swung open the door.

"Franklin! Lieutenant Calder! What are you doing here?"

Franklin stepped into the room and wrapped her in a hug. "What kind of a greeting is that? Last time I checked, this is where my parents live." He gestured toward Lieutenant Calder. "Mama invited Ward to visit at any time."

Luellen blushed at how ungracious she'd sounded. "You're most welcome. Both of you." She sent Franklin a mock frown. "Did Mama and Papa know you were coming? They didn't say anything to me."

"Christmas is next week. I wanted to make it a surprise."

Belle stood at the worktable, holding the spoon and watching their exchange. Franklin glanced at her, then took a second look, a smile lighting his eyes. "I'm Franklin, Luellen's brother."

"Happy to meet you. I'm Belle Brownlee." Her cheeks pinked. "Luellen talks about you all the time."

Luellen swiped a hand over her forehead. "Where are my manners?" She introduced Lieutenant Calder to Belle and turned to Franklin. "Why don't you take your things upstairs while we get this cake in the oven? Tap on Mama's door to let her know you're here. She'll be ecstatic."

"Why is Mama in her room?"

"She said she was tired."

"You got here just in time for the festivities on Friday," Papa said to Franklin at supper. "Jack Bryant has made the second floor of the hotel available for a Christmas party for you young people. There'll be games and dancing. I expect the ladies will bring Christmas treats, if it's anything like last year."

Mama put down her fork. "We were in the mercantile today, and Ben didn't say a word about it. Usually he's the first to know about parties and such."

"Jack stopped by late this afternoon. His wife's been ailing, and he wasn't sure she'd want all the commotion. But she loves parties, and insists she's well enough to oversee the plans."

Luellen looked at her lap, focusing on the woven pattern in her napkin. She'd hoped there'd be no party this year. As a recently married, then divorced, woman, there was no place for her among the single adults in the community. Nor did she belong with the married girls.

"I put up several jars of mincemeat this fall," Mama said. She turned to Luellen. "We could make pies. Nobody has your light touch with pastry—they'll be the best desserts on the table."

"I used to wait all year for my mother's mincemeat pies," Lieutenant Calder said. Sadness flashed over his face. "She only made them at Christmas." His eyes met Luellen's across the table. "I haven't had a taste of mincemeat in many years. I'll look forward to sampling yours, Miss McGarvie."

Luellen flushed. "I hope you won't be disappointed." He'd given her an idea. She could spend the evening of the party overseeing the refreshment table. If Mrs. Bryant's health was poor, she'd no doubt welcome the help.

"If your pie is as good as this ginger cake, I'm sure I won't be," Lieutenant Calder said, drawing her back to the conversation.

"Belle and I worked together on the cake. She deserves much of the credit."

Franklin gazed across the table at Belle. "I knew there had to be a reason this cake was so tasty."

Luellen fought an unexpected surge of jealousy. Franklin was *her* brother. Belle was *her* friend. She didn't want to share. The intensity of her reaction surprised her.

Frowning at her task, Luellen picked threads from the waistband of her best dress. By opening the side seams, she could add gussets so the rose taffeta garment would be suitable to wear to the party on Friday. Since she had to attend, she wanted to look her best for the prying eyes she knew would scrutinize her.

Mama poked her head into the small sewing room. "This would be perfect with your dress." She held up a silvery gray silk cape, trimmed with black ribbon. "It will conceal the gussets."

Luellen stood and slipped the garment over her shoulders. Tied at the neckline, the shimmering folds fell below her waist. "It's perfect, but this is your best cape. Are you sure?"

"I want you to feel equal to the other girls. If you look pretty, you'll feel pretty."

"Oh, Mama." Luellen handed her the cape before her tears stained the silk. "I wish I didn't have to go."

"Belle's your guest. You need to entertain her. Friday's her last day with us—let's make it special."

"Franklin's making it special enough for both of us, mooning over her the way he is." Luellen brushed at her tears with the back of her hand. "Ever since he came home, neither one of them has much time for me."

"You sound like one of the children you hope to teach." Mama jammed her hands on her hips and gave Luellen a stern look. "'Rejoice with them that do rejoice.' You should be happy your friend likes your brother. What if they'd taken an instant dislike to each other? Think how awkward we'd all feel."

Luellen bent her head to her stitches, picking at broken threads. "It feels awkward now. Franklin is so busy following Belle around that poor Lieutenant Calder is left to his own devices much of the time."

"I don't think he minds. He seems content to work on the reports he brought with him." She patted Luellen's shoulder. "This attitude isn't like you."

After Mama left, Luellen rested her hands in her lap and stared out at the cloudy sky. Skulking around the house feeling sorry for herself gained her nothing. As soon as Christmas was over, she'd work at the hotel until time to return to Allenwood. That way she could recover what she'd spent on fabric and have a start on next year's savings.

Hung with swags of greenery, the ballroom at Bryant House looked like an illustration from Dickens's *A Christmas Carol*. Men and women in bright clothing mingled throughout the capacious room. Luellen watched the chattering guests from her position behind the refreshment table. On a raised platform against the opposite wall, musicians tuned their instruments. Fiddles scraped, a harmonica screeched, and a fife player piped high notes before they swung into the first tune of the evening, "Camptown Races."

Couples filled the floor for the lively polka. Uncle Matthew's oldest sons, twins Jimmy and Johnny, joined in the dancing with their wives. Their younger brother, Harrison, danced with his current ladylove. Luellen smiled to herself. Her uncle had certainly mellowed since the Shakespeare fiasco that happened when she was a girl. Then, he wouldn't allow his family to attend a play, much less a dance. Now here were her cousins, dipping and swaying to the music.

She ignored the stares and whispers of a group of young women nearby. She assumed everyone believed she'd come with Lieutenant Calder, even though she'd left him with Franklin and Belle to take her post receiving and arranging the desserts. She stood, listening to the bouncy tune and wishing the evening were over.

"Mrs. O'Connell?" A familiar-looking man who appeared to be in his midthirties, with a receding hairline, stood in front of her. His arms were folded across his stomach, fingers of one hand drumming against the opposite forearm.

"It's Miss McGarvie, if you please."

"Oh. Sorry. I heard—"

"Daniel Griffith, isn't it?" Franklin appeared beside him, holding out his hand. "Haven't seen you in a coon's age. Where've you been?"

"Here and there. Took over my folks' pottery business when they died, but no one around here wants that old brown crockery anymore. So I'm on the road peddling the stuff most of the time." Daniel's nervousness evaporated while he talked to Franklin. "Heard you was an Army scout." His gaze took in Franklin's blue trousers and dress coat. "You look pretty well turned out—'cept for them moccasins. Never did get over being with them Indians, did you?"

"I learned a few tricks that've come in handy." He turned to the refreshment table. "Like never passing up food when it's offered." His hand closed over the edge of a plate containing a generous slice of mince pie. "How many desserts can I have?" he asked Luellen.

"One." She grinned at him. "At a time."

The band slowed the tempo from "Camptown Races" to a waltz. Several couples stopped by the table and selected desserts, taking cups of punch with them back to their chairs. Fewer dancers filled the floor.

During the lull, Daniel Griffith sought Luellen's attention. "Would you like to dance with your old neighbor?" A blush flared across his face.

Surprised he would ask, Luellen said, "You're very kind, but I prefer to watch." She couldn't imagine running the gauntlet of gossips if she were to take to the dance floor. Why would Daniel seek her out? He'd been almost grown before she ever started school. Surely he had a wife and children someplace. Uncomfortable, she turned away and pretended to be absorbed in watching the dancers.

Franklin and Belle swirled past, deep in conversation. Luellen fought down jealousy. If it weren't for Belle, her brother would be keeping her company at the table. She rearranged dessert plates, filling empty spaces with fresh cut slices of pie or cake.

"May I have this waltz?"

Irritated, Luellen glanced up, expecting to see Daniel repeating his request. Instead, Lieutenant Calder smiled at her and held out his arm.

She shook her head. "See all those busybodies watching me? They're just waiting for something new to gossip about."

He placed her hand on his arm. His wool coat felt warm under her fingers. "Keep your chin up and look them in the eye, remember?"

Conscious of people staring, Luellen allowed him to lead her to the edge of the dance floor. He clasped her right hand in his left and placed his right hand lightly against her back above her waist.

Smiling, she settled her left hand on his shoulder. "Might as well be hanged for a sheep as a lamb." Together they slipped into the flow of the music.

Lieutenant Calder danced her near the gawking girls at the back of the ballroom. "Let's give them a good look," he said, a mischievous twinkle in his blue eyes.

She shook her head in mock disapproval. "I have to live here after you go back to Missouri, Lieutenant."

"Please call me Ward. We've spent enough time in each other's company to consider ourselves friends, don't you think?"

"Ward it is." She appreciated his no-nonsense personality. "Heaven knows, I could use a friend right now."

"So could I."

❧

The following morning, Luellen sat in the guest bedroom watching while Belle tucked the last of her belongings into her traveling bag. "I so appreciate the invitation to spend these weeks with your family. All of you made me feel so welcome."

"Especially Franklin?"

Hurt darkened Belle's eyes. "You're my dearest friend. I assumed you'd be pleased that your brother and I got on so well."

"Don't tell me you spent all week in his company for my sake."

"What's got into you?"

Luellen's mouth curved in a wry smile. *Now there's a leading question.* "I thought you were my friend. But you've ignored me in favor of my brother for days on end."

"That's simply not true. We've taken walks, shopped, read,

sewed, cooked—what more do you want?" Belle tightened the strap on her bag with a vigorous tug. "I don't understand you."

Franklin tapped on the door frame. "I came to get your baggage. The buggy's waiting out front. I'll drive you to the depot."

A flush appeared on Belle's cheeks. "That will be lovely. Luellen, will you come with us?"

"No, thank you." She kept her tone formal. "I'm sure you'll manage without me."

Franklin seized Belle's travel bag and turned toward the stairs. "We'd better leave. The train will be here soon."

Belle planted a kiss on Luellen's cheek. "See you in two months—let's try to start fresh then."

Luellen gave a noncommittal nod.

After they left, she walked into the front bedroom and pushed the curtain aside. Mama and Papa stood on the walk, waiting while Franklin assisted Belle into the buggy. If she hurried, she could still accompany them and make things right with Belle. She took a step away from the window. No. If they really wanted her company, they would have tried harder to persuade her.

She lifted the curtain again, watching until the buggy traveled out of sight.

On Christmas Eve, Luellen leaned over the worktable in the kitchen, rubbing lard into a bowl of flour with her fingers. Mama stood at the stove, watching to be sure the pumpkin didn't scorch as it cooked. Three pie pans waited to be lined with pastry and filled. Since Ward had expressed a fondness for mincemeat, Mama decided they would have two mince pies in addition to Papa's favorite, pumpkin, for their Christmas dinner.

Mama removed the pot from the heat and stirred in ginger

and cloves. The spicy aroma reminded Luellen of the cake she and Belle had been making the day Franklin and Ward arrived. She swallowed regret at her treatment of her friend. If only she could turn time backward and keep her jealousy to herself. Once they returned to Allenwood, Belle would forget about Franklin. For his part, Franklin would be off on a new adventure with no room for a woman in his life.

If she could turn time backward, where would she stop? Before Brendan? She'd be wishing her baby away. And she'd never have known Belle's friendship at all. She rested her hands on the side of the bowl and stared into its floury depths.

"Are you woolgathering?" Mama's voice cut through her self-recrimination.

Luellen sprinkled cold water over the flour mixture and tossed it with a fork. "I was thinking about Belle. I'm afraid I treated her unkindly before she left."

"She'll understand. Women in your condition are often moody."

"Belle doesn't know about the baby."

"My goodness, why not? If you insist on going back to Allenwood, you'll need to have an ally. God forbid, what if something goes wrong while you're far from home?"

"I just couldn't bring myself to say anything to her. I already feel like an outsider. My extra studies kept me from making friends. Now to be with child and trying to finish the term—I was afraid she'd want nothing more to do with me."

Mama slipped an arm around Luellen. "So you drove her away before she could hurt you," she said in a soft voice.

The fork clinked against the side of the bowl when Luellen dropped it. She turned to her mother, eyes blurred with tears. "Yes."

# 13

Luellen leaned over Uncle Arthur's shoulder and placed a cream-garnished wedge of pumpkin pie in front of him.

"This is the best part of Christmas dinner." He brandished his fork. "With Matt's family gone to Quincy, that leaves only six of us to eat these pies. So I can have another helping." He glanced at Franklin and Ward. "That is, if you boys don't eat every bite first."

"Keep your eye on Franklin," Ward said. "I'm enjoying the mincemeat. Best I ever tasted."

"Thank you." Mama spoke from her place at the foot of the table. She looked at Luellen. "Why don't you stop fussing and eat your dessert? The clutter in the kitchen will wait."

As she slid into her chair, Uncle Arthur turned to her with a question in his eyes. "You look like you're filling out, Lulie. Any chance that no-good O'Connell left you in the family way? Be nice to have a young'un close by."

A pulse pounded in Luellen's throat. Not now. Not here. She wanted to tell Franklin when the two of them were alone.

Before she could respond, Mama leaned forward. "Uncle. That's not a proper question for mixed company."

"Why not? We're all family, 'cept for the lieutenant here, and he's not likely to run through town spreading the news."

Ward's eyes met Luellen's. "You've no reason to be ashamed. It will be a fortunate child indeed to be born into such a fine family." *Hold your head up*, his expression said.

"Is it true?" Franklin stared at her. "You told me you're going back to Allenwood. How can you do that?"

She bristled. "Easily. Buy a ticket and board the train."

He opened his mouth to say something further, but Papa intervened. "Franklin. I know you're surprised, but could we please discuss this later? I want to enjoy my pie without the two of you bickering at each other."

Uncle Arthur slipped his hand over Luellen's. His caterpillar eyebrows bunched together in a frown. "Didn't mean to upset you. Figured everyone knew."

One thing about Arthur, the older he got, the more outspoken he became. Goodness only knew what he'd blurt out when he was eighty. She patted his hand. "I would've told Franklin sooner or later. You saved me the trouble."

She took a bite of her dessert, avoiding her brother's wounded expression.

Sounds of Christmas melodies being played on a fiddle drifted into the kitchen. Through the frosted window, the backyard appeared silvery-blue in the late afternoon light. With her hands deep in warm water, Luellen scrubbed the last bits of gravy from the roasting pan. She welcomed the time alone to regain her composure.

Franklin acted crushed that she hadn't confided in him, but it was his fault. If he hadn't spent all his time with Belle, she would have found an opportunity to tell him. She'd talk to him tonight, after they took Uncle Arthur back to his farm.

"Would you like a hand in here?" Ward lifted a towel from a hook on the wall, and scooped up a handful of knives and forks from the draining rack.

"This is woman's work," she said, flustered. "I'll be finished soon."

"Please let me help. Before my father died, I did all the kitchen work. I never thought I'd say this, but I miss cooking and cleaning up."

"Didn't your mother—"

"My mother died when I was a youth. My father never remarried." His gaze met hers, open and without self-pity. "I was just glad to have a home."

Interested, she waited for him to say more. He dropped the dry tableware into a wooden cutlery tray and wrapped the towel around the roasting pan. "Let's hurry. You're missing your uncle's music. He's an enthusiastic fiddler, isn't he?"

"Some of my earliest memories are of him playing for us at Christmas."

"Sounds quite different from my Christmas memories."

"How did your family celebrate?"

Ward appeared ready to answer, then he folded his lips together and shook his head. "Some other time." He placed the roaster next to the range. "Come. Let's enjoy the carols."

When they entered the parlor, Uncle Arthur lowered the bow and smiled at them. A fire snapped on the grate, spreading ribbons of flame over blackened firebricks. Lighted candles blazed on the mantel. Luellen wrapped her arms around her middle, hugging the pleasure of the moment to herself. Ward took a chair next to the fire and she settled beside Franklin on the divan.

Franklin glanced at her, his expression cold. "When were you planning to tell me about the baby?" He spoke in an undertone.

"First, Mama has to write me that you're married—you were too busy to do it yourself. Now, you would've let me go back to Missouri not knowing I'm going to be an uncle. Don't I matter to you anymore?"

Stung, Luellen placed a hand at her throat. "Of course you do. I didn't realize it mattered that much."

"Why wouldn't it?" His voice climbed a decibel. "I've always—"

Papa cleared his throat. "Do you two want to listen to music, or argue?"

Franklin folded his arms over his chest and stretched his legs out in front of him. "Music."

"Luellen?"

"Music." She angled her shoulders so she faced away from her brother.

Uncle Arthur slid the bow over the strings. "It's getting late. This'll be the last carol." The gentle strains of "Silent Night" filled the room.

Hands folded in her lap, Luellen closed her eyes and thought of a baby born centuries earlier in Bethlehem. She felt a stirring inside. Her eyes flew open when she felt movement again. *The baby's quickened!* She turned to Franklin to whisper the news, but he met her gaze with a stony glare.

Tears prickled. How could she make things right with him? She couldn't let him return to Missouri without mending their relationship.

On Saturday afternoon, Mama and Luellen spread the wool challis yardage on the dining table. Following a muslin pattern, Luellen cut into the golden brown fabric. By moving the waistline higher on the bodice, she'd be able to wear the dress for some time before she needed to add the matching sacque to the costume. While she worked, her mind strayed to Franklin. He hadn't said two words to her since yesterday evening. Her brother was not one to hang on to anger, so she must have hurt him deeply.

"I wish Franklin didn't have to leave Monday," Mama said, putting Luellen's thoughts into words.

"So do I." She cut around a section of wide pagoda sleeve. "He's angry with me for keeping the news about the baby from him."

Mama raised an eyebrow. "You didn't tell us, either. How long were you planning to wait?"

"I didn't have a plan." Luellen laid cut sections of fabric aside. "I was so tired and distressed I just didn't think."

"Tell that to Franklin. He'll understand."

"First I have to get him to listen to me. You saw how he took Ward and went riding this morning. He's avoiding me."

"Oh, I don't believe—" Mama swayed forward, grabbing the edge of the table. Her fingers caught the golden wool. She slumped to the floor, pulling the fabric down on top of her.

"Mama!" Luellen dropped the scissors and raced to her mother's side. She slid an arm around her waist, helping her into a sitting position. Mama's skin was pasty white. Small droplets of perspiration dotted her forehead.

"I'll be all right in a moment. Just let me get my breath."

"Can you sit in this chair?"

She nodded, and Luellen lifted her into an armchair next to the wall. "I'll go get Papa. You just be still."

"No. I don't want to worry your father."

"He'd be more than worried if we didn't tell him. I'll be right back." She ignored her mother's protests, dashing through the kitchen and out to Papa's office. Frozen needles of grass glittered in the late morning light. Once she reached the door, she saw his printed "Out of the Office" sign placed in the window.

She wheeled toward the house, trying to think of where she could go for help. She didn't dare get too far away. Who knew what might happen in her absence?

A carriage rumbled along Adams Street. Luellen ran to the front, waving her arms. She could send the occupants to get Uncle Matthew. No. He'd gone to Quincy. Maybe Mr. Wolcott could come. "Wait! Help!"

The carriage moved past without the driver noticing her.

She stood on the walk, staring down the icy street. Should she go to one of the neighbors? What could they do? They didn't know any more about medicine than she did. The new physician, Dr. Gordon, had an office on Washington Street, but that was blocks away, and what if he wasn't there either? Her heart pounded in her throat.

The sound of horses' hooves rang from the frozen ground. Two riders turned a corner and headed in her direction.

"Franklin!" She stepped into the street. "Thank goodness you're here."

He reined in his animal. "What are you doing out with no cloak? You'll freeze to death."

"It's Mama." Luellen placed a hand over her racing heart, trying to get enough breath to talk. "She collapsed. Papa's gone on a house call."

Ward rode up beside Franklin. "You go with your sister. I'll take care of the horses." He shot a concerned look at Luellen. "You'd best get inside. This cold is wicked."

She looked down, realizing she wore her thin leather slippers. Chill air crept through her calico dress. Shivering, she wrapped her arms around her middle.

Franklin swung off his horse and strode toward her, unbuttoning his overcoat as he approached. "Here." He dropped it over her shoulders. Instant warmth enveloped her. He took her arm and they hurried up the steps.

Mama rested in the chair, her head tilted against the back. She looked up when Franklin entered with Luellen. "My goodness. Both of you." She tried to smile. "I'm a little tired. If you'd help me up the stairs, I believe I'll lie down for a bit."

Brother and sister exchanged a worried glance, their enmity forgotten. Neither one could remember a time when their mother needed their assistance.

Once in the bedroom, Franklin excused himself while Luellen helped Mama out of her dress and into her wrapper. After propping pillows against the headboard, Mama settled on the bed, smiling when Luellen tucked a quilt around her shoulders. "This is good practice. Soon you'll be looking after a baby."

"Babies are one thing, you're another. I'm worried. Has this happened before?"

Mama hesitated. "No. Well, not like this." She took Luellen's hand. "I haven't been sleeping much, and you know how busy things are at Christmas. A nap is all I need." She sighed, her eyelids drooping shut. "Will you see to dinner?"

"Of course." Luellen tiptoed from the room.

Franklin and Ward were waiting at the foot of the stairs. They both looked up when she appeared.

"What do you think is wrong?" Franklin asked.

"I have no idea. She says she's just tired." Luellen rubbed her forehead. "I hope that's all."

"Fatigue can have that effect," Ward said. "I've seen men collapse on the parade field after an intense drill."

Hope brightened Franklin's expression. "Mama does go at

119

things like she's killing snakes. She'll probably be back on her feet by suppertime."

Luellen wasn't so sure.

Papa rose from the breakfast table Monday morning and cupped a hand over Mama's cheek. "You're to stay off your feet until office hours are over. Rest." He bent down and kissed the top of her head. "I'll be back in plenty of time to take Franklin and Ward to the depot."

He turned to Luellen. "I don't see why you're so set on seeing Jack Bryant this morning. It's brutally cold. At least let Franklin drive you to the hotel."

"I walked there winter and summer for the past four years. A cold morning won't stop me."

"You might as well let her go, Karl," Mama said. "You know how she is when her mind's made up."

Luellen sent her a grateful smile. "I won't be gone long. Just have to find out what time he wants me there tomorrow. I'll come right home." She studied her mother's face. Pink colored her cheeks, and the fatigue lines around her eyes had softened. "Maybe we can sit together and sew later?"

"As long as you work downstairs," Papa said. "When I say your mother's to stay off her feet, I mean it."

Wrapped in a cloak and wool mittens, Luellen stepped with care along the board sidewalk. She hoped her hours at the hotel wouldn't be too long. Papa had ordered total rest for her mother for the next week, so Luellen would need to do the cooking at

120

home before and after work, as well as keeping up the house. Her pace increased as she pondered her schedule.

Trees lining the town square stood black against a gray sky. Snow clouds hovered. She caught sight of the lighted front windows of the hotel across Madison Street and tightened her grip on the front of her cloak. As she moved to the edge of the walk, her foot skidded on a patch of ice. She pitched headlong into the street.

Shaken, Luellen struggled to her knees and glanced around to see if anyone had witnessed her fall. Fortunately, no one approached from either direction. She brought one foot forward, testing, then pushed herself upright. Wet splotches stained the front of her cloak. The palms of her hands smarted from the rocks that had torn through her mittens.

She limped across the road, momentarily dizzy. Did her fall hurt the baby? She closed her eyes and focused inward. No sharp pains or cramps. Grateful, she stripped off her raveled mittens and used them to blot the blood that trickled from scrapes on her palms.

No reason she couldn't call on Mr. Bryant anyway. He probably wouldn't notice stains on her dark indigo cloak. If she kept her hands tucked out of sight, she could hide her skinned flesh.

When she entered the lobby, he looked up from the desk in the reception area. Strange, where was the clerk who normally greeted guests?

"Mrs. O'Connell—"

"I'm Miss McGarvie again, thankfully."

"To what do I owe the honor of this visit? Especially on such a miserable day."

She drew a chair next to his desk and sat, arms folded inside her cloak. Her palms stung. "I stopped by to see what hours you'd like me to work while I'm home on vacation. Allenwood doesn't resume classes until late February, so I'm available."

He shook his head. "Business has been slow since the bank failures. Now that winter's here, railroad work has stopped, so laborers aren't coming in for meals." He gestured around the empty lobby. "I had to let my clerk go. When we do have diners, Mrs. Dolan can handle them. I'm sorry, I don't need extra help."

# 14

Luellen left the hotel lobby, trying not to limp until she was out of Mr. Bryant's sight. Once on the walkway, she bent over and massaged her aching knees. She'd be wearing bruises by morning.

How could she have been naïve enough to believe her job would be waiting for her whenever she asked? Beldon Grove didn't exist in isolation from the rest of the country. Hard times in the eastern states now affected rural Illinois as well.

Deep in thought, she crossed the road and picked her way toward home around frozen spots. She passed Wolcott's Mercantile and paused at the corner. The shuttered schoolhouse faced her across the way. Once the Christmas holiday ended, children would be back at their studies. Would any of them need extra help with their lessons? Maybe she could offer her services as a tutor. The wages wouldn't be much, but anything would help.

Luellen backtracked to the mercantile and hobbled through the door. Mr. Wolcott sat on a stool behind the counter, making notes in a ledger. He smiled at her when she entered. "This is a surprise. Why aren't you at home with your family?" He gestured around the deserted store. "Everyone else is."

"Could you post a notice for me?"

"Certainly. What're you advertising?" Lamplight reflected off his scalp, shining between sparse strands of hair.

"I want to try tutoring. Do you think I'd have any interested families?"

He cupped a hand around his chin for a moment before answering. "Well, the Carstairs boy seems a little slow. He's around seven now, and still doesn't know his letters—or so his father says. 'Course I don't think Orville can hardly read a lick, either." He grimaced. "Don't repeat that."

Luellen smiled. "I didn't hear a thing." She rested an arm on the counter. "If you can spare a bit of paper, I'll write out the information. School doesn't resume at Allenwood for almost two months, so that would allow time for lessons."

Mr. Wolcott watched while she printed her tutoring offer. "What happened to your hands? They look raw."

"I slipped on an icy spot in front of Bryant House. It's nothing."

"You planning to tutor and work at the hotel too?"

"Mr. Bryant doesn't need extra help." Her cheeks warmed. Somehow being told she wasn't needed felt almost as humiliating as being dismissed. She pushed the completed notice toward him.

"I'll be sure folks see this."

Luellen noticed sympathy in his eyes. "Thank you."

Once inside her parents' house, Luellen shed her damp cloak and placed her mittens on the hall table. She'd unravel them later and save the undamaged wool.

Papa met her at the entrance to the sitting room. "What took you so long? We need to leave for the station soon."

"I'm sorry. Time got away from me."

He stepped forward and slid an arm around her waist. "You're limping. Are you hurt?"

"Mostly my dignity. I slipped on the ice."

"Let me look." He eased her onto a chair next to the fire and knelt in front of her.

"I'm fine," she said, sliding her skirt up enough so he could see for himself. "My knees will be bruised tomorrow. My hands are a bit skinned too." Luellen turned them over, revealing the scrapes on her palms.

Papa pushed himself to his feet. Worry lines etched his forehead. "You're fortunate you weren't more seriously hurt. I wish you'd forget this nonsense about working at the hotel."

"Mr. Bryant doesn't need help right now. I'm going to tutor children until time to return to school."

Irritation sparked in his eyes. "You've enough savings left to see you through—" Papa gasped and fumbled with the buttons on his collar.

Luellen jumped to her feet. "What's wrong?"

"Nothing. Just a little breathless. It'll pass."

"I'll get you some water." She hurried toward the kitchen.

Mama looked up from her sewing when Luellen dashed through the dining room. "Where are you going in such a rush?"

"Something's wrong with Papa. I'm getting him a glass of water."

Her mother stood, dropping the fabric on the floor. "Is he having trouble breathing?"

"Yes." Luellen cocked her head. "This has happened before?"

"Usually at night. He sleeps propped up, but sometimes he slips off the pillows." Her eyes glistened. "I lie awake listening." She took a step toward the doorway.

Luellen watched as Mama hurried away. Why hadn't she been warned about Papa's illness?

When she returned to the sitting room, he had buttoned his collar and was breathing normally. Mama hovered beside him, a hand resting on his shoulder.

"You two are making too much of this." He stood and accepted the water. "It's time to head for the station. I'll go hitch the carriage."

"Let Franklin do it," Luellen said. "I'll call him."

"No need." He strode from the room. His determination not to be coddled was apparent in the set of his shoulders.

The train waited, billowing clouds of dense steam over their heads. Light snow melted as soon as it touched the boiler on the locomotive. Ward glanced toward Luellen and her parents. They stood close together, as though bound by a secret. He wondered what had passed between them while he was upstairs. Luellen clung to her father's arm, casting worried glances at him when he wasn't looking.

Ward handed his luggage to the baggage master and followed Franklin to the shelter of the station. After hugging his mother, Franklin clasped Luellen's hands. "Will you write me often? I don't want any more surprises."

"I'm sorry. I didn't realize—"

He grabbed her in a bearlike embrace. "You're forgiven. Just take care of yourself, please."

She placed a hand on his cheek. "I will. You too."

Ward stepped closer to Luellen, missing the family he'd never had. What would it have been like to have sisters or brothers who cared about him? He cleared his throat. "I'd appreciate it if you'd drop me a letter from time to time, also. Franklin's not always at the barracks to share your news." Embarrassed, he gazed into her doe brown eyes, hoping she didn't think he was a fool for asking.

A smile tipped a corner of her mouth. "I'd be happy to. As long as you promise to answer."

Once Beldon Grove faded from view, Ward settled in his seat and opened his folding writing box. He lifted the sloping surface and extracted half-finished survey reports. How would he phrase his recommendations to discourage development of western land, yet satisfy investors' desires to extend the railroad?

He uncorked the inkwell and dipped his pen, but Luellen McGarvie's courageous face intruded. Whatever possessed him to ask her to write? Ward wiped ink from the nib and laid the pen down. A woman with Luellen's spirit didn't come along every day. He couldn't deny the admiration he felt, but he couldn't act on it, either. His goal when he was admitted to West Point was to make the Army his career, and there was no room in that ambition for a wife.

Franklin jostled his shoulder. "You're going to stare a hole in that paper. You still trying to control the future?"

His mind still on Luellen, Ward frowned at him. "What future are you talking about?"

"The railroad. Have you figured out a way to avoid our country's pursuit of 'manifest destiny'?" He spun the phrase with sarcasm.

The word settled in Ward's brain. Which destiny was he avoiding? Railroads? Or Luellen?

He shook his head. "I'm still mulling it over."

Whiskered with frost, trees lining the parade ground rose like ghosts through the fog. Shivering in spite of his heavy wool overcoat, Ward watched with sympathy as recruits practiced cavalry drills. In a few minutes he'd be inside the officers' quarters, but the men would be out in the cold for hours. If he were fortunate enough to command a post one day, he'd see to it that enlistees were treated with more respect.

Franklin nodded toward one of the buildings. "Let's get out of the wind."

Nudging their horses forward, they rode through the wide doors of the stone stable. Once inside, the musky smell of horseflesh enveloped them. A young private jumped up from a chair near the door and took the reins of Ward's mount. "I'll take care of him for you, sir."

"Thank you." Ward slung his saddlebags over one shoulder and turned to Franklin. "You'll be on the post for a few weeks?"

"Far as I know." He dismounted, grinning in the direction of the retreating soldier. "Looks like I get to put up my own horse."

"Spend a few years at the Academy and you too can have your horse stabled for you."

"No thanks. I'd never survive." He touched his hand to his forehead in a mock salute and followed the private down the center aisle.

Smiling, Ward left the enclosure and walked toward the officers' quarters. He'd finish his report for the investment company, then organize his thoughts for an upcoming class on military tactics to be taught to the enlisted men.

Luellen's goal to become a teacher set his mind adrift from his own assignment. Would she succeed? He didn't see how. No matter what she thought now, caring for a baby would bring her ambitions to a halt. "Too bad," he murmured, dropping his bags on the bed.

"What's too bad?" Mark Campion slouched into Ward's room.

Ward whirled around. "Don't you knock?"

"Not when the door's open." He dropped into a chair. "You going to the New Year's Ball on Thursday? I heard young ladies from the finishing school in town are invited." He rubbed his hands together. "Should be a worthwhile event."

"Maybe for you. I'd rather greet the New Year without a headache."

He snorted. "You're living like a monk. Who are you trying to impress with your studies and reports? You'll likely be stuck on this post for years, just like the rest of us."

Ward bit back a retort. His plans were none of his fellow officer's business. He leaned against the wall, arms folded over his chest. "You didn't stop by to discuss my career. What's on your mind?"

"Well, I figured you wouldn't go to the ball—you never do—so how about loaning me your sword belt? Mine's in sad shape. I want to look good for the ladies."

"That's all?" Ward asked, suspicious.

"All for now. Say, how's that report about the rail line progressing? I heard you're recommending against the cheaper route over the prairie." A sly look crept over his pudgy features. "I was born in St. Joseph—I don't think your suggestion will hold water. I plan to submit my own recommendations."

Anger roared in Ward's ears. "You *heard* what I'm recommending? No one knows what's in that report." He grabbed the front of Campion's shirt and lifted him from the chair. "Next time I find out you've been poking around in my papers, I'll turn you in." He released his hold on the shirt and the man stumbled backward, catching himself against the desktop.

"You don't have to get rough." His voice shredded into a whine. "I must've been mistaken about the railroad plans. You know how rumors fly." He inched toward the door. "We're still friends, aren't we? You gonna loan me that belt?"

Luellen stood at the window of an upstairs bedroom, looking down on the shoveled path between their house and her father's office. Snow lay drifted against the wall of the building. Half of January had passed and she'd received no responses to her tutoring offer. Winter chill crept around her heart when she considered her meager savings. The money Papa received from Bryant County Bank would barely last through the upcoming term.

She felt as though she were standing on one side of a snowy forest, her goal out of sight through impenetrable brush. *Lord, there must be a way.*

Mama joined her at the window. They both watched as Papa opened the door to his office and disappeared inside.

"Are you sure there's nothing wrong with him? He seemed tired at breakfast," Luellen said.

"I wish I knew. He says he has a touch of asthma. He won't go see Dr. Gordon, no matter how much I urge him."

"You can't stay awake listening to his breathing every night. You'll collapse again." She dropped the curtain and crossed the upstairs hall to Mama's sewing room, where the pieces of her green worsted dress were laid out for basting.

Mama threaded a needle and settled herself in a low rocker, fabric spread across her lap. "Most nights he's fine. He seems to have the greatest trouble when something's upset him during the day." She sighed. "I have no control over that. In spite of office hours, he still travels all over the community. You know what a doctor's life is like."

Luellen nodded. "I've always been so proud of him. Everyone loves Dr. Karl."

"They do, don't they?" Mama's face glowed. "He's been a wonderful father to you children too."

"The very best." She jumped at the sound of a knock on the front door. "Drat. Just when I thought we'd get the basting finished. I hope it's not one of the neighbor ladies come to call—that'll take hours." Luellen dropped a half-completed bodice on the table. "I'll go see who it is."

She dashed downstairs, her slippers making little sound on the polished wooden steps. Pausing, she settled her shawl around her middle, then opened the door.

"Daniel. What are—" A flush warmed her cheeks. "I beg your pardon. Please come in."

Why was he here? Luellen remembered him asking her to dance at the Christmas party. She prayed he hadn't come courting.

Daniel stepped into the entryway, his hat clutched in one hand. His rust-colored hair stuck out around his ears. "Miss Luellen, Ben Wolcott said you're a reading tutor."

"Yes. I'm studying to be a teacher. I've had practice with youngsters over these past months."

"Daniel!" Mama called from the top of the stairs. "How good to see you." She hurried toward him. "I've missed you since you moved to the other side of town. Won't you come into the sitting room? Coffee's still warm, if you want some." She patted his arm. "This is like old times, having you at the door. I've never forgotten how much you helped me when I was alone with the children."

He turned scarlet. "Glad to do it, Miz Spengler. Besides, my ma would've had my hide if'n I slacked off." His Adam's apple bobbed when he swallowed. "I thank you for the offer of coffee, but I just stopped by to see if'n Luellen would learn me how to read. I'll be proud to pay whatever it costs."

Luellen stared at him. "You already know how to read. I remember when you finished school."

"I finished by memorizing. Never could get the hang of letters too good." He dropped his gaze, rolling the brim of his hat between broad fingers. "I reckon you must think I'm stupid."

Mama's eyes met Luellen's. *Be kind.*

Tutoring adults wasn't what she had in mind. Especially someone as old as Daniel. She bit her lip to keep from smiling at the image of six-foot-something Daniel Griffith reading "The Pancake."

She extended her hand, and he grasped it. "I think it's a brave thing to ask for help. When do you want to start your lessons?"

# 15

Luellen closed the door behind Daniel and looked at her mother. "Saturday morning will be here before I know it." She blew out a breath. "I haven't had any practice teaching adults. I'm grateful for the promise of income, but this isn't what I intended."

"The Lord sends help in unexpected ways."

"That he does. I can't help but wonder, though. Why would Daniel seek me out? I pray he's not using reading lessons as a means of courtship. Did I tell you he asked me to dance at the Christmas party?"

Mama's face clouded. "If that's why he's here, his timing's inappropriate, to say the least." She turned toward the stairs. "Let's get back to our sewing. Maybe we can have that dress finished by next week."

"You go ahead. I need to look through my books and find the first reader. I'll start by seeing how much Daniel already knows."

On Saturday after breakfast, Luellen placed a slate, pencils, and the reader on the dining room table.

Papa watched her, thumbs tucked around his suspenders. "Looks just like a schoolroom."

"I hope so. I can't imagine teaching someone older than me how to read. I worried about it all night. What if—"

He put an arm around her shoulders and hugged her. "Don't think about your ages. Focus on your skills as a teacher. You know something you can share with Daniel. That's what you need to remember."

"You're right. Thank you." She relaxed against his side. "I don't know what I'd do without you."

"Right now you'd better answer the door. I hear footsteps on the veranda."

At a loss how to begin, Luellen stared across the table at Daniel. He'd slicked his hair back with oil, and wore a tie under his fold-down collar. "Can you write your name?" She bit her lip. How insulting. "I mean, do you know your letters?"

He avoided her eyes. "I know the ABCs. Just can't do nothing with 'em."

She printed GRIFFITH on the slate and turned it to face him. "What's this say?"

"Griffith, of course." He sounded defensive.

Luellen turned the paper to face her, and printed GRUFF.

He shook his head. "I told you, I don't know words. I can do my name because I memorized how." Daniel loosened his collar.

She studied him with compassion. He really didn't know how to read. "I'll be home for four more weeks. By that time, I promise you'll know words." She lifted the slate. "Tell me the ABCs, and I'll write them down."

With each letter she wrote, she told him the sound and had him repeat it back to her. When they reached *G*, she underlined the letter in the word GRUFF so he'd see the connection to the sound of his name. As the morning went on, she forgot she was teaching an adult, and simply enjoyed watching Daniel as he grasped the concept of sounding out letters to form words. How was it he'd completed school and failed to learn?

Belle's comment about her brother came to Luellen's mind. He'd been disciplined in school so severely as a young boy that he refused to try. She suspected that had been the case with Daniel.

Belle. As quickly as the name came to her mind, she turned it away. They'd be back at Allenwood next month. How could she make up to her friend for her unkind behavior? Did she dare trust the depth of their affection? She tucked the questions aside for later consideration.

"I think this is enough for one day," she said after two hours had passed. "Take this reader home with you and practice on the first story. Don't worry if you can't do it all—just read the words you can and copy out the ones you have trouble with. We'll go over them the next time you come."

Daniel's broad hand dwarfed the child-sized volume. He opened the book to "The Pancake." His eyes widened. "I don't know, Miss Luellen. There's a lot here."

"Take it one word at a time. You'll surprise yourself."

He stood and mopped his forehead with a kerchief. "You're a caution. Little girl like you and here you are a teacher."

"Not officially. Not yet." Her future held more questions than answers.

On Monday, Luellen woke at dawn with cramps stabbing at her abdomen. Alarmed, she felt for movement from the baby. Nothing. She rolled onto her side, swinging her legs to the floor.

She grabbed her wrapper from the foot of the bed. Gray light revealed dark stains on the sheet. *Please, no!* She tore down the stairs. "Papa!"

He emerged from the kitchen, holding a mug in his hand. "What's wrong?"

Mama followed him into the dining room. She took one look at Luellen's face and ran to her side. "Are you ill?"

"It's the baby."

Papa slammed the mug onto the table, splattering coffee. In a flash, he had his arm around Luellen, steering her to a chair. He sat facing her. "Tell me what you're experiencing."

She dropped her gaze, embarrassed to be sharing such a personal subject with her father. "I . . . I'm bleeding."

His hand rested on her forehead. "No fever. Any pains?"

"Some cramping." She rubbed her abdomen. "Right here."

"Do you hurt now?"

Luellen took a deep breath. "No." She swallowed. "They stopped."

Mama stood behind the chair, hands on Luellen's shoulders. Luellen felt her trembling.

"Karl, is the baby safe?"

"It's too soon to know." He stood. "I'm ordering bed rest for you. Stay down except to use the chamber pot. Your mother will bring your meals."

He turned to Mama. "We'll put her on the divan. It's frigid upstairs."

Too frightened to argue, Luellen asked, "How long will I have to stay in bed?"

"I don't know. Depends on what happens."

Mama took her hand. "Let's get you into a fresh gown, then you can settle down for the day."

Reclining against a stack of pillows, her Rose of Sharon quilt tucked around her, Luellen watched snow flurries dance over the street. The tedium of inactivity gnawed at her. A stack of flannel nightdresses she'd embroidered for the baby lay on the quilt, next to a half-finished lesson plan. Mama sat near the fire, stitching trim onto a tiny cambric shirt.

"I've been fine for days, Mama. Don't you think I can get up long enough to help Daniel tomorrow?"

"What's the urgency? He can come back when Papa says it's safe for you to be up and around."

"In three weeks I return to Allenwood. I want to be sure Daniel's learning on his own before I go—plus I need the money he's paying me."

"How can you even consider getting on a train and traveling all that distance after what's happened?"

Luellen laid a hand on her abdomen. As though responding to her touch, the baby bumped against her palm. "Papa said cramping is normal."

"Bleeding isn't," Mama shot back. "You're risking my grandchild's life."

"I'm not. I'll lie here as long as necessary to protect my baby, but not one second longer. If there are no more symptoms between now and next month, I'm going."

Mama pursed her lips. "We'll see what your father says." She rose and moved toward the entryway.

Remembering Papa's asthma attack the last time they'd argued, Luellen held out a hand to stop her. "I'd prefer to talk to him myself. It can wait until suppertime." Between now and then she'd decide the best way to wheedle him around to her way of thinking.

That evening, she smiled at her father across the table. "Thank you for letting me get up for dinner. Lying down for so long hurts my back."

"Being on your feet for short times shouldn't be harmful." He buttered a wedge of cornbread. "But you need to return to the divan as soon as we've finished."

Mama raised an eyebrow in Luellen's direction. "I believe Lulie has something to ask you."

Luellen frowned. She'd rather have waited until after dessert. "I'd like your permission to follow through on my appointment with Daniel tomorrow. He'll be here at ten."

"There's no reason he can't come back in a few weeks, when you're better."

Mama laid her fork on her plate, her gaze switching between Luellen and Papa. She looked ready to spring to her feet if Papa showed any sign of distress.

"We'll only be a couple of hours." Luellen prayed for the right words. "I've been up nearly that long now, without ill effects. Besides, students learn best when education is continuous. If we miss sessions, I may have to start over. It would be a shame to discourage him—he was so excited last week." She realized she was rattling and put her fingers over her lips to stop herself.

"I don't know—I'm not convinced the danger is passed."

"How about if I promise to stop the lesson if I feel any discomfort?"

"How about if I sit in and keep my eye on you?"

Luellen looked down so he wouldn't see her roll her eyes. When she lifted her head, she sent her father a sweet smile. "That would be fine. I do hope Daniel won't feel self-conscious."

Mama looked at her with a questioning expression. Luellen shook her head. The rest of their discussion would have to wait. Papa needed to agree that she was perfectly healthy before she brought up the subject of Allenwood.

On Saturday morning, Papa watched from his post near the kitchen door, newspaper in hand, while Luellen gathered her lesson papers and stacked them at one end of the dining table. He folded the *Illinois Monitor* and set it aside. "How are you feeling?"

"Quite well." She'd never admit it, but she did feel a bit weak.

"As soon as Daniel leaves, I want you to lie down."

"I know. You already said so." Arms folded, she flounced into a chair to wait for Daniel's knock.

Papa sent her a sharp look and returned to perusing the *Monitor.*

◯

Daniel stopped at the entrance to the dining room. "Doc. What are you doing here?" He looked at Luellen. "Aren't we having a lesson today?"

"We are. Papa just wanted to keep an eye on me. I . . . haven't been feeling well."

The big man's face reddened. "I'm happy to see you and all, Doc, but these here lessons are between me and Miss Luellen. I can't stand in front of another man and read baby stories." He drew the reader from inside his jacket and laid it on the table. "I'm sorry." He backed away and headed for the front door.

Luellen shot an agonized glance at her father, then dashed after Daniel. "Wait. I'm sure Papa can sit in another room." She turned. "Can't you? If I collapse, you'll hear the crash."

Daniel snickered. "You always did have a quick tongue," he said under his breath.

Papa's chair scraped against the floor as he rose. Anger chased worry from his face. "I'll be in my office." His eyes narrowed. "You're to rest as soon as you're finished, do you understand?"

She nodded, embarrassed at his tone but knowing she deserved the rebuke. Her face hot, Luellen pointed at a chair. "Let's get started." She noticed Daniel had taken pains with his appearance again. He wore a fresh white shirt and a waistcoat under his jacket. His hair had been cut into a neat trim just below his ears.

As they reviewed last week's words, Luellen's admiration for his efforts grew. She opened the reader to "The Pancake," smiling approval as he made his way through the story. They both chuckled at the ending.

"I've heard that one before," Daniel said. "Only it was a 'gator and a duck." He grinned. "Got to be careful who you trust."

"That's true." She turned to the next story and printed the practice words on the slate. Together they worked through pronunciation. By the time he left, Luellen felt drained but satisfied. Daniel was making progress—she'd been right to insist that they not interrupt the lessons. But why did he wait until now to decide to learn to read?

She climbed the stairs to her room to slip into her nightgown, pulling herself along by using the handrail. Each step was an effort. She'd rest, as Papa ordered, but wouldn't tell him how tired she was. As long as she had no further symptoms, nothing would stop her from returning to school.

Luellen folded her quilt over the top of clothing and books in her trunk. Tomorrow morning she'd add her night things and be ready to leave. Three weeks had passed and all seemed normal with her baby. New dresses hid her changing figure. Swallowing a flutter of tension, she dared to hope that she'd be able to complete the term.

Papa tapped on the door frame. "Daniel stopped by to see you. He's downstairs in the sitting room."

"We finished with our lessons on Saturday."

"He said he has something for you."

"Oh, Papa, I pray he hasn't come courting."

He smiled at her. "Instead of jumping to conclusions, why don't you go see what he wants?"

She followed him down the stairs. Daniel turned from his spot in front of the fire, his face breaking into a grin when he saw her. "Miss Luellen. I couldn't let you leave without thanking you again for helping me." He dug in his pocket and handed her a gold coin.

"Five dollars! You already paid me for tutoring. I can't accept this."

He closed her fingers around the gold piece. "I want you should have it. Because of you I have big plans for my future. When you come back in the spring, I'll have a surprise for you."

"But—"

"I got to get back to work. Good luck with school and all."

After he left, she peeked out the window and saw him drive away, his wagon loaded with wooden crates. What surprise did he have planned for her in the spring?

Shaking her head in wonder, Luellen looked down at the Liberty Head half eagle in her palm. Indeed, the Lord sent help in unexpected ways.

Steam poured from the pistons of the locomotive, hiding the wheels in a storm cloud of white. Papa helped Luellen from the carriage onto the train platform, his face set in resignation. "I hoped you'd change your mind at the last minute. I won't stop you, but you must know how worried I am about letting you go."

Luellen pressed her fingers against her lips. So much had changed since she first left for Allenwood. Was she doing the right thing? How many times could she stand up to her parents, knowing the pain she caused them? She drew a shuddering breath. "I'll be careful, I promise."

He held out his arms and she burrowed into them, tears stinging her eyes. "Thank you for understanding. No one ever had a better father."

"Bo-oard!" the conductor called. "All aboard!"

Papa walked her to the steps of the passenger car. She turned and kissed his cheek, grateful that Mama had stayed home. Two heartrending good-byes at the station would have been too many.

The train jolted forward. Through the glass, Luellen saw Papa watching. Were those tears on his cheeks?

# 16

When the locomotive rolled into the Allenwood station, Luellen peered out the window at the crowd of people on the platform, wondering if Belle might be among them.

She pressed her hand against her abdomen, concealed beneath layers of fabric. By dressing carefully, she felt sure she could keep her condition a secret. Her mind balked when she tried to think beyond her child's birth. Next year would take care of itself. For now she'd concentrate on her studies and passing the final examination.

"This your stop, miss?" the conductor asked.

"Yes. Thank you." She winced when a cramp angled across her back.

"You all right?"

She rubbed at the pain. "I'm fine. Just been sitting for too long." She prayed that was the case.

As she descended the steps, she glanced around. Snow-laden clouds crowded the sky, submerging Allenwood in gloom. She thought of the months since she first arrived, and all that had happened. Everything had been new and unfamiliar. Now she felt like an experienced traveler. Luellen tucked gloved hands inside her cloak for warmth while she waited for her trunk.

An omnibus driver tipped his cap as he approached. "Where are you headed, miss?"

"The Normal School." She pointed at the baggage cart. "Could you please fetch my trunk for me?"

"Right away."

When she climbed into the omnibus, she glanced at the empty rear seat where Belle had been sitting when they first met. *Lord, give me the courage to be honest with her.* The thought of living next door to each other for the next three months with a barrier between them was too much to bear. She'd swallow her pride and apologize as soon as she saw her friend.

As the conveyance traveled along College Avenue, Luellen noticed Mrs. Hawks bundled in a shawl, sweeping snow from the front porch of her boardinghouse. Inside, a lamp glowed in the front window. The hours she'd spent with the landlady were pleasant memories. As soon as she was settled in the Ladies Hall, she'd pay a visit. Maybe Belle would join her.

Luellen followed Matron Bledsoe to the foot of the stairs. "Your trunk's been delivered to your room," Mrs. Bledsoe said. "Everything's clean and ready. I checked it myself."

Luellen doubted it, considering Matron's aversion to climbing steps, but she thanked her nonetheless.

"Your friend Miss Brownlee returned yesterday. She's out right now, but I'm sure she'll be happy to see you again."

"I've missed her."

Mrs. Bledsoe gathered Luellen's hands in hers. "I've missed both of you." She stepped back. "You've gotten a bit heavier over the winter. It suits you. Lean-fleshed girls are so unappealing, don't you think?"

Suppressing a smile, Luellen gazed at the stout woman. "I've never thought about it before, but you may be right." Excusing herself, she mounted the stairs, wishing she could share the exchange with Belle.

Once in her room she hung her dresses in the wardrobe and spread the quilt over the bed. She'd finish unpacking later. Right now she wanted to meet with Dr. Alexander and register for the term.

Luellen's boots crunched on the gravel path as she strode toward Allenwood Hall. She kept a tight grip on her reticule. Through the satin lining, the gold coins felt smooth beneath her fingers. She hurried down the hallway to Dr. Alexander's office.

Mr. Price stood, his face alight. "Miss McGarvie. Welcome back. I trust your holiday was a pleasant respite." His wispy moustache had filled in somewhat, and joined a new fringe of whiskers surrounding his chin.

"Yes. I enjoyed spending time with my family." She turned toward the registrar's door. "Is Dr. Alexander in?"

"He is. I'll announce you." Mr. Price smoothed his jacket and preceded her through the anteroom. He rapped on the door. "Miss McGarvie is here to see you, sir."

"Tell her to come in."

When Luellen entered his office, he came around the desk and pulled out a chair for her. "So glad to see you back. You're looking well rested—blooming in fact, if I may say so."

"Thank you." A flush traveled over her face. Blooming was the right word. "I want to register for this term." She patted her reticule. "I assume the cost is the same as last fall's."

"It is." He turned a page in the ledger.

Opening the drawstring on her bag, she removed the gold pieces and placed them in front of him, her fingers trembling.

The money on his desk represented the majority of her savings. She'd have to watch every cent to get through to the end of the term. She squeezed her hands together in her lap and watched while he entered the amount on a half-filled page of numbers.

Dr. Alexander leaned back in his chair. "Model School resumes next week. With your permission, we'll schedule you for Mondays, Wednesdays, and Fridays. Mrs. Guthrie is most eager to work with you again."

"And I with her." Luellen smiled at the prospect of renewing her acquaintance with the children as well. She loved seeing the expressions on their faces when they learned and understood something new. "Thank you, Doctor."

"You're most welcome. Feel free to call on me with any problems you may encounter this term."

Luellen stepped outside as the bell announcing supper tolled, its resonant tone echoing across the shadowed campus. She was near enough to the steeple to feel the vibration in her bones. She picked up her pace. Even the prospect of an unappetizing meal excited her—it was good to be back.

A familiar voice greeted her when she entered Ladies Hall. "Luellen?" She whirled to see Belle smiling tentatively in her direction. "When did you arrive?"

Now's the time to make things right, Luellen told herself, but the words froze in her throat. What if she couldn't trust Belle to keep her secret?

"I got here this afternoon." She kept her voice polite but not overwarm. "I just returned from registering for the term."

Belle's eyes searched her face, the welcoming smile on her lips fading. "I did that yesterday." Her tone matched Luellen's. "Would you like to sit with me at supper?"

"I'd be happy to." A splinter broke away from the wall Luellen had built around herself. She'd risk the friendship for as long as it lasted—but she wouldn't share the truth about her situation.

Once seated, with a bowl of salted beef and potatoes in front of her, Luellen glanced around the dining hall. "There are fewer girls here than there were last fall."

"I expect our difficult economic times have forced some of them to miss this term." Belle cut her stringy meat into bite-sized pieces. "My father is very dour about the prospects for the coming year." A smile lifted her lips. "At least I was able to come back—and so were you. We still have our same rooms."

"I wondered about that." Taking a deep breath, she plunged ahead. "I was afraid you wouldn't want to room next to me after I treated you so unkindly."

Belle's face softened. "I know you were worried about your mother. We all say things we don't mean when we're upset."

Shamed, Luellen looked down at her food. Leave it to Belle to forgive before she was asked. She raised her eyes. "That's no excuse for rudeness. Are we still friends?"

"We've never stopped being friends as far as I'm concerned. My visit to your family was a joy. I'm so glad I got to meet your brother. He reminds me so much of you. Smart, amusing, cheerful. His homecoming must have been a special surprise."

"It was."

"He sent me a letter just before I left Springfield. He and the lieutenant had an uneventful journey to Missouri." Belle blushed. "He said he'd like to see me again."

Luellen choked down a lump of beef. Was Franklin the reason Belle was so eager to continue their friendship?

On Monday morning, Luellen slipped her petticoats over her head and tied them above her abdomen. The baby turned and kicked while she stepped into her wool challis dress. Cupping her hands around the movement, Luellen paused, relishing the sensation. "Good morning, my baby," she whispered.

When she pushed her arms into the matching traveling sacque, she noted with satisfaction that it covered her from neckline to below her hips. Today would be a test. She couldn't wear her cloak while teaching in the Model School. Would Mrs. Guthrie notice the difference in her appearance? Nerves twitching, she stepped into the corridor.

Belle joined her on the way to breakfast. "You're wearing your new outfit. I remember when we selected the fabric." She stepped back and surveyed Luellen. "That color is lovely on you. The braid trim around the jacket is especially attractive."

Relieved, Luellen nodded her thanks. "Mama and I spent many days sewing after Christmas." She didn't mention that most of the garments had been for her baby's layette.

"I'd love to have a new dress." Belle smoothed the pleats on her plaid wool skirt. "But my father told us we'd have to make do until times get better."

Luellen thought of her friend's extensive wardrobe. Making do wouldn't be much of a hardship. Her own challenge would be keeping her two dresses fresh-looking for the next two and a half months.

After breakfast, Luellen threw on her cloak and stepped into the cold, windy morning. Across Chestnut Street students filed into the Model School. She hurried along the path, crossing the road and climbing the steps of the school building.

As she reached for the door handle, a series of cramps jabbed her side. She bent forward, hands resting on her middle. Papa had explained that cramping meant her body was changing to accommodate the baby, but each time they occurred she felt a fresh pang of alarm. She waited several moments for the squeezing sensation to pass before stepping into the schoolroom.

Warmth and the faint odor of burning coal greeted her. Ice crystals etched the windows with feathery swirls, bathing the room in white light. Mrs. Guthrie glanced up from her desk. "Look who's here, children. Miss McGarvie will be teaching you this morning."

Luellen sought the faces of the children she remembered from the previous term. Joshua, Elizabeth, Cassie, and nearly a dozen others sent her welcoming smiles.

She unfastened her cloak and draped it over a peg in the entry. With her back to the room, Luellen adjusted the folds of the traveling sacque so that it hung smoothly over her dress.

When she turned, Mrs. Guthrie stood watching her, a quizzical expression on her face. She opened her mouth as if to say something, but closed it and handed Luellen a book. "We're doing sums this morning. Did you bring your lesson plan?"

"No." She gulped. What a terrible beginning to the term. "I was preoccupied with . . . I just forgot. I'm so sorry." She reached for her cloak. "I'll go get it right now."

Mrs. Guthrie laid a hand on her arm. "No need. You can show it to me on Wednesday. Meantime, mine's on the desk. You may refer to that."

Luellen felt her face flame as she took her position in front of the room. She shouldn't allow personal distractions to affect her work. She opened the arithmetic book to the marked page and copied a series of addition facts on the blackboard, grateful for the time to gather her thoughts.

Lifting the pointer from the instructor's desk, she tapped the first problem. "Who can tell me the answer to this one?"

To her surprise, normally eager Joshua sat still while several other children waved their hands in the air.

"I know, Teacher." Cassie leaned forward.

Luellen darted a glance at Mrs. Guthrie. She sat near the rear of the classroom, writing in a notebook. She didn't appear to be paying attention.

"All right, Cassie. Please recite the answer."

"Three plus four equals seven."

"Correct." She wrote the number after the equal sign and moved the pointer to another set. More hands shot in the air, but Joshua's wasn't among them. Luellen noticed him counting on his fingers. She frowned. By now, he should have these sums memorized.

She called on another child, received the correct answer, and continued along the row until all the answers were written on the board.

"Take your slates and copy these sums for practice." She checked the lesson plan. "We'll have reading next."

While the children were busy scratching numbers on their slates, Luellen walked back to Mrs. Guthrie. "Should I spend extra time with Joshua?" she whispered. "He's not keeping up with the others in arithmetic."

"Let's wait and see. If he doesn't improve in a week or so, perhaps you could find room in your schedule to work with him after the other children leave in the afternoon." Sounds of murmurs and muffled giggles rose from the front row. Mrs. Guthrie nodded toward the mischief makers. "For now you'd best regain control of the class."

Luellen returned to the front of the room, folded her arms, and waited for quiet. To her dismay, one of the boys paid no attention to her and continued whispering to the child next to him. Luellen looked up and caught Mrs. Guthrie watching.

Taking a deep breath, she strode to the boy and picked up his slate. Instead of numbers, he'd drawn a picture of an animal with what looked like a tree growing out of its head. She cleared her throat. "This doesn't look like your arithmetic lesson, Jackie."

"It's a deer, Teacher," the boy next to him said. "He's showing me how to draw."

Luellen remembered her own school days. The schoolmaster would have pulled Jackie from his seat by his ear and whipped him in front of the class. What discipline did Mrs. Guthrie expect? They hadn't discussed corporal punishment.

She tucked her hand under Jackie's arm and lifted him from the seat.

"What're you going to do?" His voice sounded fearful.

The classroom was quiet, each child watching to see what would happen. Mrs. Guthrie had her head tilted to one side, hands folded in her lap.

"Come with me." Luellen marched him to a desk with only one child sitting in it—a girl. "You'll spend the rest of the morning right here."

Jackie slumped into the seat, looking mortified.

She walked to the board and wiped it clean. "Open your books to page seventy." Her voice wavered. "Who can read the first sentence for me?"

While she listened to the children take turns reading, part of her mind remained on Jackie. How should she have disciplined him? What would Mrs. Guthrie say?

When the morning's lessons were finished, Luellen gave the children permission to get out their dinner pails and then hurried to escape, her confidence shaken.

The classroom instructor joined her at the door. "Would it be convenient to meet with me after your classes? Say around five?"

# 17

Luellen opened the door of the Model School. Lighted lamps hung from the ceiling, illuminating rows of empty desks in the chilly room. Mrs. Guthrie leaned the broom she'd been using against a wall.

"Please come in. We'll sit over here." She led the way to two chairs in front of the stove. "I let the fire burn down after the children leave to conserve coal."

Luellen settled into one of the chairs, loosened her cloak, and laid her portfolio over her knees. "I brought my lesson plan if you want to see it."

Mrs. Guthrie's blue eyes twinkled. "No need. You did well following the plan I prepared. That's a good quality if you're called to substitute for a teacher who's ill."

"Then you asked me here because of Jackie." She clamped her hands together, nails digging into her palms. Would she be denied a teaching certificate because she refused to whip a child?

"I did." She rested her hand over Luellen's. "Corporal punishment is favored in many schools. You'll hear more discussion on the subject in your classes next year. However, I feel it's rarely necessary. The way you handled the incident with Jackie this morning is exactly what I'd have done."

Relief swept over Luellen. "I'm not being written up?"

"Not at all. I want to commend you. Children learn better in an atmosphere of trust rather than fear."

"I worried all afternoon."

"I'm sorry. I should have said more before you left." Mrs. Guthrie leaned forward. "I know how hard you studied to be able to return for this term. Finishing the full two-year course was a struggle for me too." For the briefest moment, her gaze dropped to Luellen's middle. "Please don't hesitate to come to me if you need to talk . . . about anything."

"Thank you." She could hardly breathe. Was Mrs. Guthrie being kind, or did she suspect? Luellen stood, wanting nothing more than to be alone in her room to think.

The instructor rose and patted Luellen's shoulder. Her voice changed from intimate to brisk. "See you Wednesday."

Once outside, Luellen waited at the curb while a carriage passed by, lanterns glowing beside the driver's box. She'd need to be careful crossing the street in the dark. On the campus, lamps mounted on poles cast yellow circles over the gravel paths between buildings.

The carriage rattled down Chestnut Street, but Luellen remained at the curb. She fought the impulse to run back into the school building and share her dilemma with Mrs. Guthrie. What a relief it would be to have someone to confide in. She shook her head. Too risky.

Squaring her shoulders, she stepped across the street. Once on campus she was startled to see Mr. Price appear out of the gloom. His pale face shone in the lamplight. "Miss McGarvie? It's rather late for you to be out unescorted. May I see you to your residence?"

Pools of darkness spread between each light. Since the Ladies Hall lay on the far side of campus, she'd be foolish to refuse his offer. "Thank you. It is terribly dark tonight."

"And icy." He clasped his gloved hand under her elbow.

She moved to her left, opening a space between them. "Do you always work this late?" she asked as they walked toward her building.

"I was going to ask you the same thing. The students at the Model School were dismissed two hours ago. Is Mrs. Guthrie a harsh taskmaster?"

"No—far from it."

"I remember when she was a student here. Most unusual. She obtained special permission to attend. As a widow, she could be considered a single woman and still be allowed to teach."

Luellen disliked his gossipy tone. "She told me."

"Did she tell you she had a child shortly after she graduated?" His voice squeaked with incredulity. "She certainly wouldn't have been permitted to attend had anyone known that little tidbit."

"Aren't you supposed to keep students' information confidential?" She stopped under a streetlamp. The Ladies Hall was a few steps away.

He turned to her, an ingratiating smile on his lips. "While they're students, yes. For instance, I've said nothing about your conversation with that big redhead on the steps of my building last fall."

Fear prickled along her arms. "Oh, that? It was nothing. A misunderstanding." She kept her voice casual.

"It didn't sound that way." He moved closer, his greatcoat billowing in a sudden gust of wind. "If you ever have any problems—and you don't want to trouble Dr. Alexander—I hope you won't hesitate to come to me."

Luellen sat on the edge of her bed, quilt wrapped around her shoulders. How much had Mr. Price heard? What would happen if he spoke to Dr. Alexander?

She paced. On the other hand, maybe he was bluffing just to make himself seem important. Flopping back on the bed, she covered her face with her hands. *Lord, show me what to do.*

If only she had someone to talk to. She couldn't ask her parents, they'd advise her to come home. Best not to worry them.

Ward Calder's compassionate face came to mind—he'd invited her to write to him. In the weeks it would take to receive a reply, she hoped her problems would resolve themselves. In the meantime, maybe if she put her worries on paper, she would find her answers while she wrote.

She rose and lit the lamp. Uncorking an ink bottle, she took up her pen.

> *Dear Ward,*
>
> *I have no one here in whom to confide. Today has been most distressing as regards two matters, and I pray you will indulge my ramblings. I cannot share my concerns with my family. As you are no doubt aware, they are most unhappy with me for choosing to return to school.*
>
> *To reassure you, I'm quite well physically—but my emotions are in turmoil. To begin with . . .*

Her pen scratched over the paper as she poured out her fear that Mrs. Guthrie knew she was expecting a child.

> *She said I could talk with her about anything, but I'm afraid whatever I say would go on my record.*
>
> *Then coming back to the campus tonight, I encountered the registrar's assistant. He offered to escort me to the Ladies Hall, and on the way . . .*

Luellen told Ward about Brendan's visit to the campus in late October, and Mr. Price's surprise intrusion on their argument. Paper rustled as she set the completed pages to one side. She concluded with Price's implication that he'd heard her mention the divorce. Could she be dismissed from school for falsely claiming to be a single woman when she registered? How should she respond, if at all?

> *I know nothing will happen overnight, but the simple act of writing to you has relieved my mind. Thank you for considering my difficulties. Any suggestions you may offer will be gratefully received.*
>
> *Please convey to Franklin that I am well, and will write soon.*
>
> *Yours sincerely,*
> *Luellen McGarvie*

She blotted the ink on the final sheet and folded the letter into an envelope. If she posted it in the morning, he might receive it within the next week or two. Until he replied, she'd go about her days as though nothing had happened. If Mr. Price spoke to Dr. Alexander—well, she'd cross that bridge when the time came.

Ward's hand fastened on the letter in his mail slot. He seldom received correspondence, and when he did it usually came from the manager of his father's estate. This one, however, was addressed in unfamiliar handwriting, with "Allenwood, Illinois" written in the left-hand corner of the envelope. He smiled. True to her promise, Luellen had written him.

Once in his room, he flopped in a chair under the window and ripped open the envelope. Several sheets covered with flowing Spencerian script greeted him. He skimmed through the pages, then went back, reflecting on what she'd said. Pleased as he was that she'd trusted him with her concerns, he also felt the responsibility of being her confidant. Two weeks had passed since she posted her news. By now, anything could have happened.

For the first time, he wished he were out of the Army and able to travel at will. He'd go straight to Allenwood. He dropped the letter in his lap, shocked at the thought. Wish himself out of the Army? He'd invested too much in his career.

"Come on, Calder, you're forgetting yourself," he said aloud. "All you can do is write back with encouragement. Get on with it."

He dragged his chair to the desk and opened a drawer, then stopped in midmotion. Someone had been rummaging through his papers. He remembered leaving his military tactics manual squared on top of the maps he'd drawn of proposed railroad routes. Now the book was shoved to one side. The map on top had smudges around the edges, as though it had been clutched in grimy fingers. Two sheets, showing proposed routes through St. Joseph, were missing. Warning Lieutenant Campion had served no purpose.

Ward stalked down the hall and banged into Campion's room.

The lieutenant leaped to his feet, face the color of paste, and shoved a cluster of papers into a drawer. His eyes darted between the desktop and Ward. "Thought you were the proper officer—never enter without knocking."

Ward shouldered past him. "What've you got in there?" He jerked the drawer open and flipped the pages. He held up his two missing maps. "This is my work." He shuffled through the rest of the papers. "You're writing a report based on stolen information."

"I can explain."

"I doubt it."

Ward stalked out and slammed the door so hard it bounced open. He grabbed the handle and slammed the door again.

His boot heels thudded on the stone floor as he strode to Captain Block's office. The post commander looked up when he entered. "What is it, Lieutenant?" He shoved a pile of forms to one side, a harassed expression on his face.

Ward stood at attention. "I've brought my report regarding a rail line from Independence to St. Joseph, sir."

"Why are you in such an all-fired hurry?" Captain Block slammed his hand on the desktop. "Biddle and Grisson don't expect to hear from us until April. In case you missed it, today's March eighth." His jaw set in an angry line. "Come back in a few weeks. Right now I've got to finish this confounded budget requisition."

"Sir, I can't wait. Something has come up with a fellow officer that threatens my work."

Sighing, the captain ran his fingers through his bristling gray hair. "That's a serious charge. At ease, Lieutenant. If it were anyone else coming in here with accusations, I'd be inclined to ignore them, but you've never given me reason to doubt your word."

"Thank you, sir." Ward opened his portfolio and laid the maps in front of the captain. "You can read the full report when you have more time. The gist of my recommendation is that the new rail line be routed through the communities between St. Joseph and Independence, rather than across open prairie."

The captain blinked. "I don't see the urgency here." His gaze strayed to the requisition forms.

Ward's heart hammered. Once he reported Lieutenant Campion,

he couldn't retract the words. One or the other of them would be disciplined, depending on the outcome. He took a deep breath and straightened his shoulders. "Lieutenant Mark Campion has been copying my work for his own ends. He threatened me with blackmail last fall."

"Blackmail! Why didn't you report him at the time?" Captain Block studied him through narrowed eyes. "You're not paying, are you?"

"No. I refused, believing that would be the end of it. But he's planning to submit a report of his own regarding this rail line, accusing me of using false information." Ward pointed out smudges around the maps. "Lieutenant Campion entered my quarters and took these maps. I discovered them in his room."

The captain leaned back in his chair, arms crossed over his chest. "Any witnesses?"

Ward felt his courage drain away. "No, sir."

Turning toward the window, the captain stared out onto the empty parade ground. A long silence stretched between them. Finally he swiveled around and met Ward's eyes. "I need to think about this. Leave your report. We'll talk again."

"Yes, sir." He saluted and left the room. Instead of returning directly to officers' quarters, he walked past the ordnance depot and out the east gate to stand on a bluff overlooking the Mississippi River. He'd taken an irrevocable step. After a moment he thought of Luellen's letter. She'd said she had no one in whom to confide. Neither did he. Franklin was a close friend, but as a civilian he'd never understand Ward's dilemma.

The next afternoon the door to Ward's room banged open. An enlisted man in sergeant's garb stood in the doorway. Surprised at the intrusion, Ward turned from the letter he was writing to Luellen.

"It's customary to knock, Sergeant, before entering a superior officer's quarters."

"My apologies, sir." He stood at rigid attention, his youthful face flushed. "Sergeant Grover, Second Cavalry, at your service. Lieutenant Campion has challenged you to a duel. He's appointed me his second."

"Is he mad?" Ward pushed his chair back and eyed the gangly soldier. "Dueling is forbidden, he knows that."

"Sir. You have damaged his reputation, and he seeks satisfaction."

"The lieutenant damaged his own reputation by his actions. Tell him I refuse."

"He instructed me not to accept a refusal, sir. Name your second and your conditions."

Ward rested his forehead on his palm. "Very well. My second will call on you tomorrow."

Once Sergeant Grover left, Ward sagged in his chair. Perhaps he could reason with Campion. He picked up his pen and scribbled a hasty conclusion to his message to Luellen.

He'd post it on the way to Campion's room.

Standing outside the man's door, Ward clenched and unclenched his right hand several times before knocking. "Campion?"

"Talk to Sergeant Grover. I have nothing to say to you."

Ward opened the door and stood on the threshold. "You have to cancel this absurd duel. We could both be dismissed from the Army if Captain Block hears about it."

Campion's eyes narrowed to slits in his pudgy face. "Are you going to run and tell him? You're good at that."

"You left me no choice. A duel with me won't change anything now."

"It's your word against mine. If you're not here to testify, no one will be able to prove a thing. I'll say you challenged me."

Ward clenched his teeth so hard his jaw hurt. "I'm giving you the opportunity to withdraw. No one will find out."

"You've blackened my name. Campions are proud people. We don't back off from a fight." He rose and pushed Ward into the hallway, banging the door behind him.

Ward stomped down the stairs and out into the chill Missouri dusk, praying he'd find Franklin in his quarters. He covered the distance to the enlisted men's barracks in double time, clattering in the front door as the men were filing into the mess hall for supper. When he spotted Franklin, he mouthed, "I need to talk to you."

As soon as Franklin joined him, Ward rested a hand on his shoulder and guided him outside. "I'm in serious trouble. Lieutenant Campion challenged me to a duel, and he won't back down."

Franklin stared at him, mouth agape. "That weaselly little petunia. He could get you both thrown out of the Army." He cocked his head. "What brought that on?"

"I had to tell Captain Block about Campion stealing my reports. Campion thinks the only way out is to eliminate me—that way no one can testify against him."

"I can. You've told me all along what he's been up to."

"That's hearsay. Won't stand up."

"What do you want me to do?" Franklin pushed the sleeves of his shirt up his forearms. "I can make him forget the whole thing."

Ward shook his head. "I want you to act as my second."

"You're going through with it?" Franklin took a backward step. "You're as cracked as he is."

"I can't back down from a challenge. Campion's a coward, through and through. I saw him get close to fistfights when we were at the Academy, but he always turned tail. You watch. He'll fire into the air. That way his honor will be satisfied—in his own mind, anyway."

"But if Captain Block learns about this—"

"Who's going to tell him?"

Early Saturday, when all colors were shades of gray, Ward followed Franklin through the north gate toward a clearing behind the post. Frost crunched underfoot as they made their way through the half-light to the designated meeting place.

"You ready?" Franklin asked.

Ward rested his hand on the butt of his Colt revolver. "Ready as I'll ever be." His palms were clammy.

Two shapes emerged in the distance. "That you, Calder?" Sergeant Grover's reedy voice piped.

"We're here," Franklin said. He put a hand on Ward's chest. "Wait." He strode over the uneven ground until he reached the sergeant. "Ten paces, then turn and fire. Agreed?"

Lieutenant Campion spoke from several feet behind them. "Agreed. Let's get on with it."

Franklin motioned Ward to come forward. Campion's face looked bone white, but his jaw jutted forward in a grim line. "I'm looking forward to this," he said in an undertone when Ward reached him.

The muscles in Ward's arms twitched. Jesus's words came to his mind. *Father, forgive them for they know not what they do.*

". . . eight, nine, ten," Franklin and Sergeant Glover chanted in unison. "Turn and fire."

As he'd planned, Ward aimed at a clump of brush to the right of his opponent and squeezed the trigger.

A white-hot blaze of pain spun him sideways. He dropped to the ground.

# 18

Luellen heard Belle's familiar tap at the door and closed her algebra textbook, thankful for the interruption. Since they'd returned to school, Belle no longer stepped inside without being invited. On the surface, Luellen behaved toward her friend as she always had, but her reluctance to trust the friendship enough to confide in Belle dug an ever-widening gulf between them. She longed to fling open the door, draw Belle into the room, and pour out her heart.

Instead, she draped a shawl over her green worsted dress and answered the knock. "Come in. If I spend another minute with this algebra assignment, I'll go totally mad. Rational and irrational numbers? What good is any of it?"

Belle shook her head. "I can't imagine. The only good I see is that once we pass the course, we're one step closer to a teaching certificate."

"That's all that keeps me going some days."

"A letter came for you." Belle held out an envelope. "It's from Lieutenant Calder." She looked hopeful. "Maybe he has news about your brother. I haven't heard from Franklin since before school started."

Luellen would have felt satisfaction that Franklin hadn't written Belle but for the fact he hadn't written her either. She took the letter and slit open the envelope, eager to see Ward's response to her plea for advice.

Belle stood waiting. "What does he say?"

She skimmed the lines, her lips turning up as she read. He wrote like he talked—each word chosen with careful deliberation.

> *In my opinion, you are safe trusting Mrs. Guthrie. It's unlikely she's trying to trap you by offering a listening ear. Please let me know what you've decided, and the outcome.*
>
> *On the other hand, I wonder why Mr. Price is showing such an interest. I believe he has too much to lose by reporting your divorce to the registrar. You might be called to account for the earlier deception, but he would likely be dismissed if it came to light he obtained his information by eavesdropping. From what you've told me, Dr. Alexander doesn't suffer fools gladly. I suggest you keep your distance.*

Ward went on to describe the post in winter and how it compared to his memories of Pennsylvania. He stopped abruptly midway through a paragraph about an ice gorge on the Mississippi that sunk a steamboat.

When she read the next line, she lowered the letter and stared at Belle.

"What?" Belle touched Luellen's shoulder. "You look like you're going to faint."

"He was challenged to a duel."

Belle's eyes widened. "And?"

"Ward planned to calm him down. He believes the man is all bluster." Luellen's voice trembled. "He scribbled those lines at the end of the letter." She checked the written date. "He posted this two weeks ago." She walked to the window and stared out as though she could see across the distance between Allenwood and Jefferson Barracks. "Surely we'd have heard if anything serious—"

"Oh, absolutely. Franklin would have telegraphed."

Luellen's stomach churned. How could she pray for a good outcome for something that had already happened?

Belle reached to hug her, but Luellen sidestepped and took her hand instead. "I feel so helpless."

"Let's both write letters demanding news."

"It'll still be weeks before we hear."

Belle squeezed her hand. "In the meantime, we'll pray. The Lord already knows."

After her last class, Luellen hurried back to the Ladies Hall, planning to post a letter to Ward that evening. When she entered the building, Matron Bledsoe met her in the vestibule. "Mr. Price is waiting to see you in the parlor."

Mr. Price again. Had Franklin telegraphed the school? Hopeful, she looked at the matron. "Did he say why?"

Mrs. Bledsoe splayed her fingers over her chest. "I'm sure I have no idea. You know I don't pry."

"Of course not."

Mrs. Bledsoe missed the sarcasm. She patted Luellen's arm. "If you're ready, we'll join him."

Luellen had avoided Mr. Price since the evening he'd escorted her across the campus. Now he bobbed to his feet when the two women entered the room.

"Please sit, young man." The matron took her usual chair near the window.

Luellen continued to stand, her heart fluttering. A special visit from the registrar's assistant couldn't be good. "You have information for me? Have you been contacted by my family?"

Mr. Price's face reddened and he fumbled with papers clutched in his hand. "Nothing like that. The progress reports are in. I thought you'd be happy to know your grades are in the top 5 percent."

Luellen collapsed in a chair, deflated. "You came over here to tell me about my grades? Why? Won't they be posted?"

"Yes, certainly. Tomorrow." He fidgeted. "I just—"

Mrs. Bledsoe folded her arms over her bosom. "Young man, you're allowed to call on the ladies here with genuine messages from Dr. Alexander, not folderol about good news." She pierced him with a glance. "Perhaps you should return to work."

"Yes, ma'am." He rose, dropped the papers, then scooped them up and dashed from the room.

Luellen looked at the matron, for once appreciating her interfering presence. "Thank you. I can't imagine why he felt the need to deliver my grades in person."

"Nor can I. I'll have a word with Dr. Alexander. He needs to find more for that boy to do."

On Monday morning, Belle stopped by Luellen's room. "Did you write to Lieutenant Calder and Franklin?"

"I posted both letters last night." The chapel bell tolled seven. Breakfast time. Luellen adjusted the sacque over her dress and lifted her portfolio from the table.

As they descended the stairs, Belle said, "I have an idea. Let's go to the depot after you're finished at the Model School and send a telegraph to Franklin. We'll ask him to respond immediately."

Luellen's mind calculated the cost of an omnibus ride plus the fee for a telegram. Nearly a dollar. She gulped. It would be worth it if they didn't have to wait weeks for news.

Aloud, she said, "Mrs. Bledsoe would collapse if we both left the campus without a chaperone. She'd probably chain us to our beds."

Belle giggled. "I'm going to ask her permission. That way she can escort us if she wishes."

That afternoon, Luellen left the Model School with her mind more on Mrs. Guthrie than on the telegram Belle wanted to send. She wondered how much longer she could postpone confiding in her instructor. Today she'd noticed Mrs. Guthrie eyeing her closely as she moved about the room. Luellen chewed her lower lip. Soon. She'd tell her soon.

When she approached the Ladies Hall, she saw Mr. Price waiting out front, Belle at his side. She hurried toward them, bewildered. Why was he here? She thought Matron Bledsoe had driven him off for good.

Belle stepped forward. "Mr. Price is going to be our escort to the telegraph office. Mrs. Bledsoe arranged it with Dr. Alexander." She must have noticed Luellen's surprise, because she took her arm. "I'll go upstairs with you."

"Please excuse us," Luellen said to Mr. Price. "We'll be right back."

Once inside, she asked, "Why on earth did Matron pick him?" Their boot heels clacked on the stairs as they climbed to the second floor.

"She said he didn't have enough to do, so she'd find a way to keep him busy."

"I'd rather have Mrs. Bledsoe's company."

"You must be joking."

"No. Mr. Price has been—" She bit off the rest of the sentence.

To explain why she wanted to avoid the registrar's assistant, she'd have to disclose her marriage to Brendan, and that was too great a risk.

Luellen opened the door to her room and tossed her portfolio on the bed. After retrieving her reticule from a drawer, she turned to leave.

"Aren't you going to change out of that jacket? It's unseasonably warm today."

"I'm quite comfortable, thank you."

Belle drew back at Luellen's sharp tone, hurt in her eyes. "You don't have to snap my head off."

Luellen reached for her hand. "I'm sorry. I'm letting my worries get the best of me." She hoped Belle would assume she meant worry about Ward and Franklin.

Once at the telegraph office, Belle and Luellen debated what to write as they studied the blank form. "We can't come out and say 'duel,'" Luellen whispered, glancing behind her to be sure Mr. Price couldn't overhear. "Most states have laws against the practice."

Belle rolled a lock of her hair between her fingers. "How about, 'Concerned Ward's health Stop Please advise immediately Stop Luellen and Belle.'"

"You ladies going to stand there all afternoon? I'm going home in an hour." The operator snickered. "I'd hate to close up with you in here."

Luellen glared at him. His manners hadn't improved since the day she'd telegraphed her father. She glanced at Mr. Price, expecting him to come to their defense. Instead, he stared out the window, pretending he hadn't heard.

She nodded at Belle. "Go ahead and write the message. I think Franklin will understand our meaning."

Once they'd filled out the form, the telegrapher read it over, his lips moving. "That'll be sixty cents." He took their coins and dropped them into a box. "I'll send a messenger if there's a reply." Turning his back to them, he began tapping the key.

Mr. Price cleared his throat. "Perhaps we should return to school now. Dr. Alexander was very emphatic that we not delay." He opened the door and followed Belle and Luellen out.

Belle's eyes snapped with anger. Once they were out of earshot of the telegrapher, she said, "What a rude man."

"Indeed." Mr. Price turned to Luellen. "I hope you weren't overly upset by his manner."

She sent him her stoniest glare. "Rudeness doesn't bother me." Perspiration trickled inside her bodice. She wished they were back at the school so she could remove her jacket in the privacy of her room.

The next day passed with no reply from Franklin. That evening, Luellen sat brushing tangles out of her thick curls, the rhythmic strokes soothing her tumbling thoughts. She stretched out on her quilt. The baby rolled, poking her ribs with an elbow or a knee. She cupped her hands around her belly. Seven more weeks to the end of the school term. Doubts about her plan surfaced—it was becoming ever more challenging to hide her pregnancy, especially now that the weather had turned warm.

She woke to the sound of chimes. Her feet hit the floor before her eyes were fully open. Dashing through her toilette, Luellen dropped her worsted dress over her head and fastened the buttons on the bodice. If she hurried, she could get a quick bite of whatever lurked in the dining hall and still reach the Model School on time.

Belle waited at their accustomed table. "I was about to come up and see if you were ill."

"I had trouble falling asleep last night, worrying about Ward and Franklin."

"I'm worried too. Do you think we'd be called out of class if a telegram comes today?"

"I hope so. A telegram isn't an everyday thing." Luellen spooned a bite of boiled hash and shuddered. "Would you please pass the catsup?"

Belle handed her the sauce dish. "My class starts in a few minutes." She leaned forward, resting her hand on the table. "I'll look for you at dinner. By then, one of us should've heard."

Following Mrs. Guthrie's instructions, Luellen led the class through their arithmetic and reading lessons. When those were finished, she wrote spelling words on the blackboard.

Mrs. Guthrie joined her at the front of the room. Speaking in a low voice, she said, "While they practice their spelling, I'd like you to spend some individual time with Joshua. He's progressing on his sums, but he still lags behind the class. Could you take him through some drills in one of the empty desks at the back?"

"Of course." Joshua was one of her favorites. She loved his eagerness and his bright smile. Luellen walked to his desk. "Let's go in the back where it's quiet and practice your arithmetic."

He beamed at her and bounced to his feet. "Numbers make sense when you teach me." He threw his arms around her as far as they would go and hugged.

Luellen tensed. She'd allowed no one to get close since she returned in February.

Joshua jumped back, pointing at her abdomen. "You have a baby in there—just like my mama!"

# 19

Stunned, Luellen glanced between Joshua and Mrs. Guthrie. His innocent smile brought tears to her eyes. The idea that she was like his mama obviously thrilled him. He rested a small hand against her side. "Can I feel it move?"

Her fingers shook as she stroked his dark hair. "Yes."

The other children turned in their seats to look. To them babies were a routine fact of life, news greeted either with joy or dismay, depending on the family's circumstances. Their reactions didn't bother her—Mrs. Guthrie's did.

The instructor hastened to her side. "When we dismiss for dinner, I'd appreciate it if you would stay for a few minutes." Worry lines creased her forehead.

Luellen nodded. Summoning poise, she told Joshua to sit. Her heart thudded in her throat as she led him through addition facts. What would happen to her? Mr. Price's words about Mrs. Guthrie's earlier situation echoed in her ears. *She wouldn't have been permitted to attend if anyone had known.*

When the noon bell rang, she gathered her portfolio and stepped into the vestibule to wait for Mrs. Guthrie. The children's dinner pails clattered as they opened them and took out their food. Smells of onion, cheese, and cold mutton mingled with the odor of sulfur seeping from the coal-burning stove. Luellen turned her head, storing the classroom scene in her memory in case this was her last day at Allenwood. Sorrow washed over her, leaving her drenched in its wake. She had so many regrets, she didn't know which was the most profound. Her marriage to Brendan? Not leaving for school years ago, before she ever met him? Her failure to confide in Mrs. Guthrie? Luellen clasped her hands together and waited.

"I'm sorry for the delay. I wanted to be sure the class was well occupied before I left." Mrs. Guthrie took Luellen's elbow. "Let's step out onto the porch."

Once the door closed behind them, Luellen faced her. "You knew, didn't you?"

"I suspected." She shook her head. "I wish you'd come to me sooner—perhaps we could have avoided this moment. I would have kept your secret. But now that all the children know, they'll tell their parents, and it'll get back to Dr. Alexander in no time."

Luellen covered her lips with her fingers. "What will he do?"

"He'll ask you to leave. This is an institution founded on strong moral principles. He has no choice."

"I want you to know—" Luellen's breath caught in her throat. "I was married. Then he told me he already had a wife." She fought to keep tears back, but they defied her. Her words rolled out between sobs. "I didn't know I was with child until I'd been enrolled here for a couple of months. And now . . ."

Mrs. Guthrie opened her arms and Luellen leaned into her, grateful for the contact.

"Don't give up yet. I'll talk to Dr. Alexander." She stepped away, her eyes warm. "We'll see what he says."

Still in shock, Luellen returned to the Ladies Hall, barely noticing the wind that tugged at her shawl. Should she attend afternoon classes as though nothing had happened, or remain in her room and wait for Dr. Alexander's summons?

Dashing in the front door, she almost flattened Belle. "Oh! Excuse me."

"Surely our menu isn't so tempting that you're rushing to the table?"

"No, I—" Now would be the time to confide in her friend, but she couldn't force the words out. "Let me run up and put my things away, and I'll join you in a moment."

Belle caught her arm. "Did you hear from Franklin?"

She shook her head. Joshua's remark in the classroom had chased all other concerns from her mind. Now her worries about Ward returned with the force of a blow. "The longer the silence lasts, the more worried I become."

"Do you suppose no news is good news?" Belle tried to smile.

"I've never found it so." Luellen polished her glasses on the edge of her shawl. "We'll just have to wait. I don't know what else we can do." Fear whirled through her mind—the idea that Ward had been injured circled the thought that she'd be dismissed from Normal School before nightfall. "I'll see you in a moment. We'll walk to psychology class after we eat."

Luellen spent the next hours trying to keep her mind on the theory and practice of managing children. Every now and then she glanced over her shoulder, expecting to be summoned to the registrar's office. When the day passed with no incident, she felt almost lighthearted. Perhaps Mrs. Guthrie had persuaded Dr. Alexander to allow her to remain.

Holding to that thought, she arose the next morning and left for her classes. Perhaps no news *was* good news. But when she entered the Ladies Hall at midday, Mr. Price waited in the foyer.

Startled, she looked around for Mrs. Bledsoe. "Where's the matron? Does she know you're here?"

He smoothed a corner of his scraggy moustache. "I'm here at Dr. Alexander's request. He asked to see the matron, so she dashed off. But I have something for you." He reached inside his coat and removed a folded envelope.

Luellen had never received a telegram before, but she knew what it was. She reached for the missive.

Mr. Price took a step closer. "Not bad news, I hope?"

Anxious to get to her room, she withered him with a glance. "It's none of your concern, is it?"

"Whatever affects the students concerns me."

Luellen wondered how such a pompous young man had ever found a job with the school. Surely there were more qualified people in a town the size of Allenwood.

The door swung open and Belle stepped inside. Luellen held up the telegram so Belle could see it and nodded toward the staircase. "Thank you for bringing the message," she said to Mr. Price. "Please excuse us now."

Once upstairs, she stopped in the hallway and slit open the envelope, holding the contents so Belle could read them too. "*Ward wounded Stop Recovery hopeful Stop Letter follows Stop Franklin*"

"At least . . ." Luellen gulped. "At least he's not dead."

Belle studied Luellen's face and opened the door to her room. "You look like you're going to faint. Come in and sit for a moment."

Luellen settled into a chair, embarrassed by her reaction. "It's a relief to know he's alive. When we didn't hear right away, I expected the worst." She tried to sound detached. "Franklin said Ward's recovery is 'hopeful.' That means they're not sure."

"I know."

"So now we wait for Franklin's letter." She remembered how Ward had supported her through her difficulties since they'd first met. "The lieutenant's such a kind man. Why'd this have to happen?"

"You sound like you're growing attached to him." Belle cupped a hand behind her ear. "Do I hear wedding bells?"

"Marriage is the farthest thing from my mind. I'm here to become a teacher, not to find a husband. You know most schools won't hire married women."

"I know. But sometimes I think it would be nice to do both."

"Not for me." How could she trust her own judgment after the disastrous mistake she'd made with Brendan? She pushed herself to her feet. "I'd better get some studying done before dinner."

Once in her room, she dropped her jacket on the bed and raised the window, letting a cool breeze surround her. A pile of books waited on her desk. She opened the algebra text and stared at an equation, forehead resting on her hand. Images of Ward blocked the symbols on the page. *Father, I don't know how badly he's injured, but you do. Please heal him.* She forced her attention to algebraic formulas. Mastering them felt like trying to pound a worm down a hole.

"Miss McGarvie!" Matron Bledsoe's voice bellowed from the hallway. "Come out here right now."

Luellen covered herself with her jacket and flung open the door. "My word, Matron, what's wrong?"

"Don't act innocent with me." Red-faced, she stood on the threshold, her bosom heaving. "Passing yourself off as a maiden, and you're expecting a child! Well, not under my roof!"

Luellen fought for breath. She'd expected to be called to the registrar's office, not assaulted by Mrs. Bledsoe. "P-please come in. Let me explain."

"We can talk right here, thank you. I don't wish to sully myself with the likes of you."

Doors opened up and down the hall. Shocked faces peered at her, Belle's among them. Luellen stared into her friend's eyes, then turned her gaze to Mrs. Bledsoe, her temper rising. "My baby has nothing to do with my conduct here, and you know it."

"Nonsense. How do I know what you were up to all those times you left for town without a chaperone?"

Luellen reeled. "That was months ago."

"Exactly." Matron's jowls quivered. "I'll leave it to Dr. Alexander to decide whether you remain enrolled, but as for me, I want you out of Ladies Hall by tomorrow evening." She reached past Luellen and grabbed the door, slamming it with a frame-rattling crash.

Where could she go? Fingers pressed against her temples, Luellen stared at the floor as though she might find an answer carved in the wooden planks.

Voices buzzed in the hallway. Gradually she heard doors closing as the other women returned to their rooms, no doubt to continue speculating about her.

*Tap, tap, tap. Tap tap.* Would Belle add her recriminations to those of the matron? Luellen shook her head. She couldn't take any more abuse right now. If she ignored the sound, Belle would go away.

The door swung open. Her friend stood in the hallway, tears streaming over her face. She held out her arms. "I'm so sorry."

Luellen walked into the embrace, laying her cheek against the top of the shorter woman's head. Belle's characteristic rosewater fragrance filled her senses. "I didn't think you'd want to associate with me."

"Whatever has happened, I'll help you see it through." Belle stepped back, dabbing at her eyes. "All this time and you never told me. Why?"

Taking her hand, Luellen drew her into the room. "How could I tell you? What must you think of me?"

"What do you think of *me*, that you couldn't trust my friendship?"

"I was afraid. So much has happened since we met. You've been a bright spot in some terrible days—I didn't want to lose that."

Belle placed her hands on her hips, her round face flushed. "A friend loveth at all times—that means during the bad as well as the good. Now, tell me what I can do."

Luellen's reserve broke. Hands over her face, she fell into a chair, sobbing. "After the way I treated you in Beldon Grove, I don't deserve such friendship."

"Let's not worry over that now." Belle handed her a lace-trimmed handkerchief with a scrolled *B* embroidered in one corner. "First things first. When's the baby coming?"

"Probably late May." She clutched her friend's hand. "One thing you must know. I was married last August. After four weeks he came home and told me he already had a wife. My father arranged a divorce. In October I realized I was carrying my husband's child."

"Oh, my dear!" Sympathy played across Belle's face.

"I was determined to see out the year." Luellen ran her hand over the skirt of her golden brown dress. "Mama helped me make these clothes to hide my condition. It worked until yesterday, when one of the children in the Model School threw his arms around me and felt the baby." She closed her eyes at the memory. "Now . . ." Luellen spread her hands. "I don't know where I'll live, but I know this. I'm going to fight to finish this term."

Belle stood, jaw set. "Count on me to be right beside you."

The sound of the noon chime rolled in the open window.

Footsteps clattered on the stairs as occupants of the second floor headed for the dining hall.

Luellen rubbed her face. "Do you suppose Matron will refuse to feed me?"

"She said 'tomorrow evening.' Do you want me to bring you a meal?"

*Chin up and look them in the eye.* "No. I'll go down with you."

# 20

The murmur of conversation ceased when Luellen and Belle entered the dining hall. Some girls stared openly, while others averted their eyes. "Looks like there's a few empty tables," Belle whispered.

"I think anywhere we choose to sit we'll find the table empty," Luellen said. Holding her head high, she waited while one of the kitchen helpers scooped a pile of overcooked cabbage mixed with boiled beef onto her plate.

"Don't let Bledsoe worry you none," the woman said under her breath. "I been where you are. People like her love to make others feel like dirt."

Tears sprang to Luellen's eyes at the unexpected kindness. "Bless you. Thank you for the kind words."

"My room's behind the kitchen. You come find me if you get hungry in the night." She winked. "I know how that is."

Buoyed by the woman's support, Luellen sat and waited for Belle.

"See. Not everyone's against you," Belle said as she slid into a chair.

Mrs. Bledsoe appeared in the doorway, arms folded across her chest. She glared in Luellen's direction.

"Just most people," Luellen said.

Luellen slipped into her afternoon algebra class and took a seat near the door as the instructor called the roll. He read "McGarvie" and moved on to the next name without waiting for a response.

"I'm here." Luellen jutted her hand in the air.

Startled, he peered in her direction, then dropped his gaze and noted her reply. For the duration of the session, Luellen felt like an uninvited guest at a party. Her presence was tolerated, not welcomed.

When class ended, Luellen walked alone to the Ladies Hall. If she obeyed Mrs. Bledsoe's ultimatum, this would be her last night on campus. She didn't have the money to live in town, and didn't know a soul with a house to share. After an uncomfortable supper in the dining hall, she returned to her room to pack her belongings. With each item stowed, she breathed a prayer she'd find a place to go. She was folding a nightdress when someone knocked on her door.

A girl she'd seen in class, but didn't know well, stood in the hall. Her gaze skated past Luellen's body and came to rest on a point close to one ear. "Matron sent me to tell you that Dr. Alexander wants to see you in his office right after breakfast."

"Did she say anything about my Model School class tomorrow?"

The girl backed away from the doorway. "That's all Matron said. Dr. Alexander first thing in the morning."

Luellen dressed with care, pleased to note that her sacque still concealed her expanding waistline. When she entered the ante-room outside the registrar's office, Mr. Price eyed her, his face flushing. "I'll announce you."

"No need. Dr. Alexander is expecting me." She swept past his desk.

"Miss McGarvie." The registrar nodded when she entered, his face carved from granite. "Please have a chair." He watched while she seated herself opposite him.

"It seems you've been leading a secret life. According to Mrs. Guthrie, you are with child—the result of an unfortunate marriage." He shook his head. "To say I'm disappointed would be an understatement. You showed more promise than most of the students I see, and now to have you leave—"

"I have no intention of leaving. I paid for this term and I'm going to finish. Didn't Mrs. Guthrie tell you the circumstances of my marriage—and divorce?"

"She did. But Matron Bledsoe made it clear to me that she thinks you're a bad example to the other girls in the Ladies Hall, and now that you're . . . in this condition, she can't condone your presence."

"Have you no influence with her?"

"Kindly watch your tone. Mrs. Bledsoe has my full confidence in her management of the girls' living arrangements. Thus, if she says you're to go, I don't see how you expect to continue your studies."

"If I find lodging, do you have any objection to my completing the term?"

A half-smile cracked the granite. "Once you get your teeth in something, you don't let go, do you?"

"No sir, I don't." She kept her voice steady. "I plan to attend classes and participate at the Model School, with your permission."

Arms folded across his chest, he studied her for a moment, as if trying to decide if she were serious. "Granted." He growled the word.

Luellen stood and took a step closer to the desk. She kept her hands out of sight under her jacket to hide their trembling. "Since

I'm being forced to leave the Ladies Hall, I believe I'm entitled to a refund of the unused portion of my room and board. According to my calculations, the sum amounts to eighteen dollars and eighty-three cents. In specie, please."

The kitchen in the Ladies Hall bustled with post-breakfast activity when Luellen entered. Heat from the oversized range drove an odor of stale grease through the room. The woman who had befriended her the day before tossed her a quick wave and went back to stirring the contents of a steaming pot. Glancing around, Luellen spied the head cook disappearing into the pantry. She hurried after her.

"May I have a word with you, Mrs. Enlow?"

The tired-looking woman spun around, her eyes narrowing when she recognized Luellen.

Her white cap drooped over one ear. "Students aren't allowed in the kitchen—even girls who are no longer students, such as yourself."

"You are misinformed. I'm still a student at Allenwood, and will be until the term ends." She squared her shoulders. "I came to ask if I might be able to stay in one of the kitchen maids' rooms out back. I'd work for my keep."

Mrs. Enlow's face pinched. "Sorry." Nothing about her expression looked regretful. "Juliet Bledsoe has told me about you."

*Juliet?* Luellen fought down a snicker at the image of Mrs. Bledsoe as Shakespeare's youthful heroine. "What she didn't tell you is that I have several years' experience cooking in a hotel. I can be useful here."

"No. I don't need any help, and you need to be out of this building."

When Luellen turned to leave, the woman at the stove beckoned to her with a tilt of her head. Up close, her face showed age lines around her mouth and eyes. From under her apron, she produced a napkin-wrapped bundle. "I didn't see you at breakfast. Here's a couple biscuits. Remember, you get hungry, come and find me."

Luellen took the offering, her eyes prickling with unshed tears. Over her shoulder, she caught sight of Mrs. Enlow approaching. Tucking the food under her sacque, she whispered her thanks and hastened from the kitchen.

The bell for the first class of the day tolled over the campus while Luellen strode toward the Model School, chewing bites of biscuit while she walked. A few more hours and she'd be forced to leave Ladies Hall. Where could she go? Her thoughts skittered in a dozen directions, but each road ended at a locked gate. Her only hope was to throw herself on Dr. Alexander's mercy and beg him to intercede with Mrs. Bledsoe. Luellen shook her head. She'd rather swallow arsenic.

She closed the door of the Model School and hung her jacket near the door. Since Mrs. Guthrie knew of her condition, she no longer needed to hide under layers of wool.

The instructor smiled when Luellen reached her desk. "Dr. Alexander allowed you to stay?" She spoke in an undertone.

"He did. Mrs. Bledsoe didn't."

Mrs. Guthrie's concern-filled eyes met Luellen's. "Are you all right? You look flushed."

"I'm well. I'm just—I don't know what to do." Luellen shook her head. "I hope I'll be able to focus on the lessons today."

Behind her, a boy's voice called, "Teacher, I'm ready for my arithmetic."

"We'll talk later," Mrs. Guthrie mouthed. Aloud, she said, "Miss McGarvie will be there in a moment, Joshua. Please sit still."

The morning passed in a swirl of spelling words, sums, and story reading. When the noon bell rang, Luellen helped the children with their dinner pails, then joined Mrs. Guthrie in the rear of the classroom. She tried not to look hungry as the other woman lifted a thick sandwich from a square basket.

Without saying anything, Mrs. Guthrie handed half to Luellen. "So, tell me about Mrs. Bledsoe."

She gulped, swallowing a partly chewed bite. "She gave me until this evening to vacate the Hall. Dr. Alexander said I could continue classes until the end of the term, but he didn't overrule Matron's edict." Tears blurred her vision. Luellen placed her food on a chair between them. "I don't have any place to go—except home, and I just can't! Not after everything I've gone through."

Mrs. Guthrie sat silent for a moment. "Can you come back this evening? I may have a solution for you, but I have to check with someone first."

"I'll be here." She blotted her eyes. "I don't care where it is, as long as I can stay in Allenwood. Thank you, Mrs. Guthrie."

"Please call me Alma."

When Luellen arrived at the school that evening, Alma hurried down the steps and took her arm, leading her south on Chestnut Street. Upon reaching the corner, Alma turned right. "It's just down here a few blocks."

"I stayed on this street when I first got to Allenwood—at Mrs. Hawks's boardinghouse."

"That's where we're going. Mrs. Hawks is my mother."

Luellen stared at her through the gathering twilight. Alma's face wore a serene expression. "I can't afford to live in a boardinghouse. My money would be gone in no time."

"I talked to Mother this afternoon. She would be willing to provide a room if you could help in the kitchen. Didn't you mention you'd cooked in a hotel?"

Swallowing a lump in her throat, Luellen bowed her head in a silent prayer of thanks. "I don't know how to repay your kindness."

"There's no need."

Unable to believe her good fortune, Luellen asked, "Does your mother have room for both of us and her boarders?"

Alma chuckled. "I live with my grandparents. They watch my son during the day. I stayed with Mother until Frederick was born, but then I went to Grandma's. Mother couldn't look after him and take care of roomers too." She turned off the walkway. Lamplight from the parlor window reflected across the covered porch. "She's expecting us."

Luellen took a deep breath. The transition seemed too easy. She hoped Mrs. Hawks wasn't taking her in out of pity.

Once inside, Alma led the way to the kitchen, where they found her mother scrubbing dishes from the evening meal. The scent of fried ham tickled Luellen's nose. Her stomach gurgled, and she remembered she hadn't eaten since the half sandwich at noon.

Mrs. Hawks turned from her chore and embraced Alma with dripping hands. The resemblance between them was plain, although Mrs. Hawks was thinner than her daughter and her sandy hair had been overtaken by gray. She smiled at Luellen. "I'm so glad you'll be able to help me." She waved at a stack of pots waiting to be washed. "By the end of the day, it's all I can do to get through the dishes and prepare for breakfast."

"I'll do everything I can." Luellen stepped forward. "I can't tell you how grateful I am to have a place to stay."

"Nonsense. I'm the one who's grateful." She rubbed perspiration from her forehead. "Let me show you your room. It's not much, but the kitchen keeps it warm, and once you're done cleaning up, you can study on the table in here." Mrs. Hawks walked toward one of two doors. "That there's the cellar," she said, pointing. She opened the second door. "This will be yours."

Not much bigger than a pantry, the rectangular space held a neatly made single bed. A washstand stood against the opposite wall, flanked by a narrow wardrobe. The small four-paned window at the end of the room was framed by tabbed blue curtains hanging from a wooden rod. Luellen could see why her study area would be in the kitchen. "It's perfect. Thank you."

"Alma said you'll be moving in this evening. Have you got someone to fetch your things?"

Luellen closed her eyes. She hadn't considered that. The thought of facing Mrs. Bledsoe again was more than she could bear. She sank into a chair and pressed her fingertips against her temples.

Mrs. Hawks rested a hand on her shoulder. "The omnibus will be along in thirty minutes or so. Do you want me to have the driver stop at the school and bring your trunk on his way back to town?"

"Please."

Later, once her belongings had been delivered, Luellen excused herself and closed the door to her tiny room. She unfastened the clasps on the trunk and drew her quilt into her arms. The downward spiral of her status at Allenwood over the past three days left her stunned. Sinking onto the bed, quilt hugged against her, she stared at the wall. The ceiling creaked as lodgers moved about overhead.

She'd need to arise at least two hours earlier to allow time to help with breakfast chores and walk the half mile to school. Tonight she had studies to think about, but weariness weighted her in place.

Was Papa right? Should she have stayed in Beldon Grove?

Several weeks later, Luellen shivered on a bench outside the Lecture Hall. Yesterday had been so warm she'd chosen to wear her yellow calico with a shawl this morning, but now she regretted the decision. The pages of the textbook she held fluttered under her fingers in the crisp wind.

Mr. Price walked by, eyes fixed on something in the distance.

"Good afternoon," Luellen said. She knew he was ignoring her, but couldn't resist jabbing at him.

He feigned surprise. "Miss . . . er . . . good afternoon." He picked up his pace.

"Indeed it is," she said to his retreating back. If anything positive could be said about her treatment on campus since the news of her condition spread, it was that Mr. Price had stopped fawning over her.

Belle dashed up, waving an envelope. "There you are. I've been looking all over for you."

Luellen marked her place and closed the book. "Is that a letter? From Franklin?"

"It is. I snatched it from Mrs. Bledsoe's grip—she was ready to send it back." Belle thrust the envelope at Luellen.

Horrified, she read "No Longer A Resident. Return To Point Of Origin" scrawled over the address. "Oh my word. Maybe that's why we haven't heard anything for weeks. Do you suppose she returned his other letters?" She broke the seal on the envelope, drawing out the contents.

Belle frowned. "Then why would he have sent another one?"

Luellen shook her head. She'd notified her parents of her move without telling them why, and had assumed they'd pass the word to Franklin. Each day she'd checked the post. The more time that elapsed, the greater her fears that Ward's wounds were so severe he'd been sent home—or worse. She didn't know why the thought of not seeing him again bothered her. After all, he was simply her brother's friend.

She patted the bench. "Sit. Maybe if we huddle together we'll be warmer."

"The bell for afternoon sessions will ring soon. Hurry and tell me what Franklin says."

Luellen unfolded the pages, scanning through her brother's careless penmanship. "He says he's sorry he hasn't written sooner. He was waiting until he had definite news for us." She stopped talking and read ahead. "Oh dear. The poor man."

"Who? What?" Belle crowded closer and peered over her shoulder.

"Ward—Lieutenant Calder—was wounded in the shoulder. The injury became corrupted and he spent more than two weeks in the post hospital. He was released on the thirtieth of March, with a crippled left arm." She glanced at the top of the page. "Franklin wrote this two weeks ago, on April 1. He says Ward's on restricted duty until he's completely healed. The doctors hope he'll be able to use his arm again, but they're not sure."

Belle covered her mouth with her fingers. "Do you suppose he'll have to leave the Army?"

"I don't know." Sorrow clenched Luellen's heart when she pictured his left arm hanging useless at his side. A person like Ward didn't deserve such a fate.

She lifted the letter and read aloud.

> *Lt. Campion, the yellow dog who shot him, has been dishonorably discharged. He was caught passing Ward's work off as his own. That's why the duel.*

*Guess he thought if he killed Ward no one could
testify against him. Didn't happen that way. Ward
fired to one side, but Campion shot to kill. Couple
inches closer and he'd of succeeded.*

*Doctor thinks Ward shouldn't move his arm,
but I'm making him use it. Otherwise he'll turn
into a tin soldier. He's going to get furlough, so I
want him to see Papa—I don't trust the sawbones
here.*

Belle's eyes pooled with sympathetic tears. "Your father can
help, I just know it. When is Lieutenant Calder going to Beldon
Grove?"

Luellen turned back to the letter. "He doesn't say. Soon, I
imagine." She pointed at the last paragraph and smiled at Belle.
"Franklin asks to be remembered to you, and hopes to get reac-
quainted one day."

"I hope you don't mind if we're friends." A worried expression
crossed Belle's blushing face.

Embarrassed over her earlier jealousy, Luellen fumbled with
the textbook before tucking it under her arm. "Not at all. I'd be
pleased."

The summons for their afternoon sessions resonated from the
walls of the stone building. As they walked to class, her mind
remained on Ward. Would he be at her parents' house when she
arrived at the end of the term?

# 21

Luellen coughed into her handkerchief before entering the dining room to clear the dishes. A new boarder leaned against the archway separating the parlor from the dining area. "Looks like Ida Hawks got herself another charity case."

She froze. "I beg your pardon?"

"I come through Allenwood every six months or so, and she's always got someone . . . in your condition . . . staying here. When'd she take you in?" His narrow face and pointed nose made him look like an inquisitive ferret.

Luellen stared him down. "I've been here six weeks. Not that it's any of your concern, but I'm a student at the Normal School and will be going home after exams."

"You've got a home to go to? That puts you ahead of most of 'em." He straightened and took a step in her direction. "You ever get lonely, come upstairs. I'm in the second room past the landing." He raised his eyebrows suggestively. "Can't get in any worse fix than you're in now, eh?"

"Get out of my sight." Her breath wheezed in her throat, and she fought down a cough. "If you come near me, I'll call Mrs. Hawks."

He sneered. "And what will she do? Throw me out? Not likely. She needs the money, or she wouldn't be running a boardinghouse, now would she?" He sauntered through the parlor and headed for the stairs. "See you at breakfast."

Hands shaking, Luellen stacked dirty plates. How dare he speak to her that way? With longing, she thought of her parents and home. Another few days and she could leave Allenwood. She prayed she wouldn't see Ferret Man again. From now on, she'd make sure to stay out of sight until all the boarders left the room.

Back in the kitchen, she sank down at the table, overcome by a spasm of coughing. She was struggling to catch her breath when Mrs. Hawks descended the back stairs.

"You sound dreadful. Why don't you go to bed and let me clean up?"

"It's just a spring cold. The May weather's been so changeable lately—I'm either chilled or too warm." Luellen stood, fighting fatigue. "I have to study for final exams. Bedtime is a ways off." She forced a smile.

Mrs. Hawks cocked her head. "Your cough sounds worse to me. Shouldn't you see a doctor?"

"My father is a doctor. I'll be home by Friday." She took a deep breath, hoping the landlady couldn't hear the rattle in her chest.

After a restless night, Luellen awakened and willed herself out of bed. Shivering, she hurried into her brown dress—the only one that still hung straight over her belly. Through the door she heard Mrs. Hawks moving about the kitchen. Had she overslept?

When Luellen walked into the next room, she felt as though she were wading through waist-deep water. Every step was an effort.

"There you are." Mrs. Hawks beamed at her. "I let you sleep. That's the best way to get over a cold."

Prickles of alarm tingled along her body. "How late is it?"

"Not quite eight. Your breakfast is waiting in the warming oven."

"Eight! I have to leave. Now. Examinations begin at eight thirty.

If I'm late, they won't let me in." Luellen fought dizziness. She had to get through this day. She lifted her jacket from a peg and reached for the door handle.

Mrs. Hawks hastened to her side. "Are you sure you're up to the walk? Why don't you wait for the omnibus?"

Through the strangling in her throat, she said, "No time. I'll ride back, I promise." Her voice sounded more like a wheeze than speech.

Leaving the landlady frowning in the doorway, Luellen set off down College Avenue. Just put one foot in front of the other, she told herself. She hadn't traveled far when she had to stop while coughs racked her body. Pain shot across her lower abdomen. Cupping her hands under her belly, she pressed upward to relieve the spasm. How would she ever get through the exams? Her body felt like it belonged to someone else and her brain was coated with dust.

Luellen wished Mrs. Hale would close the window. A chilly draft blew across her table near the back of the crowded testing room. She knew better than to ask. After handing out the exam packets, the proctor acted as though Luellen were invisible, as did most of the other girls in the room. Belle sat at the table in front of her, but after initial greetings, students weren't allowed to converse during the exam period.

She clenched her teeth to prevent their chattering and tried to focus on filling in countries on a blank European map. Exactly where did the empire of Austria end and the Ottoman Empire begin? She'd studied the atlas over and over, but now chasing the boundaries felt like grasping at fog. Her hand shook as she traced borders and identified nations. A glance at the clock told her there was an hour left in the exam period, and she had yet to tackle the section on algebra.

Luellen closed her eyes and rested her forehead in her hands. *So tired.* Could she get through another hour? Turning the page, she stared at a row of equations. The numbers blurred. She must have moaned, because Belle turned around, a worried expression on her face.

"Are you all right?" she mouthed.

"Miss Brownlee. Eyes front." Mrs. Hale rapped on her desk for emphasis.

By force of will, Luellen lifted her pencil and tackled the first problem. If she failed now, the entire year would be wasted. Each equation was a struggle through briars, and she knew she was guessing at answers. Halfway through the set, she heard the chapel bell toll three times. The examination was over, and she hadn't finished.

Mrs. Hale strode to Luellen's table and snatched her exam booklet. "You'll be notified by post. No special treatment this time." She spoke under her breath, a sneer on her lips.

Luellen nodded, afraid to speak for fear she'd start coughing again. As soon as all the booklets had been collected, Belle stood and hurried to her side.

"Let me help you back to Mrs. Hawks's. You never should have come today—you're terribly ill."

"Had to. Everything I've done—" Luellen doubled over, her chest burning.

Belle slipped an arm around her back and helped her to her feet. "Can you get to the bench out front? We'll wait there for the omnibus."

Once they reached the boardinghouse, Mrs. Hawks brewed a pot of tea and sat at the table with them. Speaking to Belle as though Luellen wasn't in the room, she said, "She's going home tomorrow. I'm worried. I think she's too ill to travel."

Mrs. Hawks and Belle swam in a gray haze. "I have my ticket," Luellen said, her voice raspy. "I want to go home."

"And you shall." Belle took her hand. "What time does the train leave?"

"Early. Seven."

"I'll be here—we'll go together."

Tears filled Luellen's eyes. "I can't ask you—" She coughed, heart pounding.

"You're not asking. I'm telling." Belle's dimples appeared at the corners of her smile. "You rest now. I'll be here to fetch you in the morning."

As soon as Belle left, Mrs. Hawks bustled around the table. "Come, let me help you to bed." She laid a hand on Luellen's forehead. "You're burning with fever. I pray this doesn't harm the baby."

Luellen wrapped her arms around her abdomen. "So do I."

After the landlady left the bedroom, Luellen huddled under two blankets and a quilt, shivering. Points of light danced behind her eyes. When she took a breath, she heard rattles in her chest.

At some time during the evening, Mrs. Hawks came in carrying a bowl of broth and helped her spoon the steaming brew into her mouth. Once finished, Luellen fell back on the pillow.

"You sleep now," Mrs. Hawks said. "I'll wake you when it's time to get ready to leave."

"My trunk . . ."

"I'll pack your things."

"Thank you." Luellen wasn't sure whether she'd spoken aloud or not. She rolled onto her side and slept.

"Time to wake up, dear."

Drenched in perspiration, Luellen attempted to focus on Mrs. Hawks's face. "Is it morning already?"

"Miss Brownlee is here with a hired buggy." She handed Luellen a cup of tea. "I added some honey—the sweetness will help your cough." Stepping back, she asked, "How are you feeling this morning?"

"My chest hurts." Luellen stood, placing the teacup on the washstand. Her haggard face reflected back at her in the mirror. Dark circles painted the area under her eyes and two bright dots of color highlighted each cheek. "Please tell Belle I'll be dressed in a moment." She splashed water into the basin.

As soon as Mrs. Hawks left, Luellen removed her nightgown, observing her swollen belly. "Not much longer," she said to her baby. "We just have to get home." A cough tore her throat.

"Luellen?" Belle called through the door.

"One moment. I'll be right out."

True to her word, Mrs. Hawks had packed the trunk, leaving a fresh shift and her traveling costume hanging in the wardrobe. Luellen folded her quilt and placed it atop her belongings, then fastened the hasp.

She entered the kitchen, resting a hand on the wall to keep her balance. "Thank you for coming, Belle. I don't believe I could get through the trip by myself."

"You'd do the same for me." She held out her arm. "Are you ready?"

Luellen clung to her elbow and nodded.

"I'll have the driver load your trunk."

The trip to the station seemed to take only minutes. The train had already arrived and was taking on water and coal. Belle busied herself seeing to the luggage while Luellen rested on a bench. At the edge of the platform, a little girl stood next to her mother, tossing bread crumbs at rufous-striped sparrows. Luellen watched, thinking of the day she'd show her own child how to feed birds. She prayed she'd be able to manage school and a youngster as well as Alma did.

Belle interrupted her reverie. "Time to board. I've arranged seats for us."

The conductor met them at the steps. "Right this way, ladies." Once inside, she noticed Belle had chosen two facing seats and arranged a blanket and pillow on one of them.

Tipping his cap, the man said, "You let me know if you need anything. We should be at the relay station in time for noon dinner."

Luellen nodded thanks and slipped into her seat, wrapping the blanket around her shoulders. "You are such a thoughtful friend," she said to Belle.

"Hush now. You'll start coughing." She fluffed the pillow and tucked it behind Luellen's shoulders. "I brought a book. Would you like me to read aloud?"

"Please." The train jerked into motion, gradually settling into a rhythmic clicking as the wheels rolled along the tracks.

On the facing seat, Belle reached into her satchel. "Have you read Mr. Hawthorne's *The House of the Seven Gables*?"

"No. I read—" She struggled for breath. "*The Scarlet Letter*. Didn't like it much."

"This one's supposed to be better." Belle opened the cover. "Chapter one. 'Halfway down a bystreet . . .'"

Luellen closed her eyes. Belle's voice blended with the train sounds, then faded away.

❧

Papa stood in the aisle, his face masked with fear. "Why didn't you come home sooner?"

*Was she dreaming?* "Papa?"

His arms went around her, helping her rise. "My little girl. Let's get you home. Mama's right outside."

Supported by Belle and her father, Luellen descended the steps onto the platform in Beldon Grove. The sun dangled in the western sky, washing the town with the last rays of afternoon.

Mama dashed over. "Belle telegraphed us about your illness. Thank the Lord that you're here safely." She placed a hand on Luellen's cheek and kissed her.

Turning to Belle, she said, "Bless you for accompanying her. I know you've delayed your own homecoming."

"I couldn't let her make the journey by herself." She sent a mock frown in Luellen's direction. "And she would have, I'm quite sure."

"Once she makes up her mind . . ." Mama's voice trailed off.

Papa helped Luellen into the buggy. "You wait here. We'll leave as soon as the baggage is unloaded."

Her arrival at the house wasn't marked by the festivities that greeted her at Christmas. Papa drove the buggy around to the back door and helped her inside. To her surprise, Franklin and Ward waited in the kitchen. Vaguely, she remembered Franklin's letter mentioning a planned visit to Beldon Grove.

Her brother blanched when he saw her. "You look like you been chawed up and spit out. Belle telegraphed that you were sick, but—" He sought Papa's face. "What's she got?"

"Soon's I know, I'll tell you." He clipped off the words. "First we need to get her to bed."

"Let me help you, sir," Ward said, stepping forward. He'd lost his ruddy look, and appeared thinner. His left arm hung straight from his shoulder.

In spite of her own misery, Luellen felt a pang when she met his haunted eyes. What happened to the confident officer she'd first met?

Mama entered the bedroom, carrying a vase laden with late-season lilacs. Their heady fragrance filled the air. "Ellie stopped by with these before church. She sends her love, but couldn't stay for a visit. I'll put them on the bureau."

"Tell her thank you." Luellen pushed herself up on one elbow. The effort left her trembling. Morning sun flared across the bed, igniting the flowers on her quilt in a blaze of crimson. "I'm sorry you and Papa had to miss services."

"The Lord will understand." Mama smiled. "Belle went with Franklin and Ward, so our family will be represented."

"When did Papa say Dr. Gordon is coming?"

"Any minute now. Do you want me to help you into a fresh gown?"

"Please." She leaned forward while Mama tugged off her damp nightgown and replaced it with one smelling of sunlight. Exhausted, Luellen fell back onto the pillow. "I'll sleep until he arrives," she murmured, eyes closing.

A short while later, voices in the hallway roused her. Papa entered the room first, followed by Beldon Grove's new doctor. A small man, he sported a beard and a head of carroty red hair. He wore a wrinkled black jacket over a blue-striped shirt with a fold-down collar. In one hand he carried a bulging satchel, which he plopped on the bureau next to the lilacs.

"Pleased to make your acquaintance, Miss McGarvie. I'm Dr. Gordon. Angus Gordon to my friends, like your father here."

Luellen sought Papa's eyes, still mystified as to why he wouldn't treat her.

"I don't trust myself, Lulie," he said, reading her mind. "I'm too close to you to be objective."

"Don't you worry, lass. Karl and I went to the same school of medicine. I finished two years ago, so I know some new tricks." He grinned and drew a stethoscope from his bag. "I need to ask you to unfasten the ribbons at the neck of your garment, please."

His manner changed from jocular to professional when he placed the cold chest piece of the instrument against her skin. "Take a deep breath now."

Luellen sucked air into her lungs and immediately bent double, coughing. Dr. Gordon spread his fingers across her back and supported her until the spasm ended. Once she was resettled on the pillow, he patted her hand and turned to Papa. "Lung fever, without a doubt."

"I thought so too. She's been sick most of the week, according to her friend. Fever and chills. Coughing fits."

"If it's been that long, she may be near the crisis point." He angled his gaze at Luellen. "I'd say you'll be on the mend in a few more days." His eyes strayed to the mound of her pregnancy under the quilt. "With your permission, I'd like to examine you further. When is your baby expected?"

"Before the end of the month." Luellen paused to take a shallow breath and then gave voice to her deepest fear. "Has my . . . lung fever . . . harmed my child?"

Dr. Gordon folded the bedding aside and laid his hands on her nightgown-covered abdomen. His fingers probed the position of the baby. "I feel movement. I believe your child will be perfectly healthy. But it's too soon to know for certain."

He replaced his stethoscope in the satchel. "I'll be back to check on you in a day or two. In the interim, you must observe complete rest—for your sake and the child's."

# 22

Franklin sprawled on a chair next to Luellen's bed, moccasined feet stuck out in front of him. "Things are too quiet around here since Belle went home."

"I miss her too." She shifted to relieve an ache in her lower back. "Mama said you went strolling together in the evenings. I'm glad you were here to entertain her." As she said the words, Luellen knew she meant them.

"No hardship, I assure you." He sat forward. "Now that your fever's gone, will the doc let you come downstairs?"

"I have to wait until after the baby comes. He said I could walk up and down the hallway to keep my legs strong, but no stairs." She scooted higher on the pillows, wincing when a spasm crossed her abdomen.

"That doctor looks like a leprechaun, doesn't he? Short and red-haired. All that's missing is a little green cap." Franklin's eyes sparkled with mischief.

Luellen giggled. "Don't let Papa hear you. He thinks highly of Dr. Gordon."

"Not highly enough to see him about his breathing problems."

She sobered. "He's worse than he was when I was home this winter." She felt heaviness in her belly and sudden warmth between

her legs. Muscles in her groin rippled. Luellen clutched the edge
of the quilt. All the horror stories she'd heard about childbirth
pounded through her mind. "I think the baby's coming. Call Papa."

The chair clattered backward as Franklin sprang to his feet,
face pale. "Stay right there." He dashed from the room.

Luellen couldn't help but smile. Where did he think she'd go?

Franklin's voice spiraled down the staircase. "Mama! Luellen's
having the baby. Right now! Where's Papa?"

Mama's voice followed Franklin's into the room. "Papa's in his
office. After you tell him, go get Dr. Gordon. And Franklin—"

"What?"

"Babies take awhile. Slow down and catch your breath."

After a moment, Mama arrived in the doorway. "Are the pains
close together?" She stepped next to the bed and smoothed Luellen's hair away from her brow.

"Every couple of minutes. I thought I was just having settling
pains this morning, but—" She paused while a contraction seized
her abdomen. "My water broke. I'm scared, Mama."

Her mother's soft palm rested against Luellen's forehead. "You're
going to be fine," she said, but her voice wavered. "Papa should
be here soon."

"I'm here now." Her father strode to the bedside, his pale face
telegraphing concern. "How are you feeling, Lulie?"

"The pain—it's worse by the moment."

His hand shook when he reached for hers. "That's normal,
unfortunately. Dr. Gordon's on his way." Papa's blue eyes misted.
"I'll stay right here with you, but—"

"Papa is too attached to you to be much help, is what he's trying to say." Mama patted her husband's cheek. She pointed to the
chair that Franklin had upset when he dashed from the room.

"Why don't you sit, Karl? I'll run downstairs for towels and put

---

the kettle on." She raised the window. "This breeze should help you feel comfortable," she said to Luellen.

May air stroked Luellen's perspiring face. "Thank you." She drew a deep breath and waited for a contraction to pass.

When Dr. Gordon arrived, he plopped his leather satchel on top of the bureau. "So, here comes the little one. How far apart are your bearing pains?"

"Seems like every minute—I'm not sure."

He tipped his head toward Papa, who still clutched her hand. "Aren't you timing them?"

"No. I didn't think of it." He fumbled in his pocket and withdrew his watch. The gold case glinted in the morning light when he clicked the cover open.

Dr. Gordon scrutinized Papa's face. "I don't want two patients. Maybe you'd be better off downstairs with your son and his friend."

He drew a shaky breath. "I promised Luellen. I'm staying here."

A pungent odor of sweat lingered over the bed when the doctor laid the squalling infant on Luellen's abdomen. "He's a healthy lad. Just listen to those lungs."

Exhausted, she touched the baby's mop of wet black curls with a trembling fingertip. "Hello, David. You're beautiful." Luellen didn't think her heart could hold all the love she felt for this tiny red-faced boy.

Mama bent over her and cradled the baby in a towel. "I'll bathe him and bring him right back." The setting sun cast a rosy glow over the two of them as she slipped from the room.

The spot where David had rested on her belly felt cold and empty. "Hurry," Luellen whispered.

Papa stood to one side, shirt collar unbuttoned, while Dr.

203

Gordon completed his ministrations. Once the doctor left the room, Papa leaned down and gathered Luellen in his arms. He rested his cheek against her hair. "Thank you, Lord, for giving us a strong baby and preserving our daughter." The balm of his fervent prayer washed her in peace.

The next morning Ward hovered in the doorway when Franklin came into the bedroom. "May I see him too? I don't want to intrude."

Mama had freshened the room, putting a bouquet of climbing roses on the bureau and folding the quilt over the foot of the bed. Cuddling her blanket-wrapped son in the crook of her right arm, Luellen smiled a welcome. "Please do. David wants to meet my family and friends."

"You named him David." Ward approached the bed. "David what?"

"David Karl O'Connell."

Franklin reared back. "O'Connell! Why would you want any connection to that . . . that . . ."

"He needs a father's last name. He can't go through life with people thinking he was born on the wrong side of the blanket." She held the sleeping infant toward her brother. "Would you like to hold him?"

Franklin clasped David around his shoulders and lifted him straight into the air, the way he would land a fish.

"Not like that." Ward pushed next to him and slid his right hand under the baby's head, supporting the body with his left palm.

Alarmed, Luellen watched the exchange. Would Ward's injured arm be able to withstand David's weight? She straightened, ready to gather her son back in her arms, just as Ward settled into one of the chairs.

"I've got him. Don't worry."

"Where did you learn how to hold a baby?" Luellen couldn't keep the surprise from her voice.

"Well . . . I . . ."

"I've got to hear this too," Franklin said, perching on the edge of the bed. "It's a safe bet they didn't teach this at the Academy."

Ward kept his eyes on David's sleeping face for a long moment. "I was abandoned as an infant—not much bigger than this little scrap." He swallowed. "I grew up in a foundling home. When I got to be seven or eight, I was put to work caring for the little ones." His voice trailed off. When he looked up, his eyes met Luellen's. She felt she was seeing into his soul.

"I wasn't adopted until I was twelve, so I had plenty of practice." He shifted his left leg so his knee supported his weakened arm.

Once Ward had David steadied, she asked, "And then?"

"Obadiah Calder and his wife wanted me. They were older, in their sixties, and needed a son to carry on the Calder name."

David whimpered.

"Shh, little fellow." Ward rose and laid the baby in Luellen's arms. His gaze swept her face. "This little boy is blessed to have a family like yours."

"Ward—" She reached for his hand.

"I have to work on a report." His color high, he fled the room.

Franklin stared after him. "All this time I've ragged him about making the Army his home, and I never knew . . ."

"You meant no harm." The open trust in Ward's eyes had touched a current within her. No wonder he understood how it felt to be the object of gossip and speculation. Undoubtedly he'd experienced many critical slurs as an orphan adopted into a wealthy family. "He wouldn't have told us about himself if he didn't feel safe in doing so."

Her brother nodded. "It's good for him to be here. The reaction on the post to that duel has hit him hard. Campion's friends think Ward should've been discharged too."

"Why? Didn't you say he was copying Ward's reports?"

"He was. But Campion's friends don't know that. Ward won't say anything in his own defense. Feels he'd be kicking a man when he's down."

Luellen thought of the rumors that circulated through the Normal School when her pregnancy came to light. People believed what they wanted to believe.

"I'm glad you brought him home. How long will you stay?"

"He has a week left on medical furlough. Papa's helping him strengthen his arm. Those quack Army doctors told him not to work it, but Papa says that's a sure way to end up with a useless limb."

"He's the best doctor anywhere. He knows." Luellen looked down at her sleeping son and dropped a kiss on his dark curls. "Your timing was perfect. You got to meet your nephew—and see Belle."

Franklin smiled at the mention of Belle's name. "And I got a bonus today."

"A bonus?"

"Yes. Now I know how to hold a baby."

Dr. Gordon allowed Luellen to go downstairs on the last day of Franklin and Ward's visit. Papa supported her with an arm around her waist, and Mama followed, carrying David. By the time she reached the sitting room, Luellen's legs trembled with fatigue. The family watched while she grasped the arms of the rocking chair and lowered herself into it. Trickles of perspiration slipped down her temples.

"Why am I so weak?"

"You've been bedridden for weeks. You have to get your strength back," Papa said. "Give it time."

She reached for David and cuddled him under her chin. Wiggling, he made sucking noises against her neck. "I hope you can help me get stronger the way you've helped Ward's arm. I've made plans for earning money this summer."

Mama and Papa exchanged a glance.

"Earning money for what?" Mama asked.

"To finish school." Luellen looked up and noticed Ward watching from the doorway.

His worried eyes were fixed on David. "I realize this isn't my concern, Luellen, but your baby needs you right now."

"I know that, for heaven's sake. But I also know a woman who completed her schooling *and* cared for her infant. If she can do it, so can I."

He stared at her for a moment, then turned and walked away.

"What's gotten into you?" Mama asked. "You shouldn't speak rudely to a guest in our home."

Heat climbed Luellen's cheeks. "I'm sorry. No one understands how much it means to me to finish. I've sacrificed to get this far. I won't quit now."

"No doubt Ward's aware of your ambition." Mama put her hands on her hips. "What you don't realize is how much a baby will change your life. These early days of being awakened in the night are just the beginning. From now on, the baby *is* your life."

"I can do both." She looked out the window at a carriage traveling toward the train depot.

Ward spoke little during supper, and excused himself after the meal to complete his packing. Luellen knew she couldn't let him return to the post without apologizing for her sharp-tongued remarks.

Once she'd tucked David into his cradle, she crossed the hallway and knocked. "Ward?"

He opened the door, his expression guarded. A valise rested on the bed with a stack of clothing folded nearby.

"I want to apologize for my rudeness this afternoon. I had no call to speak to you like that."

"No apology necessary. I was out of line to interfere in a family matter." His voice was as stiff as the high collar of his white shirt.

She remembered the times he'd stood up for her. Without his support, the past months would have been far more difficult. "You weren't interfering—you were concerned for David." Her tone pleaded for forgiveness.

"I do have a soft spot for that little fellow." Ward's expression mellowed. "I know how it feels to have no parents."

Luellen bristled. "David has a parent. I promise you, I'll never do anything that would lead to his harm."

Ward gripped her shoulder with his left hand. "Of course you won't. But if you ever need help—of any sort—please let me know."

Warmth from his hand traveled down her side. She moved a step closer, drawn to the depth in his blue eyes. Her arms ached to wrap themselves around his sturdy body.

What was she doing? A few kind words and she was ready to . . . what? She bit her lip and moved back.

"Th-thank you for the offer." She turned and escaped to her room.

# 23

Luellen hurried around the dining table, placing the reader next to a slate. Her first student, Oswald Carstairs, would arrive any moment. It had taken a month to find a family interested in having a child tutored. She believed without Mr. Wolcott's help she'd still be searching.

She glanced at the cradle through the open door of the sitting room, hoping David would sleep for the next hour. If the Carstairs were pleased with their son's progress, perhaps they'd tell other parents. The money the registrar returned to her had dwindled with the cost of omnibus and train fares. As things stood now, she'd need every cent to return for the fall term, if indeed she could return.

When she heard a knock, Luellen smoothed her gored brown skirt and opened the door. Penelope Carstairs stood on the veranda, holding her eight-year-old son's hand. Her bonnet was tied in a prim bow under her chin. She studied Luellen with dubious eyes.

"Mr. Wolcott assures me you have trained as a teacher. Is that correct?"

"Yes. Won't you come in?"

Mrs. Carstairs propelled her son forward. "No, thank you. I

need to do my marketing. You may send Oswald home when the hour has passed." She surveyed Luellen again. "He just needs a bit of help with reading, is all. I'm sure he'll learn quickly."

Luellen closed the door behind her and leaned against the frame. Her student's posture bristled defiance. Summoning a cheerful voice, she said, "Well, shall we get started?"

Oswald glared at her. "I don't need to read. I'm going to be a blacksmith when I grow up, like Mr. Pitt."

"I happen to know Mr. Pitt can read." She took his hand. "Come with me. We'll start by writing your name."

Once at the table, he scrunched over the slate and printed his name in large capital letters. "There. Can I go now?"

Her thoughts flicked to Daniel and his earnest desire to learn. Why had she assumed that all pupils would be as eager? With a sigh, she turned to Oswald. "Your mother paid for an hour, and we will use every moment. Now, print the alphabet and tell me the sounds of the letters, please."

Groaning, the boy picked up the pencil and scrawled an *A*. After writing the next several letters, he came to a halt and fished in his pocket. He placed a marble on the table and watched while it rolled to the edge and plunked on the floor. Before Luellen could stop him, he dove after the white sphere and put it back on the table, where it repeated its race to the edge.

Luellen clamped a hand on Oswald's shoulder. "Please leave the marble where it is and attend to your letters. You may retrieve it after your lesson."

He glared at her, shoving his fingers through his cowlicky brown hair. "I'm going to tell my mother you're mean."

"Fine. I'll tell her you're disobedient."

While Oswald printed and grumbled, she heard a whimper from the sitting room. "Excuse me a moment. I'll be right back."

She seized David and dashed up the stairs to the guest room. "Mama. Can you watch him for me until my student leaves?"

Her mother turned, brushing tendrils of hair from her forehead with the back of her hand. A pile of blankets lay over a chair. "He's hungry. I'm afraid you'll have to tend him yourself. Lily and Edmund will arrive this evening and the room's not ready." She unfurled a sheet over the mattress.

David's whimper grew louder. His little fists clutched at the front of Luellen's dress. She felt a responsive pulse within her breasts. What would she do with Oswald? Carrying the now-wailing baby, she plodded down the stairs.

The boy sat rolling the marble back and forth, the slate pushed aside.

"We'll have to stop for now. You may go home. Please ask your mother to bring you here a little earlier next time."

Oswald jumped to his feet. "I'll tell her if I remember." He bolted for the door.

Luellen sagged onto a chair and unfastened her bodice. At this rate, how would she ever manage to return to Allenwood?

Luellen flung open the front door when she saw Papa's carriage stop by the front walk. She hadn't seen her sister since Lily's wedding nearly a year ago. Letters weren't the same as time spent face-to-face.

Edmund descended first. The sun polished his straw-colored hair with bronze. Frock coat slung over one arm, he reached up to assist Lily. When she stepped to the walk, Luellen dashed forward, eager to engulf her in a hug.

Hoopskirts swaying, Lily reached toward her with gloved hands. "I've missed you so. You look wonderful." She studied

Luellen's face. "Are you feeling well? Mama wrote that you had lung fever before your confinement."

"I've entirely recovered, thank you. A little tired sometimes, but with an infant that's to be expected."

"We can't wait to see him, isn't that right, Edmund?"

"Yes. In fact—"

Lily jabbed him in the side with her elbow. "Let's get out of the sun, shall we? It was fearfully warm on the train, and leaving the windows open only served to soil my traveling costume." She brushed at gray coal dust that covered her gathered skirt.

Her arm looped through the crook of her sister's elbow, Luellen turned toward the house. Mama joined her, and the three of them ascended the steps to the veranda. Edmund trailed behind, carrying a leather valise.

Mama paused at the top of the stairs and looked at Edmund. "Would you please help Lily's father with the baggage? Take the heaviest pieces if you will."

"Certainly." He placed the valise in the entry and returned to the carriage.

Concern crossed Lily's face. "Is Papa ill? He's never needed help before."

"He's been rather fatigued lately. He says he has a touch of asthma."

Lily glanced at Luellen for verification.

"Later," Luellen mouthed.

Once inside the house, Lily hung her flowered bonnet on the hall tree and whirled to face Luellen. "Where's David? I can't wait to see him."

"In here." She stepped into the sitting room and gathered her son into her arms. He blinked and yawned, waving his fists in the air. Cuddling him close, she nuzzled his soft neck before handing him to her sister.

212

"He's absolutely adorable. He's got your black curls. And look at those blue eyes—just like Brendan's. Do you think they'll stay that way?"

"I hope not. I pray he'll look like a McGarvie through and through."

"Yes. So do we." She bounced David in her arms and tickled him under the chin. He rewarded her with a toothless smile.

The next afternoon, Lily joined Luellen in the sitting room while Edmund accompanied Papa on his rounds. The previous night's supper had been filled with excited conversation, as the family caught up with all the news that hadn't been written in their letters. Now the two sisters were ready to talk out of earshot of their parents.

Lily leaned forward in her chair, adjusting her lilac-sprigged muslin skirt around her ankles. "How's Papa, really? He looks so pale."

A knot of apprehension formed in Luellen's chest. "I'm frightened for him. There are times he fights for air. I wish he'd let Dr. Gordon examine him."

Lily's eyes widened. "Mama didn't write me any of this."

"She probably didn't want to worry you." Luellen shook her head. "While I was away she didn't write about his health to me, either. Now that I'm home—"

"But you're not staying. Mama says you're determined to go back to school, no matter what anyone says."

"I can't quit now."

Lily had always been her ally. Thankful to have her sister on her side, Luellen continued. "I need your help. Somehow we have to convince them without upsetting Papa." She explained how Alma Guthrie had managed an infant and schooling. "Last year was such a struggle—hiding my condition, fighting weariness—the coming term is bound to be easier."

"How can you say that? Since I've been home you've spent more time with David than you have with me. Surely you can't take him with you to classes."

"I'll find a nurse."

"School is so important that you'd leave your son with a stranger?"

Luellen flushed. "He won't be left. David will be with me all the time unless I'm in class."

"After what happened with Brendan, you deserve to reach your goal." Lily pursed her lips. "I just don't understand why you can't wait until your son is older."

"What difference does it make? I'll still have David to care for, no matter how old he is. Besides, if I stay away too long, I'll have to start over."

Lily rested her index finger against her cheek. "I may have a solution."

Luellen watched as she left the room. Leave it to her sister to come up with a plan.

⬯

Penelope Carstairs studied Luellen with a dubious expression. Oswald stood behind her on the veranda, a scowl etched across his broad forehead.

"I'm happy to try to help you with your finances, but Oswald tells me your baby interrupted his lesson time. How can you expect him to learn when your attention is elsewhere?"

Luellen strove to look professional, which wasn't easy with David clinging to her neck and cooing. "I'm sure it won't happen again. My son normally sleeps for two hours or more after he's eaten. I was just about to put him in his cradle when you arrived."

To emphasize her remarks, David gave a huge yawn. His eyelids drooped.

"Well . . ." Penelope hesitated.

Lily joined them at the doorway. "I'll be happy to watch him while Oswald's here." She lifted David from Luellen's arms and cuddled him close. "You go ahead with your lessons. Don't worry about a thing." With a swirl of muslin, she swept into the parlor and closed the door.

Penelope blinked. "In that case, go along, Oswald. Miss Mc-Garvie is ready for you."

As she led her pupil into the dining room, Luellen seethed at Penelope's implication that hiring her as a tutor was a charitable act. What had Mr. Wolcott been telling people? She'd have to produce outstanding results with this boy in order to gain credibility.

He slumped in a chair and propped an elbow on the table. "Are you going to make me do the alphabet again?"

"Yes. Do you like to draw pictures?"

"Sometimes." His lower lip protruded.

"Can you draw an apple?"

"That's an easy one." He shot her a scornful look and picked up a pencil.

She pushed the slate in his direction. "After you draw the apple, make a picture of a bell—like the one in the schoolhouse belfry."

"I get to ring that if I've been good in class all day." Smiling, Oswald completed a sketch of a bell. "What next?"

"How about a cat?"

By the end of the hour, he'd illustrated the alphabet and read each of the identifying names Luellen printed below his drawings. He grabbed the filled slate. "Can I take this home to show my ma?"

Luellen smiled a secret smile. "Certainly."

After Oswald left, she opened the door to the parlor and peeked inside. Lily sat in a high-backed armchair, cradling a sleeping

David in her arms. When she heard Luellen enter, she lifted her head. Her eyes were shiny with tears.

"What's wrong?" Luellen hurried to her sister's side. "Have you and Edmund quarreled?"

Lily blinked rapidly. "Everything's fine. I'm a little tired, that's all."

"I'll take David now." She looked at her sister with mock severity. "You'll spoil him, holding him all the time."

With apparent reluctance, Lily relinquished her hold on the baby. "We've only been here a few days. A little attention won't spoil him." Her voice was edged with criticism.

Luellen cocked an eyebrow. "You think I don't pay enough attention to my son?"

"You're busy with lessons. What would you have done if I hadn't been here to watch him while you were with your student?"

"He'd have slept whether you were here or not." Her voice rose. "You've been home for a week and you think you know more about David than I do?"

Upstairs, Luellen settled the still-sleeping infant in his cradle. The letter she had tucked in her pocket crackled when she straightened. Biting her lower lip, she drew out the report that had arrived from Allenwood. She'd failed the algebra examination. The words jumped off the page and struck her across the face. She'd never failed courses in Beldon Grove.

Her other passing marks—geography, psychology, literature— weren't enough. Even the commendation from Alma Guthrie on her student teaching didn't lift her spirits. The thought of approaching Dr. Alexander to ask for special treatment again made her stomach twitch. After everything that had happened over the last term, he was unlikely to grant her any more favors. In fact, she'd be lucky if she could enroll at all.

Sighing, she dug her algebra textbook from her trunk and carried it to a chair next to the window. She *would* learn these equations. The sun shifted to the western sky while she studied, but she paid little attention. When David whimpered, Luellen moved her foot so she could rock his cradle and continue reading.

"How can you ignore him when he cries?" Lily stood in the doorway, her mouth pinched in disapproval. Edmund hovered behind her in the hall.

Luellen marked her place with her finger and looked up. "He's fine. I'll pick him up when he really gets serious."

"May I?" Without waiting for an answer, Lily lifted David from the cradle and felt his bottom. "He's wet. I'll change him for you."

"That's not necessary. I'll do it." Luellen snapped the algebra text closed.

Lily shrugged her away and plucked a folded diaper from a stack on the bureau. When David was clean and dry, she perched on the edge of the bed with him in her arms. She nodded at Edmund, who entered the room and closed the door behind him.

"We have a proposition to offer," he said. "Since becoming a teacher is so important to you, we would like to help by taking David and raising him as our son."

Luellen gasped. "No!"

"We can give him a better life than you ever could. I make a comfortable living at my father's flour mill. The boy wouldn't want for anything." Edmund rocked back on the heels of his shiny brown boots.

"And he'd have a mother and a father," Lily said. She dropped a kiss on David's dark curls. "How can you even consider raising a child on your own?"

Luellen snatched the baby from Lily's arms, startling him. She glared at her sister. "Our father died before you were born. Where would you be if Mama had decided not to keep you? She could have given you away, but she didn't. And I won't let David go."

She brushed past Edmund and flung open the door. "Please get out of my room—and stay away from my son."

Edmund tugged on the hem of his checkered waistcoat, smoothing it over his trim physique. "The offer is open. We'll see how you feel once you've struggled at Allenwood for a few months." He laid an arm around Lily's shoulder and guided her from the room.

# 24

Luellen slammed the door behind Lily and Edmund. The bang started David howling.

"Shh. Mama's got you. You're safe." She patted his back until he relaxed, then reclined against the head of the bed and took him to her breast. While he nursed, she fingered his curls and stroked the outline of his tiny ears. "You're all mine to love," she whispered. "No one will take you away from me."

Her stomach tightened when she considered her sister's offer. Was she doing the right thing by keeping David? What if she couldn't manage? *Lord, help me.*

When the day arrived for Lily and Edmund to return to Springfield, Luellen felt sadness mixed with relief. She'd anticipated spending pleasant hours with her sister, but their time together ended on a note of strained politeness.

Now, standing in the depot next to her parents, she stiffened when Lily approached.

"May I hold him one last time?"

Their mother watched the exchange. Luellen sensed Mama noticed the restraint between them, so she kept a pleasant expression on her face. Inside, she counted the moments until she could reclaim her son.

When the train left the station, Luellen heaved a deep sigh.

"What happened between you and your sister?" Mama asked while Papa walked ahead to untie the horses and bring the buggy around to the edge of the platform. "You didn't spend much time together this week."

"She and Edmund wanted to take David and raise him as their own." She enfolded David's head with one hand and kissed him. "They think if I go back to school, I won't be a proper mother."

"She said as much to me."

"What did you tell her?" She held her breath.

"I told her God gave David to you, not her."

Tears burned Luellen's eyes. "Thank you, Mama. I pray I'll be worthy of his trust."

"At the same time, you must do your part."

"My part?"

"Take care of yourself so you can take care of your son. If you get lung fever again, Lily might feel justified in her position. You could hardly tend to a babe as sick as you were in May."

Luellen opened her mouth to protest. She believed she'd stay well, but then, she'd assumed the same thing last term.

Papa stood in the kitchen doorway. "Someone's here to see you."

Luellen paused in setting out papers. "My new student? Why would she come to the back entrance?"

"I'm an old student." Daniel stood behind her father. His height made Papa appear small.

Flustered, she dropped a handful of pencils. "It's been a long time."

His hair was trimmed and combed back. He wore a loose-fitting white shirt tucked into a pair of linsey-woolsey trousers. "I told you I'd have a surprise for you this summer."

"Yes. You did." She waited.

Papa spoke in the ensuing silence. "Daniel stopped by my office for permission to take you to see the house he's built. I told him I'd come along to keep things proper."

"This isn't a very good time. I have a new student coming later today. And I shouldn't leave David."

"Bring him with you," Daniel said. "I heard about your little one. Guess I'm not the only person with a surprise, eh?" He chuckled.

Luellen shot a pleading glance at Papa, hoping he'd see her reluctance.

He met her gaze, amusement twinkling in his eyes. "You can spare an hour. It's a cool morning for August. Be good for you to get some fresh air." The two men acted as though they shared a secret.

She heaved a deep sigh and scooped the pencils from the floor. "I'll get David ready and be with you in a few minutes." She wouldn't upset Papa by arguing with him.

Luellen braced her feet against the floorboards of Daniel's wagon to keep from being bounced off the stiff plank seat. Why would Papa think she needed to see Daniel's new house? She prayed he wasn't matchmaking.

David wiggled and she adjusted his cap to keep the sun from his eyes. He waved his hands in the air until he found his thumb, which he poked in his mouth.

"Bright little fellow, isn't he?" Daniel's hazel eyes rested on her for a moment. "He takes after his mama."

"Thank you." Luellen resisted the urge to tell him all the ways she believed David to be advanced for two and a half months old. A man his age wouldn't be interested in babies.

They passed the hotel, the smithy's, and the cottage she'd shared with Brendan. The bitter taste of betrayal rose in her throat. As time went by, she thought of Brendan less and less, but the scene of her folly brought his laughing face back to her memory. *You and those glasses—you should be happy you had this much time with a man.* She clenched her teeth, fighting back a wave of anger.

Papa slipped an arm around her shoulder, as though sensing her thoughts. "You're better off," he murmured. "I'm proud of you."

She leaned against him, bolstered by his nearness.

A young woman Luellen didn't recognize sat on a bench in front of the cottage. She lifted her hand and waved at Daniel as they rolled past. He removed his hat and waved it back at her, a wide grin filling his face.

After passing an expanse of empty acreage, he stopped the wagon before a square clapboard building. Newly milled lumber gleamed yellow in the sun. Daniel jumped from the wagon. Papa followed, reaching up to help Luellen.

Like a child with a new toy, Daniel bounded ahead and flung open the door. "Miss Luellen, I want you should see this." He disappeared inside.

"What?"

"Wait and see." Papa took her elbow and supported her over the rough ground in front of the stoop.

The fragrance of freshly cut wood filled the small room. Daniel stood next to a table in the center of the living area. The corner of a tall bedstead showed through the doorway behind him. "D'you think a lady would like this house?"

"I'm sure she would." Luellen strove to keep her tone neutral.

"Look at this. I made it special." He pointed to a step-back cupboard against one wall. One of the open shelves contained a row of books.

Curious, she moved closer to read the titles. He had a full set of *Leatherstocking Tales*, a volume by Edgar Allan Poe, and several books of poetry. She couldn't hide her surprise. "You read all these books since last spring?"

"I'm working on it. I bought all them because of you."

Her heart plummeted. "Daniel, I—"

"If you hadn't learned me to read, yon Prudy Gibbs wouldn't never have agreed to marry me. She's almost smart as you are."

"Prudy Gibbs?" She swung a glance at Papa for clarification.

"The young woman outside your former cottage." He looked delighted at her surprise. "Daniel asked me how best to give you the news, and I thought it might be a good idea to tell you this way."

"I can't thank you enough." Daniel stepped forward, holding his hat in front of his chest. "I've had my sights on Prudy for a long time, but never guessed she'd have me."

"I'm happy for you." Luellen's face heated. When would she learn not to jump to conclusions?

Another lesson to take back to Allenwood. Perhaps she was too hasty in assuming she couldn't ask Dr. Alexander to allow her to retake the algebra exam. It wouldn't hurt to try.

Luellen filled a valise with David's gowns and diapers for the journey. She stepped back, surveying her bedroom. An open trunk, piled with both her clothing and clothes to accommodate a growing baby for the next three months, rested under the window. David lay on top of the bed watching her movements. She flopped down beside him.

"This will be your first train ride. Are you excited?"

David gurgled and blew a spit bubble around his thumb, his blue eyes filled with trust.

Her stomach churned. What if taking her baby with her caused him harm? She pushed her fears away. She'd come too far to back down now.

"Are you almost ready?" Mama stood in the doorway.

"Another twenty minutes. I just need to get us both dressed for travel."

"I'll take care of David for you." Mama lifted him, kissing his cheeks. "It's been a joy having a baby in the house." She slipped a white muslin gown over his head. "I confess I was worried about you taking him away from us, but I've watched how you've balanced caring for David with tutoring your students. He's thriving. You'll do well at Allenwood."

Luellen exhaled, unaware until that moment that she'd been holding her breath. "Your confidence means everything to me." She slipped into a new royal blue skirt and fastened hooks and eyes on the matching flowered bodice. After sweeping her hair into a twist at the back of her head, she took a straw bonnet from a peg and tied the blue ribbon under her chin.

"You look ready for anything."

"I pray you're right."

Boarding the train brought back memories of Belle escorting her home last May. Luellen was bursting to show David to her friend. One more day and they'd be reunited—during classes at least. The rest of the time Luellen would be living at Mrs. Hawks's and caring for David in her free time. In hindsight, her early days at Allenwood were carefree by comparison.

The passenger car reeked of overheated humanity. Luellen

struggled to carry David and a heavy valise while searching for an empty seat. When she found a spot, she dropped the bag and sank onto the hard wooden bench. Her son wiggled and whimpered.

"Hush." She peered out the open window for one final wave as the train lurched into motion. Good-byes never got easier. Swallowing a lump in her throat, she settled David on her lap and draped her shawl over the two of them. He howled in earnest while she hurried to unfasten her bodice.

Once he quieted at his meal, she looked around at the other passengers. Across the aisle, a saggy-jowled older woman locked eyes with her. "I hope that child isn't going to cry throughout our journey." Her face pinched into a frown.

Luellen wiped perspiration from her forehead. "I hope so too." She held her gaze until the other woman dropped hers. It was going to be a long ride.

Sunset unfurled orange ribbons across the station as the train rolled into Plymouth Mills for a supper stop. Brakes screeched along the track. Luellen rocked forward, slamming backward when the car came to a halt.

Startled awake, David wailed, earning a glare from across the aisle. The woman gathered her skirts and plunged out of the car, muttering under her breath about mothers who ought to stay home with their infants.

Luellen set her jaw. "Come on, let's go for a walk." She slid her reticule over her wrist and patted David's back, praying the activity would quiet him.

On the platform, passengers jostled their way into the station house to eat a meal in the fifteen minutes allowed while the train took on water and coal. Luellen sent a mental thank-you to her mother for packing ample food for the journey so she wouldn't have to be part of the demanding mob.

The community of Plymouth Mills lay east of the station. She walked past the locomotive to a point where she had an unobstructed view of the prairie. Sienna-brown grassland stretched westward, sparking a longing to explore, to live as her parents had in new territory. She squinted into the setting sun. Perhaps once she had her certificate, she would take David and make a fresh start somewhere.

He squirmed on her shoulder and she turned him so he could see forward. "Beautiful, isn't it? Someday we'll go see what's past the horizon." She walked toward the passenger cars. "For now, let's have some supper."

The omnibus driver deposited Luellen and David at Mrs. Hawks's. A swath of stars covered the ebony sky as she trudged up the walk, arms aching from holding David for so many hours. Mrs. Hawks opened the door and stood silhouetted against the light. "Welcome back. Let me see this little lad."

Luellen handed over her sleeping son and flexed her shoulders, grateful to be relieved of the weight.

The driver huffed up the stairs behind them, carrying her trunk. "Where do you want your baggage?"

"Inside the door, please." Luellen dug in her reticule for a gratuity.

When the omnibus left, Mrs. Hawks led the way into the sitting room, placing David on the sofa. Luellen sank down next to him and worked open the buttons on her boots.

"You look exhausted. I'll bring some tea."

"Thank you. That sounds ideal." She leaned against the flowered gold upholstery, running her fingers over the worn brocade fabric. After the wooden bench on the train, the softness of the padding tempted her to fall asleep beside David. She closed her eyes.

"Here you are, dear." Teacups clinked when Mrs. Hawks placed the tray on a round table near the arm of the sofa.

Blinking, Luellen sat forward. "Cinnamon cookies. You remembered."

"I've been counting the days. Miss Brownlee has too. She'll be here in the morning." She lifted her cup and sipped. "Your room is ready. Alma brought over Frederick's outgrown crib."

"Bless her. What a godsend."

"She hoped you'd be pleased. In the meantime, I expect you want to know about the woman who'll be watching him while you're in classes."

The thought of leaving David with a stranger turned the cinnamon sugar to sand in her mouth. She washed it down with a swallow of tea.

"Yes. Please tell me." Her cup rattled when she replaced it in the saucer.

"Her name's Leah Holcomb. She stayed with me before you came. Leah had a daughter in March, and unfortunately the father has denied the child. She now serves as a companion to Elsie Garmon, an elderly neighbor of mine. Since I knew you were coming, I asked if she'd be willing to care for David for part of each day. She agreed, gladly."

Through tears, Luellen studied David's face. Her plan had seemed easier from a distance. She dug her nails into her palms. "What kind of a person is she?"

"Well, she's not someone you'd normally expect to find in Allenwood. I'll say no more—I want you to make up your own mind."

# 25

Belle sat beside the kitchen table, watching while Luellen removed a pan of biscuits from the oven. She cuddled David on her lap. "Hurry. I want you to open the present I brought."

"I'll only be another moment. The boarders are waiting for the rest of their breakfast." Luellen cast a fond glance at her friend as she placed the biscuits in a bowl, setting two aside. She pushed the door open with her shoulder and entered the dining room.

An older couple and a stubble-faced man sat at the long table, busy helping themselves to browned sausages and fried eggs. She placed the bowl next to a dish of butter. "Anything else you need, just give me a call."

The guests nodded acknowledgment and continued with their meal. Luellen blinked. Over the summer, she'd forgotten what it felt like to be invisible when she served diners. At least invisible was better than being singled out for ribald attention.

She ducked into the kitchen, sitting beside Belle. "We should have a few minutes to ourselves while they finish eating." She reached for the package, feeling softness under the paper wrapping. "You didn't have to bring me a gift. Seeing you again is a gift in itself."

Belle squeezed her arm. "I've waited all summer for this day."

She dropped a kiss on David's head. "I could hardly wait to see this little fellow. He's adorable—so chubby and healthy-looking."

"He's a wonder and a blessing." Luellen dropped her gaze, thinking ahead to the rest of the day.

"What's wrong?"

"I don't know how I'm going to bring myself to leave him during classes."

"Have you made arrangements already?"

"Mrs. Hawks did. I'm going to take David to a woman named Leah Holcomb after I clean up here. She lives across the street."

"I'll go with you." Belle tapped the package. "Now open your present."

Luellen untied the red cord holding the paper together and lifted out the contents. "A knitted sacque for David. How perfect." She stroked the soft blue wool, admiring the yellow embroidery on the ribbon trim, then slipped the garment on her son to measure the size. It fell to his diapered bottom. "Just right. This will keep him warm during the winter." She leaned over and kissed Belle on the cheek.

Belle looked pleased. "I made it myself—with Mother's help. This is the first time I ever knitted anything." She pointed to the rows of stitches. "They're a little close together. I had trouble holding the needles—I kept tugging the yarn, like making knots."

"Just the fact that you wanted to do this for me means everything. I'll treasure it."

The door between the kitchen and dining room opened. The stubble-faced man stuck his head into the room. "Where's Mrs. Hawks this morning? We're waiting for coffee in here."

Luellen jumped to her feet, startling David to tears. She plunked him in Belle's lap. "Mrs. Hawks is busy elsewhere. I'll be seeing to your breakfast from now on." She lifted the coffee server from the back of the stove.

"Well, hope you're not always this slow—and keep that baby quiet, can't you?"

Luellen circled the table pouring coffee, all the while listening to David howl. What would she do when Belle wasn't here to help?

◯

Luellen tugged David's cap over his curls as she and Belle crossed the street in front of Mrs. Hawks's house. Her landlady had been emphatic when she told Luellen to go to the rear entrance of the elaborate brick home where Leah Holcomb worked as a hired companion, so they walked past the carriage building and climbed narrow steps to the door. She supposed Leah Holcomb to be related to the owner of the house, sent away when her pregnancy became an embarrassment to her family.

"Makes me feel like a delivery boy," Belle whispered when Luellen knocked.

"Me too. Wonder what—"

The door opened and a tall black woman wearing an immaculate white apron peered out at them. As soon as she noticed David, a smile spread across her face. "You must be Luellen McGarvie. We're expecting you."

"I'm here to see Leah Holcomb. Could you please tell her I'm here?"

The smile disappeared from the woman's face. "I'm Leah." Her voice was cold. She stepped aside. "Come in."

Luellen tried to disguise her astonishment. Slavery was outlawed in Illinois. In her limited travels through Allenwood, she'd not seen another black person. "You're indentured?"

Leah's eyes narrowed. "I was born in Middletown, to free parents. That makes me indentured to nobody."

"What are you doing here?"

Belle poked her in the side.

"I mean . . ." She tried to smile. "How did you come to Allenwood?"

"Does it matter? Do you need a nurse for that baby or not?" Her expression didn't soften.

"Yes. I do." Luellen couldn't see a way out of the hole she'd dug for herself. "Mrs. Hawks said you have a daughter just a couple of months older than David."

"She's correct. She very kindly provided a home for me until Frannie was born. My skin color didn't seem to bother her."

"It doesn't bother me, either. I was just surprised, is all."

Leah ignored her remark and held out her arms. "May I hold your son? We'll see if he's happy with me." She pointed to chairs grouped around a scrubbed table. "You and your friend can sit if you wish."

Luellen handed David to her, watching to see how he'd react. He settled into Leah's arms and grabbed for one of her green glass earrings.

The woman chuckled. "That's the first thing Frannie does too. Loves the sparkle."

Luellen glanced around the well-lit kitchen, thankful she didn't have to clean the embossed designs covering the sides of the shining cookstove. They reminded her of the pressed glass her mother owned. A generous-sized worktable stood under a window and shelves stacked with plates and bowls lined the facing wall.

"Where is your daughter?"

"In here. I'll show you. This is where David will be sleeping while you're at the Normal School."

She and Belle followed Leah into a room off one side of the kitchen. A crib was stationed opposite a single bed, and a bright red and yellow braided rug bloomed in the center of the floor.

Leah held a finger to her lips. "She just fell asleep," she whispered.

Frannie lay on her stomach, her face turned to one side, a fist against her mouth. Her skin was several shades lighter than her mother's—pecan colored, Luellen thought. "She's beautiful."

"She is, isn't she?" Leah's voice softened as she looked at her daughter. Turning businesslike again, she said, "Let's go back to the kitchen and you can tell me when you'll bring David each day. Then we'll set a fee."

"I was hoping you could keep him for an hour or so now, while I go register at the school. If it's not too much trouble."

"Today?" Leah shot a glance toward a doorway that Luellen assumed led to the rest of the house. "Mrs. Garmon—" She cleared her throat. "All right. What time do you think you'll return?"

"She doesn't like me," Luellen blurted as she and Belle walked toward the school.

"Well, you treated her like a servant when she opened the door."

"I didn't mean to. I was just taken aback for a moment."

"I must confess, I was surprised too. Even if she's free, she's not safe in Illinois."

Luellen nodded, remembering the slave woman who had been her mother's friend in Missouri when Luellen was a child. Betsy had escaped to Canada. From the few letters they'd received over the years, she knew Betsy and her husband Reuben had settled on a small farm in a community called Buxton. Why would Leah remain in an area where slave catchers could claim a black person as a runaway, born free or not?

Clouds bunched overhead, throwing shadows across maple leaves that littered the walkway. A pulse ticked in Luellen's throat. So much had changed since she'd registered last year. Where did her earlier plans fit into her altered life? The campus buildings rose ahead of them, gray in the subdued light. Her steps slowed.

When they approached the intersection between the main building and the Ladies Hall, Belle stopped and squeezed Luellen's hand. "I pray all goes well when you meet with Dr. Alexander. I don't think it's a bit unreasonable for you to ask to take the algebra examination again."

Luellen hugged her. "Thank you. I spent all last year asking him to make exceptions. I dread beginning this term the same way."

"Come and see me after you've talked to him—I want to know what he said. I'll wait in the parlor."

Luellen glanced at the Ladies Hall. "Is Mrs. Bledsoe matron again this year?"

"Indeed she is. In all her glory, I might add." Belle giggled. "I know she'll be thrilled to see you."

In spite of her worries, Luellen laughed. "No doubt."

She waited a moment while Belle walked away, then climbed the steps of Allenwood Hall. *The highest object of education must be that of living a life in accordance with God's will,* the bronze plaque set into the entry wall reminded her.

Luellen took a deep breath. However Dr. Alexander responded, she'd try to remember those words.

When she reached the registrar's office, Mr. Price sprang to his feet. "Miss . . . er, Mrs. . . . ." He coughed. "This is a surprise. I didn't think you'd be back."

She ignored his stammers. "Is Dr. Alexander in?"

"Yes, but—"

"Thank you." She brushed past him and entered the registrar's office. The clutter looked unchanged since the previous spring. An open ledger rested on a corner of his desk, surrounded by stacks of papers. Beside his chair a tower of books listed toward the floor.

Dr. Alexander glanced up. His jaw dropped when he recognized her. "Miss McGarvie."

"I'm here to register for the second-year term." She opened her reticule, closing her fingers around a ten-dollar gold piece.

"Correct me if I'm wrong, but I seem to recall you failed the final examination in algebra." He shook his head. "You're not qualified to begin senior studies." He rose and stepped toward the door.

She moved in front of him. "I was extremely ill at the time. If you'll permit me, I'd like to take the examination again before classes begin." She clutched the gold coin.

One corner of his mouth turned up. "Didn't you have a similar request last September? I'll say this for you, you're one persistent young lady."

Luellen relaxed. Once he smiled, he was on the way to giving in. "So, I have your permission? You'll schedule the examination?"

"Be here at seven on Monday morning. Mrs. Hale will meet you in the testing room."

Her hopes deflated. "I can't. I'm working in a boardinghouse—it's my job to serve breakfast to the guests. Could I do it later?"

"If you want to take the examination, you'll be here at seven. And Miss McGarvie—"

"Yes?"

"This is the last time. Don't ask me to make any more exceptions."

An hour later, Luellen knocked on the back door of Mrs. Garmon's house. Leah answered, holding David with one arm. Tears streaked his face.

"He just woke up," Leah said. "He's frightened. He doesn't know where he is." Her tone accused.

Luellen took David in her arms, guilt racing through her. "Mama's here." She kissed his damp cheeks. Her poor baby. He'd gone from the security of her parents' home to being jostled on a train and carried from one bed to another in the course of a little over twenty-four hours. No wonder he was upset.

"Thank you for taking him on such short notice."

"You're welcome. After this, I'd appreciate more warning. Mrs. Garmon isn't the most pleasant person when her schedule is upset."

"It won't happen again." Luellen turned to leave, then stopped, remembering. "May I bring him over before seven on Monday?"

Leah frowned. "Seven? That's smack in the middle of break-fast. Mrs. Hawks said you wouldn't be ready mornings 'til after eight."

Tension crawled across the back of Luellen's neck. "Yes, after eight. Every weekday." She injected apology into her voice. "It's just this Monday that he'll be here early. Please. I need to take an examination."

"All right." Leah tilted her head, eyebrows raised. "As long as you don't make a habit of early mornings."

How could she? Leah wasn't the only one who had breakfast to serve. Luellen mumbled thanks and marched across the street. There must be someone else in town who could help with David. She'd ask Mrs. Hawks.

The landlady rested her hands on her hips and frowned. "Why would you want someone else? You're blessed to have Leah close by. Allenwood's not exactly spilling over with women willing to nurse another woman's child."

Luellen paced the kitchen, jiggling David in her arms. She

lifted her voice to be heard over his cries. "She doesn't like me. I'm afraid she'll take her feelings out on David."

"My word. Aren't you letting your imagination run away with you?" She fitted a silver thimble over her finger and lifted a napkin from her mending basket. With expert precision, her veined hands worked a needle through a rip in one corner of the fabric.

"It's not my imagination. You should have heard how she spoke to me."

"I'm not talking about whether or not she likes you—although I wonder why she was hostile. She's a dear girl." The needle flashed in the light that spilled through the open rear door. "I mean your imagining that Leah would be unkind to David. I know her. I'd trust her with my own flesh and blood if the need arose. As far as whether she likes you or not, that's up to you, isn't it?"

Shamed, Luellen sat. David stopped wailing and relaxed against her, one hand clutching her sleeve, his mouth soft on her neck. She hugged him close, loving the sensation of his curls against her cheek. What Mrs. Hawks said made sense. Somehow she'd have to overcome her unfortunate first meeting with Leah. She had no choice at the moment.

Late that evening, Luellen lay in bed listening to her baby's steady breathing. Tired as she was, her mind wouldn't settle down to sleep. David. Monday's examination. Classes. She swung her feet to the floor and padded over to the bureau where she kept her writing materials.

Once in the kitchen, she laid several sheets of paper on the table, along with a pen and bottle of ink. The stove ticked as the fire retreated to glowing coals. Luellen lowered the lamp on its chain and touched a lucifer to the wick. Yellow light flared over the work surface. She sank into a chair, her hair falling over her shoulders.

*Dear Ward,*

She paused. Should she burden him with her discouragement, or spin a tale of a successful transition back to Allenwood? Luellen dipped the pen and wrote.

# 26

Ward stood at the north border of the post, his mind on the letter he'd received from Luellen. She was having as much trouble as he adjusting to an altered life. How could he encourage her when he found each day a struggle?

Footsteps crackled in the dry grass. He pivoted, wary.

"Didn't expect to find you here." Sergeant Grover's face stretched in a thin-lipped grimace. "Thought this was the last place you'd want to visit."

"Just out for a walk."

"Don't look like it to me, sir. I been watching you for a spell. You ain't moved a twitch."

Cicadas chirred in the clearing outside the north gate. The sumac wore late-summer burgundy leaves and red fruit clusters. When he squinted, Ward imagined the ragged hole his bullet had torn through the dense shrubs. He thrust out his jaw. "If you've got nothing better to do than follow me around, I can assign you some duties."

"No, sir. I don't need no more duties."

"Then I suggest you get back to work."

"Yes, sir. But first I got something to say."

Ward folded his arms across his chest. "You have one minute, Sergeant."

The gangly soldier stepped closer. He held his hands open at his sides. "I want to thank you for not reporting me to Captain Block. I'd of been discharged too, and I need the Army pay. There's no work back home."

"No need for thanks. The sooner this whole affair is forgotten, the better."

"Yes, sir." Grover saluted. "For an officer, you're all right. I don't care what nobody says." He turned and ambled back toward the post.

Ward tracked his retreat, asking himself the question he'd asked since he returned to Jefferson Barracks. What drew him out here every day?

He squared his shoulders, wincing when his left side twinged. Campion's discharge tormented him. All his what-ifs couldn't change the outcome of that March morning. He tried to imagine how he'd feel, as a West Point graduate, if he were forced to leave the Army. Wherever he went, the stigma would follow.

Ward carried his own stigma—not that of being forced to leave the Army, but of being allowed to stay. He lifted his chin. So be it. He strode across the parade ground and entered a closed-off area on the first floor of the officers' quarters. He'd rather be on a survey assignment, not stuck in an airless classroom.

Feet shuffled as a dozen noncommissioned officers straightened in their chairs.

"Gentlemen." Ward drew a copy of Mahan's *Out-Post* from the bookshelf behind his desk. "I trust you've familiarized yourselves with today's passage."

"Over and over, sir," said one of the students. "Do you really think Napoleon has anything to teach us?" His voice was one note below insolent.

"You're soldiers. You never know when you may be called upon to lead in battle. My job is to relay tactics I learned at the Academy."

The men watched him, expressions cold. From the back of the room, he heard a loud whisper. "Tactics must be how he got Lieutenant Campion discharged."

Ward drew himself up to his full height. "I'm sorry, Sergeant. I didn't hear you. Would you mind repeating your remark?"

The man stood, hooded eyes defiant. "It ain't worth repeating, sir. A mere observation."

"Observation means something you've seen." Ward walked around his desk and glared at the soldier. "Tell us what you've *seen* regarding the lieutenant's untimely departure from the post." He fought to keep anger from his voice.

The sergeant's eyes shifted away from Ward's face. "I never saw nothing, sir."

"How about the rest of you? Anything to contribute to the discussion?"

The wall clock ticked in the silence.

"I'm only going to say this once." Ward planted his feet apart and stood with hands clasped behind his back. His voice boomed over the men. "Lieutenant Campion got himself discharged for breaking several Army regulations. I'm sorry it happened. From this day on, I don't want to hear another word about him, either in my classroom or on the field. Is that understood?"

Heads bobbed.

He cupped a hand behind his ear. "I can't hear you."

"Yes, sir!"

"Good. Class dismissed. Be back here tomorrow ready to work."

After the men left, Ward tucked his copy of *Out-Post* under his arm and left the room. Angry with himself for losing his temper, he stalked toward the stairway leading to the second floor. His image of a perfect officer was one who remained calm in all circumstances. He shook his head. *You've got a ways to go, Calder.*

When he passed the mail slots in the hallway, he noticed an envelope in his box. His mood lifted. Another letter from Luellen so soon would be a bright spot in a brutal day.

He plucked the message from the slot and stared at the envelope, disappointed. Standing in front of the boxes, he read a summons to Block's office for late that afternoon. He shook his head. It wasn't possible that news of his classroom outburst had reached headquarters already. What did the captain want?

The door to the headquarters building opened and a dark-haired woman emerged, carrying an infant. Sunlight glinted off the gold frames of her glasses.

Ward held his breath. Could Luellen have come all this way to seek him out? He stood bolted in place, unprepared for the surge of joy that filled him. That's why Block had summoned him—to tell him he had a visitor.

The woman hurried in his direction on the stone pathway. Ward swept his hat from his head and felt a grin spread across his face. "Lu—"

When she was twenty feet away, he realized she was a stranger, probably the wife of one of the other officers. She looked at him curiously as she passed.

"Ma'am." He clapped his hat on, hoping his embarrassment wasn't obvious. Head down, he walked to the headquarters entrance, berating himself all the way. What was the matter with him? He couldn't allow himself to become attached to Luellen McGarvie. Her plans didn't include marriage and neither did his.

Once inside the stale-smelling building, Ward turned down

the corridor leading to the commander's office. He drew himself to full attention when he entered.

Captain Block swiveled around in his chair. "At ease, Lieutenant. Have a seat."

"Thank you, sir." Ward sat, resting his hat on his lap.

"You've had a rough few months since you returned. How's the shoulder?"

"Better, thank you."

"And your dealings with the men on the post? I understand there's been some resistance to your presence here."

Sweat prickled his forehead. "I'm working to overcome that, sir."

The captain nodded, shuffling through a stack of papers on the corner of his desk. Finding the one he wanted, he laid the sheet in front of him. "Feel like you could handle yourself on a plains assignment?"

"Another survey? I look forward to the opportunity."

"Not a survey this time." He turned the paper around and Ward saw it was a map. Captain Block put his thick index finger on a point near the center of the page, and traced a line from left to right. "You're looking at the Smoky Hill Trail in Kansas Territory. Six years ago the Army established Fort Hook here." He indicated a circle drawn on the map.

Ward waited. The captain disliked being rushed.

"Your orders arrived this morning."

His eyebrows shot up. "Orders, sir?"

"You're being transferred to Fort Hook—as post commander."

Ward's mouth dropped open. "I'm only a lieutenant."

"Not any longer. I recommended you for a captaincy." Captain Block lifted an envelope from his desk. "Here's the approval."

Stunned, Ward leaned back in his chair.

The captain's eyes crinkled at the corners. "You're an outstanding soldier, Calder. Dedicated. Reliable. This post will suit you."

"Sir, after everything that's happened, how could you possibly—"

"You know how slow the Army can be. I sent my recommendation right after the first of the year. What occurred this spring has no bearing on these orders." He leaned back in his chair, hands braced against the edge of the desktop. "You're not turning them down, are you?"

"No, sir. Thank you, sir." He straightened his shoulders. "When am I to leave?"

"You're to report on New Year's Day, so you've got three months to prepare."

Swamped by conflicting thoughts, Ward left the commander's office and walked toward the officers' quarters. He wished his father had lived to see this moment. His ambitions for Ward were embodied in the designation of post commander.

Ward could picture his father's excitement upon hearing the news—sightless eyes filled with tears, face wreathed in a broad smile. He could almost feel the strong arms pounding his back.

"You're the reason I've worked so hard," he said to the memory. "This is for you."

A passing soldier saluted, looking puzzled, and Ward realized he'd spoken aloud. He returned the salute, slowing his steps as the impact of the promotion washed over him. Kansas Territory. Instead of one long day's train ride, he'd be nearly a week away from Beldon Grove. No railroads. Barely a trail in places. Mail service unreliable.

How would he tell Luellen? Would she care?

Luellen woke at the first suggestion of daybreak on Monday. She tiptoed to the kitchen and fed wood into the cookstove, then broke eggs into a large bowl. A pan of ham custard should satisfy the boarders' breakfast needs for this one morning. Mrs. Hawks hadn't been pleased at the idea of Luellen departing early, so she wanted to leave nothing undone prior to taking David to Leah.

She gave a mental shiver at the idea of facing an unhappy Leah on the heels of leaving an equally unhappy Mrs. Hawks. After this morning's examination, the days should smooth out.

Once Luellen had assembled the minced ham, torn bread, and eggs, she slid the combined breakfast in the oven to bake. The clock on the wall ticked toward six.

She hurried into her bedroom. David lay on his back in the crib, arms flung outward, eyes closed. Luellen stroked his hair off his forehead. He stirred, smiling and lifting his arms when he saw her.

Luellen swung him from the crib, nuzzling his soft cheeks. After changing his diaper and slipping a fresh gown over his head, she sat to nurse him.

A few minutes later, Mrs. Hawks stopped by the open door. "Are you minding the clock? Don't you have to be at the school by seven?"

"What time is it?" She held David at her shoulder, patting his back.

"Going on six thirty."

"Oh, mercy." Luellen scrambled to her feet, grabbing her portfolio and David's blanket on her way out.

The sun hovered below the horizon, its glow forming a crescent in the early morning haze. She sprinted across the street and pounded up the back steps of Mrs. Garmon's house. The fragrance of baked apples drifted toward her when Leah responded to her knock. She thrust David into the other woman's waiting arms, thanked her, and dashed down the steps.

"When will you be back?" Leah called.

Luellen paused. "Dinnertime. I'll have almost an hour—that is if I pass this examination. Otherwise—" She shook her head. "Much sooner than that."

Leah's impassive expression didn't change. "Good luck." The words sounded perfunctory.

"Thank you." She matched Leah's tone.

She entered the administration building as the chapel bell tolled seven. Mrs. Hale had her hand on the latch preparatory to closing the door of the testing room when Luellen slipped inside. Several students sat at the tables, men on the right, women on the left. She didn't recognize anyone she knew. So she wasn't the only person asking for favors.

She took a seat and waited while the proctor sorted through papers on her desk, evidently seeking the appropriate examination for each student. She dropped a page covered with letters and symbols in front of Luellen. "You have an hour to complete these equations. Use the extra sheet to show your work." She walked among the other tables, leaving pages along with instructions.

Luellen filled her lungs, exhaled slowly, and lifted her pencil. Weeks of study. An hour to get everything on paper. She shoved her fingers into the hair at her temples and focused on the first set.

Pencils scratched and chairs creaked as students bent over their work. Mrs. Hale padded up and down the aisle, ready to pounce on anyone caught cheating.

The end of the hour came all too soon. The proctor swept through the room gathering examinations. With reluctance, Luellen surrendered her papers. She needed more time to review her answers.

"Wait here, please, while I grade your work," Mrs. Hale said to the group at large. "I have schedules for each of you if you pass."

Luellen leaned back in her chair and picked at a snag on one fingernail. The muscles in her shoulders twitched. She'd gambled by returning to Allenwood with no assurance that she'd be admitted for the final term.

What if she lost?

Luellen climbed the back steps of Mrs. Garmon's house and knocked.

No response.

She knocked again, louder this time.

After a long moment the door opened and a querulous voice asked, "Who are you?"

Luellen's gaze dropped to a tiny woman leaning on a cane. Her white hair was arranged in an elaborate coiffure and glittering rings encrusted the bent fingers. Her mouth turned down at the corners.

"I'm Luellen McGarvie. Leah Holcomb is caring for my son." Her voice faltered. "Where is she?"

"If I knew that, I wouldn't be answering the door now, would I?"

Luellen's heart lurched. "She's not here?"

"Of course she's not here. Are you deaf? I just said I didn't know where she was."

She sagged against the porch railing. "But I thought she worked here. Are you Mrs. Garmon?"

"She does and I am. But she's free to come and go when I have no tasks for her—as long as my meals are served on time." The woman squinted up at Luellen, her face a map of wrinkles. "I expect she'll be along."

"She's got my son. I can't just sit."

"Up to you. You can run all over town, or you can wait here 'til she comes back. Makes no difference to me." She turned from the doorway and waved her free hand in the direction of the kitchen table. "Have a chair. I'm going back to my reading, and I won't welcome another interruption."

Dry-mouthed, Luellen shook her head. "I'd rather stay outside and watch the street."

"As you please." Mrs. Garmon headed for the connecting door, her black taffeta skirt brushing the floor behind her.

After she disappeared, Luellen reconsidered and stepped inside. Maybe Leah decided to nap while the children slept and didn't hear her knock.

She tiptoed to the doorway of the back room. No Leah. The crib stood empty. How far could the woman go carrying two babies? And why would she leave? Luellen retreated to the porch and tried to rein in her racing thoughts. First she'd check the boardwalk along College Avenue. Perhaps Leah had a friend nearby and had gone for a visit.

Dry leaves shattered beneath her boots as she retraced her steps to the street. Near the campus she saw a group of people walking in the direction of the chapel. At the other end of the block, a man wearing a straw hat raked leaves into a pile. A current of autumn flowed beneath the sun's warmth, chilling her. *Where's my son?*

She heard creaking behind the house and spun around. Leah came into view, pulling a long-handled wagon.

Luellen flew toward the alley, the pounding of her heart choking her. "David?"

"He's right here." Leah stopped the wagon next to the carriage house and pointed at the two babies, pillowed together inside the rough wooden conveyance.

"Praise God." Luellen's skirts billowed as she knelt next to her son. A bonneted Frannie nestled next to him. She touched David's cheek with a fingertip and was rewarded with a smile.

She faced Leah. "I was frightened out of my wits when I found you gone. You should have told me—"

"You're early. As you can see, I'm here in plenty of time to prepare Mrs. Garmon's dinner." Leah gestured toward the sky. "It's good for babies to be in the sunshine. I took them for a walk."

"In an *alley*?"

"D'you think I'd dare parade down College Avenue? What if someone decided to report me as a runaway slave?" She lifted Frannie and held her with one arm. "Soon's I save the money, we're going to Canada. Meantime, I get fresh air only when it's safe to be out."

The mystery of Leah spun through Luellen's brain. If she was afraid to be seen on the street, how did she expect to travel to Canada?

She pushed herself to her feet. "How will you get there?"

Leah studied her for a moment, distrust in her eyes. "You don't need to know." She strode toward the house, talking over her shoulder as she went. "Bring the boy with you and come in. I need to cook dinner."

Luellen scooped David from the wagon and trotted after her. What would she have to do to get into Leah's good graces? The woman took offense at everything she said. She sighed, feeling David's hungry mouth pressing on her skin. "You're ready for dinner, aren't you?" she whispered.

When she entered the kitchen, Leah had propped Frannie in a tall armchair. "You want to sit a spell and feed the boy, go ahead." She opened the oven and removed a covered roasting pan.

"His name's David."

"What?"

"You keep calling him 'the boy.' His name's David."

Leah raised an eyebrow. "You came back early because you failed that test, didn't you? That why you're so snippy?" A cloud of fragrant steam billowed out when she raised the lid of the roaster. Luellen bit back a caustic retort. If they continued bickering, they'd never be friends. "I'm sorry. I spoke more sharply than I intended." She drew a chair away from the table. "I appreciate your offer."

"Well. Make yourself comfortable then." She speared a browned chunk of meat onto a platter and bestowed a half-smile on Luellen. "After I serve Mrs. Garmon, would you like a slice of this beef?"

"Yes, please."

Leah folded her arms across her middle. "Now tell me about the test. What happened?"

"I passed—barely. My score was seventy-nine percent." Humbled, she shifted her gaze to the floor.

"That's good enough to be enrolled, isn't it?"

"Yes."

"Then why the hangdog face?"

Luellen tightened her jaw. "I studied hard. I wanted to prove to Dr. Alexander—"

"You know him?" Leah caught her lower lip between her teeth.

"He's the registrar. He's the one who says whether I stay or go."

Leah's eyes narrowed. "He's good at telling folks to go. Him and—" She turned her back and slashed a knife into the roast. "You mind yourself over there. Things isn't always what they seem."

# 27

On her way to the campus, Luellen pondered Leah's words. Who else did she refer to in her warning? She filed the question away in her mind for later.

Ahead, clusters of students streamed toward classrooms. By squinting, she could discern Alma Guthrie on the steps of the Model School and hurried toward her.

"Welcome back." Alma's eyes shone. "As soon as class is over, I want to hear all about your baby. Mother says he's a wonder."

"He's a joy, no doubt about it." Luellen followed the instructor into the classroom, noticing new faces filling some of the desks.

To her surprise, Belle stood next to the blackboard. She waggled her fingers in greeting.

"Did I mistake my assignment?" Luellen whispered. She dug in her reticule for the schedule she'd been handed when she left the examination room.

Alma laid a hand on her arm. "Not at all. We're doubling up our second-year student teachers to allow each of you plenty of practice time. You'll alternate sessions. Miss Brownlee will teach arithmetic to the older children while you start the first-year pupils on reading. They're waiting for you there on the right." She rubbed her hands together. "It's going to be a busy term. All the Model School classes are full."

Luellen glanced around the room, seeking familiar faces of pupils she'd taught last year. Elizabeth and Cassie shared a desk in the third row. From his seat farther back, Jackie faced her with a challenging expression. But someone was missing.

"Where's Joshua?"

"His father lost his job, so he moved the family to Chicago. I heard he's working for one of the railroad lines."

Luellen tensed. She could keep Brendan from her thoughts most of the time, but the mention of Chicago unlocked a door to memories. Would she ever forgive herself for her impulsive leap into marriage? The worries she faced today wouldn't exist if only she'd waited.

Belle's sharp voice penetrated Luellen's self-reproach. "I've explained this several times. Aren't you paying attention?"

The object of her scolding, a girl near the rear of the classroom, sat with a flushed face, eyes shiny with tears.

Luellen stared at her friend. It wasn't like Belle to be unkind, particularly to a child. Alma hustled toward them, settling her hand on the girl's shoulder. "Martha, why don't you work on your penmanship for now? You can study arithmetic tonight at home." Sniffling, Martha reached for her slate pencil and complied.

Alma turned to Belle. "May I have a word?" She pointed toward the cloakroom. To Luellen she said, "Please keep the children occupied for a few minutes."

Luellen nodded, wishing she could accompany Belle for moral support. Instead, she strode to the front of the classroom, nerves jumping. First day of the term, and Alma left her in charge. What if she couldn't occupy the students' interest? A copy of *Robert Merry's Museum* lay on one corner of the desk. She riffled through the pages of the children's magazine until she found a story she thought they'd all enjoy. "Have you heard 'A Very Odd Grandfather'?"

The children shook their heads, some of them grinning with anticipation. She threw a glance toward the cloakroom door, then folded the magazine open and began to read. She'd reached the conclusion of the little piece by the time Alma returned—without Belle.

The instructor joined her at the front of the room. "You start with the new students, as we discussed. I'll handle Miss Brownlee's assignment."

What happened to Belle? Much as she'd like to ask, there wasn't time. Luellen selected a first reader from the shelf and crossed to the youngest pupils. "Today we'll start with our letters. Who knows the alphabet?"

Of the half-dozen children, four raised their hands.

"Excellent. Let me hear you recite." While she listened, Luellen peeked out a window hoping to glimpse Belle across the street, but couldn't see her. Had she returned to the Ladies Hall? Or been sent to the registrar's office?

When time came to dismiss classes, Luellen handed in her notes and hurried out the door. She wished she could find Belle to ask what happened in the cloakroom, but didn't dare return to the boardinghouse too late to cook supper.

She never expected to miss living in the Ladies Hall. Right now she did. Belle needed her friendship, and she wasn't there to provide a listening ear.

Luellen turned in front of Mrs. Garmon's house and trotted up the graveled drive to the kitchen entrance. The door opened in midknock, Leah's floury hand clasping the knob. A mound of dough rested on the worktable under the window. "After this, just come on in," she said, her voice curt. "I can't be stopping what I'm doing all the time to open the door."

Luellen recoiled. What happened to the armistice they'd reached earlier in the day? She forced a smile. "All right. Thank you."

Leah returned to her task while Luellen stood in the kitchen wondering how best to ask about David without drawing another sharp remark. Since she didn't see either baby, and didn't hear crying, she assumed they were asleep. A long moment passed. Muscles in Leah's forearms knotted and released as she worked the dough.

"I'll go get David now," Luellen said, taking a tentative step toward the bedroom.

"Try not to wake Frannie. I just got 'em both to sleep a few minutes ago." Leah slapped the pile of dough into a flat rectangle, the sound popping across the room. "Can't get nothing done when the babies cry. One gets the other started."

"I'll be careful."

Once in the bedroom, she paused a moment at the sight of the two infants in the crib, both with dark curls plastered to sweaty heads. Slipping her hands under David's body, she lifted him to her, inhaling his sweet baby smell. He nestled close.

Frannie's eyes opened when the crib jiggled. Seeing Luellen, she scrunched up her face and howled.

"Shh." Luellen stroked the child's head.

Frannie wailed louder.

Footsteps pounded from the kitchen and Leah appeared in the doorway, a scowl across her brow. "This isn't going to work."

"It has to. Please. Give us a few more days. They'll get used to each other."

Leah sniffed. "I'll try it through Friday." She hoisted Frannie to her shoulder. "That way you can pay me for a full week."

After the supper dishes had been stored away, Luellen bent over her *Science of Education* textbook, but her thoughts tugged her back to the scene with Leah. Even if she could hire another nurse, how likely was it she'd find one close to the school? Today's ten-minute walk each way demonstrated how little time she'd have with David during the noon recess. Any farther away and she wouldn't be able to see him from morning until late afternoon.

She stood and paced the kitchen. Somehow, she'd just have to make it work.

*Tap, tap, tap. Tap tap.*

Luellen flung open the door. Lantern glow gilded Belle's face. "I'm so glad to see you!"

"Me too." Belle stepped into the room. "I miss having you next door."

Luellen peered into the dusk before closing the door. "I hope you didn't walk here. It's getting dark."

"I rode the omnibus. I'll stay until he comes round again." She looked at the books and papers on the tabletop. "*Science of Education.* I tried studying tonight, but . . ." Slumping into a chair, Belle rested her face in her hands. "I feel like such a failure."

"One afternoon doesn't make you a failure." Luellen slipped an arm around Belle's shoulders. "What happened when you left the class?"

"Mrs. Guthrie said I needed to go to the Ladies Hall and rest. She thought I was just tired."

"You weren't?"

Belle fixed round blue eyes on Luellen. A shimmer of tears reflected on their surface. "If teaching means I can't marry, I'm not sure I want to be a teacher anymore."

"Marriage is off in the future somewhere."

"No, it isn't. Franklin and I have been corresponding since I went home with you in May." Belle drew a folded piece of paper from her pocket, her cheeks pink. "This letter was in my postbox today. He's planning to come to Springfield after the first of the year to meet my parents. He's going to ask my father for my hand." Her face brightened.

Luellen stared, trying to make sense of the words. Franklin married? Whenever she pictured her brother, he was riding a horse across open grassland, wearing buckskins and moccasins. What would he do with a wife?

As the silence between them lengthened, Belle's smile faded. "I was afraid of this. You don't want him to marry me."

"Oh Belle, I can't imagine anything better than having you as part of my family." She drew her friend into a tight embrace. "I'm just having trouble imagining Franklin settling down. He's been scouting for the Army so long, I guess I thought he'd always be out there on the prairie."

Belle's dimples reappeared. "He's going to look into finding work in Springfield during his stay. I'm sure my father will help him." She drew a deep breath. "Now do you see why I don't care if I become a teacher or not?"

"If you got that letter today, I know why you were distracted at the Model School." She faced her friend. "You can't quit. God forbid, what if something happens to your plans? Education is too important. Even if you don't use what we're learning here to teach in classrooms, think how well you'll be able to train your own children." She seized Belle's hands. "You'll regret your decision if you don't use this opportunity."

"You're making a speech."

"I'm sorry. I think you'd be the best wife in the world for

Franklin, but . . . things happen that we don't anticipate. Education is never wasted." Her pulse drummed in her throat. She had to make Belle understand.

"I hoped you'd be happy for us." Her friend moved toward the door.

"I'm overjoyed. Truly." She placed her hands on Belle's shoulders. "The thought of having you for a sister-in-law is a dream come true. I just don't want to see you leave in the middle of our training."

Belle ducked around her. "The omnibus will be here any moment." She stood on the porch framed in blackness, lamplight illuminating her over-bright eyes. "Good night."

When Luellen awoke the next morning, her eyes felt sanded. She'd tossed for hours worrying that Belle might make the same impulsive decision she'd made. Allenwood Normal School was one of the few institutions to admit women. Her friend couldn't toss away her golden opportunity for something as uncertain as marriage.

David rustled in his crib. Luellen tiptoed over and gathered him into her arms, covering his blanket-warmed face with kisses. Every moment of her struggle to care for him would be worth it when she received her certificate and could support the two of them on her own. If Alma could do it, so could she.

Once she cleaned up after the boarders' breakfast, she bundled David into his hooded cape and carried him across the street to Leah's. While she walked, she rehearsed what she'd say to calm yesterday afternoon's turbulent waters.

*I'm sorry I made Frannie cry.* No, that wouldn't do. *Could David maybe sleep somewhere else?* That was just silly. Still pondering, she opened the back door of Mrs. Garmon's house and entered the kitchen.

Leah turned toward her, smiling. "Glad you came back. I was afraid I ran you off with my bad temper." She took David from Luellen's arms. "It's just my way—I get upset and spread the gloom around. You'd best learn to ignore me when I get like that."

Luellen blinked. What could have upset her, stuck away as she was in the house all day?

Leah propelled her toward the door. "You run along. We'll see you at dinner, won't we, David?"

# 28

Luellen hastened toward the campus. She had enough time to stop at the Ladies Hall and see Belle before classes at the Model School. Last night she'd worried Belle would leave school without graduating—now she worried she'd been so forceful she'd alienated her. A long shadow spread before her on the walkway. She looked up, surprised. "Good morning, Mr. Price. You're out early. Are you going to town?"

He halted, eyes wide. "Miss . . . Mrs. . . . . I had no idea you lived in this direction."

She let the remark pass.

"Town?" He ran his finger around his collar. "Yes. I must be on my way." He tipped his hat and dashed past her, his boots thudding on the boardwalk.

Luellen watched him for a moment, her curiosity piqued. What was so important that he couldn't wait for the omnibus? She shook her head. Thankfully, it had nothing to do with her.

When she arrived at the Ladies Hall, she straightened her shoulders and sailed through the front door as though she had every right to be there. Sounds of cutlery clinking on dishes, along with the bland odor of boiled oats told her she'd arrived in time for the students' breakfast. The trick would be to catch Belle in the dining hall without encountering Mrs. Bledsoe. She balled her hands into fists, nails pressing into her moist palms, and stepped across the threshold.

A quick survey showed Belle sitting near the center of the room. Mrs. Bledsoe was nowhere to be seen. Luellen moved around crowded tables and slipped into a chair beside her friend. "I came to tell you again how happy I am about you and Franklin." She kept her voice low.

Belle studied her for a moment with red-rimmed eyes. She blinked, a smile glimmering at the corners of her mouth. "Really?"

Luellen slipped an arm around Belle's shoulders. "Really. I'm afraid I was much too forceful last evening."

"And I was too quick to take offense." She pushed her half-eaten bowl of oatmeal toward the center of the table. "I thought about what you said most of the night."

"What did you decide?"

"I'm going to write Franklin and see what he thinks."

Deflated, Luellen drew her arm away and rubbed the bridge of her nose. Franklin had paid little attention in school. She imagined he'd be no help in urging Belle to stay in Allenwood long enough to obtain her certificate.

"You may not receive a reply for a month or more. What will you do in the meantime?"

Belle's dimples showed. "'When in Rome, do as the Romans do.' As long as I'm here, I'll attend classes and Model School training."

Luellen did a quick mental calculation. By the time Belle received Franklin's letter, they'd be only a few weeks away from winter vacation. Maybe she could coax Belle to finish this semester.

Her neck prickled. She looked up to see Mrs. Bledsoe standing behind them, arms folded under her bosom.

"Miss McGarvie? I don't recall seeing your name on the list of students residing here. Visits are to be accomplished in the parlor, not during meals."

Luellen stood, her height placing her several inches above the matron's head. She looked down at the line of white scalp that parted the woman's graying hair. "That rule applies to male visitors." Out of the corner of her eye, she saw Belle conceal a smile with her napkin.

Mrs. Bledsoe's face reddened. "It applies where I say it applies. I will not have you upsetting my girls again this year."

The room grew silent.

Luellen had come to talk to her friend, not antagonize the matron. She took a deep breath and held it for a moment. "It won't happen again. My apologies."

Belle stood, taking her arm. "We must get to our class, Matron. Please excuse us."

Once they were out the door, Belle snickered. "She didn't know what to say when you apologized."

"I could hardly believe it myself. I wanted to yell at her." Adapting a casual tone, she said, "So, are you coming to the Model School with me?"

"For now."

❦

The kitchen door at Mrs. Garmon's house stood open to the warm fall afternoon. Luellen stepped inside, stopping at the sight of Leah slumped in a chair, weeping. Her hands covered her face.

Luellen hastened to the woman's side and laid a hand on her shoulder. "What's happened?"

Leah jumped at Luellen's touch, shrugging her hand away. "Land sakes. You scared me. Past noon already?" She swiped at her eyes with the corner of her apron. "I best finish Mrs. Garmon's meal or she'll be having a fit." From her swollen face it appeared she'd been crying for some time.

David and Frannie played on a blanket spread between the stove and worktable—David trying to catch his waving toes and Frannie gnawing on a wooden spoon. "The children are all right?"

Leah bristled. "Of course. I wouldn't let anything touch the babies." She stalked to the cookstove, poking at the contents of a steaming pot with a fork.

"Let me help. I'll feed David in a couple minutes."

"It's not your job to work in this kitchen."

"Maybe not, but you're upset. Together we can get this meal ready quicker than you can do it alone."

Tears filled Leah's eyes again. "Thank you. You're nicer than you seemed at first."

Embarrassed, Luellen eyed a simmering brisket surrounded by potatoes and carrots. "I can slice the meat if you want."

Leah nodded, stepping around the children's blanket and placing a gold-rimmed china plate on the worktable. "Put the lean pieces here. Mrs. Garmon won't eat fat. I'll get a tray ready."

Once the meal was served, Luellen took David into the bedroom and changed his diaper. She had seated herself at the table, her son at her breast, when Leah returned to the kitchen.

After fetching Frannie, she slid into a chair next to Luellen. "Hope you don't think I'm flighty. Most times I'm not a crier, but this morning—" She shook her head, her earrings swaying.

"I'm happy to listen if you want to tell me."

"You know about me going to Canada soon as I save the money."

Luellen nodded.

"A person was going to help me." Leah's expression hardened. "Well, now he's not. I should've known better. If I hadn't believed him in the first place, I'd never be stuck here in Allenwood." Her eyes flashed. "Twice I fell for his promises. Never again."

Luellen thought of her own limited funds. "If I can find a tutoring job, I'll increase what I pay you for David's care. It wouldn't be much but—"

Leah held up her hand. "You said you'd listen. I'm not asking for money. I just want to talk. It's so hard living away from my people. No one understands."

"I'm sorry. You're right. I can't understand." She shifted David to her shoulder, patting his back. "But I do know how difficult it is to care for a child without a father's help."

"Frannie has a father." Leah stalked across the room, her daughter under one arm, and flung cooking utensils into the washbasin. "Trouble is he's a lying, sneaking, good-for-nothing milksop."

While she walked back to school, Luellen couldn't help but smile at Leah's description of Frannie's father. Except for the milksop phrase, the woman had echoed her sentiments about Brendan. She kicked at a pile of fallen leaves. What made women so eager to believe a man's words?

Ward Calder walked across the parade ground toward the enlisted men's quarters, the cape on his overcoat billowing in the brisk November wind. A few red leaves clinging to oak trees fought a battle against approaching winter. When he entered the stone building, he found Franklin tipped back in a chair near the door.

"You took your time," he said, rising to his feet and stretching.

"Had a class to teach. I don't spend my days lolling around the post."

Franklin grinned. "I'm leaving in the morning. Captain Block's sending me to scout the Smoky Hill Trail one last time before you travel to Fort Hook. He wants to know about any new Indian camps."

"A camp you find in November could be gone by January."

"Maybe. Maybe not. Anyways, you need to be forewarned." Franklin tossed his coat over his shoulders. "Let's walk."

They started across the grounds toward the east gate. After several moments, Ward said, "I know you didn't ask to meet so you could tell me about a scouting mission. What's on your mind?"

"After Christmas I'm planning to ask Belle Brownlee's father for her hand." Franklin's black hair whipped across his face.

Ward stopped and stared. "Well, I'll be. You sure kept that quiet." He gave Franklin a teasing look. "Somehow I can't picture her camped on the prairie while you chase Indian trails."

"That's another thing. I'm going to find work in Springfield. No more trails."

Envy mixed with loneliness caught Ward by surprise. Without realizing it, he'd counted on having Franklin with him in Kansas. The thought of his friend settled in a cozy home with a bride left him bereft.

As post commander, private housing awaited him at Fort Hook. But achieving his career goals felt hollow with no one to share his accomplishments. His right hand stole inside his coat and touched Luellen's most recent letter, folded in his breast pocket. If Belle was willing to give up her education, perhaps Luellen had similar thoughts.

Aware Franklin was waiting for him to say something, Ward clapped him on the back. "Congratulations! How'd you convince her to quit school to marry you?"

Franklin shook his head, his expression gloomy. "We won't marry 'til after she graduates. I can thank my sister for that. When Belle told her our plans, Luellen went to work convincing her to finish." He bent down and picked up a woolly worm that inched across their path. It curled in his palm. "Going to be a cold winter." He placed the insect in the grass and watched while it bumped away. "I wanted to set a date before spring, but Lulie talked her out of it. Told Belle not to trust marriage to protect her."

Ward's hopes plummeted to his boots. So she didn't trust marriage. In a weak voice, he said, "Your sister has good reason to feel like that after what happened to her."

"She does. Belle doesn't. I don't have another wife tucked away."

They continued pacing toward the river. When they reached the gate, Ward turned. He wanted time alone to think. "Must be about suppertime. You ready to go back?"

Franklin caught his arm. "You still planning on spending your furlough in Beldon Grove?"

"Some of it. First I have to go to Pennsylvania to meet with the manager of my father's estate. Why do you ask?"

"Would you talk to Lulie? Convince her it wouldn't hurt Belle to leave school. What good will a teaching certificate do a married woman?"

Ward waved his hand in the direction of the post chapel. "There are exceptions. Captain Block's wife teaches soldiers' children there during the week." He trained his gaze on Franklin. "Besides, I doubt I could convince your sister of anything. She knows her own mind."

Luellen took a last look around Mrs. Hawks's kitchen.

"If you don't hurry, you'll miss your train." Mrs. Hawks cuddled David in her lap.

"I can't thank you enough for holding my room for me until

after vacation." She leaned over and kissed the older woman's cheek.

"Go on with you." Mrs. Hawks's eyes misted. "Leah promised to come over at least once every day. We'll manage."

Luellen knew the extra money Leah received would be a welcome addition to her travel savings. For a moment her mind lingered on the mystery surrounding the woman's presence in Allenwood. In the three months since she'd known her, she'd gotten no closer to learning about her past.

Mrs. Hawks gave her a slight push toward the front door. "If you carry the valise, I'll bring this little darling. The omnibus will be along any moment."

They stepped onto the porch, pausing next to Luellen's trunk. Mrs. Hawks adjusted the hood on David's cape to protect him from blowing rain. "Both of you take care," she said as the omnibus driver stopped at the curb. "I'll miss you."

"I'll miss you too."

Luellen ducked through the rain, climbing into the waiting conveyance. The interior reeked of wet wool. Steam covered the windows. As she'd hoped, Belle held a seat near the front. Luellen made her way down the aisle past passengers clinging to drippy umbrellas and damp parcels.

Sliding onto the seat beside Belle, she said, "I'm glad our trains are leaving near the same time. Gives us a few more minutes together."

"I'm glad too." Belle held out her arms and David reached for her. Grasping his sides, Belle stood him on her lap. "Much as I miss my family, I wish I were going to Beldon Grove."

"You're just in a hurry to see Franklin," Luellen teased.

"I confess I am. Letters are a pale substitute. But I'll miss you and this little fellow too. I'm used to being Auntie Belle." She bounced David up and down on her knees, eliciting a chortle of delight.

Luellen leaned against her. "The good thing is, David will always have his Auntie Belle."

When they reached the station, a locomotive was stopped at the platform taking on water. "Oh my. That must be my train." Belle jumped to her feet. "I need to hurry."

"You got time," said a passenger behind them. He cleared a space on the steamed glass and pointed. "The luggage cart ain't been loaded yet."

Passengers exited the omnibus in a slow shuffle as people stood and blocked the aisle. Luellen sensed Belle's anxiety. "Calm down," she whispered.

"I'm nervous all of a sudden. What if my parents don't like Franklin?"

Luellen raised an eyebrow. "Of course they'll like him. Everybody does." She followed Belle across the platform to the steps of the waiting passenger car.

Belle turned, hugging her. "Have a blessed Christmas." She grabbed the handrail and climbed into the car.

"Remember your promise to come back," Luellen called. "I'll see you in February."

# 29

Bundled against the December cold, Luellen sat close to Franklin in their father's carriage. Sleet pounded the iron railroad tracks. She shivered, huddling lower under the lap robe. "I don't see any sign of the train."

"You're the one who wanted to leave early. We could've stayed home for an extra ten minutes or so."

"What if Ward arrived in this miserable weather and no one was here to greet him?"

Franklin eyed her. "Sounds like you're sweet on him."

"I'm not. He's your friend. I'm just showing hospitality."

"Uh-huh." He released the brake. "I'll try to get us out of the wind." When he shook the reins, icy particles showered from the horse's back. After maneuvering the carriage closer to the station, he set the brake again and leaned back in the seat, tucking his gloved hands under his arms. "How long since you've heard from Ward?" His tone was one of idle curiosity.

"A letter arrived just before I came home, so it's been almost four weeks."

"Did he have anything to say about me and Belle?"

"No. Why would he? Now that I think of it, he didn't say much of note. Just that he was going to Pennsylvania and would visit here the week before Christmas." She poked him in the side. "Are you going to ask him to be your best man when you get married next summer?"

Franklin shot her a sidelong glance and then leaned forward, pointing. "The train. See the smoke?"

She jumped to her feet. "Let's go. He'll never see us way over here."

"You *are* sweet on him."

"I'm not. Stop saying that."

The locomotive clanged into the station, clouds of steam obscuring the blowing sleet. Luellen scrambled from the carriage, eager for a glimpse of the man she'd come to know through his letters over the past six months. Franklin's boots crunched on the ice as he hurried to her side. "Hold on to me. The platform's slick."

The cloak on Ward's dark blue overcoat billowed in the wind when he descended from the passenger car. He paused below the step and glanced around the station. Upon spotting them, he strode toward the shelter of the depot and seized Luellen's hands in his. "It's been a long time. You're even prettier than I remembered." His ruddy complexion radiated pleasure.

"Thank you." Warmth from his strong grip traveled up her arms. Flustered, she took a step backward. "We've been looking forward to your visit."

Franklin whistled and pointed at two black silk braids decorating the lower edge of Ward's sleeve. "I see your promotion's official."

"Promotion?" Luellen glanced between the two men.

Ward threw his shoulders back, his eyes seeking hers. "I'm a captain now." Pride tinged his response.

"Why didn't you mention the news in your letters?" Luellen heard the whine in her voice and bit the inside of her lip. He didn't owe her an explanation.

"I wanted to tell you in person. I swore Franklin here to secrecy."
Luellen wished she understood more about Army life. What
did it mean when an officer was promoted, aside from higher pay?
She forced an enthusiastic response. "Congratulations. I know
your career is important to you."

"It is, certainly, but—"

Franklin clapped him on the shoulder. "Tell her the rest."

"There's my trunk. Want to give me a hand?" Ward took Franklin's arm and steered him toward the baggage cart. Luellen studied
them as they crossed the platform. She couldn't hear their words,
but Ward was shaking his head, his lips moving rapidly.

Papa watched, a surprised expression on his face, as Ward and
Franklin struggled up the stairs with Ward's trunk between them.
"I thought he was only staying through Christmas," he murmured
to Luellen. "Looks like he's planning to settle here."

She nodded. "I wondered about that myself. We can't ask him.
That would be horribly impolite."

"Maybe I can find out without asking." Papa hastened across
the entryway and started up the stairs. After the first three steps,
he stopped, gasping for air.

Luellen dashed to his side. "Once a day up these stairs is plenty,
Papa. They'll be down in a few minutes." Anxious, she waited
while his breathing returned to normal.

He pressed a hand to his chest before responding. "No need
to hover over me. One fussy female in the house is plenty." His
smile took the sting from his words. "If you have to fuss, maybe
you better look in on David. I think I hear him." Papa turned on
the stairs, gripping the railing. "It's time for office hours, anyway."
He pecked her cheek. "See you at supper."

Luellen watched him walk toward the back door, her heart heavy. Every week he looked more worn. His thick blond hair had turned white over the past year. Now she noticed his shoulders hunched when he walked. Why wouldn't he go see Dr. Gordon?

Frustrated, she ascended the stairs to care for her son. Across the hallway, Ward and Franklin had shoved the trunk into a corner. They stood with their backs to her, gazing at the sleet rattling the window. Over David's increasing wails, she heard Ward say, "I'll wait for the right time. Maybe she won't—"

He turned and saw her, a smile crossing his face. "May I join you? I'm eager to see your son again."

"He's hungry." Luellen's cheeks warmed. "Can you wait?"

Ward's ruddy face turned redder. "Of course."

"We'll be in the kitchen," Franklin said. "Sampling Mama's baking."

Luellen eased the door shut after they left and lifted David from his crib. She studied him with fresh eyes, trying to see him as he might look to Ward after six months.

His dark curls covered his head in a wavy cap. Dimples creased his cheeks, his wrists, and his elbows. His chubby feet, encased in knitted boots, kicked free of his long gown. No one could say her baby went hungry.

Once he finished nursing, she smoothed his hair with a soft-bristled brush and slipped a fresh sacque over his shoulders. "Are you ready for company?" she asked, tickling his round belly.

When she entered the kitchen, Ward jumped to his feet. "Would you mind?" He held his arms out toward David.

Mama turned from the stove, smiling. "My grandson's very sociable."

David flung himself in Ward's direction. Luellen held tight to her son's waist, laughing. "He's ready to say hello."

Ward lifted the baby, one hand under his bottom and the other behind his head. His left arm showed no sign of weakness. "Look at him. He's thriving." He sat, standing David on his lap. "Brown eyes. When did they change?"

"Gradually over the last month. He's trying to crawl now too."

Luellen felt happiness bubble inside as she sat in the warm kitchen and shared David with Ward. The spicy fragrance of holiday baking filled the room. When Ward's eyes met hers, a tingle sparkled in her throat.

What was she doing? She looked down. She couldn't allow her heart to rule her head again.

Mama brought a plate from the counter and placed it in the center of the worktable. "There's time before supper to sample the shortbread. Luellen baked it," she said to Ward.

Luellen cleared her throat. "Mama."

Eyes wide with innocence, her mother looked at her. "What?"

David reached for the treats, and Mama moved his chubby hand away from the platter. "Not yet, young man. You need more teeth first."

Ward helped himself to a piece of shortbread, tipping his head away from David so he could take a bite. "Delicious. I'll try to leave some for Franklin and Dr. Spengler."

Pleased in spite of herself, Luellen said, "There's plenty more. We've been baking for the Christmas party at Bryant House tomorrow night. Franklin's going to deliver our efforts in the morning."

Mama gestured toward the pantry. "Luellen made some mincemeat pies. We remembered you favor those."

"How thoughtful." His eyes rested on Luellen.

"It was Mama's idea." Luellen wished she could kick her mother under the table.

"I hope you planned on attending our local celebration. I

know you young people had an enjoyable time last year." Mama smiled at Ward. "Perhaps you can convince Luellen to attend. She's been living like a hermit ever since she came home from Allenwood."

"I don't fit in anywhere in Beldon Grove. Why should I go?" Luellen stood and leveled a meaningful stare in her mother's direction. "Perhaps Ward is tired from the journey. We don't want him to feel obligated."

Ward cleared his throat. "I'm not tired at all. In fact, I'd hoped you would consider allowing me to escort you—if it's not presumptuous of me to ask so close to the event."

She thought of the town gossips. How they'd cackle at the sight of a divorced woman carrying on at a public function. Well, let them. In May she'd graduate and find someplace to live far from Beldon Grove. She lifted her chin. "I'll be pleased to have you as my escort. Thank you."

The next evening, Luellen stood in front of the mirror in her parents' room while her mother adjusted her gray silk cape over Luellen's rose taffeta dress. Layers of petticoats extended the skirt in a fashionable bell shape. "You look lovely." Mama pulled tendrils of hair loose around Luellen's temples. "I know you'll have a pleasant evening. Don't worry about David. Papa and I will take good care of him."

"I'm not worried about David." She looked at her mother's reflection in the mirror. "It's just hard to face everyone, knowing what they think of me."

"After the first few moments, no one will be thinking about you at all. Most of those girls will be all atwitter at the sight of Ward in his uniform."

A surge of possessiveness seized Luellen. Why should she care if other girls fluttered around Ward? She had no claim on him.

He stood at the foot of the stairs when she descended. No doubt about it—the girls would flock around him. Gilt buttons on his frock coat shone in the light from the overhead lamp. His high black boots were polished until they glittered. He bowed theatrically, one hand over his heart. "Miss McGarvie."

Luellen tucked her glasses into her reticule. She didn't want to spoil her mother's efforts. Ward stepped through the blur in front of her and placed a hand on her arm. "Glasses are part of your charm. Please put them back on."

Franklin joined them from the sitting room, wearing loose wool trousers and a brown flannel shirt. He carried a folded newspaper under one arm. "Ward's right, Lulie. You look downright pretty."

"That's a compliment, coming from you." She smiled at him. "I wish you'd change your mind and join us."

"I'm promised to Belle. Wouldn't be fair to our understanding for me to go out dancing while she misses the holiday frolics in Springfield. I'll be there in time for the New Year's celebration. We can dance together then."

Luellen's taffeta dress rustled when she moved to her brother and slid an arm around his waist. She glanced at his feet, clad in boots rather than moccasins, and wondered how well he'd fare in Springfield. Pushing her misgivings aside, she said, "Belle is fortunate to have you. I'm proud you're my brother." She kissed his cheek, the end of his wide moustache tickling her nose. She shook her finger at him. "Just remember, she needs to finish at Allenwood first."

He nodded, impatient. "I heard you before." Franklin turned to Ward. "Quick. Take her to Bryant House before she gives me any more orders." He swatted Luellen's backside with the newspaper. "Enjoy yourself. I'll be fine right here."

Luellen took a deep breath when she entered the ballroom. The air was heavy with the mixed aromas of cedar boughs, mulled cider, and wood smoke from the box stove in one corner. She tightened her hold on Ward's arm.

Several people stood at the refreshment table, chatting and nibbling on sweets. One young woman noticed them and leaned over to whisper to the girl next to her. If the music hadn't been so loud, Luellen knew she'd have heard them buzzing their condemnation.

Ward guided her toward the platform where the musicians labored at producing a Viennese waltz. Taking her right hand in his, he placed his left against her back. She remembered their dance last winter and how comforting his presence had been. Luellen felt that comfort even more now. "I'm glad you convinced me to join you tonight," she said, settling her left hand above his silver-barred epaulette.

They swirled into the midst of the dancers. "It's my pleasure." Ward's breath was warm on her face. "After all these months, I feel I know you from your letters. I'm going to miss—" He cleared his throat.

"What?"

"Later. Let's enjoy the music."

The musicians segued into the closing notes of the waltz. After waiting for polite applause, they burst into a polka.

Ward grinned at her. "Are you feeling energetic?"

She tapped her right foot in time to the music. "I am if you are."

They swung into the promenade of dancers whirling around the perimeter of the dance floor. She laughed with delight as Ward twirled her out and back to him as they circled the room. "I'd forgotten how much fun this is." Luellen had to raise her voice to be heard over the thumping beat.

He squeezed her hand. "So had I."

When the last notes died away, Ward led her toward a pair of vacant seats along one wall. Perspiration dotted his forehead. "May I bring you a glass of cider?"

"That would be lovely." Luellen fanned herself. "I need to catch my breath."

Heads turned as he approached the refreshment table. The girl serving the punch took her time filling two glass cups. Another young woman sidled next to him, tossing her curls and smiling coquettishly.

Luellen couldn't help the satisfied smile that crossed her lips when he settled into the chair at her side. No matter what others thought of her, she was the one the handsome officer had escorted to the party.

When the band played the opening notes of another polka, Ward said in an undertone, "Shall we sit this one out? I'd like to talk to you."

Her heartbeat, which had slowed after the dance, increased. "Of course. What is it?"

He took her empty cup and placed it with his on the table behind them. "Let's go somewhere quieter."

Mystified, she took his arm and allowed him to lead her from the ballroom. The rhythmic thud of the music followed them downstairs to a guest parlor where several ruby-colored plush armchairs were arranged in front of a fireplace. An upright piano stood against one wall. Except for the hotel clerk in the reception area, they were alone.

Ward waited while she seated herself, then took a chair facing her. "I told you about my promotion, but there's more."

She clasped her hands together. "I pray it's nothing serious. Has something adverse happened because of that duel?"

"No. Far from it." He closed his eyes and took a deep breath. "I'm being given command of a post."

"That's wonderful news." Luellen surveyed Ward's worried features. "Isn't it?"

"The post is in Kansas Territory—Fort Hook."

She nodded, uncomprehending. "And?"

"There are no railroad lines west of St. Louis. I doubt I'll be able to visit with any frequency. I'll write, but several weeks may pass before my letters reach you—or yours reach me."

Luellen leaned back in the chair, stunned. Her connection to Ward shivered on a fraying thread. "You're going?" She didn't stop to analyze the depths of her disappointment.

"Of course I'm going. This is the opportunity I've waited for." He placed a hand over hers. "The Army is my profession. I go where they send me." He swallowed. "I'll still write, and hope you'll answer." His grip on her hand tightened.

A log in the fire broke in two, sending a shower of sparks up the chimney.

Luellen met his gaze, blinking hard to keep tears at bay. "Certainly I'll answer your letters, but this is good-bye, isn't it? After Fort Hook, where might the Army send you?"

Ward stood and bent over her chair, tucking his thumb under her chin. "Luellen, I—"

Her breath caught in her throat at the pleading in his eyes. It would be so easy to raise her lips to his. But she knew a kiss would only make it harder to say good-bye.

Instead, she turned her head away. "We'd better return to the party. People will be wondering where we are."

# 30

Ward's horse's hooves struck sparks on ribs of exposed rock as he rode onto the parade ground at Fort Hook. Stone buildings surrounded him, some squat, hugging the bare earth, others two stories high. The largest of these stood alone at the left rear of the compound. Ward assumed the limestone edifice to be headquarters, and rode in that direction.

After exhausting days on the trail from St. Louis, he longed for nothing more than a bed and a hot meal. But first he needed to assess his command. Except for a trunk, which traveled on the supply wagon following him, all his possessions should have been delivered to his house on Officers' Row.

Ward saw few soldiers on the grounds. Given the below-freezing temperature and bitter wind, he couldn't blame them. He tied his mount to a hitching rail and climbed the stairs to the principal floor of the building. Right now the fort displayed no accumulated snow, but he knew that a second-floor entrance would be a necessity during blizzards, which he'd been told often swept the hilly area surrounding the outpost.

The heavy plank door screeched when he shoved it open. Warmth blasted his face from an iron stove in the center of the room.

"Sir!" A fresh-faced soldier hastened out from behind a desk. He saluted. "Welcome, Captain. I'm your aide, Corporal Robbins. We've been expecting you for several days."

"My trip was delayed by storms." Ward nodded toward the desk. "Looks like you've been running things in my absence."

Blushing, the young man moved toward a table stacked with papers. "No, sir. No one's been in charge since Captain Seevers left last month—officially, that is. Lieutenant Green has seen to discipline when necessary." He shrugged. "Otherwise, we're muddling along."

He seized a handful of documents. "These are awaiting your signature. Captain Seevers felt his replacement should make the decisions."

"Thank you, Corporal. I'll look at them in the morning." Ward glanced at the deepening twilight through the window behind his desk. "If you'll show me to my quarters, I'm in need of rest and a meal."

"Yes, sir." He scrambled to open the door. "Right this way."

Corporal Robbins chattered over his shoulder while he led Ward toward a two-story frame house fronted by a covered porch. "I'm afraid I didn't know when to expect you, so no one's built a fire. Sorry. My wife will bring you a meal from the mess hall soon as the food's ready." Robbins paused at the bottom step of Ward's house. "She's a laundress here. She'll cook for you, too, until your wife arrives."

"I don't have a wife."

"Too bad." Robbins winked. "It gets mighty cold at night."

Ward raised an eyebrow and stared at him until the grin faded from Robbins's face. "I'd appreciate it if Mrs. Robbins would cook my meals. She can get my rations from the quartermaster."

"Yes, sir." The corporal turned on his heel and strode back to the headquarters building.

Ward's footsteps echoed when he entered his new home. Frost swirls covered the windows. He noticed that the wing-back chair he'd shipped from his father's house had been placed near the box stove in the sitting room. Before starting a fire, he opened a door to his left and found his father's mahogany bed and bureau waiting in the bedroom. He retraced his steps through the sitting room into the kitchen where a square table and two caned chairs sat across from the cookstove. Wooden crates were stacked near the back door. Inventory complete, Ward gathered a handful of shavings and poked them into the firebox. His breath fogged in the freezing air.

He struck a lucifer against the side of the stove and held it to the shavings until they blazed, then crossed kindling over the flames. While he waited for the wood to ignite, he returned to the sitting room and repeated the process in the box stove. The fragrance of burning cedar filled the air.

His few pieces of furniture did little to make the place feel like home. Ward shook his head, recalling Corporal Robbins's assumption that he'd be married. Right now his prospects looked dim. Luellen had treated him with cool politeness once he told her of his reassignment, as though his leaving was deliberately intended to put distance between them. How could she blame him for accepting a promotion? Considering how single-mindedly she pursued a teaching certificate, she should understand the importance of reaching one's goals.

Ward tossed chunks of wood into each firebox and settled into his father's armchair to wait for the cold to retreat. The horsehair stuffing crackled under him. He tipped his head back. Here he sat in the captain's quarters—his quarters. Why did this moment feel so hollow?

"Yes, Doctor?" Ward pushed a stack of supply orders to one side, frustrated. Every time he tried to make headway on the accumulated business of the fort, someone interrupted him.

"Two wagons came off the trail this morning seeking medical assistance. Several of the travelers are seriously ill." Dr. Oliver Marshall threw his coat over a peg and sprawled in a chair opposite Ward's desk.

"Immigrants? In the middle of winter? Where are they going?"

"To Denver City. Chasing after a gold discovery up there."

"The snow won't be off the mountains for months." Ward shook his head in disbelief. "Why are they traveling now?"

"Gold makes fools of men." Dr. Marshall tugged at his goatee. "One of the fellows said they wanted to be ready to file claims by first runoff in the spring. In the meantime, I've got a hospital full of what looks like typhus."

Ward scrambled to his feet. "Typhus! Are you sure?"

"I saw cases in tenements in New York before I came west."

"How many men are there? Any women or children?"

"Nine men. No women. No children." The doctor took his time standing. "Haste won't change anything, Captain. They'll recover or they won't. I've already dosed them with calomel and rhubarb extract."

"I'm concerned about keeping the contagion from spreading through the post. We need to put the hospital under quarantine." Ward shoved his arms into his overcoat. "We have nearly two hundred men here. Were any soldiers in the ward when these immigrants arrived?"

"Just one. I think he was malingering. I sent him back to the barracks."

"Quarantine him too." Ward strode across the parade ground toward the two-story hospital building.

When he opened the door, the doctor put out a hand to stop him. "Will you put yourself under quarantine?"

Ward shrugged him off. "Not unless I feel it's necessary." The stench of vomit assaulted him as soon as he stepped inside. Beyond the doctor's office, the door to the infirmary stood ajar. Ward pushed it open and stepped into a stomach-turning scene.

The patients lay on cots lined up on both sides of the narrow room. Sheets draped their bodies from the waist down. Most appeared half-conscious, their exposed skin covered with a blotchy rash. At the foot of each cot lay a pile of clothing.

Ward stepped to the nearest pile and lifted a pair of trousers with the toe of his boot. The filthy garment drooped toward the floor. He turned toward Dr. Marshall. "Burn their clothing. I want it out of here."

From the cot nearest him, a wheezy voice said, "You cain't do that. I ain't got no other clothes." Sweat plastered the man's hair to his scalp.

"We'll outfit you from the storehouse when you're ready to travel." He bent over the bed, refraining from touching the patient. "What's your name?"

"Earl Cribbins."

"When did you get sick, Earl?"

"We was a ways out of St. Louis when Pinky over there took a bad turn." He pointed at a man with white-blond hair at the end of the row. The man's breath rattled through slack jaws.

Earl's voice grew thready as he continued. "Seemed like we was dominoes. One after t'other, we went down. This here fort looked like a vision of heaven, let me tell you."

Ward smiled. "Pretty far from heaven, but the doctor here will pull you through if anyone can."

"Sure hope so. We gotta get to that gold." Earl's eyes fluttered shut.

Motioning for Dr. Marshall to follow him, Ward left the infirmary. As soon as they were out of earshot of the patients, he stopped. "We'll set up a tent next to the hospital for any soldiers who come to you with ailments. Your assistant can deal with them. It would be best if you slept upstairs instead of going home."

The doctor nodded. "I wouldn't want Millie and the boys sick."

"How long do you think before this passes?"

"Maybe a week—couple of them are pretty far gone. I'm not so sure they'll make it."

"I'll keep an eye on your family." Ward put a hand on the doctor's shoulder. "The mess sergeant will bring meals. Tell him what you'll need for these men."

Once outside, Ward lifted his face to the sky, welcoming the bite of freezing air on his skin. He prayed he'd made the right decisions. Now he had to put them into effect.

Her steps light with anticipation, Luellen hurried toward Allenwood Hall to pay the tuition for her final term. Four more months, and she'd have her certificate in hand. She breezed through the double doors and into Dr. Alexander's reception area.

Mr. Price's face tightened when he saw her. Behind him, the registrar's door stood ajar.

"Dr. Alexander is busy with another student now. You'll have to wait."

"I don't hear any voices in there."

"Nevertheless, he's busy."

"I just need to pay my tuition and get the schedule for the term."

"In that case, you don't need to see Dr. Alexander at all. I'm authorized to accept tuitions." His posture radiated condescension. "I've been given increased responsibility this year."

"How nice for you." Luellen ran her eyes over him. Some people wore authority well—Mr. Price wasn't one of them. She opened her reticule and extracted two gold half eagles. "Ten dollars, isn't that correct?"

"Yes." He opened a ledger. "What name are you using this term? Are you still Miss McGarvie, in spite of . . . ?"

She dropped the coins on the desk next to his left hand. He scrambled to catch one that teetered at the edge. "My name hasn't changed," she said through clenched teeth. "If you'll give me the schedule, I'll be on my way."

His cheeks reddened under his skimpy beard. He dug through a stack of papers, eyes not meeting hers. "Here's your chart. You'll be in the senior session." He ran his finger down a column. "For you, Model School every morning at eight—that includes today."

"What time is it now?"

Mr. Price glanced at the clock behind her. "Ten minutes past. You should have stopped in earlier."

"I just returned last night. This was my first opportunity." She turned toward the door.

His voice stopped her. "Are you living on College Avenue again this term?" His casual tone rang false. When she looked at him, he dropped his gaze and fiddled with the papers on his desk.

"I don't believe that's any of your concern. Now please excuse me, I'm late for my first session." She strode down the hall, the sound of her boot heels hollow against the plaster walls. Four more months. Thankfully, she wouldn't have any future dealings with the registrar's office before May.

Her mood lifted when she crossed the campus toward the Model School. She'd only received one letter from Belle during their vacation, and that before Christmas. Once they finished practice teaching for the day, they'd have time to visit and catch up on each other's news.

Alma Guthrie sent her a welcoming smile when she entered the classroom. A young woman Luellen didn't know stood at the blackboard, apparently in the midst of a spelling lesson. The children scratched each word on their slates as she read from Webster's blue back speller.

Luellen slipped next to Alma and whispered an apology for being late.

"I'm thankful to see you," Alma whispered back. "I wasn't sure you were returning. I assigned Miss Clark the spelling, since it requires no advance preparation. This is her first time at practice teaching." She smiled. "I hoped you'd be here. Arithmetic is next. That's where you shine with the students."

The two women walked toward the cloakroom. Behind them, slate pencils squeaked. February's gray light filtered through the narrow windows. Luellen inhaled the atmosphere of the classroom—burning coal, children's bodies, beeswax polish. "It's good to be back." She took another look around. "But where is Belle Brownlee? I'd hoped we'd be scheduled together again this term."

"Miss Brownlee hasn't registered yet. I'm just happy to see you. I stopped at the registrar's office before opening the school today and didn't find either of your names entered in the ledger. I scheduled you both anyway, hoping you'd arrive."

"I was delayed at home. My parents felt last week's storm made travel unsafe."

"They were right. A passenger train was snowbound overnight on the Galena–Chicago Line. The travelers were quite hungry and cold by the time rescuers arrived." She touched Luellen's arm. "You wouldn't have wanted to expose David to such privation."

"Indeed not." Luellen felt a sense of relief. "Perhaps Belle was delayed by—"

A little girl screamed and jumped from her desk. "Jackie has a snake!"

Several other girls shrieked and scattered away from the center of the room.

Miss Clark's eyes widened. She dropped the spelling book and clambered onto a chair. "Where is it?" Her voice squeaked.

Alma shielded her mouth with her hand and spoke into Luellen's ear. "Would you tend to Jackie while I calm Miss Clark?"

The boy turned and watched Luellen cross the room, a smirk on his face.

"Where is this snake, Jackie?"

"Under Priscilla's desk." He pointed.

A desiccated snakeskin, rattles attached, lay stretched on the floor. Hiding her revulsion, Luellen picked up the dead reptile. "He's lovely." She rested it on her open palms. "Girls, resume your seats. See, he's harmless." She turned to the boy. "Step up front. You can tell the class all about your snake—where you found him and how you cured the skin."

A chair scraped as Miss Clark climbed down, trying to keep her hoopskirt under control. She picked up the speller and retreated to one side of the room.

Jackie looked alarmed. "No. I ain't going up there."

Luellen placed the snakeskin on the instructor's desk. "Of course you are. I assume you want him back when you go home this afternoon." She shot a glance at Alma and saw her nod confirmation.

The boy scuffed to the front of the row, head down. "Well, one day me and my pa was plowing." The children listened as he continued, boys fascinated, girls grimacing. Once Jackie saw how much attention he received, he warmed to his tale. Luellen allowed him five minutes, then thanked him and took up the arithmetic lesson.

By the time the dinner bell rang, her thoughts had wandered to David, waiting for her with Leah in Mrs. Garmon's kitchen. If she hurried, she'd have time to stop at the registrar's office on her way to ask what news the school had from Belle.

Belle had to come back. She promised.

Luellen wrapped her cloak around her and plunged into the noontime chill. She dreaded having to meet with Mr. Price again. She'd hated having him fawn over her when she first arrived in Allenwood, but his supercilious attitude now was even harder to bear.

Mr. Price's chair was empty.

Luellen let out a sigh of exasperation. She didn't have time to wait—David would be hungry. She'd try again between classes this afternoon.

"Miss McGarvie. This is a surprise. More special requests?"

She whirled to see Dr. Alexander standing behind her. "No. I just stopped in to ask Mr. Price if your office had heard from my friend Miss Brownlee. I expected her to be at the Model School this morning, but Mrs. Guthrie told me she wasn't registered yet."

"Miss Brownlee . . ." His voice trailed off. He stepped over to Mr. Price's desk and riffled through a pile of papers. "This is all the student correspondence we've received so far this term. I don't find that name here." He dropped the papers back in a tray. "Not every student possesses your determination. Perhaps your friend decided not to return. In any case, she has until the end of this week to register. After that—" Dr. Alexander shook his head. "It'll be too late."

# 31

Leah turned from the stove where she'd been stirring the contents of a large kettle. "Would you like a taste?"

The fragrance of chicken and curry swirled through the kitchen, making Luellen's stomach rumble. "Yes, please." She held David over one shoulder and patted his back. Frannie toddled over to them, tugging at the hem of David's gown.

Leah placed a filled bowl and spoon on the table, then swept Frannie into her arms. "This soup is for Mrs. Garmon's supper. She got the recipe on one of her trips out east. I don't like the flavor of those foreign spices myself."

After shifting David to her left side, Luellen tried a spoonful. "This is very tasty. Mrs. Hawks has curry powder in her cupboard, but she doesn't use it much."

"Mrs. Garmon collects recipes on all her travels. Pretty soon—" Leah cleared her throat. "She's leaving on another journey." She rose and paced to the stove and back again. "Once the weather improves, that is."

Luellen glanced at the curtain of snow obliterating the landscape. Was bad weather all that had prevented Belle from returning? Luellen posted a letter after the first week passed, but so far had received no reply. Without the distraction of her friend's cheerful outlook, the days blended into one another, each one lonelier than the last.

Leah continued to pace. "Least he could do is come see his baby," she muttered.

"Who?"

"Frannie's no-good father. I sent and told him, 'We're not staying here forever. You'd best come while you have the chance.'" She stopped and faced Luellen. "D'you think that moved him? Not a whit. I should'a known." Leah resumed her trek back and forth across the kitchen.

"Did you meet him here in Allenwood?" Luellen held her breath. Would Leah answer?

Leah laughed, a harsh, scoffing sound. "Not hardly. How would I meet anyone in this place?" She shook her head. "We met in Middletown, when Dr. Alexander was president of Middletown Academy. I worked for his daughter, taking care of her babies. When the families moved here, she wanted me with her."

Luellen's mouth dropped open. "Dr. Alexander?" Stunned, she stared at the other woman.

"Oh, gracious no. Not him. I never hardly saw him at all—until he fired me for being in the family way. I came here because Frannie's father did. He said pretty soon we'd go to Pennsylvania. He said we could get married there, all legal like. He said he'd take care of me." Tears clouded her eyes. "He never meant any of it." She slumped in a chair next to Luellen's. "I feel like the dumbest person on earth. Why'd I believe him? Soon's I told him about the baby, he gave me Mrs. Hawks's address. Now he pretends we're nothing to him."

"Who is he?"

"Doesn't matter now, does it? Besides, it's my word against his." Leah held out her hands, palms down. "See this dark skin? Think anyone would take my word against a white man's?"

Luellen stood David on the floor. He teetered on his feet for a moment, then plopped on his bottom. She turned and took one of Leah's hands. "I'll pray for you." The words sounded weak. Surely there was more she could do.

Leah bowed her head. "Thank you. No one's said that for a long time—not since my mama and papa left." They sat in silence for a moment. Leah gathered her normal reserve around her and stepped to the window. "Good thing you don't have far to walk. Snow's piling up."

Recognizing dismissal, Luellen dropped her cloak over her shoulders, tucking David underneath its folds. "We'll see you in the morning."

She picked her way to the board sidewalk and waited while an omnibus and two carriages rolled past. Their lanterns illuminated whirling flakes. Once across the street, she climbed the steps of the boardinghouse and stamped her feet to dislodge packed snow.

The door flew open. "I hoped that was you," Mrs. Hawks said. "I've been worried."

David wiggled out from under Luellen's cloak and reached for the landlady. She took him in her arms, kissing his reddened cheeks.

Luellen wiped moisture from her glasses. "I'm sorry you worried. I spent more time with Leah than I'd planned. She was upset over Frannie's father."

"Poor girl. I'm glad she has you to talk to. That man has treated her shamefully. He should be horsewhipped." She shook her head. "I'll be happy when she's able to join her parents in Canada."

They walked through the deserted dining room and into the kitchen. A chunk of salt pork, onions, and half a dozen potatoes waited on the worktable. "Potato soup tonight?" Luellen asked.

"I only have three guests right now—no sense cooking a big

meal." Mrs. Hawks sucked in her lower lip. "Soon as the weather clears, I expect I'll have a full house. Hope so, anyway. I did last year." Tired lines fanned around her mouth. She settled in a chair and bounced David on her knee. "I'm grateful for your help."

"I'm grateful for my room and board." Luellen sliced strips of salt pork.

"Did you look through those potatoes to be sure there are no bad spots?"

Surprised, Luellen glanced at Mrs. Hawks. Why would she set out the potatoes without checking them first? Luellen slid the cutting board out of the way and grabbed a potato. Something white showed underneath. Pushing the rest of the vegetables aside, she saw an envelope addressed to her in Belle's familiar handwriting.

Mrs. Hawks's eyes twinkled. "I went to the post office today before the snow got bad. I know you've been waiting to hear from your friend."

"Thank you." She tore open the envelope and extracted several thin sheets of paper. "My word, she's written a book." Her eyes ran down the first page. Heart pounding, she turned to the second sheet.

"What's kept her from returning? Is she ill?"

Numb, Luellen shook her head and continued reading. When she reached the end, she stared unbelieving at Mrs. Hawks. "She and Franklin were married on the fifth of February. Almost a month ago—before school ever started. No notice, no invitation, no nothing." Tears seeped from the corners of her eyes. "My best friend and my brother. I knew they had plans to marry, but I believed they'd wait until after graduation. And I assumed I'd be asked to stand up with them." She wiped her eyes.

Mrs. Hawks looked surprised. "This must have come as a blow to your parents."

"My parents. Do they even know?" Fear squeezed her throat. "Papa's health is poor. No telling how he'll handle a shock like this." She sank into a chair and ran her fingers through the hair at her temples. Now she knew how Mama and Papa felt when she and Brendan eloped. Cheated. And to have it happen again with Franklin . . .

Luellen's tiny room felt like a prison holding her in Allenwood. Three months before she'd be free to go see her parents. How were they taking the news? She ached to have someone in whom she could confide. If Belle's tardy missive was any indication, she and Franklin were far more occupied with each other than with thoughts of her. Would it do any good to write to Ward? So far he hadn't replied to any of her letters.

Rolling onto her side, she stared through the blackness in the direction of David's crib. His soft baby snores quieted her whirling thoughts. The image of Ward carrying her son up the stairs in her parents' house slipped into her mind—David's head resting on Ward's broad shoulder, his baby eyelashes brushing his chubby cheeks as he slept. Had she ever told Ward how much she appreciated his help?

Luellen swung her legs to the floor. It wouldn't hurt to write him again. Even if he didn't answer, at least he'd know she was thinking of him.

She hugged her quilt around her shoulders as she tiptoed into the kitchen. The door to the firebox on the stove screeched when she opened it to throw a stick of wood on top of the banked coals. Sparks shivered over the split pine, rippling along the splinters at the edges. After lighting the lamp, she gathered pen and paper from the cupboard.

Luellen addressed the envelope to Jefferson Barracks, as Ward had instructed. He'd assured her that couriers carried messages to the outposts whenever enough mail accumulated.

She stared at the blank sheet of paper in front of her. Should she tell him she missed his letters? No—that would sound like a reproach.

> *I never thanked you for helping me with David at Christmas. I think he misses you now.*

She stopped herself from adding, "*. . . and so do I.*" Tapping the pen holder against her teeth, she visualized herself talking to Ward face-to-face.

> *I had a shock today—I learned that Franklin and Belle were married the first part of last month. Did you know they had such plans? I must confess I was distressed to receive the news. Selfishly, I wanted to be part of their wedding day. And to have Belle quit her studies when she was so close to finishing is a terrible disappointment. I fear she'll be sorry later.*

Luellen told him about her classes, her progress in practice teaching, and her loneliness without Belle. She concluded:

> *Only three months to go. Commencement exercises are scheduled for the twentieth of May. I'm hoping to hear of a teaching assignment nearby so I can continue to have Leah care for David. She's very good to him. After an uncomfortable beginning, which I told you about at Christmas, we are becoming friends.*

*I pray your command at Fort Hook is all you hoped it would be.*

*Most sincerely,*
*Luellen*

❧

Enough people had traveled along the walkways the next morning that the snow had been trampled down. Broken clouds hung overhead. Luellen stepped into the classroom at the Model School, grateful she'd arrived ahead of the children. Her eyes burned from lack of sleep.

Alma sat at her desk, making notes in her grade book. "Are you ready to give the arithmetic test today?"

"I am." Luellen opened her portfolio and removed the textbook. "I'll have the problems copied onto the blackboard before the children arrive."

"I should have known better than to ask. You're always well prepared."

Luellen sighed, remembering how hard it had been to focus on the lesson plan when her mind was filled with thoughts of Franklin and Belle. "Some days are better than others."

"That's true of all of us, but you never let outside distractions take precedence over the children."

"Children are the reason I want to teach. So much potential is wasted by poor educators. If my mother hadn't helped us, I don't think we'd have learned a thing." Chalk powdered Luellen's fingers as she wrote the addition problems out. "Our teacher knew nothing but rote and the rod."

"That's changing. Enrollment here at Allenwood grows each year." Alma stood, arms folded over her middle. "There's talk of another class being added to the Model School curriculum next year. They'll be looking to hire an instructor." She tilted her head. "I plan to recommend you."

When the morning session ended, Luellen floated back to Mrs. Garmon's, buoyed by the hope of a position with the Normal School. She could maintain her current living arrangements with no disruption to David or herself. She looked up and breathed, "Thank you, Lord," aiming her voice at a break in the clouds.

When she turned in front of the woman's house, she caught a glimpse of a shadowy figure disappearing down the alley. Was it Frannie's father? She hurried toward the rear of the property, but by the time she got there the person had vanished. Perhaps he'd been a nearby resident, taking a shortcut to his home. She shrugged. Whoever it was, he couldn't dim her excitement about the future.

Luellen flung open the kitchen door. "I have the most exciting news." Her voice trailed off. Leah and the children weren't there. She peered into the small room off the kitchen and saw Leah sitting on the rug, resting her back against the side of the bed. David and Frannie were nestled on her lap while she hummed a lullaby. She turned her head when Luellen appeared on the threshold.

Her eyes held a faraway look. "Some days all I want to do is hunker down with my baby. I'm so tired of being in a place where no one cares what happens to me."

All at once Luellen's news didn't seem so important. She knelt beside Leah and lifted David from her lap. The woman's despair filled the room, thick enough to be touched. "I care, Leah," she said in a gentle voice. "So do Mrs. Garmon and Mrs. Hawks." She sat on the edge of the bed. "I know how it feels to be lonely."

"You're trying to be nice." Leah rose, holding Frannie, and

looked down at Luellen. "There's lonely, and then there's lonely. All you got to do is hop on a train and you're home in a day, your mama and papa waiting for you." She closed her eyes for a moment. "Me, I can't even get to Canada without looking over my shoulder every second. Why I didn't leave with my parents—" Leah walked out of the room, still talking. "When I make a mistake, it's a big one."

Luellen watched her retreating back. She needed Leah in Allenwood so she could accept the teaching position. What would she do without her?

She flushed. Had she grown so self-centered that her needs were the only ones that mattered?

Grateful she had only one class that afternoon, Luellen slipped into a vacant seat in the lecture hall. When she returned to the boardinghouse, she'd ask Mrs. Hawks about continuing her room and board if she were hired by the Model School next year.

Glowing lamps hung at spaced intervals from the ceiling. She placed her *Science of Education* text in a pool of light and waited for the professor to take the lectern. Murmurs and giggles drifted from one of the tables near the back. She recognized Miss Clark's voice from the Model School.

"To see them together, you'd think they were sisters."

"Well, they certainly have a lot in common." The second girl snickered. "Did you hear what Mrs. Bledsoe said about her?"

"No. What?"

Their voices dropped to whispers. Luellen cocked one ear, wondering who they were gossiping about. She hadn't seen Matron Bledsoe at all this term, but from the sound of things the woman hadn't muted her sanctimonious personality.

"Matron needs to tell Mrs. Guthrie what she knows." Miss Clark's voice gained volume. "Someone like that shouldn't be teaching innocent children."

Hot pinpricks swept over her body. Were they talking about her? No telling what embellishments Mrs. Bledsoe had spun since Luellen left the Ladies Hall.

She swiveled in her seat, made sure the girls saw her, then rose and walked toward them.

# 32

Ward walked to the window in his office. Beyond the fort, the undulating hills wore a cloak of emerald. Early spring brought unexpected beauty to what he'd termed a bleak and desolate landscape when he first arrived.

He paced back to his desk. Dr. Marshall's request for an addition to the hospital stared up at him. Ever since the need for a quarantine during the typhus scare, the doctor had appeared weekly with requests for more space and increased supplies.

The post hospital spent more time on doctoring immigrants than soldiers, Ward learned. The warmer weather brought a steady influx of gold seekers heading north to Denver City. They often arrived hungry, poorly clothed, and sick.

He hadn't planned on operating a field station for treasure hunters. He'd expected to command troops according to West Point standards, but instead found himself dealing with soldiers whose sole reason for enlisting was a need for a job and food. Today would be no different. An hour of fatigue duties and an hour and a half of drills, then the troops would assemble for noon mess with more enthusiasm than they'd shown all morning. No wonder the previous commander asked for a transfer.

The door swung open and Dr. Marshall poked his head inside. "Have you got a few minutes?"

"Another requisition, Oliver?"

The goateed man raised his eyebrows in mock surprise. "Me? Certainly not." He dropped into a chair facing Ward. "We've got a difficulty over at the hospital."

"What is it now?"

"That immigrant wagon that came in yesterday—the fellow died."

Ward gripped the arms of his chair, poised to jump to his feet. "Nothing that will spread around the post, is it?"

"No. Lung fever. I don't know how he made it this far."

"So, send a burial detail out. The ground has thawed enough."

"Burial's not the difficulty." The doctor fingered his salt-and-pepper whiskers. "He had a daughter with him. What should we do with her?"

"Perhaps one of the officers' families can take her in until we can find a way to send her back to her people. Do you know where they came from?"

"She's been hysterical since her father died. I can't get her to tell me anything."

Ward stared at the ceiling for a moment. The father must have been her only parent. Surely no mother would allow a child to travel to the goldfields. He pushed his chair away from the desk.

"I'll go see her. Maybe she's settled down by now."

A skeptical expression crossed Dr. Marshall's face. "My assistant's doing his best, but perhaps she'll warm up to you."

The two men skirted the edge of the parade ground where trainees performed weapons drills. They passed the laundresses' quarters, where a dozen or so children played tag under lines of drying clothes. Ward glanced at the doctor. "Wasn't your wife going to keep the youngsters inside for lessons during the week?"

"She tried. Some people are cut out for teaching—Millie's not. She can hardly manage our twins." He winked. "She's a good cook, though."

Ward looked over his shoulder at the children once more before entering the hospital. Something needed to be done.

Sergeant Brainerd, Dr. Marshall's assistant, met them inside the door. "Got the girl calmed down," he said. "She's resting." A flush covered his thin cheeks. "I was just going to the enlisted mess to fetch something for her to eat. I told her I'd be right back."

The doctor nodded. "Go ahead. Captain Calder wants to talk to her for a moment."

Inside the infirmary, Ward scanned the empty cots. "Where's the child?"

A young woman of sixteen or seventeen rose from a chair at the back of the room and walked toward him, barefooted. She stood no taller than Ward's shoulder. Her eyes were swollen. "If you mean Abel Lampy's child, that's me. I'm Rilla Lampy." Coppery hair hung in limp strands around her haggard face. She studied Ward, fear in her gray eyes. "Guess the doc told you about my pa dying. That must be why you're here."

Ward tried to hide his surprise. "It is." He clasped his hands at his waist. "My condolences."

She nodded. "What's going to happen to me now?"

Dr. Marshall stepped around Ward. "You're welcome to stay with my family until you're able to return home."

Rilla frowned. "What if I don't want to go back? Took us a month to get this far. We was leaving Arkansas behind, if you get my meaning. Denver City was a new start. Pa had everything figured out. He'd find gold and before long, we'd have a fine house. Now . . ." Her crooked teeth tugged at her lower lip. "I just need to think up something else."

✑

Ward entered his office and cast an apprehensive glance at his desk. A covered plate rested on top of the requisition forms he'd left when he went home the night before. He lifted the napkin. Molasses balls rolled in brown sugar. Still warm, their cinnamon-clove fragrance made his mouth water.

"I hope you like them." Rilla's voice pursued him across the room. "I made them special for you."

She stood on the threshold. He'd be flattered if he didn't know she'd spent the last two weeks bringing treats in rotation to all the unmarried officers. "Thank you. I'm sure Mrs. Marshall appreciates your skills in the kitchen."

Rilla stepped into the room. Her green calico frock emphasized her shining curls. "My pa liked my cooking. He always said I'd make some man a fine wife."

Ward moved so that the desk formed a barrier between them and looked pointedly at the door. "Corporal Robbins will be here soon. I'll share these with him."

"The corporal has a wife." Her lower lip stuck out in a pout. "These are for you."

On cue, Robbins's boots clattered up the stairs. He took one step into the room and stopped, his eyes darting between Rilla and Ward. "Excuse me, sir. I didn't know you were busy." A leather dispatch bag hung from one hand.

"Miss Lampy was just leaving."

"I'll be back later for the empty plate." She flounced toward the door, hips swaying. The black look she gave Corporal Robbins as she left didn't escape Ward's notice.

The corporal watched her leave. "That must be why Sergeant Brainerd was hanging about downstairs. I reckon the doc doesn't know why his assistant is gone half the time." He turned to Ward. "Think I should tell him?"

"Not as long as Brainerd's doing his job. Miss Lampy won't be here much longer. Next time wagons pass this way going east, she'll go with them."

"She don't act like she plans to go east."

"We don't always get what we want." Ward held out his hand. "Now, can I see what's in that dispatch bag?"

Corporal Robbins stood while Ward dumped the contents of the bag over his desk. He separated a communication from Jefferson Barracks and flipped through the rest of the envelopes, stacking aside letters addressed to the troops. "Distribute the mail, please, Corporal. I imagine the men have been waiting ever since the courier rode in."

"Yes, sir." Robbins sat at a table and proceeded to arrange the envelopes in alphabetical order.

Ward smiled at his aide's methodical habits. He suspected the man kept his life in the same order. Did he have his spouse listed by her first name, or under "w" for wife? Grinning, he reached for the official document and broke the seal.

"Sir? This one's for you."

"It is?" His heart thumped when he saw the handwriting on the envelope. *Luellen*. His reaction jolted him. After nearly three months with no word, he'd resigned himself to her going ahead with her plans to find a teaching position. That's what she wanted, wasn't it? Like he wanted to command an Army post. In Kansas. Alone.

With eager fingers, he spread her letter open on his desk.

*I never thanked you for helping me with David at Christmas.*
*I think he misses you now.*

Little David, with his mother's curls and liquid brown eyes.
Ward missed him too. He read on through the news about Franklin
and Belle. His eyes stopped near the end of the missive.

*Commencement exercises are scheduled for the twentieth*
*of May.*

What if he surprised her by attending the graduation? Even if
her future didn't include him, Ward wanted to wish her well. If
anyone deserved to achieve their goals, it was Luellen.

He could leave the post in Corporal Robbins's hands. Nothing
important ever happened here anyway. Smiling, he folded her
letter and tucked it into his breast pocket. He'd put his plan in
motion immediately.

His mind still on Luellen, he turned to the communication from
Jefferson Barracks. Captain Block's bold penmanship scrawled
across the page:

> *General Kinner is due from Washington on a tour*
> *of the western outposts. He will likely arrive at Fort*
> *Hook the third week in May. Have all in readiness.*

"I don't know how you do it," Miss Clark gushed to Luellen
as they left the Model School together. "You're always ready with
your lesson plan, and you have that baby to care for too. It must
be very difficult."

Luellen shrugged. "I keep my eyes on my goals, not how hard
it is to reach them. You'd be surprised at how much you can
accomplish if you don't stay your thoughts on what you can't

do." She kept her tone neutral. Miss Clark was seeking gossip fodder for her companions in the Ladies Hall. She'd seen them whispering together in the weeks since their confrontation in the lecture room.

"But how *do* you do it? I get so distracted." Miss Clark waved her hand at the separate columns of men and women moving toward classes on campus. "So many young men, and we aren't allowed to mix with them."

Luellen felt older than her twenty-four years. Had she ever been so giddy? They crossed the street, avoiding patches of ice. "I got distracted once. The results were disastrous, with the exception of the birth of my son. If you really want an education, you need to put on blinders and focus on your studies."

"But two years here? I'll be twenty before I'm finished, practically an old maid."

Luellen grinned. "You'll be twenty in two years whether you finish here or not."

Miss Clark shot her an impatient glance. "It's easy for you to talk. Your life is already over." She spoke as one stating a fact. Excusing herself, she dashed toward a group of girls waiting near the chapel.

Stung by the barb of truth in her remarks, Luellen plodded toward Mrs. Garmon's house. She'd seen a teaching certificate as a beginning. Instead, was it the end?

Mrs. Hawks scurried into the kitchen, where Luellen put finishing touches on the evening meal. "Do you have everything ready? We're filled up tonight, and I don't want to disappoint my new boarders."

Luellen backhanded perspiration from her temples. "Beef pie, biscuits, cabbage slaw, and apple pudding. They won't go away hungry."

"Thank you." The landlady wrapped a towel around her hand and took the pie from the oven. "I'll carry this in. Would you bring the biscuits and slaw?"

"Certainly." Luellen squatted in front of David, who sat on a blanket gnawing on a piece of dried bread. "You stay right here while Mama helps serve." She kissed the top of his head. "That's a good boy."

The door to the dining room swung shut behind Mrs. Hawks. Luellen slid the biscuits into a napkin-lined bowl and followed her.

Eight men looked up when she entered. Luellen froze, her eyes locked on the one with chestnut curls seated nearest the door. The bowl of biscuits slipped from her nerveless fingers and crashed to the floor.

"Brendan."

# 33

Brendan looked as stunned as Luellen felt. Red crept up his neck as the others in the room stared at him. He pasted an artificial-looking smile on his face. "I never expected to see you here. You're looking well."

Luellen ignored him and turned to Mrs. Hawks. "I'll clean this up right away." Her hands shook. Brendan O'Connell was one of the new boarders? Please, no.

Understanding filled the landlady's eyes. "No need. Why don't you work up more biscuits while I sweep the floor?"

After pushing broken shards of pottery aside with her foot, Luellen fled to the kitchen. David toddled over to her and grabbed her knees. Her first instinct was to run to Leah's and keep him there until Brendan left. She drew a breath. No. With David's dark hair and eyes, no one would ever suspect that the ruddy, blue-eyed man in the dining room was his father, least of all Brendan himself. David was hers, and hers he would stay.

Mrs. Hawks slipped into the room. "Is that him?" She nodded toward the closed door.

"Yes." Perspiration prickled under her arms. "How long is he going to be here?"

"I don't know—he's part of the railroad crew." She moved to

the stove and took a waiting pan of biscuits from the warming oven. "You certainly baked these quickly," she said with a wink.

"I made two pans full." In spite of her jumping nerves, Luellen managed a smile. "As you well know."

Late that evening, she sat at the kitchen table attempting to write a lesson plan for the next day. She'd advised Miss Clark to keep blinders on to avoid distractions. Now blinders weren't helping her at all. What would she do if Brendan stayed at the boardinghouse for the weeks remaining until commencement? Could she really block him out of her thoughts? How could she keep him from learning about David?

She rested her forehead in her hands. *Lord, please help me.*

"Luellen?"

She swung around.

Brendan stood in the doorway. "May I come in?"

"You're fine right there. What do you want?"

"I want to tell you I'm sorry for what happened." Blue eyes shone from his smooth face. "The last thing I expected was to see you here, sure. But it's providential, I'm thinking." He took a step into the room.

He hadn't lost any of his charm. The scene reminded her of the times he spent with her in the kitchen at Bryant House—before she knew he had a wife.

She stood, gripping the back of her chair. "And how is Mrs. O'Connell? Shouldn't you be at her side in Chicago?"

Brendan ran his fingers through his thick curls. "That's over and done with. Her father . . ." He cleared his throat. "It was a mistake from beginning to end."

"You were the mistake, for both of us. Now go away and leave me alone." Luellen kept one ear tuned to the bedroom, praying David wouldn't wake at the sound of their voices.

"Can't say I blame you." Brendan's eyes moistened. "Good night, then."

The next day after classes, Luellen sat in Leah's kitchen holding a cup of tea. "I really should go home and start supper, but I can't think how to avoid him."

"He's your baby's father. Maybe you should tell him. Railroads pay good—he could help so you don't have to work so hard."

"He lied to me in the worst way possible. I don't want him in our lives." She shuddered. "Just the thought of him makes me ill."

"I'd give anything if Frannie's father came here and said he was sorry." Leah clutched her cup. "All I'm saying is give him a chance. People change."

At suppertime, Luellen spooned mutton and rice into a tureen while she considered Leah's advice. Had Brendan changed? After slicing a loaf of bread, she filled a dish with apple jelly and set it beside the hot food. Changed or not, she wasn't ready to see him again.

"Looks tasty," Mrs. Hawks said. "You stay out here, I'll serve."

"Thank you."

The landlady patted Luellen's shoulder. "Once upon a time, there was a Mr. Hawks. Lucky for him, he never came back." She pushed the swinging door with her elbow and carried the tureen to the diners.

Once Mrs. Hawks had supper on the table, she hung her apron on a hook near the door. "Are you sure you don't mind cleaning up? I promised Alma I'd be there as early as I could for Frederick's birthday celebration."

"Go and enjoy yourself. Once I hear the boarders leave, I'll clear the dishes."

"I don't know what I'll do without you after the term ends."

"Maybe I'll stay here." Luellen smiled, but the remark reminded her she'd forgotten to ask about a permanent arrangement if she got the position at the Model School.

While the boarders ate, Luellen held David on her knee and fed him spoonfuls of mashed rice and carrots. The murmur of conversation from the next room rose and fell and eventually she heard chairs scraping across the wooden floor. Heavy boots clumped up the stairs.

Luellen wiped David's face and set him on his blanket. "Here's your doggie." She tickled his nose with a soft, rag-stuffed toy. He chuckled, grabbing at his favorite plaything.

"Well, who's this?"

Luellen jumped. She hadn't heard the door swing open.

Brendan stood looking at her, a quizzical expression on his face. Part of her mind noted his clean shirt and the comb lines drawn through his curls.

She stood, concealing David behind her skirt. "Boarders aren't allowed in the kitchen."

"We're not to help ourselves to food, but I'm thinking we can talk to each other." He turned his head toward her side. "That lad yours?"

The pounding of her heart threatened to choke her. Under her apron, she dug her nails into her palms. "Yes, he is."

Brendan slid a chair out from the table. "Well, now. You've been busy since we parted."

Luellen exhaled with a whoosh. "You might say that." *Let him think what he will.*

"Where's the mister?"

308

"I don't have a husband."

"I've got to give you credit for more gumption than I thought you had. Woman alone with a baby. Can't be easy." His Irish lilt polished his words.

"Life isn't easy."

"'Tis true." Brendan leaned back. "Mind if I stay here, have a chat? A boardinghouse is a lonely place."

The sound of his voice beguiled her, as it had in the beginning. "I need to clear the table and wash up."

"I won't be in your way."

What harm could it do? "All right then." She propped the swinging door open and carried plates into the kitchen.

Brendan's voice followed her as she moved back and forth, telling her of his job with the railroad. "One of these days, I'd like to operate a lodging house like this one. Follow the rails west. If I'm lucky, I'll find someone who can cook like you do. We'd be a team."

Luellen splashed water over the dishes in the basin. His voice went on, spinning his dreams. She closed her eyes, remembering the early days of their courtship and marriage. Listening to him ignited a spark she'd thought to be dead.

When the last pot had been dried and hung on the rack, Brendan rose. "Thank you for your company. D'you mind if I come back again?" His broad hands rested on the back of a chair.

"I have studies." At the disappointment in his eyes, she relented. "But for a while after supper, a visit would be fine."

"Good night, then. See you tomorrow."

After he left, she gathered a sleepy David in her arms and carried him into their room. "What am I doing?" she whispered. "Heaven help me, I'm looking forward to tomorrow evening."

Luellen sat at the rear of the Model School classroom while Miss Clark led the children through their reading assignment. She scanned over the subtraction test she'd prepared, her thoughts occupied with Brendan rather than numbers. Could she trust his friendship? Three weeks had passed since he appeared at the boardinghouse. If he hadn't changed, surely some trace of the old Brendan would have popped up by now.

The latch clicked open and a young man stepped into the foyer, a leather pouch slung over one shoulder. At the disturbance, the children swiveled in their seats, reading lesson forgotten.

"I'm looking for a Miss McGarvie."

Luellen stood. "I'm Miss McGarvie. How may I assist you?"

He thrust a yellow sheet of paper at her. "Telegram."

"Thank you." There must be a mistake. Who would send her a telegram?

As soon as the messenger left, she ripped the envelope open.

> *Come home at once stop Papa dangerously ill stop Mama*

Alma hastened toward her. "You look like you're going to faint. Sit down."

Luellen slumped in the chair and handed her the message.

"Oh mercy. Your father." Alma turned back to the class. "Go on with the lesson, Miss Clark. I'll be with you in a few moments." She slid a hand under Luellen's arm and guided her toward the door. "There's a train south tomorrow. You must go. I'll talk to Dr. Alexander for you."

"Thank you, but I want to tell him myself. After all the times he helped me, I owe him that much."

Their eyes met, understanding passing between them. If Luellen went home now, she would lose her chance at a teaching certificate.

The loss didn't matter. She pictured Papa—laughing, carrying her on his shoulders when she was small, his wise counsel through her maturing years, and most of all, his support after Brendan left. She'd be on that train.

She gathered her portfolio and cloak and dashed across the street to Allenwood Hall.

Mr. Price sat with his head bent over a ledger. Luellen cleared her throat. He looked up, feigning surprise. "What brings you here in the middle of the morning?"

"I need to speak with Dr. Alexander immediately, please."

"I'm sorry. Unfortunately he's away at a trustees' meeting." The expression on his face was anything but regretful. "I'll be happy to give him a message."

"When do you expect him to return?"

"Wednesday or Thursday."

Luellen fought tears of frustration. By Wednesday, she'd be back in Beldon Grove. Of all times for Dr. Alexander to be gone, why did it have to be now? She drew a deep breath.

"Please tell him that I've been called home. My father is gravely ill." Her voice shook. "Be sure to thank him for all the help he extended to me."

Mr. Price gaped at her. "You're withdrawing? Commencement is next month."

"My father's more important."

He shook his head. "You amaze me. You've been here countless times begging to be allowed to continue, and now you leave with a certificate practically in your grasp."

His sneering expression wavered through her angry haze. "I

doubt you were hired to pass judgment on students. I suggest you do the job you were assigned—keep records. Good day, Mr. Price."

Luellen stalked from the building, body trembling. Once outside, she slumped on a bench and buried her face in her hands. *Lord, forgive me for losing my temper. Please, please, help me get home in time.*

⟡

Luellen sat in Mrs. Garmon's kitchen, David on her lap. Frannie played on the floor at her feet. "We're leaving in the morning."

Leah placed her hands on Luellen's shoulders. "I'll miss both of you." She stepped back, her face drawn. "You don't know how lucky you are."

"Lucky? My papa—"

"You *know* about your papa. You can board a train and be home tomorrow." Leah's green earrings gleamed in the light. "I'd give anything to be in your shoes."

"I wish there was something I could do for you."

"Can't think what it would be. Tell Mrs. Hawks I'll work if she needs me." Leah clutched her in a fierce embrace. "Go with God. I'll pray for your papa." Tears flavored her words.

"I'll be praying for you too." Sobs choking her, Luellen fled down the steps and crossed the street.

She burst into Mrs. Hawks's kitchen, still weeping.

The landlady dropped the broom she was holding. "Why are you here in the middle of the morning? Did something happen to David?"

Luellen reached into her pocket and handed her the telegram.

"Your father. Oh my word. There's a train south tomorrow."

Controlling her sobs, Luellen said, "I know. I plan to be on it." She wiped her eyes.

"But this means you're gone for good." Mrs. Hawks sank into a chair, sniffling. "Things won't be the same without you. You've become like a daughter to me."

Once again, tears trickled over Luellen's cheeks. She waved a hand in front of her face. "I'm sorry. I wasn't prepared for all these good-byes today."

"We're never prepared for bad news, dear. It attacks us like a mad dog." She stood David on the floor. "Do you need help packing?"

"No, thank you. I've packed and unpacked my trunk so often I could do it in my sleep."

A few minutes later, the landlady tapped on her door.

When Luellen opened it, Mrs. Hawks handed her a handkerchief with the ends tied together. "I want you to have this."

Inside rested a gold half eagle. "Five dollars. I can't take this."

"Yes you can. I was planning to give it to you when you graduated. Anyway, you'll need this for the trip home."

Mrs. Hawks guessed correctly. Luellen barely had enough left from her tutoring income to buy a ticket, with little to spare. Overcome, she bowed her head. "I don't know how to thank you."

"There's no need. The Lord put us here to help each other." She patted Luellen's shoulder. "Now get busy with your packing. You have a train to catch tomorrow."

That evening, Luellen dragged the trunk toward the front door so it would be ready for the omnibus driver to load in the morning. Brendan stopped her halfway through the dining room.

She jumped, surprised to see him.

"And where are you going with that?" He stood close enough to touch her, but his hands remained behind his back.

For much of the day, she'd been so distracted she'd forgotten he lived in the same house. "Home. I'm going on the train in the morning. Papa's very sick."

"I'm sorry to hear that, sure. Your father's a fine man."

She shuddered to think what it would do to Papa to know she'd spent time with Brendan, no matter how innocent their conversations. She took a step away. "So, I won't be seeing you again." Her tone conveyed dismissal.

"I'll be out front with my wagon in the morning to take you and the lad to the depot." He touched his lips with his fingers and brushed her cheek. "Sleep well."

# 34

Franklin and Belle were waiting next to the depot. They stood side by side, not touching, the bloom on their faces showing their connection more clearly than if they'd been holding hands. Belle glanced up at Franklin, and together they moved toward the train.

Luellen turned from the window and gathered David's blanket, his red calico doggie, and her traveling case. David whimpered, tugging at her skirt.

"We'll get off in a moment. Stop whining."

"Lulie." Strong arms grabbed her from behind. Franklin spun her around in a hug.

She buried her face in his shoulder, inhaling the aroma of wood smoke and leather. She glanced down at David in time to see him escaping down the aisle. After dragging him, howling, back to their seat, she seized Franklin's hand. "What's wrong with Papa? How is he?"

"Dr. Gordon says he has edema of the lungs. He's holding his own. The next day or two will be critical." Franklin lifted her belongings and led the way down the aisle.

Belle waited at the bottom of the steps. Her wide smile emphasized the deep dimples at either side of her mouth. "I've missed you so." She held out her arms.

"I've missed you too." Keeping a firm grip on David's hand, Luellen moved into Belle's embrace, kissing her pink cheek. "I should be angry with you for getting married without me, but I'm too happy to see you." She sent Belle a teasing smile. "I'll get upset later."

"My mama was especially put out. She wanted to plan a big wedding." Belle took Franklin's hand. "But once we had my father's permission, there was no reason to wait. In my heart, you were there with us. After all, if not for you I'd never have met your handsome brother."

She bent down to David's level. "Is this my nephew? This boy standing on his own two feet?"

David chewed on his doggie's ear and sidled closer to Luellen. "It will take him a moment to warm up to you," she said. "It's been almost five months." She turned to Franklin. "How did you know I'd be on this train?"

"We planned to meet every southbound until you arrived. Luckily, this was the first one. Belle and I dropped everything and caught yesterday's train out of Springfield. Lily and Edmund will be here as soon as he concludes some business."

"And James?"

"Our big brother is on his way from Philadelphia. You should've seen Papa's face when the telegram came this morning. Knowing he'd see James did him more good than any of Dr. Gordon's medicine."

Luellen felt a smile spread over her face. James hadn't been home in four years. "I imagine Papa's overjoyed." She scooped David onto her hip. "Now, please take me home."

"I'll let you out here," Franklin said, stopping the buggy in front of their parents' house. Inside the picket fence, dogwood leaves displayed glossy spring green. Flowering red and yellow columbine crowded against the front steps. From the exterior, the house appeared unchanged. But the moment Luellen opened the front door, the illusion shattered.

Sickroom smells filled the entryway. In the sitting room, Papa leaned against a stack of pillows on a narrow cot. His eyes widened when he saw her. "My Lulie." He tried to sit up, but fell back coughing—a dry, hacking sound. His body was swollen to the point where he was almost unrecognizable.

Luellen dropped to her knees beside the cot and took Papa's hand. Her fingers left white indentations in his skin. "I'm here, Papa." The fire on the sitting room hearth burned into her back.

He turned his head. "I'm sorry . . . you had to . . . leave school."

Tears stung her eyes. "You're more important."

He shifted on the pillows. "Where's . . . the . . . boy?"

"Right here," Mama said, leading David forward. "Look, he's walking already."

Luellen lifted her son so Papa could see him better. "He can say 'mama.'"

"Smart . . . like you."

David handed his doggie to Papa. "Doo," he said.

Papa's face broke into his familiar grin. He took the toy and pretended to stroke it. "Thank you." He coughed, struggling for breath.

Luellen laid a hand on his forehead. "You rest now." She closed the curtains, her heart heavy with grief. This couldn't be the end. Papa was only fifty-four.

Footsteps dragging, she followed her mother into the entry hall. "How long has he been this bad?"

"The swelling came on Sunday. At first he wouldn't let me telegraph you children, but I insisted." Mama's face was gray with fatigue. "As you can see, he has to try to sleep sitting up. I made myself a bed on the divan so I could stay beside him. It was a blessing that Franklin and Belle were able to come yesterday." She clasped Luellen's arm. "And you today. I don't know how I'd get through this without you children."

"What would you like me to do?"

"Pray. Dr. Gordon will be here soon with a decoction he believes will take the swelling down. If he's successful . . . well, he thinks Papa may have a chance."

Luellen slipped David's nightgown over his head. Twilight painted the scene outside the bedroom window with shades of purple. Any other time she'd have admired the changing colors of the evening. Today she watched without caring. Where was Dr. Gordon? Why wasn't he here treating her father?

David's eyelids fluttered shut. "It's been a long day," Luellen whispered. "You've been a very good boy." She tucked him in bed with his doggie. "Sleep now. I'll be back soon."

Once downstairs, she followed the sound of murmuring voices into the dining room.

"Dr. Gordon. I didn't hear you arrive. How's Papa?"

"Miss McGarvie." He rose and gave her a half bow. "I just administered a digitalis decoction. He'll get another dose presently." A flask rested on the table and a satchel sat on the floor next to his chair. "I plan to stay with him overnight to monitor the effects. There's a fine line between therapeutic and poisonous. But if it works as I believe it will, within a week or so he may be back on his feet."

Luellen's knees wobbled. She grabbed a chair and sank into it. "Truly? You mean he's going to get better?"

The doctor raked his fingers through his disheveled red hair. "No promises. We'll have to wait and see."

When Lily and Edmund arrived on Saturday, Papa shuffled to the door to greet them. The swelling in his legs and feet had subsided enough to allow him to wear his leather slippers. Mama walked at his side, supporting him with one arm.

Luellen stood with Franklin and Belle while her parents were embraced by their youngest daughter and her husband. "It's a miracle," she said in a low voice. "I didn't think I'd see this moment."

Franklin nodded. "When we got here, I was afraid James and Lily would be too late. Now it looks like James can take his time."

"It takes my father a week or so to get to Washington from Springfield," Belle said. "Your brother ought to be here any day."

Lily advanced toward Luellen and kissed her on the cheek. "I'm so glad Papa's recovering. I wanted to leave as soon as we received the telegram, but Edmund—"

"Edmund what, my dear?" Lily's husband stopped next to her.

"You had pressing business." She turned to Franklin and Belle and embraced them in turn. "He wouldn't let me travel alone. Edmund thinks it's unwise."

Luellen bit her lip. The more she saw of Edmund, the less she liked him. How did he think she traveled to and from Allenwood—transported by angels?

Franklin cut a glance in her direction and winked. He clapped a hand on Edmund's shoulder. "Let me help you with your bags. Mama put you in their bedroom since she's staying downstairs with Papa at night."

Unfastening her bonnet while she walked, Lily followed their parents into the sitting room. "I saw David playing in here the minute I came through the door. My, he's grown." She knelt in front of him, her green and white taffeta promenade dress billowing as her hoops collapsed. "Come see your aunt Lily."

"Give him a moment . . . to get used to you," Papa said. His eyes twinkled. "Likely he's never seen . . . so much clothing . . . on one person before." He settled in an armchair and propped his feet on an ottoman.

Thankful to hear him teasing, Luellen closed her eyes. Every sign of her father's recovery was a reason for praise. When she opened them, she caught Belle watching her, her face a reflection of Luellen's gratitude. She squeezed her friend's hand. Belle squeezed back.

David toddled past Lily and grabbed Luellen's leg. She swung him high in the air, kissing his cheek. "Show Aunt Lily your doggie."

He grabbed the calico toy from the hearth rug and thrust it at Lily. Taking it between two fingers, she turned it over with a forced smile. "Very nice." She struggled to her feet, hoopskirts swaying. "I'm glad you're going to be home all the time," she said to Luellen. "Now you can be a proper mother to him. Not that you weren't already, of course. But Edmund says a mother's place is with her children at all times."

"Indeed." Luellen smiled sweetly. "You have domestic help in your home, don't you? Do any of those women have children?"

"Well, cook does."

"Are they with their mother in your house?"

Lily's face flushed. "No."

"My goodness. What does Edmund say about that?"

From her chair next to the fire, Mama cleared her throat. "Luellen, I'm sure Lily and Edmund would enjoy tea and some of that ginger cake you and Belle made last night."

Luellen noticed her sister's lip trembling and slipped an arm around her shoulders. "I'm sorry. Please forgive my sharp tongue."

"I'm sorry too. Sometimes I speak without thinking. Edmund says—" She clapped a hand over her mouth. "There I go again." She took a step toward the kitchen. "Let me help you with the tea."

❧

The following Monday, Luellen spread her textbooks on the dining table. David toddled toward the sitting room, where Mama sat knitting next to Papa's cot.

Luellen followed her son. "Would you be able to keep an eye on him while I study?"

"Let me." Lily hurried down the stairs and joined her in the doorway. "Mama needs to pay attention to Papa."

"Why don't you play with him in here?" Mama said. "We can all watch him." She tilted her head toward Luellen. "You brought your school books home with you? What for?"

"I want to finish what I started. Even though I won't get a certificate, at least I'll know as much as any of the graduates. And maybe someday—"

Lily snickered. "You and your books."

Papa swung his feet to the floor. "Go study, Lulie." He drew a breath. "Education is never wasted."

Lily settled in a chair next to the window, her wire hoops clicking together as she sat. "Edmund says it's wasted on women."

When had her sister turned into such a ninny? Luellen shook her head, tired of listening to Edmund's pronouncements. "I'll be in the dining room. Call me if David gets fussy."

Out of the corner of her eye, she saw the station hackney coach stop in front of the house. A tall man wearing a loose-fitting black coat stepped out. When he faced the house, Luellen's heart jumped. "James is here!"

She ran down the front steps. James's face broke into a grin when he saw her. "Lulie." He grabbed her under the arms and lifted her for a kiss on the cheek.

Once back on the ground, she smiled up at his moustached face. "I'd forgotten you were so tall."

"Six foot four. I take after the McGarvie side." He lifted his bags. "I got here as fast as I could. How's Papa? Is he—?"

"He's better, praise God." She pointed at the open front door where their parents stood. "See for yourself."

Upon reaching the veranda, he dropped his luggage and bent to embrace Papa.

When James straightened, Papa had tears on his cheeks. "I haven't been . . . this happy in years. All our children . . . home at once." He turned to Mama. "I should get sick . . . more often." A grin hovered at the corners of his mouth.

James scrutinized Papa's face. "You need to get off your feet. Your color looks good, but it sounds like you're not getting enough air. Who's the doctor in charge? What's his diagnosis?" He pointed at a black satchel. "I have my medical bag with me. Once I get settled, I'd like to examine you."

Papa's face glowed. "It would be my privilege, Dr. McGarvie."

That night, Papa joined the family at the supper table. Luellen and Belle bustled back and forth from the kitchen, serving stewed hen with dumplings, boiled greens, and applesauce.

James leaned back in his chair. "After a week of eating in hotels and railroad depots, this meal is ambrosia. You've always been a gifted cook, Lulie."

She patted his shoulder. "Thank you—but Belle deserves equal credit."

Belle dropped a mock curtsy. "My pleasure. It's a joy to meet the brother I've heard so much about."

"You'll have the opportunity in the future to form your own opinion." James placed his hand on Papa's wrist. "I told my colleagues in Philadelphia I was leaving. I'd always planned to come home and join your practice. When I got Mama's telegram, I prayed I hadn't waited too long."

"I don't know what to say." Papa took a deep breath. "This has been my hope . . . since you went to medical college."

Mama burst into tears. "Thank you, son." Her voice caught on a sob. "You can't know how happy you've made us."

Luellen sank into a chair and pulled David onto her lap. James home to stay? Papa's blue eyes shone. She imagined she could see him growing stronger by the moment.

Excited conversation swirled around her. Under her lashes, she studied each sibling in turn. They'd all found their places in life—Franklin a saddlemaker, happy with Belle; Lily seemingly content with stuffy Edmund; James a doctor, joining Papa's practice—she was the only one still drifting. Without a teaching certificate, was she doomed to eke out a living as a tutor in Beldon Grove?

# 35

Luellen snapped her history text shut. Since she arrived home, she'd read through her course material more than once. Next week seniors at Allenwood would take their final examinations in preparation for Friday's commencement. She'd been so close.

Mama strolled in from the kitchen and took a chair opposite Luellen. "The house is quiet with Franklin and Lily back in Springfield."

"David makes up for their absence."

"He has been fussy, hasn't he?"

Luellen winced. Mama didn't look pleased. "I hope he hasn't disturbed your rest."

"Well, last night I confess Papa and I were both awakened."

"James, too, I imagine. He looked tired at breakfast." She scooped her books into a stack on one corner of the dining room table. "I don't think my presence is helping Papa now that he's up and around. Having James with him spares him house visits at all hours, but my son interrupting his sleep could cause a setback." She massaged her temples. "I don't know how to keep David quiet. He's cutting a new tooth and he's cranky as a bear." Luellen pointed up the stairs. "Except now, while he's napping."

Mama smiled at her, sympathy in her eyes. "I well remember pacing the floor with you children when you were babies." She glanced at the stack of books. "Isn't graduation next week?"

Surprised at the change of subject, Luellen nodded.

"Have you thought about returning? There's time."

Luellen stared at her mother. "You must be clairvoyant. How did you know?"

"I know you. You're not one to leave a job unfinished—especially after working as hard as you have." Mama leaned across the table. "You can take Saturday's train and be there for examinations. Papa and I will buy your ticket as a gift. We'll never forget you were willing to forsake your dream for us."

The weight of Luellen's disappointment took wing, leaving her buoyant with relief. She scrambled to her feet. "Thank you for believing in me." She planted a kiss on Mama's cheek.

"You've found what you were born to do." Mama gave her a mock shove. "Now go do it."

Luellen grabbed her books and ran up the stairs. Her mind raced ahead to Dr. Alexander's warning that she not ask for any more favors. One more time. It wouldn't hurt to try.

What if Mrs. Hawks found someone to replace her? Where would she stay? Just go, she told herself, remembering a verse from the book of Joshua. *Put your foot in the waters and they will stand up in a heap.*

James drove her to the station on a balmy May morning. "I wish we could all be there for your graduation."

Luellen's initial excitement rolled into a knot of anxiety. "You can't be sure I'll persuade the registrar to let me sit for the examinations."

The corners of his moustache twitched. "You could persuade a fish to walk on land if you wanted to. You've always had your own way."

"Even when I was wrong," she said, thinking of Brendan.

James tapped the back of her hand. "Sometimes wrongs turn out right. Life's not in our hands, is it?"

A column of smoke appeared on the southern horizon. Allenwood grew more real with every rotation of the approaching iron wheels. The knot in her stomach twisted tighter. Dr. Alexander could say no as easily as he might say yes. As James said—the decision wasn't in her hands.

After he set the brake on the buggy, she leaned against him. "I'm frightened."

"So was I. I threw up before every examination—worried I'd fail and disappoint Papa and Mama."

"You? I thought you sailed through."

"More like rowed into a headwind." He smiled at her. "You can do it. McGarvies are tough."

The locomotive whooshed as it came to a stop. James carried David on his shoulders, depositing him inside the vestibule of the passenger car. Luellen gripped her son's hand. "I'll let you know what happens."

"I already know. Next Friday you'll leave Allenwood with a teaching certificate folded in that bag of yours."

As the train rolled north, her brother's words repeated in her head with every click of the wheels. She drew a textbook from her valise. She'd use the time to review chemistry formulas.

Luellen trailed the omnibus driver onto Mrs. Hawks's porch. In the twilight, the house appeared gray and unwelcoming. He lowered her trunk to the floor. "You sure someone's here? We got hotels in town."

She shifted David to her hip and handed the driver the fare, compensating him with an extra coin for handling her heavy trunk. "I've been here before. The landlady's probably in the kitchen." She prayed she was right.

"I'll be back this way later. Wave me down if there's no one home. G'night, ma'am."

After the omnibus rolled away, Luellen stood for a moment, then rapped on the door frame. To her relief, she heard footsteps approaching.

"Glory be, you're back." Mrs. Hawks pulled her close. "How's your father?"

"Better, praise God. My oldest brother's a doctor—he's with my parents now." She took a deep breath. "I hope I can stay here until graduation."

"You'd make me happy if you stayed longer than that." Mrs. Hawks took a sleepy David from her and led the way into the kitchen. "I'll have one of the boarders fetch your trunk off the porch tomorrow morning."

"Is Brendan—Mr. O'Connell—still here?"

"He's been in Chicago this past week—just got back yesterday." Mrs. Hawks raised an eyebrow. "He's a charmer, that one. You want to be careful." She chuckled. "Guess I don't have to tell you. 'Once burned, twice shy,' eh?"

"Indeed." *Chicago.* Furious with herself, Luellen marched into the little room off the kitchen. She dropped her valise beside the washstand and rolled her shoulders to loosen the tension that seized her muscles. Would she never learn?

Mrs. Hawks lowered David to the floor. "This little one is asleep on his feet. We'll talk in the morning." She eased the door shut behind her.

Luellen had finished unpacking her valise when she heard a knock at the door. She opened it a crack.

"I'm sorry to disturb you, dear." Mrs. Hawks handed her three envelopes. "These all came on the same day, soon after you left. It's a good thing I hadn't got around to taking them back to the post office—otherwise they'd be going to Beldon Grove and you'd be here."

Luellen's hands tingled when she saw Ward's careful script. "Oh, thank you."

"Good night." The latch clicked.

As soon as David was tucked into the crib, she scanned the postmarks. They'd been stamped in St. Louis on the same date in April. But when she opened the envelopes, she noticed Ward had written the first one shortly after he arrived at Fort Hook in January. Puzzled, she checked the next two. The second was dated in late February, the third in mid-April. The envelopes looked grimy. Where had they been all this time? Had he received her letters?

Blinking away tears, Luellen moved the candle closer to the edge of the washstand. *I wish he'd never gone to Kansas.* She read the January missive slowly, hearing Ward's voice in her mind. He described his journey, the Army post, and went into detail about the quarters he'd been assigned.

> . . . *The other officers have wives. I envy them when I enter this cold house every night.*
>
> *Yours sincerely,*
> *Ward*

She unfolded the next letter. More about the post and the bitter weather. Ward told of a wagonload of immigrants arriving with typhus, and the measures he'd taken to prevent it from spreading among the troops. He concluded,

*I think of you often and wish you would write.*

*Yours fondly,*
*Ward*

Luellen lifted the April message, hoping to learn he'd received some of her letters. Spring had arrived in the hills around the post, he wrote. The men were busy preparing for a visit from a general, scheduled to take place toward the end of May.

*You must be too occupied with your studies to write. I find myself thinking of you more and more.*

*Your devoted*
*Ward*

She pressed the paper to her chest. Poor Ward, on that post thinking she'd dismissed him from her life. Luellen reread each message, then folded the pages and tucked them under the pillow. She'd wait to reply until after she met with Dr. Alexander.

She heard footsteps in the kitchen and a soft tap at her door. *What else did Mrs. Hawks forget?* Tucking her loose hair behind her ears, she turned the knob. "Did you—"

Brendan stood in a shaft of moonlight. "I heard you and the landlady talking earlier. I couldn't wait to see you." He stroked one of the curls that fell over her shoulders. "Ah, that lovely hair."

Luellen slapped his hand away. "Don't touch me."

He took a step backward, an injured expression on his face. "One minute we're friends, now you strike me. Why?"

"How was Chicago, Brendan?" Luellen closed the space between them until she was less than a foot from his face. She planted her hands on her hips. "Did you have a fine visit with your wife?"

His face darkened. "Don't get high and mighty. That lad in there says to me you're not all that hard to come by."

"He's your son." The pulse in her throat threatened to choke her. Why did she tell him?

"Hah! Don't try to stick me with your brat. I know your kind."

Vibrating with anger, Luellen clenched her fists. "Get out. Out of this kitchen, out of my life." She put a hand on his chest and shoved. "I never want to lay eyes on you again."

"That makes two of us, dolly." He punched the swinging door open and stamped upstairs.

She watched him go with narrowed eyes. Tomorrow, she'd ask Mrs. Hawks to evict him. Tonight, she'd block her door.

The next morning, Mrs. Hawks bustled into the kitchen where Luellen stood stirring flapjack batter. "The boarders will be down soon—except for Mr. O'Connell. I sent him on his way." She gathered a stack of plates and carried them to the dining table.

Luellen paused at her task. With the poison of Brendan out of her system, she felt as though she'd recovered from a lengthy illness. "Thank you. You're a blessing."

"And he's a snake. We're both better off without him."

Luellen placed a cast-iron griddle on the stove. "After church, I'd like to see Leah for a few minutes. I'm counting on her help with David this coming week."

A shadow crossed the landlady's face. "Leah's gone. I was going to tell you after breakfast."

"What?" Luellen turned, mouth agape.

"She left last week."

"For Canada?"

"I hope so."

"How did she—"

"She accompanied Elsie Garmon as her traveling companion, of all things. You'd never think that old woman had it in her, but evidently Leah's plight touched her stony heart. Elsie told me she would see Leah all the way to Buxton." Mrs. Hawks carried the bowl to the stove and spooned batter onto the griddle.

"Buxton?" For a fleeting moment, Luellen remembered Betsy. "Leah was miserable here. I'm thankful for her sake that she's going to be with her family." Luellen hugged her arms around her waist. "But what will I do with David tomorrow?"

"Leave him here. I can manage for one day." She reached into a drawer and handed Luellen an envelope. "Leah left this for you. She said you'd know what to do with it."

Luellen unfolded the slip of paper inside. It contained two words—*Sumner Price.*

After breakfast Monday morning, Luellen dressed in her royal blue skirt and matching flowered bodice. She swept her curls to the back of her head, covering them with a blue silk net.

Mrs. Hawks leaned on the doorjamb. "You look quite lovely. Dr. Alexander is sure to grant your request." She waggled David's doggie at him. "We're going to have a fine time this morning, aren't we?"

"Mama." He clung to Luellen's leg.

She plucked his fingers loose, mindful of Lily's remark that she could only be a proper mother if she stayed home with her son.

"Go to Mrs. Hawks." She knelt in front of him. "I'm trying to do what's best for us," she whispered. "I'll be back soon."

David's howls followed her out the door.

On her way to the school, Luellen rehearsed what she wanted to say to Dr. Alexander. She'd need to be her most persuasive. Should she remind him how hard she'd worked to reach this point, or would that only serve to bring up all the times she asked for other favors? Perhaps she could mention her high marks and her skills in the Model School.

And how would she handle the information with which Leah had entrusted her?

Before Luellen knew it, she stood at the stone steps in front of Allenwood Hall. She took a deep breath. Now. She pushed open the door and marched toward Dr. Alexander's office. In the anteroom, Mr. Price held up a hand. "Dr. Alexander is quite busy this morning. I don't think he has time for former students."

Luellen lowered her head and glared at him over the rims of her glasses. "What you think doesn't interest me in the least." She swept past.

The registrar glanced up when she reached his door. "Miss McGarvie. This is a complete surprise. Mr. Price said you'd withdrawn with no explanation."

"Mr. Price misspoke. I asked him to convey my regrets and thanks to you for your assistance to me in the past." She moved to the front of his desk.

His expression didn't soften. "You withdrew. Why are you here now?"

"I left because my father was seriously ill. Thankfully, he has recovered sufficiently for me to take the examination for a teaching certificate. I'm here to ask your permission."

"You've requested exceptions to almost every rule this school has in place. I'm inclined to refuse. It's time you learned that our high standards are more than empty words." Dr. Alexander leaned forward, palms of his hands flat on his desk. "Where would we be if the Lord granted exceptions to his commandments?"

Luellen sucked in a breath. "Right where you are today, I expect." She drew the slip of paper from her reticule and placed it in front of him.

"Sumner Price? What's this about?"

"Do you remember the black girl who looked after your daughter's children? The one you dismissed when you learned she was in the family way?"

Color rose in his cheeks. "Leah. Yes. Why?"

Luellen pointed at the slip of paper. "That's the name of the baby's father. He refused to support or acknowledge his child after promising to do so. He broke Leah's heart. Fortunately, a kinder soul than yourself has seen to it that she's now safe with her family in Canada." She clasped her hands together. "Now, what did you want to teach me about adhering to high moral standards?"

Dr. Alexander slumped in his chair. "Sumner Price is the father? My assistant? *He* dallied with my grandchildren's nurse?"

"Apparently. What did you think would happen to her when you turned her out on the street? Especially here in Allenwood?"

"I don't know. I didn't think." He rubbed his forehead. "What are you going to do with this information?"

"Nothing. It's what you do with it that matters now."

He waved a hand at her. "Take the examinations, and good luck to you."

"No. That's not why I gave you his name. I did it for Leah." Luellen turned to leave.

"You're a remarkable woman." He studied her, something

deeper than admiration in his eyes. "Your name will appear on the roster on examination day. I have a feeling you'll excel."

She extended her hand and he took it in both of his.

"Thank you."

"Good day, Miss McGarvie."

As she left the building, Luellen heard Dr. Alexander bellow, "Price. Come in here. Now."

# 36

Luellen paused with her hand on the doorknob. "Thank you for watching David again, Mrs. Hawks."

The landlady pursed her lips. "You haven't eaten breakfast. How will you concentrate on the questions if you're hungry?"

"My stomach's in knots. Everything I've learned over the past two years comes down to this examination. I feel dizzy just thinking about it."

She stepped forward and kissed David's cheek, forcing herself to ignore the tears pooled in his eyes. "I should be back right after the noon bell."

Once inside the administration building, Luellen turned toward the testing room. Mrs. Hale waited in the hallway. "I have to hand it to you, Miss McGarvie. You're a plucky one. Dr. Alexander informed me you'd be joining the other seniors today." She pointed to a table near the front. "There's an empty seat over there."

"Thank you," Luellen said. She sensed other students watching her as she crossed the room. Their stares didn't matter. She needed to pin her thoughts on her studies.

Once they had permission to begin, she opened to the first page. History. In her mind, she pictured the text she'd spent hours studying while at home. Heart pounding in her throat, she took pains with her answers, reading and rereading before going to the next question. Chemistry followed history, then geometry, literature, and elementary physics. Chewing her lower lip, Luellen forged through each topic. Perspiration tickled her temples.

When she reached the final question, she shot a glance at the clock. Twenty minutes remained. She flipped the booklet over and skimmed through each page, double-checking for errors.

Mrs. Hale rose. "Time. Please pass your work forward. Your grades will be posted in the registrar's office tomorrow morning."

Luellen sucked in a deep breath and handed her packet to the student in front of her. The results were in God's hands now. She'd done her best.

The next day, Luellen strode down the hallway of the administration building and stepped into the anteroom outside Dr. Alexander's office. A stranger looked up from behind the desk Mr. Price had occupied. "May I help you, miss?"

"Are you one of the students?" Foolish question. He appeared to be at least a decade older than she was.

He straightened in his chair. An amused expression hovered at the corners of his mouth. "No. I taught here several years ago. Dr. Alexander asked if I'd take the job as his assistant until a permanent replacement could be found."

"Mr. Price is gone?"

"As of Monday."

Luellen hid a smile.

"Did you wish to see the registrar?"

"No, thank you. I'm here to learn the results of the final examination." She turned toward the notice board, her face warm. She ran her finger down to the midpoint of the list of graduating seniors.

*Kerrigan, Charles.*

*Koberly, Esther.*

*Longberg, Mark.*

*McGarvie, Luellen.*

She hadn't realized she'd been holding her breath until her head began to pound. A perfect 100 percent. She closed her eyes, exhaling with a whoosh.

"Is anything wrong, miss?"

"No." She whirled to face the assistant. "Everything's wonderful." He probably thought her addled. She didn't care.

The murmur of conversation in the auditorium ceased. Gowns rustled as Luellen and the other members of her graduating class took their seats on the platform. Her gaze roamed over the assembled families who had come to celebrate their students' accomplishments, her eyes stinging with unexpected tears. If only her parents had been able to attend.

At the rear of the room, one of the double doors opened and Mrs. Hawks entered carrying David. Luellen glanced at her and smiled in gratitude. Her Allenwood family was here.

Speeches by the school's founder, department heads, and Dr. Alexander droned on for over an hour. Luellen's face ached from trying to appear attentive while wishing they'd stop talking and distribute the certificates. Finally Dr. Alexander turned to the graduates. "It is with deep pleasure that I award Allenwood Normal School diplomas and State Teaching Certificates to the future educators of Illinois's children."

From a tray on the podium, he took one envelope after another, identifying each student as he did so. When Luellen heard her name, she walked toward Dr. Alexander.

"I know you'll succeed in whatever you do," he said under his breath as he handed her an envelope.

The silence in the auditorium was broken by the sound of clapping and a voice calling, "Mama, Mama, Mama." She turned toward Mrs. Hawks, hoping the landlady could quiet David. The woman's arms were empty. Behind her, under a candle sconce at the back wall, an Army officer stood with her son on his shoulders.

*Ward.* It took all of Luellen's determination not to run to him. Instead she resumed her seat, hands trembling. While the remainder of the graduates stood to receive their diplomas, Luellen tried to calm herself.

As the students left the platform, they were surrounded by well-wishers. Luellen moved through the throng to Ward, heart in her throat.

He swung David to the floor when she approached. "Well done. What a remarkable accomplishment."

"I can't believe you're here." She clasped his hand, feeling a tingle jolt through her at his touch.

"Surprised?"

"I never dreamed—isn't a general visiting your post?"

"I expect he is. I'm gambling my career that my aide will give him a satisfactory tour of the fort."

Stunned, she asked, "You left without permission?"

"I sent a dispatch to headquarters. They should have it by now." He tugged her closer. "I couldn't miss your graduation. You've worked harder than anyone I know to get to this point."

Mrs. Hawks joined them, beaming. "We did it, didn't we?" she said to Ward.

Luellen turned to her, bewildered. "Did what?"

"The captain's been my guest since yesterday. He didn't want

ANN SHOREY

you to know he was here." She grinned at him. "Just don't expect
meals in your room anymore."

He squeezed Luellen's hand. "I'd rather eat in the kitchen with
the cook."

The crowd in the auditorium thinned. Luellen scooped David
into her arms and followed Ward and Mrs. Hawks into the window-
lined hallway. Outside, lamps illuminated the paths across the
campus.

"I imagine you young people would like to have some time to
yourselves," Mrs. Hawks said. "I'll take David home and have a
celebration supper ready when you arrive."

"Thank you." Ward took Luellen's arm. "We'll be along directly."

Luellen felt warmth flood her face. Once they were alone, what
would they say to one another? They stepped out into the moon-
washed evening and stood for a moment watching Mrs. Hawks
walk David along the street.

Ward leaned near Luellen. "Is there someplace quiet we could
go? I have something to tell you."

She led him toward her favorite bench outside the Lecture
Hall, apprehension tickling her throat. "The last time you had
something to tell me, you were going to Kansas."

"This is better, I promise."

Once they were in the shadows of the building, Ward took
her chin between his thumb and forefinger, bending his mouth
to hers. Heat from his lips spread through her body. She clung to
him, wishing she'd never have to let go.

He sighed and took one step away. "I've wanted to kiss you
since the first time we danced together."

"Is that what you wanted to tell me?"

He chuckled. "No, but that's a big part of it. You remember I
wrote you about the children on the post?"

339

Luellen nodded. Later she'd let him know she didn't get his letters until last weekend.

"They need a teacher. The Army doesn't care if you're married or not, as long as you're willing to live at Fort Hook."

She stared at him, speechless.

He put his hands on her shoulders. The intensity of his gaze bored into her. "I think about you day and night. Will you marry me? Come with me to Kansas?"

She placed one shaking finger over her lips and frowned, as though she were in deep thought. "Marry you? And a teaching position? Both?" She felt sure he could hear the pounding of her heart.

"If you'll have me."

She took his face between her hands and brushed his lips with hers. "How would you feel about a wedding in Mama's parlor—on our way west?"

# Acknowledgments

When I started writing this book, I didn't know how much I didn't know. Many people answered questions without laughing at my lack of knowledge. Donna Abraham, of Abraham's Lady in Gettysburg, Pennsylvania, explained how much fabric was required to create the voluminous garments women wore in the late 1850s. Nancy Shaner, one of my readers living near the fictional community of Beldon Grove in Illinois, responded in detail to my questions about the history and natural features of that part of the country. Thank you, Nancy! Thanks, too, to Deborah Vogts for supplying me with information about Kansas. Medical questions were answered by two fellow members of American Christian Fiction Writers, Ronda Wells, MD, and Anne Love, NP. If I got any facts wrong, it's my fault, not theirs.

And speaking of ACFW, many thanks to the members who specialize in nineteenth-century information. What a blessing you are.

I'm grateful to my critique partners, Bonnie Leon, Diane Gardner, Billy Cook, Julia Ewert, B. J. Bassett, and Judy Gann, for unsparingly pointing out areas that needed attention in my chapters. Special thanks to Sarah Schartz and Sarah Sundin, who went the extra mile by offering to critique the final portion of the book over the Christmas holidays. I'm in your debt.

My husband, Richard, has supported my writing since day one. Having a wife who's more preoccupied with imaginary friends than putting dinner on the table can't be easy. God truly blessed me when he brought us together.

Working with my editor, Vicki Crumpton, along with Barb Barnes, Michele Misiak, and the entire team at Revell, has been a joy. Your love of the Lord and your encouraging words keep me going.

Hugs to my agent, Tamela Hancock Murray. I so appreciated your prayers while I worked to complete this story during a family crisis. You're always there with guidance and counsel. Thank you.

I never forget there's not a word on the page that the Lord didn't first put into my mind. To God be the glory.

**Ann Shorey** has been a story collector for most of her life. Her writing has appeared in *Chicken Soup for the Grandma's Soul*, and in the Adams Media Cup of Comfort series. She made her fiction debut with *The Edge of Light*, released in January 2009. When she's not writing, she teaches classes on historical research, story arc, and other fiction fundamentals at regional conferences. Ann lives with her husband, Richard, in Oregon. *The Dawn of a Dream* is the third book in her At Home in Beldon Grove series.

Contact Ann through her website at www.annshorey.com.

Meet Ann Shorey at

# www.AnnShorey.com

Learn more about Ann, sign up for her newsletter,
and catch the most recent news about Ann's books.

Connect on with Ann on Facebook
**f** Ann Shorey

# When tragedy strikes, how will Molly McGarvie survive?

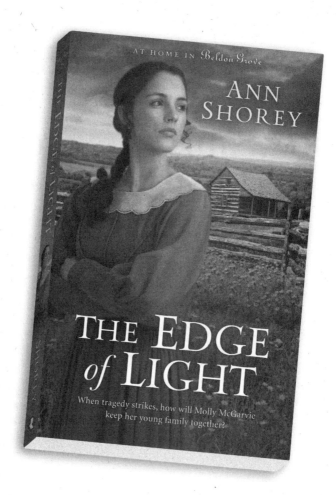

Experience the wonder and hardship of life on the prairie with Molly McGarvie as she fights to survive loss and keep her young family together.

Revell
a division of Baker Publishing Group
www.RevellBooks.com

Available Wherever Books Are Sold

# When loss drives them apart, can their faith bring them back together?

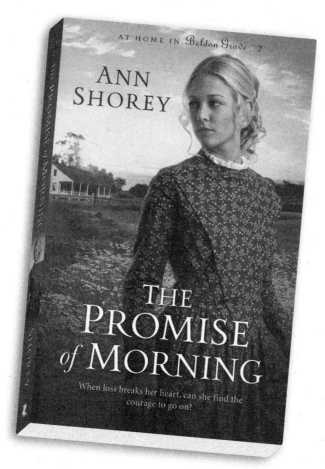

AT HOME IN *Beldon Grove* 2

## ANN SHOREY

# THE PROMISE *of* MORNING

When loss breaks her heart, can she find the courage to go on?

# Don't miss any of the

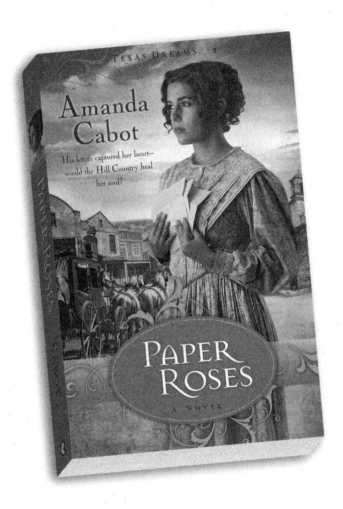

His letters captured her heart—
would the Hill Country heal her soul?

# TEXAS DREAMS series!

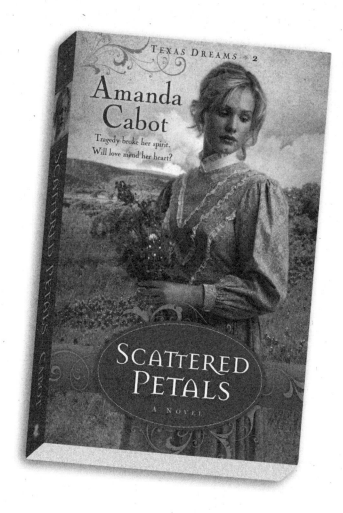

Tragedy broke her spirit.
Will love mend her heart?

Revell
a division of Baker Publishing Group
www.RevellBooks.com

"Amanda Cabot's characters and storytelling create the extraordinary out of this Texas tale. I'm in love with her books."

—Laurie Alice Eakes, author, *Lady in the Mist*

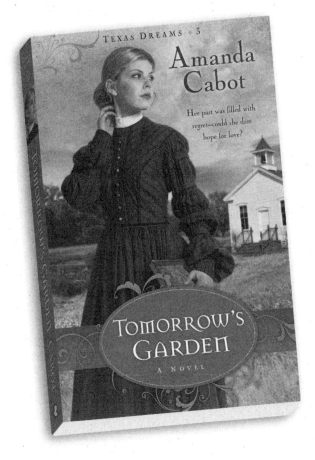

Readers will love this story of overcoming powerful odds and grabbing hold of happiness.

Revell

*a division of Baker Publishing Group*
www.RevellBooks.com

Available Wherever Books Are Sold

*"You'll disappear into another place and time and be both encouraged and enriched for having taken the journey."*

—Jane Kirkpatrick, bestselling author

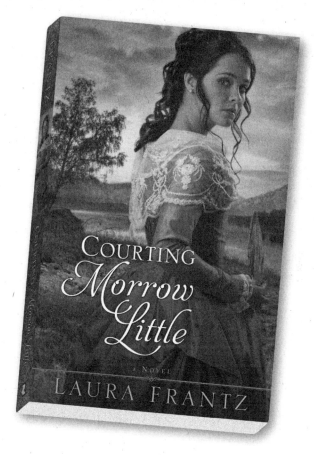

This sweeping tale of romance and forgiveness will envelop readers as it takes them from a Kentucky fort through the vast wilderness to the West in search of true love.